THE IONA CONSPIRACY

BY

G.L. GREGG

The Iona Conspiracy
Copyright © 2011 Gary L. Gregg

Published by Winged Lion Press
Cheshire, CT

Winged Lion Press titles may be purchased for business or promotional use or special sales.

10-9-8-7-6-5-4-3-2-1

ISBN-13 978-1-936294-14-5

In memory of Gary Ronald Welke,
who first introduced me to Iona Academy

895 A.D.
A PREFACE

The boy sat on soft ground in front of the cold grey stone. He had chosen it months before as his favorite spot from which to watch the sea. The soft green moss was long gone from his slouching and squirming. The seas rolled; the sun bounced off the water hypnotically. Leaning his head back against the stone, he wallowed in his dejection.

Family lore told of his great-uncle having come with Columba himself to this little island in the Scottish Hebrides. His kinsman had served the Saint in the darkest hours of bringing the new word to Scotland, and had helped stack the very stones of the monastery where the boy now lived. He had served and been a hero. Now young Cullum longed for his own day. He was frustrated at being sent out, day after day, to sit on the hill by the shore and watch for trouble coming from the sea. Though he had heard of the Viking raids that happened before his arrival, he only half believed the tales. Had the monks just sent him to the hill to get him out of their way? He didn't have the skills they had, true, but he was sure he could do more than this. He longed to feel useful, to contribute.

He bounced the leather pouch that lay on his lap, fiddling with one of the three tassels that hung from the old leather. It was said that this sporran pouch belonged to his great-uncle, and he hoped the story was true. He shifted it back and forth absent-mindedly upon the leather strap that hung it from his waist, and looked up at the clouds being puffed along overhead by the eastward wind.

When will my time come? I hate just sitting here.

Under the warming sun, his eyes closed. They were shut for what he thought was just a moment. In that time, however, the world had turned.

The first ships had already been beached. A pair of large painted dragons glared up at him from the front of the two ships being pulled further onto shore. With a clank of arms and cursing, men scrambled up the stony beach of Iona. Other ships were in the shallows and coming quickly toward the shore. The boy's heart jumped, his stomach turning. He dropped sideways onto the ground, hoping with no reason to hope that the broad men with wild hair and unkempt beards had not seen him. Crawling behind his stone, he peeked over the edge and saw the first group beginning to walk up the path from the sea.

"Boy!" one of them shouted.

The boy in the brown wool robe of a monk's apprentice froze.

"Boy!" the man bellowed again.

Cullum jumped to his feet and without looking back he ran as fast as his legs would carry him down the other side of the hill. He ran and ran. His brown robes waved in the air and his sporran bounced ferociously against his loins. As he approached the monastery, he began to yell. "Vikings! Brothers, the invaders have come! Vikings!"

The monks scrambled. Having been raided before, they were ready. Each sprang to his own emergency role: Some threw stores of food down into the holes hidden beneath their floors while others took treasures out to be hidden amidst the rocks and in secret crevices behind stone walls in the unadorned buildings.

Cullum kept running as he yelled the alert. He burst into the chapel, fearing the monks in prayer might not have heard his calls. They had heard, and only one man still stood in the center of the room. Cullum approached the Abbott. Out of breath and frightened, the boy knew he had failed in his duty to give ample warning of the terrible Norse warriors. He should not have allowed himself to drift off in a daydream. He should not have closed his eyes. He could now understand that he had been given an important job; he had not performed it well.

"Do you still have a bit of swiftness left in those legs, Cullum?" the Abbott asked, his head bowed to look into the boy's eyes.

Cullum nodded in the affirmative, though he was still catching his breath.

The Abbott turned, picked up a large book that stood on the center table in the chapel, and rubbed his hand across its cover with a mixture of admiration and deep dread. "This, lad, is Columba's great book. Some will call it the *Leabhar Cheanannais*. We have labored many years in the scriptorium to create this book." The man wiped a small tear from his right eye and the act confused the boy. The Abbott brushed his hand across the ornate cover, fingering the gold lettering and the jewels. He paused and traced the shape of the solid silver cross that came together at the exact center of the cover.

"Lad, the pages are of the finest vellum, but what is on them is more important still. This cover is inlaid in gold and set with jewels, but its leather is more important still. Can I trust you with it?"

Cullum could feel the pride rising in his chest. "Yes, teacher. In the name of my uncle who served Columba in his time of need, you can trust me."

The two were startled by the sounds of a skirmish from the courtyard outside. The Abbott ran to the wooden door and slammed a thick plank across it and into the stone frame. There was yelling and screaming and the sound of the pounding of boots, hammers and shields against doors.

The Abbott turned to Cullum. "This, lad, is why you were born. This is your destiny. This is your story, just now beginning to unfold. Take this book and guard it with your life. It must not fall into the hands of the evil men of our age or any other. It is not just a book. It holds secrets more important than the gold leafed upon the pages. It holds a truth more powerful than the jewels on the cover. Share its story with anyone, but protect its secrets from everyone."

A slight rattling at the door made the two turn. Finding the door blocked, the invaders then began pounding with sledges on its thick wood. The hammering rattled the formerly peaceful air of the chapel.

"You have no time, Cullum. Back here. Quickly. Out this window and then down to the beach. I've hidden a small boat down amidst the bushes by the sea. Take the boat and go. Don't look back. Just row as fast as your arms can move. Get to another of the islands and run. Find a place to hide. Tell no one what you carry. Let no one see it. Make your way then to Kells in the land of Patrick. There you will find an abbey. Trust our brothers at Kells. They know what we have done. They will then protect the book. Don't come back here. Stay at the abbey at Kells and never return to Iona. Your destiny is elsewhere."

Cullum stood confused. Was he being sent away? Why couldn't he come back? This was to be his new home since his parents had passed away in the cold winter of 894. He was to serve where his great-uncle had served. A great cracking in the wood of the door sent splinters flying into the chapel, giving focus again to his thoughts. The Abbott pressed the great book tight into the boy's chest. Cullum's arms folded around it. The man leaned down and kissed the boy in the center of his forehead.

When the door finally shattered off its hinges, the Viking invaders entered to find a lone man kneeling in prayer in the center of the chapel.

Almost twelve centuries have passed since the boy rowed off the island into a web of destinies not completed even now.

PART I

IONA ACADEMY

Iona Academy

The baseball spun as it rose through the air and then descended again to land in Jacob's hand. With each toss the boy lying on the bed tried to get the ball closer to the ceiling without it actually making contact. The game had left several cupped indents in the plaster and the occasional black eye when his concentration had slipped.

Mr. Nibbles lay between the boy's feet. The pug dog had learned to get safely out of the way when Jacob tossed a baseball. Once, a ball had awakened the little dog the hard way when it came crashing down on his tiny brown and black head. He jumped off the bed and was half way down the stairs by the time he realized the house was not falling in on him.

It had been almost a year since Professor Chadwick von Niblick had given Mr. Nibbles to Jacob at the end of his stay in Edinburgh, Scotland. It had also been almost a year since the magic sporran had arrived on his doorstep, bringing him into the mystical world of the Order of the Sporrai. He had kept up with professors Hammish, MacGregor and Chadwick von Niblick by letters exchanged through his magic sporran pouch. Mr. Nibbles occasionally acted more strangely than the average pug dog and sometimes disappeared in the night for hours at a time. Otherwise, the past year had gone pretty much like any other year.

He had turned thirteen the previous October and, when he deserved it, now enjoyed a bit more independence from his parents. He was lying on his bed now because he had snapped at his mother when she told him to take care of his homework before he went to play basketball with his friend Will.

The rap of knuckles on the door agitated him again. "What?"

"Mail call!" Mr. Boyd announced as he opened Jacob's door, tossing a envelope onto Jacob's chest.

"Thanks, Dad."

"You're welcome. Come down to get some dinner when you cool off."

Jacob picked up the envelope and caught a whiff of nutty vanilla that reminded him of Professor von Niblick's pipe tobacco. There was no return address on the envelope but a red rampant lion stamp was in the upper left corner with the letters "IONA" in fancy letters below it. He turned it over to find the package was sealed with red wax with the same four letters pressed into it.

Hmm. . . Iona? I wonder what this is?

"Nibbles, what do you think?" Jacob tore open the package as the dog walked up the bed to inspect the contents with him.

Inside the envelope was a burgundy colored folder with a rampant lion in gold on the front below which was written those four letters again "IONA." He opened the folder as Mr. Nibbles leaned over to look for himself. In the left pocket was a brochure for a boarding school called "Iona" located in a rural area outside the little town of Aberdeen, Kentucky. There were pictures of young boys and girls playing sports, having class, and taking a meal in a large dark paneled dining hall.

The right pocket held an application for enrollment in the school for the upcoming summer term. The application was on a heavy parchment paper with a red wax seal at the bottom. Like any standard application, there were blanks for name, address, phone numbers, grades, interests, parent information, medical concerns, and food allergies. *Just junk mail,* he thought.

Jacob tossed it on the floor beside his bed, deciding to head down the stairs to apologize to his mother, get dinner, and start his homework. "Come on, Mr. Nibbles, lets get something to eat and take you for a walk," Jacob said as he rubbed the pug's head and got up from his bed.

❖ ❖ ❖

Later that evening, Jacob returned to his room and prepared to turn in. Mr. Nibbles, as always, was right at his heels. As they did almost every night, Jacob sat in the chair by his desk and Mr. Nibbles got up on the bed. Jacob tossed a ball into the air just out of the small dog's reach. The pug leapt out and caught the ball in his mouth, often followed by a stunt man-style roll across the floor. The dog trotted back over to Jacob and dropped the ball so the game could start all over again. His little legs were only good for a few of those a night, but Mr. Nibbles never wanted to miss them.

Jacob switched on the reading light by his bed and switched off the overhead light on the ceiling. Mr. Nibbles curled up next to him and Jacob reached down to take a closer look at the package he had received in the mail that day. He opened the folder from Iona Academy and removed the brochure. He dropped the outer folder back onto the floor.

Jacob began to open the brochure when a strange thought crossed through his mind. *Weird.* Something seemed different about the folder. He picked the folder up again and opened it. Just as quickly, he slammed it shut and tossed it across the floor. His heart raced and Mr. Nibbles jumped up, cocking his head in confused concern for his master.

The folder flopped open as it landed. From across the room Jacob's eyes confirmed his first impression. *I'm sure it was blank earlier today! I know it was!* In dark black ink that looked handwritten, his name now appeared on the application: Jacob Thomas Boyd.

He reached for a cracked old wooden baseball bat from beside his nightstand and stretched to reach the folder. Its slick cover slid easily across the floor and slipped safely under his bed. Jacob laid back down, staring at the ceiling and petting Mr. Nibbles nervously. It had been almost a year since anything really out of the ordinary had happened in his life.

Jacob feared the magic was seeping back in and he wasn't sure he was ready for it all to start again. *I'm a teenager now! I have things I have to do! I have things to live for, now!*

THE IONA CONSPIRACY

Still, the thrill of adventure and the smell of danger forced a half smile across his face as the memories of his time in Scotland flooded over him. Until the waters of sleep overwhelmed those of memory, he was back in the catacombs among the battling dragons and in von Niblick's study sharing hot chocolate and listening to his stories of the ancient Order of the Sporrai.

Scholarship

In the year since he had been in Scotland, Jacob had devised some ways to keep his Sporrai gifts with him always, as Professor von Niblick insisted he do.

He had received the sporran as a gift from his father who had gotten it from a small antique shop in St. Andrews, Scotland. The ancient pouch was made from an even older piece of leather. Its origins were still a mystery to Jacob, but its importance had manifested itself clearly in his life. Its mottled brown leather was accented with three horsehair tassels and had the tip of a deer's antler that served as the button that closed its flap. He wore it around his waist on a long sword belt of leather with gold rings at one end. It was not beautiful or expensive-looking, but it *was* a treasure, hunted for centuries by men from around the world.

To keep the magic sporran with him, he had created a false bottom in his backpack by cutting apart an old one and sewing a piece of it to the nylon inside of his good backpack. He did a good enough job, he thought, that anyone just casually looking inside would think it was empty.

The treasure he loved the most, though, was Isildane's ring. He loved looking at it and polishing its gold. He would look through the inside of the ring and out through the red jewel that now sat in its center. On one side was a shield with three lions on it and a diagonal band across it on which the word "Sporrai" was written. On the other was a unicorn rearing back on its hind legs. In one of its front hoofs, it carried a St. Andrews flag. In the other hoof was a shield with a rampant lion. Around the unicorn's neck was a crown.

Jacob wished he could wear the ring all the time, but no one at Buckner Middle School wore rings like that. The one day he had worn it, he had been teased by a couple of older bullies who had tried to take it. If the bus driver hadn't seen what was happening, he was certain he would have lost it. He wore it now mainly when he was working on homework alone in his room, or sometimes when he was going to visit his grandparents, or dressed up and going to church.

To keep the ring safe, he had sewn a small pocket inside the front flap of his backpack. In there, a calculator or notebook easily covered it and kept it out of sight. He often sat looking at it, fantasizing about its power and what secret chamber it might be the key to opening, as Niblick had told him was the legend.

It took everything he had not to put the sporran on, then the ring, and then make a wish and reach into the pouch. In the catacombs beneath Edinburgh the sporran had produced the sword that saved his life. He wondered what else he could get out of the pouch. Fear of the dangers and a sense of being responsible for great things kept him from doing it … most of the time.

Occasionally, particularly when Jacob would get angry with his parents, a teacher or other students, he would sit alone and wish for the sword. He would reach into the sporran pouch and grasp its powerful handle. The sword is like no other that ever existed. The hilt is made in the shape of the head of a golden lion, its mouth open to bear its teeth and its mane flowing back as if in the wind. The handle itself is made of two twisting dragons. Their bodies combine to make the grip and their heads emerge to form the crossbar. The heads are hideous and Jacob never cared for their look, but their bodies are soft, jelly-like and comfortable to hold.

Mostly, he would just hold the handle but keep the blade in his pouch, lest someone catch sight of it. Each time, however, he felt the pain in his shoulders and down his arm that Professor von Niblick told him was called "the quickening." The pain was particularly intense when he was angry or frustrated and it helped keep him from abusing the powers he had been given.

The little black leather book von Niblick had given him as he left Edinburgh was called "enchiridion." When he had first inspected it on the plane while his father was asleep, he had taken it for a notebook since its pages were all utterly blank. When he first tried to write down some things on his mind, however, the words soon disappeared and a day or two later a reply came back on the pages. As it turns out, the "enchiridion" is a magical blank book that allows Keepers like Professor Chadwick von Niblick to write to apprentice Bearers like Jacob and give them words of advice to study and remember. Over the last year, the book had been half-filled with advice and information from Hammish MacGregor, Chadwick von Niblick, and a variety of other members of the Order of the Sporrai.

When Jacob had a question, he could write it in the book. His note would soon disappear but, sometimes within hours and sometimes within a few days, an answer would come to him from some more knowledgeable member of the Sporrai.

According to Professor von Niblick's first note, such little books had been used for hundreds of years as a way for young leaders to be instructed on how to act ethically and honorably in difficult situations. enchiridion, he told Jacob, is Greek for "little dagger" and centuries ago some hung a little book like it from their belt like a knife. Jacob, however, just kept his book in his pocket or backpack.

In the past year, Jacob and Mr. Nibbles had become very close friends. The dog went everywhere (except to school and church) with his master. He was at the bottom of Jacob's bed when he fell asleep and was always there when the boy awoke. Well, almost always. There were a few nights during the past year when Jacob woke up and Nibbles was nowhere to be found. By morning, though, Nibbles was usually back in bed with Jacob, and so the boy had learned not to worry about his little dog.

After school the day after he received the package from Iona, Jacob reached under his bed and slid out the brochure for the Academy's summer program. He wondered if anything would be different. He soon had the answer and it was not one he hoped for. Now his address and phone number were filled out in the same handwriting and ink that had put his name on the application the evening before. A tingling shiver ran up his arm.

He paused, gathering his courage. *Well, might as well see where I might be going this summer … unless I can help it!* Jacob removed the brochure from the burgundy Iona folder and slid the application and cover back under his bed. He wanted it out of sight. He sat down at his desk and began to read about the school.

The school itself was started by a group of Scottish Presbyterians in the early 19ᵗʰ century. It was originally a boarding school to train the children of wealthy Virginia and Kentucky aristocrats, but had evolved to have a diversity of programs and a wider variety of students. Through all the changes, however, the school had maintained the traditions and beliefs of its Scottish founders.

Looks pretty cool. Could be fun, I guess, but I have things to do here. I have friends here and a life! I have a baseball career to think about and clubs and all my stuff.

Jacob took the brochure and slipped it on top of the Iona folder under his bed. It was several days before Jacob again took much time to think about the Iona school or the application. Occasionally it would creep into his mind, but just as soon as it did he would push it out with *"I'm too busy for that now!"*

Arriving home from school one afternoon, his mother was sitting at the kitchen table, Mr. Nibbles sitting at her feet.

"Afternoon Mom, what're you doing?"

"Looking at this neat brochure I found on the table this afternoon." Mrs. Boyd was holding the Iona brochure. "Where did you get it, Jacob?"

Jacob paused, momentarily speechless. "Well, it came in the mail the other day, but I don't know how it got to the table. I left it under my bed, I thought." Jacob slowly and carefully replied as he approached his mother to give her a kiss on her head.

"So, do you want to go?"

"Me? No. I have too much to do around here, Mom."

"Well, it looks really interesting to me," his mom said, waving the brochure.

"Well, I'll think about it," Jacob replied as he took the brochure and turned to walk back up to his room. He didn't intend to seriously think about it at all, but figured his mother would soon forget about it anyway and that would be the end of it. He shoved the brochure back under his bed and then took Mr. Nibbles out for a walk.

The next evening he was sitting watching TV with his mother when his dad emerged from his study with papers in his hand. He sat next to Mrs. Boyd and said, "Honey, we've raised quite a fine young man, you know! Have you seen his essay and application for Iona Academy summer program?"

My essay? My essay! I didn't do an essay or application! Jacob sank into the couch as his mind raced, searching for something to say.

"No. I didn't know you decided to apply, Jacob," his mother said as she reached for the papers his father was holding.

Jacob sat silently, pretending to watch TV as she read. His father stared at him. The guilt of knowing he didn't write the essay burned in his stomach.

Finally, she finished reading the application and said, "Jacob, this is an excellent essay about Scottish history. I knew you were somewhat interested, but didn't realize how much you knew. This stuff about the Battle of Culloden is really cool."

"I agree," his dad concurred. "So, where's the rest of the information on this place so we can look at it?"

Jacob didn't reply, pretending not to hear the question. He stared gloomily at the TV across the room.

"Jacob?" Mr. Boyd repeated.

"Yes, Dad, well, it's upstairs I think, I guess. But, I'm sure it's much too much money, and I really have too much to do this summer anyway. Let's just forget it."

"Nonsense! Now, go get the rest of the materials and let's have a look," his dad insisted.

Jacob slowly lifted himself up from his seat and puttered his way up the stairs to his room. Mr. Nibbles followed, hard on his heels. "Little dog," Jacob said as he paused at the top of the stairs and looked back at Mr. Nibbles, "if you're responsible for leaving these things from Iona around the house for Mom and Dad to find … so help me, your chewy bone supply is cut off!" The little dog just kept walking.

When Jacob came back downstairs, Mr. and Mrs. Boyd were sitting at the kitchen table talking in a manner that Jacob recognized as the dreaded "family meeting" experience. He slipped the materials on the table between his parents. As he sat, he insisted, once again, that he really didn't need to go and wasn't that interested in the school.

"Now Jacob, I can tell by reading that essay that you aren't telling us the truth here!" his dad insisted.

They looked over the papers and then came to the price of the summer program. The school was very expensive and to Jacob's great relief his mother finally said, "I'm sorry, but I don't think we can afford to send you this summer. This is just too much money for us right now."

"Fine!" Jacob said with a note of excitement in his voice that he quickly tried to squelch with "Oh, well, of course I'm disappointed, but that's just fine. I understand. And, besides, I have a big summer of baseball and things planned here. Now, how about some ice cream?"

His parents both looked at him and shrugged their shoulders. "You're a good boy, Jacob," his dad said and added, "How *about* some of that ice cream, then?"

Jacob was thrilled that he had dodged a bullet and to make sure it didn't happen again, he dropped all the application materials into the trash in the kitchen.

A week later, Jacob arrived home from a particularly good day at school and greeted his mother with a big kiss before starting up to his room.

"Wait just a minute, son! Guess what came in the mail today?"

Jacob paused in mid-step and turned. "What, Mom?"

"Well … well … I wanted to wait until your dad got home and could share in our excitement, but I just can't hold it any longer!" She was as excited as Jacob had ever seen her.

His mother pulled from behind her back an envelope with a red lion stamped on its front that he instantly recognized as being from Iona. His heart sank as his mother pulled a letter and began to unfold it.

"Oh, I'm just so proud of you, Jacob!" his mother said as she began to read the letter.

> Dear Mr. and Mrs. Boyd,
>
> We have received Jacob's fine application for the summer program here at Iona. It is a truly excellent application and the essay shows an extraordinary interest in Scottish history.
>
> Because of his excellent application, we would like to offer Jacob a full-tuition scholarship to our summer program this year.
>
> We at Iona look forward to taking care of Jacob this summer and giving him a learning experience he will never forget.
>
> Sincerely,
> *Ramos Kirk Ph.D*
> Dean of the Faculty

Jacob sat down on the stairs and looked into his mother's proud eyes, wondering how the application got from the trash to Iona and how he could get out of going away for the summer. A tinge of guilt also itched at the back of his mind, but he didn't know how to tell his mother the truth when he wasn't even sure what the truth was.

The Plumpkin Boys

In the weeks that passed, Jacob made numerous attempts to get out of going away to school that summer. Jacob's resolve eventually melted and inevitability set in. He wasn't quite himself during baseball season or in school. His teachers and his coach had all commented that he seemed distracted. Truth be told, he was.

When he had first come back from Scotland a year ago, he had been energized by the evolving role he was being called to play in the secret Order of the Sporrai. Then his contacts with Professors MacGregor and von Niblick eventually subsided. Occasional notes would come through his little "enchiridion" book, but they slowed down too, as the year went by. The notes coming in his sporran had also declined and then stopped. Sometimes he started to wonder if it was all a dream. It was as if the magic was bleeding out of his life.

Now, the mysteriously appearing application to Iona Academy was bringing it all back in and his mind was torn by the turn of events. That is, he was torn about it all until one Saturday evening in late May. He had been out near dusk walking Mr. Nibbles and was paying little attention to the world around him. Mostly, he was kicking the cinders that remained on the edge of the road from the county's attempt to make it more passable after winter snows.

Suddenly, a boot appeared where he was preparing to kick another small group of black nuggets. He stopped his descending foot just in time to keep himself from kicking the foot that belonged to Bobby Plump. Plump was a new kid who had moved to town during the last year and quickly built a reputation for unqualified nastiness. Respectable kids avoided having anything to do with him and that seemed just fine to Mr. Plump. He did have his gang of hooligans—"Bobby Plump and the Plumpkin Boys," as they were known around town.

Occasionally, Plump had messed with Jacob at school or on the bus. He had knocked him into a random locker now and then or "accidentally" swung a backhand into Jacob's head when Plump got off the bus. But Jacob was not Plump's favorite quarry and Jacob was glad of it. He occasionally daydreamed about wielding his sporran blade at this bully and setting him straight, but was also relieved that he had never needed to do so. He knew Professors von Niblick and MacGregor would not be pleased with him if he had used the power for such a minor thing as a school bully.

Plump extended his log-like arm directly into Jacob's chest, stopping his momentum. Jacob took a slight step back, trying not to show any fear. He had watched Plump and knew the bully thrived on the fear he could engender in others.

"Hi, Plump," Jacob said, lifting his chin slightly.

"You almost kicked my foot, Boyd! Why don't you watch where you're going?" The boy had learned to deepen his voice to appear older than he was.

"Well, Bobby, I guess I was just watching the road, that's all. Uh, I need to go now." Jacob stepped to the side and moved to continue past Plump when he noticed several of The Plumpkin Boys hiding in the hedges just up the road.

"Not so fast, Boyd Boy!" Plump extended his right arm and blocked Jacob's path. "My associates and I have decided we could use a quiet 'goody-goody' kid with us and so we've decided to make you one of our friends."

"Yes, well, that's nice of you. And I'm really happy to have as many friends as possible," Jacob said, and again tried to pass Plump on his right.

"Not so fast!" Plump was getting angry now and pushed Jacob menacingly.

"Plump, just leave me alone. I'm not one of your little punks and never will be!" Jacob said with a tone of slight defiance balanced with a hint of fear.

Plump pushed Jacob again and he stumbled backward over Mr. Nibble's leash, which then slipped from his hand.

"Leave me alone, Plump!" Jacob shot back and exerted as much energy as he could to rock the bully back on his heels. Jacob knew he could be in for a pummeling, but adrenaline had taken over.

Then something happened that Jacob would not understand and Bobby Plump would never forget.

Mr. Nibbles, now behind his master, stepped to his side to be in full view of the bully and barked. Bobby Plump looked down at the little pug dog and spit out: "Shut up, you little puke!"

Before Jacob could react, the look in Plump's eyes changed from arrogant anger to shock and then to great and intense fear.

Mr. Nibble's head swelled to three times its size. His teeth grew huge and white. His nostrils flared. His head grew again as if being filled with air like a hairy black and brown balloon with bulging marble eyes.

Plump stumbled backwards. His eyes were like the bloated and confused eyes of a dead carp. The bully tripped over his own feet in panic. Slipping in the loose cinders on the side of the road, his feet shot forward while the rest of his body fell backward. His arms flailed. Up came his feet and down went his head and upper body into the drainage ditch that ran beside the road. He lay there unconscious as a small trickle of muddy water parted his hair and slimy dead leaves matted themselves to the back of his neck. The mud-encrusted bottoms of his old brown boots were all that could be seen from the road.

Jacob turned to Mr. Nibbles just as his head was shrinking, as if a valve had been pulled and the air was rushing out through his nose. He stepped back as his heart raced. Momentarily, he thought of running, then Mr. Nibbles rolled over on his back as his head shrunk to normal. Jacob recognized the gesture as the universal dog-sign of submission and non-aggression.

Just then, Plump's cronies streamed out of the bushes. "What've you done to Bobby?" they yelled as they approached Jacob. Jacob stood watching the five boys come toward him. They were all smaller than Bobby Plump, but they were every bit as mean. As the first approached, he noticed Bobby's boots and then the rest of their leader lying motionless in the muck.

"Guys, check this out! It's Bobby!" the first goon announced to the others then turned toward Jacob.

They are sure to jump me now! Jacob thought as he watched them with concern and confusion.

"Guys, he knocked out Bobby! No one ever has beaten Bobby!" one of the boys announced. The gang stood murmuring to themselves, looking down at their fallen champion.

"Look, Boyd. . . I mean, Jacob," another started, "we don't want any more trouble with you, OK?"

Jacob noticed their tone and demeanor changing. Now, they clearly respected, and probably even feared him just a bit. He decided to take advantage of the moment with a gamble.

"Unless you each want to end up in that ditch, I suggest you get him out of there and stay out of my way from now on!"

The five nodded their heads as two of them grabbed Bobby Plump's boots and started to drag his unconscious body up and out of the muddy ditch. Jacob slowly walked by the scene, trying to appear as confident as possible. When he finally got around the corner and out of sight he grabbed Mr. Nibbles, tucked him under his arm like a football, and ran as fast as he could down the road toward home.

Dragon Pug

Jacob placed Mr. Nibbles on his bed. He shut the door and then sat in his desk chair across the room. Catching his breath, he stared at the little dog in wonder with a pinch of fear.

The little dog lay down and looked back across the room with the same "Have I done something wrong, pal?" expression that Jacob had seen many times before.

For the longest time the two sat staring at each other but making no sound. Then Jacob broke the silence with a question. "Well, dog, what do you have to say for yourself?" Even as he said it, the question seemed childish and unworthy of the situation.

"Mr. Nibbles, what's going on? What just happened?" he pleaded.

Of course there was no answer and no movement from the dog—except Mr. Nibbles blinked.

Jacob asked questions in several ways and tones then he realized what he was doing. *What the heck? Am I really expecting an answer from a dog? Not cool, dude. Not cool. I must be losing my mind!*

Mr. Nibbles got down off the bed and walked to Jacob's dresser where he stood up on his hind legs. Jacob followed him with his eyes and then let his eyes climb up the dresser until he realized the meaning of the dog's actions. His eyes focused on his backpack sitting on top of his dresser.

"Of course! You want me to contact Professor von Niblick, don't you boy? Of course, if there is something strange about you, he'd know!"

Jacob went to his backpack to get his sporran. He had communicated with a boy named Ian through his sporran as well as having been able to communicate with von Niblick and Hammish MacGregor. But he quickly put it down. *No, I can't wait for a note to come, or not, through the sporran. The enchiridion is too slow, too. I need to know now.* "You wait here!" he ordered. "And, don't do that … *thing* you did! *Please.*"

Jacob had gotten into trouble calling Scotland without permission once before. But, this was really an emergency and he reasoned that he would be at the Iona school before the bill came anyway. *Mom will miss me so much by then that she won't be upset!*

Mr. and Mrs. Boyd were sitting in the living room reading as he slipped into the kitchen and grabbed the portable phone.

"Jacob, is that you?"

Darn!

"Yes, Dad, it's just me." Jacob answered as he paused just out of sight in the kitchen.

"You know," his dad called from the other room, "I was thinking … maybe you had better write to Professor Niblick to let him know how Mr. Nibbles is before you head off for the summer."

Jacob saw his opening and took it. "Yes. Good idea, Dad! Well, since it's your idea, Dad," Jacob said as he walked into the living room with the phone in his hand, "how about I make just a quick phone call to tell him myself?" He waved the phone back and forth.

Mr. Boyd looked at his wife and shrugged his shoulders.

"Ok, Jake, but make it quick," his mother answered.

Jacob bounded up the stairs and back into his room where Mr. Nibbles was lying on his bed.

The pug dog watched as his master dialed the number to call the dog's old home in Edinburgh, Scotland. Mrs. Lafoon, the housekeeper of Niblick House, answered and after some brief chitchat, called the professor to the phone.

"Jacob, my lad!" the professor answered in an excited tone, "so good to hear from ya. Where have ya been and why have ya not written?"

Jacob explained that he *had* written but hadn't gotten anything from

Professor von Niblick or his friend MacGregor in months.

"Something is going wrong, Jacob. We haven't heard from ya. Something must be blocking our messages. Is there anything out of the ordinary going on there?"

"Out of the ordinary? Are you kidding?" Jacob's tone made clear his annoyance at such a question coming out of the mouth of the wizardly guy who had introduced him to the mystical world of the Sporrai. "Well, as a matter of fact, the head of the dog you gave me just grew to the size of a moose and he scared the life out of the biggest jerk in town!"

"Aye," von Niblick responded followed by a very audible exhalation of air. He let another breath from his body with a loud whoosh into the phone. "It's time you found out, it seems."

Jacob waited silently. After several seconds, the professor spoke again.

"Son, Mr. Nibbles is a very special creature. Remember I told you he was from China?"

Jacob murmured an affirmation to the question.

"Maybe ya should sit down," the professor paused for a few seconds and then continued. "Well, he is actually a very special pug from the Isle of Agathon. He is from an ancient line of creatures that were bred to protect the people and the emperors of China."

As Jacob stared curiously at Mr. Nibbles lying innocently on his bed, the professor unwound a story spanning centuries. As the last few dragons were nearing extermination in Asia, the Chinese discovered a way to breed their best traits into a race of dogs. They chose the pug above all other dogs because they are themselves descended from an older breed of canines that were believed to have magical powers. Being so small, they also provided great cover for the project. "Who would believe such a little package could possibly contain such a powerful force?" von Niblick said with a touch of humor in his voice.

The professor told Jacob that to protect them from the world and to protect the world from their power falling into the wrong hands, the dragon pugs were sent to live on the misty island of Agathon. Agathon is an island in the North Sea that is seldom found, as a deep and dense fog that lifts only once every Chinese year of the dragon shrouds it. The dragon pugs are reared and cared for by Chinese children on that island where no adults are permitted even to visit. The children learn to trust and rely on the dragon pugs and those creatures learn to love and protect the children selflessly.

"Jacob, Mr. Nibbles came to me many years ago to aid in my protection. He is older than he looks or acts. I gave him to you because you are now in more danger than am I. As a Bearer, you are marked and it is only a matter of time before you will be in danger again. None of us Keepers can be with you all the time, but I hoped Mr. Nibbles might be able to aid you in your time of need."

Dragon pugs, dragon pugs, the phrase was traveling through Jacob's mind as he listened to the professor and stared at the dog across the room. "Dragon pug?" he finally blurted out. "It was Mr. Nibbles, wasn't it?" He didn't wait for an answer. "It was Mr. Nibbles that entered the catacombs and saved me when I was in danger from that golden-eyed beast, wasn't it?"

"Aye, Jacob, that was Mr. Nibbles. Well, actually, 'Mr. Nibbles' is just his name when he's a dog. His deeper, truer self, prefers to be called by his formal name. Don't use it, though, unless you are in need of his help or if you are communicating something very important to him, which should not be done regularly. In fact, you should not contact him through this name except when you *really* need him."

"Well, Professor, what is his true name?" Jacob asked anxiously.

"Frankly, Jacob, I don't think I should say it. In a few minutes, though, I will write it to you. Get your enchiridion notebook out and be ready. I will send instructions as well. Let's hope those messages are not blocked."

"OK, Professor, thank you."

"Jacob, be careful and be sure you are ready before you move forward," the professor said in a melancholy tone that made Jacob grow fearful.

"Oh, professor…" Jacob had remembered he wanted to ask von Niblick about Iona Academy and get his reading of what was happening. A click followed by a dial tone, however, told Jacob the professor was gone.

Jacob sat staring at Mr. Nibbles, still lying on the bed across the room. "Dragon pug, huh?" Jacob said as he nodded toward the dog. Mr. Nibbles blinked his black marble eyes but otherwise made no move or reaction. The master and dog watched each other silently for several minutes before Jacob walked to his backpack and removed his enchiridion notebook. The note was there. He read:

Jacob,

Be sure not to try this until you are ready to sleep tonight. It will exhaust you like your energy has never be tapped before. It will become easier with time, but tonight it will be painful and exhausting for you.

When you are ready, you must lay down and close your mind to the world. Your mind must become clear and open to transcendence. Don't take this lightly. Even being truly quiet is difficult for us in the modern world. To have a clear and open mind that is uncluttered by the rubbish of the world is nearly impossible. At the moment of blank clarity, utter the name "Nibblus Maximus."

Be strong, lad. And, pray, give my regards to my old friend.

Chadwick von Niblick

Jacob read the note several times, keeping half an eye on his dog as he carefully thought about the professor's instructions. "You stay here," he finally said to Mr. Nibbles as he got up and locked the door. He spent some time with his parents and then wished them goodnight. He didn't want to give them any excuse to come check on him and accidentally discover him communing with a dragon!

He returned and sat silently looking at the dog and gaining the courage to attempt a connection with the inner beast of the small curly tailed pup. He closed his eyes and tried to shut out the world. Noises and thoughts kept creeping in: thoughts of school and friends; thoughts of dragons and the day the dragon came to save him in the catacombs of Edinburgh. Daydreams kept sliding into his mind followed by thoughts and memories.

He shook his head several times as if he could rattle the distractions out onto the floor. He tried to concentrate and grew increasingly frustrated. He tried and tried to clear his mind. Over and over he would try to say "Nibblus Maximus" and then he would peek but the little dog just looked up at him silently.

Presently, he began to slip toward sleep. As his will let go and his mind stopped trying to clear itself, the distractions lifted and the name emerged effortlessly into his mind; "Nibblus Maximus."

"I am here, Bearer of the sporran," the words echoed around his skull and he began to struggle to wake himself. "Don't fight, Jacob, I'm here with you. You'll be safe. Let the world go and join me."

From somewhere outside his consciousness, Jacob could feel the pug snuggle its nose against his face and lay down with its head nestled under his chin. The boy felt his muscles go limp and sink into the bed.

"Bearer, I am Nibblus Maximus, a dragon pug from the 300th age of Agathon. I have been here to protect you and the power you bear. We both saved each other's life already. I saved you beneath the sod of Scotland and you saved me with the healing waters of the catacombs. Our lives are entwined now, and it is time for you to join in that understanding."

Jacob felt as if his mind had slipped from his body and something beyond his own will was pulling the strings of his thoughts. He heard himself say, "Can I see you?"

"Not now, Bearer. This is already too much for you. In an evening or so, perhaps we can connect more completely. For now, you must be quiet and work to remember this path from your mind to mine. Crossing it must become as easy as a random thought or daydream."

The next morning, Jacob awoke and realized he had not moved a muscle all night. He still felt tired and his body ached slightly from fatigue. He half wondered if the experience he had was but a dream. Mr. Nibbles was asleep at his feet.

First Flight

Jacob found it difficult to pay attention at school. His mind was fatigued and his body tired. He nearly fell asleep twice during English class. His best friends Jenny and Will could tell something wasn't right. Jacob just brushed off their questions and concerns.

The evenings passed and each night the Bearer and the dragon connected for a bit longer. The dragon shared with Jacob a bit of his history and his longing to again visit the Isle of Agathon where he had been born and raised. Jacob shared some of his inner thoughts and fears. The two became closer with each passing night.

On the seventh night since the bridge was first built between the two, Nibblus Maximus asked Jacob to open his eyes. Jacob struggled to pull open his eyelids. When they finally lifted and his eyes adjusted to the light, standing above him he saw a huge dragon filling his room. He knew it was Nibbles and yet the sight scared him and caused him to try to push away. The dragon leaned down and rubbed its black nose against Jacob's cheek and his tongue licked from the boy's ear across his cheek, then retracted into its mouth. Jacob relaxed and the dragon backed into the middle of the room.

It's all right, Bearer. I am your servant and friend Nibblus Maximus. You know I am not capable of harming you. Rise up and join me.

The dragon was communicating with the boy through his thoughts and Jacob responded by standing and searching the awesome creature with his eyes.

Jacob, I am just your old friend. Please don't be afraid. Come on.

Pet me and rub behind my ears, just like you do when I am as the dog. The dragon turned his face away from the boy and lowered his head in hopes of making him feel more comfortable.

Jacob approached the creature and touched its side slowly and gently. He felt a tingle in his fingertips and then a shudder through his neck and down his right arm—a feeling he recognized as "the quickening." He had felt it many times the year before when he was in Scotland. The brownish-blue scales of the dragon's sides were softer than he had guessed. He always imagined a dragon would have hard and brittle scales that might cut a human's skin. Instead, the dragon felt more like the sides of a catfish freshly pulled from the muddy river bottom; soft and not uncomfortable to the touch.

Slowly, Jacob brushed his hand down the side of the beast and then moved his hand progressively higher with each pass. Finally, his hand started just behind the dragon's right ear. In the reflection of the darkened window, Jacob could see Nibblus Maximus' mouth turn upward at the corners in a smile. A soft purring sound emanated from the dragon's chest and with it Jacob's apprehension melted away.

He threw his arms around the neck of the beast and exclaimed, "Old friend, forgive me for being afraid, I know you're just Mr. Nibbles!" His cheek sunk into the gelatin-like flesh of the dragon's neck and he squeezed.

I have longed to share this secret with you Jacob, but it was not the time. My kind has been persecuted to near extinction and we can only show ourselves under the most extreme need. The dragon was speaking through the mental bridge that had been created between it and the boy.

Jacob did not attempt to return the thoughts but backed up to take in the full measure of Nibblus Maximus. Sitting on its back end, his black-faced head would have pushed through the ceiling if he had straightened up. His face was flat with bulging black eyes. He might now be a dragon, but the remnant of his other self as a small pug colored everything about him. His brown chest, tinged with a deeper blue, was wide and strong. His feet ended in four long claws. His white teeth were large and burst through his pink and brown gums. Two wings blended into the colors of his body and were held tight at his side. Jacob had to climb over his bed to get around the back of the dragon and rubbed his hand over its curled tail as he turned and came back up the side.

Got a good look yet, Bearer? The dragon turned his head back to look Jacob in the eye.

"Why can't you talk out loud, if you can talk inside my head?" Jacob asked.

Ever known a dog or a dragon that could speak, Jacob?

"Are you trying to be funny?" Jacob asked, as he walked over toward the window and glanced out at the night.

Just clear your mind and connect with me, Bearer. Anyone can hear you if you speak aloud, but no one can know the secrets we will share through our minds. With the task you have been given and the times that are to come, we will need our secrets, Jacob. Now, take me for a walk.

What? Jacob answered silently but trying as he could to push the word with his imagination out of his own head and toward the dragon. He felt as if his brain was a large bulb that, if he squeezed hard enough, would send his message flying out.

Come now, don't make me say it—you know why Mr. Nibbles needs to go out for a walk!

But, its very late, and you know Mom and Dad won't let me leave the house at this time of night.

Jacob, open the window. The dragon turned his body, knocking over Jacob's chair and pushing his bed hard against the wall.

Open the window, why?

Just open it, and look carefully out at the lawn, the dragon answered sternly.

Jacob shrugged his shoulders and moved toward the window. He pulled it open and leaned out into the cool night air.

What? Jacob said and then suddenly felt Nibblus Maximus' head ram hard into the rear end of his blue striped pajama bottoms. The dragon-sized head butt sent him flying out the window and high above the front lawn below. "Ahhhhhhhhhhhhhhhhhhhh," Jacob screamed as he tumbled through the crisp night air.

Nibblus Maximus exhaled and sucked his body as small as was possible. His strong back legs launched him through the window, barely scraping his sides against its frame, but bringing down the curtain as he crossed into the night. With one quick backward thrust of his wings, the dragon dropped down and scooped Jacob up onto his back just before the boy splattered in the grass.

"What the heck are you doing?" Jacob yelled as his fingers dug into the dragon's neck.

Use your mind, Jacob, remember, your mind! It's the middle of the night, how are you going to explain being out here with a dragon if someone hears you?

Put me down! Put me down! Please!

The dragon banked left around the house as it glided and then landed in the back yard. Jacob lost his grip as Nibblus Maximus hit the ground. The boy went toppling over the neck of the beast and landed hard in the grass. He jumped to his feet, angry and hurt that his friend had endangered him.

"What did you do that for? You could have killed me!" Jacob was yelling in Nibblus' face.

A low bellowing laugh burst out of the dragon's mouth. Dragon spittle followed the laugh and splatted on Jacob's face. He spit back and wiped the dragon spittle from his cheeks and chin. A giggle crept up through his insides and burst out.

I guess that was kind of fun!

Sometimes, young Bearer, you just need to take a leap into the dark and hang on for the ride!

As the two walked back to the house, Jacob communicated, *So, how is it that I'm supposed to explain grass stains on my pajamas?*

The dragon snorted.

They paused at the garage door and the dragon took in a big breath of the night air, closed the open link that had connected his thoughts to Jacob's, and began to shrink down into Mr. Nibbles once more. The little dog jogged over to the bushes where he lifted his hind leg and watered them. Jacob shook his head and laughed.

After that first night, Mr. Nibbles never again transformed himself in the house. In the days and weeks that followed, Jacob and Nibblus Maximus took progressively longer flights and spent hours practicing communication. The dragon told Jacob more about his life from being a pup on the Isle of Agathon to his time being the protector of Chadwick von Niblick in Edinburgh.

During one night flight over the fields away from the lights of town, the dragon's mind grew particularly serious. Jacob could feel a grave sense come over himself in response.

I'm here for you, Jacob. Always remember that my role is to protect you and by doing so to serve the Sporrai. Try to keep me near, but even if I am not, our bond will get stronger and stronger until you will be able to reach me nearly anywhere at anytime by calling for me by my true name: Nibblus Maximus. But, Jacob, you must promise me that you will never hesitate to put me in danger. For, you are the Bearer and must be protected. I, like you, am but a servant of the higher power. But unlike you, my role is to protect you and what you carry.

I understand, Jacob answered as he watched the treetops pass below them. *But,* he continued, *you're my best friend. I can't put you in danger. I won't put you in danger.*

We are all born to serve; you and I and everyone else. I know my station and you would do well to know yours. Mine is to protect you up to the point that it costs me my life. Yours is to stay alive and protect what you bear until your duty has been completed. You will not hesitate to call upon me when danger comes. Is that clear?

Jacob felt chastised by the tone of the dragon's orders and knew better than to argue with a two-ton mystical beast at 5,000 feet above the ground. He said nothing more than, *You're my friend,* and lowered his head onto the dragon's neck.

It had been several days since he had stopped becoming ill on these evening flights. Now the thought of Mr. Nibbles being in danger, of another veiled reference to his own life being at stake, and the dance of the city lights off in the distance as the dragon's wings beat, was all too much. He pushed his head aside from Nibblus Maximus' neck, arched his back involuntarily, and sent his half digested dinner dropping at several hundred feet per second toward the houses below.

Sheep's Head

Several more evenings passed with Nibblus Maximus and Jacob working on their communication link and Jacob's ability to fly without getting sick or falling off. Jacob noted that a saddle would have helped very much and "Nibblus," as Jacob had come to call his friend, told him about the saddles that the members of the Sporrai once made. But that was when there were more dragons and more of their Order. Over the years, the dragons had been hunted and some members of the Sporrai had lost faith and fell from their duty. The craft of saddle making was all but lost.

Early one Saturday morning, just days before school was out for the summer, the doorbell rang at the Boyd house. It was the third or fourth ring before Jacob heard it. He and Mr. Nibbles started down the stairs and found his father already at the door talking to a man on the porch. The man's hair was white and as thin as his body. He stood in old boots and wore blue overalls stained with dirt and grease.

Mr. Nibbles ran to the door, paused, barked, and then ran out into the grass. Jacob followed him to the door.

"Sir," his dad was saying to the farmer standing on their porch, "I'm sure I don't know what you're talking about, and I'd appreciate it if you got that *thing* off my porch!"

As Jacob got to the door, a sense of nausea came over him. In the man's hand was a sheep. Actually, it wasn't a whole sheep, but merely a sheep's head held by the tuft of fur between its ears. The white fur was stained with red splotches of blood and its eyes were gray and cloudy.

Mr. Boyd called the dog back into the house and dismissed the man. Before the door closed, the farmer peeked in and caught a glimpse of Jacob, making the boy feel uneasy.

"Dad, what was that about?" Jacob asked as Mr. Nibbles scampered back into the house and up to Jacob's room.

"Seems that man has lost some sheep recently and thinks there is some flying, sheep-eating beast living in the area!"

Jacob backed into the railing of the stairs. A look of panic crossed his face.

His dad laughed loudly. "Don't worry, son! There haven't been dragons in these parts in …" he paused, "well, in forever, I guess!" He laughed again.

Mr. Boyd rubbed Jacob's already messy hair as he passed into the kitchen. As he did, Jacob's knees grew weak and he slid down onto the first stair. Blankly, he stared through the floor into nothingness for a moment and then turned and ran up the stairs to his room. There he found Mr. Nibbles standing on his hind legs on the bench below the window. He was looking down at the farmer who was across the street with his sheep's head in hand.

"Nibblus!" Jacob announced as he entered the room. "What have you done?"

The dog turned its head and looked at his master.

Jacob closed his eyes and concentrated on opening the communication link to Nibblus Maximus, but it was difficult. The dragon was resisting. Finally, Jacob sat down on his bed to conserve energy and sent a mental probe toward the dog's inner consciousness.

Jacob … a dragon's gotta eat you know! Nibblus Maximus answered even before Jacob communicated anything.

Gotta eat? Nibblus, that was a whole sheep!

Not really! The mind of the dragon answered. *I never eat the heads! You're sick!*

I'm a dragon; don't judge me by the standards of a boy!

Jacob could tell his friend was both a bit embarrassed and angry that he would question his nature or needs.

OK, OK, Jacob answered in a tone meant to calm the dragon's emotions and to back himself out of the situation. *So, tell me about it, then.*

Jacob learned that Mr. Nibbles had been sneaking out a couple of nights a week since coming to America to practice his hunting skills and, when no wild game was available, terrorizing some of the local livestock.

That farmer must have been watching last night and followed me back to the neighborhood, he said.

Jacob went to the window and looked out to see if the farmer was still in the area. He could see the man three houses away. Another man in a black car had pulled over and was talking to him.

"Mr. Nibbles, what do you make of this?" Jacob said as he pointed to the man getting out of the car and talking to the farmer who was still holding the sheep head in his left hand.

Mr. Nibbles came back over to the window and looked out.

Quick, open the window so I can hear!

Jacob raised the window and the dog leaned out. As Jacob watched the men talking, a shock suddenly shot down his neck and into his right arm.

Jacob, quickly, shut the window and get down! Nibblus Maximus had forced an opening of communication unlike Jacob had ever felt between them before.

I felt something, too, what's wrong? Jacob and Mr. Nibbles were both on the floor under the window.

Jacob, I heard the man in the car. He told the farmer that he could help him with his "little problem." He told him he heard of a dragon living in the area and terrorizing people's property and he had come to stop it. Jacob, no matter what he says, that man is here not for me—but for you. I'm sorry. I am here to protect you and instead have called attention to your existence here! How stupid of me! Will you ever forgive me, Bearer!

You're my friend, Nibblus, there is no need to forgive you for being yourself and doing what dragons do. I understand that, I guess.

The two sat peeking out the window until the man in the black car drove off. Finally Nibblus broke the silence.

Bearer and friend, you must leave this place. It is not safe here for you anymore.

Jacob reacted with a tinge of anger in his mind. *I'm going nowhere. I can't leave with that man in my community. If he is here, he can hurt anyone unless I'm here to protect them.*

No Jacob, he is here because he thinks you are here. He doesn't care about anyone else. He wants to find me and by finding me he hopes to find you and your sporran. If you are gone, he will soon realize it and will leave the area undisturbed. If the farmer can't help him find us, it's only a matter of time before he runs into Bobby Plump—and then the game is over. We'll be caught.

The two discussed the situation through the morning, skipping breakfast as they worked out a plan. When Jacob emerged from his room, he found his parents in the back yard cleaning around the flowerbeds and removing the spring weeds from the small vegetable garden his father tended near the back fence.

"Mom. Dad. I just want you two to know that I'm very excited about going to Iona Academy this summer and thought maybe we could take a little family vacation before it starts next week."

"What do you have in mind, Jacob?" his mother asked as she looked up at his father with a gentle smile.

"Well, I thought that since the summer program starts in a week, and my school is out on Tuesday … maybe we can go early and spend a few days easing me into the area and seeing what's around. That would really make me feel better about being away in a strange place for so long."

Jacob felt silly even saying the words. He wasn't a little kid and had been trying to earn his independence to do things on his own, but desperate times called for desperate measures. This time called for him to appear insecure in order to get out of the area before he put himself and the rest of his family in danger.

"Sounds good to me," his dad said as he gently swung his hoe over toward his wife's back end, which was hanging out of the flowerbed she was weeding. "How does it sound to you, honey?"

"Sounds splendid! I hear there are some great antique shops in

Aberdeen!"

Jacob thanked his parents and he turned with Mr. Nibbles to go into the house when his dad caught his attention.

"Oh, but honey, maybe our boy is just afraid of the dragon!" His dad said with another laugh as he tossed a bundle of weeds into his wheelbarrow. "Dragons, indeed!"

"Right, Dad! Dragons!" Jacob said and walked into the house with Mr. Nibbles on his heels.

SHADOW MANSION

Jacob and Mr. Nibbles were exceptionally careful over the next few days. Jacob went to school and acted as inconspicuously as possible. Mr. Nibbles stayed pretty much alone in Jacob's room watching out the window during the day. At night he caused havoc on farms far away, hoping to lure the stranger to another town. The day before school ended, Jacob saw the black car of the man who had been talking to the farmer. It gave him a scare. Otherwise, the days passed uneventfully as he packed and said goodbye to his friends.

Jacob was still not very excited about leaving home for the summer, but now that this 'hunter' was in the area he knew more than ever that it was the right thing. Hopefully, he reasoned, his absence would at least draw the danger away from his family and friends. And besides, his best friends Jenny and Will hadn't been particularly close to him since he came back from Scotland last year. They had been with him when he first discovered some of the power of the sporran, but when he wouldn't share any more of the secrets he discovered and wouldn't even let them see the powerful pouch, they had become jealous and accused him of being selfish.

He knew, or at least he thought he knew, it wasn't selfishness that motivated him, but concern for them and a new sense of responsibility that came with discovering the secrets of the Sporrai. *If I can't be trusted not to tell my friends, how can I be trusted not to spill the secrets when my life is in danger from an enemy,* he wondered.

Jenny and Will came to say goodbye the morning he and his family left for Iona Academy. Will offered to watch Mr. Nibbles, but Jacob politely declined, as he had already made arrangements to take the dog with him. Jenny said she would look after the house and water Mrs. Boyd's flowers and Mr. Boyd's vegetable garden while they were gone. The three friends stood quietly for a moment and then Will pulled Jacob aside and the three walked down the drive.

"Jacob," Will said. "Jenny and I have been talking. We haven't been very close since, well, you know, when things started happening here last year." He was kicking at some weeds that had grown up in a crack of the driveway.

"What he is trying to say," Jenny interrupted, "is that we're sorry. We wanted you to be the same and we held it against you when you weren't. We know you're dealing with things none of us can understand and we should've tried to be more understanding."

Jacob began to smile and said, "If you only knew!"

The three laughed and for the first time in a year all three reached their right hands together and did their super secret handshake they called "battle dragons," which resembled a thumb wrestling battle royal. All three laughed again at the silly feeling they got from doing something they had each clearly outgrown. Still, it felt good and Jacob left home that day happier than he had been in a long time.

Iona Academy was a three-hour drive and after stops for lunch, dinner, rest areas, and some shopping, the Boyd's arrived in the tiny little village of Aberdeen. Most buildings in Aberdeen date from the late 18th century and the ones that don't are made to look like they do. The colonial flair of the place made his mother more excited than he was. She loved the colonial period of American history and marveled at every storefront they passed.

Only one main road went through the village and about halfway through, as dark descended upon them, Mr. Boyd announced that he had seen the sign to Iona.

"Thar' she blows!" he announced, as he pointed to a brown and white sign with an arrow pointing to a side street. Jacob's nerves began to flutter in his stomach and he started petting Mr. Nibbles furiously.

Mrs. Boyd turned around to share the excitement with Jacob but instead declared, "Jacob! You're gonna pull the hide off that dog!"

Jacob looked down to see his petting stroke had ironed out every wrinkle in Mr. Nibble's face and even his eyeballs were stretched up and back in his head. "Oh, sorry guy!"

They passed Mosby's tavern and numerous beautiful horse farms on the long, winding road from the village. "Now these people have money!" Mrs. Boyd emphasized as they all gawked at the mansions and stately farmhouses that dotted the road. Some homes couldn't even be seen, but the closed gates gave the passersby some idea of what they might look like.

Jacob sat on the edge of his seat. Mr. Nibbles was behind him with his paws on the window ledge. As they descended the hill, they saw, amidst the lengthening shadows of night, two awesomely large lions lying atop great stone pedestals. Jacob would inspect them many times in the days and weeks to come. Each beast wore a sporran around its neck and had stone eyes that somehow seemed to follow Jacob whenever he walked by the gate. They were a great symbol of the school that few who saw them ever forgot.

"And, here we are!" Mr. Boyd announced as he slowly turned the car and passed between the lions. The iron gate opened as their car entered and a guard emerged from the gatehouse. Jacob felt the tingle of "the quickening" through his neck and down his arm.

"We are the Boyds and we have a reservation at the Spur and Spoon," Mr. Boyd announced after he lowered his window and the guard looked in.

The guard was of average height and was round in the belly. He wore a dark uniform shirt at least one size too small. He carried a clipboard in his left hand and patted his gun holster with the other.

"Of course. I have your name right here. Please sign in and then proceed directly up this road, take your first right and follow it directly around. Don't turn anywhere; just keep going straight through the curves and the Spur will be the large house directly in front of you. Enjoy your stay."

Large trees lined the road and formed an ominous canopy of intertwined fingers above the car. The moon lit gently upon a gurgling stream that flowed beside the road just inside the gate. Shadows danced to the music played by the wind and the branches and Jacob's already sharpened nerves dug like daggers into his stomach. At the top of the hill was a large building with a sign out front identifying it only as "The Great Hall." On its porch were two small lions identical to the giant ones at the front gate. They passed it and followed the bending road south past some work sheds and tractors then up again by some open fields. In the distance they could see small lights and the outline of a great home.

The Spur and Spoon was the only wood clad building on the grounds of Iona and its yellow paint cast off a silvery-gold glow in the moonlight. There was no innkeeper to greet them, just a note on the door saying that they were the only guests for the night and that they should make themselves at home in Room 3 at the top of the stairs.

The floors creaked with every step. The air was cold and the pictures that hung on the wall were of people who were obviously long dead. Jacob fell in love with it at the first creak of the floorboards under his feet. Though it was drafty and damp, it felt comfortable to him. Mrs. Boyd was less happy about the draft, but a small heater in their room soon provided satisfactory warmth.

Jacob pulled the shade and looked out across the field toward the other buildings on campus. Only a few lights were on, but he could see the outlines of a dozen or more buildings on the horizon. He turned to his right and in the distance stood a coldly dark mansion. Not a single spark from the building cast any light into the night. Something made him stare at it, though, and he felt strangely drawn to the dark shadow, though his eyes could not make out any details.

One particularly dark spot near the top caught his eye and he felt as if he was being dragged toward it over the fields below. He resisted and a spike of pain dropped through his shoulder and into his arm. He pulled with his mind and the link stretched like invisible taffy and then finally snapped. He fell back to the floor, almost landing on Mr. Nibbles.

"Son, are you alright?" Mr. Boyd said as he rose out of his chair.

"Sorry ... yeah ... just lost my balance I guess."

The next few days passed quickly. On most days Jacob, Mr. Nibbles, and at least one of his parents would begin the day with a morning walk around campus. Then it was back to the Spur and Spoon where Miss Ruth, the housekeeper for most of the campus, had a continental breakfast ready for them. Most days they spent away from the school shopping in the village of Aberdeen, visiting several Civil War battlefields that are in the general area of Iona Academy, and on Thursday they spent the day at an amusement park. When he could, Jacob spent time thumbing through brochures for the school and old yearbooks that were lying around, and generally familiarizing himself with the campus.

Iona Academy is set on 150 acres surrounded by rolling horse farms and patches of woods. The village is three miles to the southeast of the school and another boarding school, the Ballardsville Academy, is about a mile north of Iona. The same stream runs from Ballardsville down to Iona and once a year all the students organize a clandestine meeting in a woodlot about half way between the schools. The adults of both schools pretend not to know about "the Rendezvous of the Picts," as it is called, but that would be impossible since a number of teachers at both schools were themselves graduates and took part in the same rituals.

Between the great stone lions that guard the entrance to Iona, is a black arch of cast iron spelling out "Nemo Me Impune Lacessit." Those first days of coming in and out of the gate with his parents, Jacob wasn't quite sure the letters spelled anything. But, one night soon he would discover exactly what it said and what it meant.

Almost every building on campus was made of red bricks with yellow trim. There was a natural feel of distress around the place. A windowsill peeled here, grass that had grown up between the stones of the sidewalk there. In general, though, Iona's campus was well kept and in order.

The Great Hall was situated at the front of the campus a few hundred yards up a small hill from the gate. To its right and slightly down the hill were some rough looking old buildings used by the maintenance crew. To the left of the Great Hall, the campus rolled out flat with half a dozen buildings; two dorms, a gymnasium, two classroom buildings and the library. Around the core of the academic and student buildings, small brick homes dotted the slight decline of land toward the horse fields that unfolded away from campus to the southeast. A narrow blacktop road ran up to the Great Hall and split, forming a circle around the academic hill and small homes.

A branch of the road to the right of the Great Hall was unpaved and ran out to the Spur and Spoon and on to the horse barns nestled against the hillside below and beyond the bend. Along that unpaved road was also a series of a dozen homes, mostly white block flat ranches in which faculty and administrators lived. From the back porch of the Great Hall, the old mansion could be seen amongst the trees on a hill across the valley. From that first night on campus, Jacob tried to avoid looking at that house for any length of time, but glanced at it often and remembered its grip as he felt it from the room that night in the Spur and Spoon.

Lucy Furangle

The morning hours brought a hard rain to Aberdeen the day
Mr. and Mrs. Boyd were to leave Jacob and Mr. Nibbles for the
summer. Being a boarding school for very elite and very rich kids
during the year, the school was fully equipped to keep the favorite pets
of the students. A one hundred-stall barn kept the horses, and heated
outdoor kennels behind it housed the dogs and cats. Jacob checked Mr.
Nibbles into the kennel before he made his way up to the Great Hall to
register himself.

Mr. Nibbles' new temporary home was homely at best. There was
a nice box with a bed waiting on him that would keep him out of the
weather and the cool night air. He had a fenced in area to run around. It
wasn't much, but Mr. Nibbles wasn't much of a dog, either. Jacob felt a bit
guilty for leaving him there and apologized several times before he turned
to head back up toward the residential part of campus.

The Boyds were among the first in line for registration. There were
forms to complete, staff people and older students to meet, and buzzing
in and out of the lines was the affable Miss Abigail Witherspoon:
headmistress of Iona. Miss Witherspoon was the descendant of the great
former teacher at Princeton University, John Witherspoon. She didn't
make too much of that, but a large painting above her desk featured the
dower looking old man surrounded by smaller paintings of his most
famous students like the fourth President of the United States, James
Madison. Today, she was mostly interested in putting on a good show for
the parents and appearing to run everything herself. Her hair was pulled

up into a tight bun on her head and she wore a tartan skirt and a purple stone brooch on her white blouse.

"Ah, Mr. Boyd, so glad to have you aboard," she said after glancing down at Jacob's nametag. "His essay," she continued, now looking up at his parents, "was extraordinary, just extraordinary! Indeed, one of the best essays on the Battle of Culloden the admissions committee has ever read."

Jacob's parent's beamed over his shoulder with pride. Ashamed, Jacob remained silent. His mother pinched the back of his arm as encouragement to thank the woman for her compliment. Guiltily, he said "Thanks," and turned away from Miss Witherspoon's glance as he rubbed the back of his arm.

With a long ride home ahead of them, Jacob's parents said their goodbyes as soon as the parent-student orientation session was complete. Jacob waved goodbye from the porch of his dormitory as a hand smacked hard into his shoulder.

"So, Newbie, word is that Miss Witherspoon—the old bat—has taken a liking to you."

Jacob turned his head to see a girl who was noticeably older and also much larger than he was. Her name was Lucy Furangle. He had already been warned to steer clear of her from a few of the students he had met during the day.

"You are some kind of prodigy in Celtic history or something. Well, I have news for you … Iona is *my* school. I run it. My dad owns it. I'm the star. If you end up in my Dirks, you can be as good as you want. If you end up in the Targes, and I pity you that, you will mind your place or I will break you! Understood?"

The girl had turned Jacob around to look him square in the face and then pushed him backward before Jacob could react. She walked away with a swagger he had never seen in a girl, but recognized from the walk of the deposed bully, Bobby Plump. Before he turned to walk back into the dormitory, he fantasized about Mr. Nibbles coming around the corner to scare this bully down a peg or two.

Roommate Surprise

Jacob turned into his dorm, glanced around, and then made the one story climb up the old wooden staircase that led to his room. The basic digs were nothing like Jacob had imagined a school for spoiled rich kids would be. In the middle of each hall there was a common bathroom with three showers and three toilets and three sinks. All were basic and old, but were clean—Miss Ruth, the cleaning lady, always saw to that.

The first floor of Jacob's dorm was where the "common area" was located. To the right of the stairs was the house library. It was well appointed in oak bookcases from floor to ceiling and comfortable furniture. There were two computer desks on the left side and a fireplace at the far end. On a table behind the main sofa, Miss Ruth would put snacks and tea for the boys each afternoon. To the left of the stairs and down the hall was a laundry room for washing clothes. (Jacob's mother had had to teach him to do his own laundry, which was not something he was looking forward to and was something he would successfully avoid for weeks.) A room with a ping-pong table, TV, and radio was next to the laundry.

Between the stairs and the laundry room was Professor Ramos Kirk's apartment and office. Kirk was the tutor of the house, which meant that he was in charge of all the boys who lived there. He was responsible for maintaining the rules, helping them with their studies, giving them advice, and taking care of any problems that might arise. Kirk was also a teacher of classics and literature and was Dean of the Faculty. He had been at Iona for more than twenty years and seemed to love his job and living at the Academy. He was pudgy and a bit shy and had the bad habit of closely inspecting his shoelaces when he was asked questions that made him uncomfortable or that he thought were not very intelligent. All of his students knew he was brilliant, but some thought him a bit strange for the late night hours he kept and for the old books that seemed to be his constant companions.

Jacob would meet Professor Kirk later that afternoon during their first mandatory dorm meeting in the library. For now, he walked into his own room to check it out and be alone. He had to gather some courage before meeting the other kids. He pushed the door open. The room was basic and old. A worn area rug covered the middle of the floor. Two iron beds lay opposite one another and at the head of each sat an old wooden desk. His bags had been delivered and were waiting on his bed. His eyes focused like lasers on the desk behind the other bed. He was not alone. There was someone sitting with his feet propped up and his hands nonchalantly propped behind his head.

"Hi, Roomie," the boy announced with a big smile crawling across his face.

Jacob hesitated. They had not told him he would have a roommate, though he probably should have guessed that he would. Jacob paused and then moved with authority toward the boy. He walked right up to him and with a forceful swipe of his left hand, he pushed the boy's feet off the desk. The boy tipped forward, as he had been resting on the back legs of his chair and yelled, "What's the big deal, *Roomie!*" He stood and shoved Jacob in the chest.

A slow smile crossed Jacob's face as he punched the boy in the arm and said "What are *you* doing here, *Will?*" It was Jacob's good friend from home. Before Will could answer, Jacob repeated the question and then added, "Why didn't you tell me you were coming?"

Will laughed happily at the surprise he had pulled off. "I didn't quite know myself until the other night. Some guy showed up at my place and offered us a scholarship to come. He said it was a surprise for you and part of a new program the school had started to bring 'clusters' of kids from the same neighborhoods."

"Did you say 'us'?" Jacob asked, with an even more puzzled look on his face.

"Sure, Jenny's here, too. She's in the girl's dorm right now." Will stopped himself. "Darn it! That was supposed to be a surprise for you at dinner. Now I've blown it, as usual!"

Jacob smiled. "Oh, I'll still act surprised, don't worry," Jacob happily reassured him.

Jacob turned back to his side of the room and went to unzip his suitcase. "Boy, this is gonna be great! Glad to have you guys here with me. It will be like old times, like …"

"Yes, like before that *thing* came and screwed up everything for us," Will finished Jacob's thought for him. It wasn't quite his thought but it was close enough that Jacob recognized it.

Jacob ignored Will and reached down to unzip his suitcase and start to unpack. As he did, he glanced over at his backpack where his sporran and the red-stoned ring of Isildane were kept.

"So, what *have* you done with that magic bag of yours?" Will asked.

"Come on, Will, you know I can't tell you that. Let's not talk about it, OK?"

"Well, I don't see why you can't trust me …" Will paused and then remembered the last time they had that conversation. It wasn't pretty. Feelings were hurt and they didn't speak to each other for a week. He didn't complete his thought but instead asked, "So, what do you think we'll have for dinner?"

In the girl's dorm next door, Jenny was getting to know her roommate Elizabeth when the door suddenly flew open. In the doorway stood a large girl with straight black hair and clothes that immediately said, "I'm rich, look at me!"

"Which one of you is Jenny?" the girl asked as she leaned her weight on the doorframe and crossed her feet.

"That's me," Jenny replied after a short pause to gather her thoughts.

"I should've guessed. I hear you're friends with that Jacob Boyd kid. Is that right?"

Jenny nodded her head but did not speak.

"Well, then. Here is a piece of advice for you. Stay out of my way. I'm Lucy Furangle."

Elizabeth nervously attempted to get into the conversation by repeating the girl's name but it came out "Lucifer Angle."

"No! Lucy! Lucy Furangle, and I wasn't speaking to you!" Lucy said as she grew agitated. But she continued, "And I don't have much use for new kids who think they're special. This is my school. I go here during the year and I go here in the summer. My daddy's on the Board and he *owns* this place. If you and your friend want to survive the summer, I suggest you stay clear of me unless you get to join my Dirks. I'll be watching you, *girlfriend*." Lucy turned toward Elizabeth and added "and I'll be watching you too, pigtails!"

Hurricane Lucy turned and left the room gutted of emotion. When she was out of earshot, Jenny turned to Elizabeth and then giggled. "Lucifer! You called that old devil Lucifer! Lucy Furangle! Lucifer Angle! What a name!"

Elizabeth just sat down on the edge of her bed and looked rather sick.

I wonder why that witch is concerned with Jacob? Why does she care about me or him? This could be a long summer with "Lucifer" around, Jenny puzzled.

REVELATION

J acob and Will met up with Jenny as often as they could those first few days of the summer camp. Most of their classes were together but some of their activities were separated with the boys going one way and the girls another.

Every afternoon the girls would get riding lessons near the stables while the boys played soccer or baseball. Archery was usually done together in small mixed groups and all meals were taken in common among the whole community including teachers, camp counselors, and regular students.

Each day was basically like the others, though there was always just enough to spice it all up and make it not feel like plain old "school."

Breakfast was always served in the common dining room between 7:00 AM and 7:45 AM. "newbies," as the first year kids were called, always sat together. The rest of the students were divided into two groups—The Dirks and the Targes. The "newbies" would be placed into one of the two groups during the First Feast of Summer, which occurred the first Friday night after their arrival.

Classes began at 8:00 AM sharp and for Jacob that meant going to "Early Celtic History of Europe" followed by "Art and Literature of the British Isles," and then "Myths and Legends" before lunch. The first period after lunch was reserved for marshal training which rotated between archery, fencing, training with the broadswords and basic martial arts training. On Thursdays, they hiked to the lake for water sports, as they did every Saturday morning that it wasn't raining.

Promptly at 4:00 PM tea and scones were served in the library of each house and then their free afternoon commenced. Most days Jacob, Jenny, and Will got together and walked down by the stables to play with Mr. Nibbles. Jenny often walked over to the stables to pet and care for her favorite horses.

Jacob's little pug dog always seemed in good spirits and glad to be let out of his pen for his daily romp in the fields. He was also sad to see them go at 6:00 PM when they were expected to be at the dining hall.

The evenings were to be spent in study for the next day's classes, though most students found time to play ping-pong or just hang out in the library or recreation room of their house. Bed check came promptly at 10:00 PM, after which the doors were locked tight and no one was permitted to leave until breakfast was served the next morning. Most evenings Professor Ramos Kirk would conduct the room check himself.

Kirk always started on the top floor and worked his way down. He would walk from room to room, making up rhymes as he went or singing old Scottish tunes considerably off-key. Each boy was to be seated during this inspection, either on his own bed or at his desk. Typically, Kirk would say nothing but tip his hat or nod as he glanced into each room. Kirk was always followed by at least two of the "Chieftains;" the oldest kids who served as monitors for the floors. They would follow along making sure Kirk never had to discipline anyone himself. If someone was out of place or not in their room at all, a chieftain would jump in to take care of the situation, reporting back to Professor Kirk when the situation had been resolved. Kirk called them his "enforcers," but always said it with a smile and a playful nod.

Kirk was somewhat round and rather short. About fiftyish in age, he had a thinning top of white hair and wore very old-fashioned black plastic glasses – the kind you seldom see except in old movies. He always wore a tie, even in the evenings and during weekend "constitutionals" into town or to the lake. Often, his ties were too short or stained with some bit of lost supper, but one always hung from his neck. It was a tradition that at the end of each term, the boys in his house would go into town and buy him a new tie. To everyone's amusement, he never seemed to have a new one on, though. Some had guessed that Kirk was making a statement with his old ties—they matched, after all, his old ideas. He had a reputation for always preferring the traditions of the school and traditional modes of education whenever his fellow teachers or students offered proposals for "change". He would often be heard saying, "Change is not reform, my friends, change is not progress. And progress is sometimes regress. And regress is sometimes progress." He seemed to delight in the confusion his riddle caused.

The first evening in the dormitory, Jacob felt like Kirk was staring at him, looking his way even as the man addressed all the boys. Jacob even felt like the professor was of two minds—he could be looking at and thinking about one thing while his mouth spoke of another. It was a little disorienting. At bed check the first night, Kirk leaned into their room and welcomed Jacob and Will. He then turned to Jacob and said "A mighty fine essay, Mr. Boyd! A mighty fine essay you completed on the Battle of Culloden." He turned and as he did said, "Almost felt like I was actually there," and disappeared down the hall.

"When did you find time to do that essay everybody's talking about, Jacob," Will asked. In the background, they could hear Kirk whistling down the hall.

Jacob paused and lay back on his bed. Staring at the ceiling, he thought about ignoring the question, but it would come up again in some way or another. He considered making up a lie and taking credit for it as he had allowed others to do for him already. But he looked over at his friend and answered, "Well, you might as well know. After all, you are here now based on it too, I guess. The truth is, I didn't write the essay. I didn't even want to come here! I threw the application away and didn't fill in a single line!"

"What? Then how did it happen? I mean, why are you … why are we here?"

Jacob just looked back up at the ceiling and that was enough for Will to realize the truth. "Oh, no! Not again! You mean, that sporran stuff again? It drug you here? It drug me here? Oh, I'm going to be sick!"

"Calm down!" Jacob urged his friend. "We don't know if we are here for any particular reason. We don't know anything. So until we do, I suggest you just do what I'm doing—have fun and enjoy the time we have."

"Does Jenny know?" Will asked.

"No. But I'll tell her during break tomorrow."

Will lay his head down on his pillow and the two boys stared in silence at the small cracks in the paint on the ceiling of Room 222 Frazier House.

Dirks and Targes

The "First Feast of Summer" was less than an hour away. Jenny and her mousy roommate Elizabeth were hurriedly doing their hair and pressing the best dresses they had brought with them. Jacob had just taken a shower and Will was headed down the hall for his. This was the moment they had all been waiting for.

The "First Feast of Summer" was the great banquet that happened at the end of the first week of camp. It was where they would discover which clan they would join. The students' nerves were stretched tight. They all had made friends, or at least acquaintances, with both Dirks and Targes but that could all change in a matter of hours. Friends would become competitors and even roommates might be pitted against one another.

Dividing the students into two camps was a long tradition at Iona. During World War I, the students couldn't go home for the summer and there was not enough money to travel and play sports against other schools. The Headmaster had decided to split the students into two groups so they could compete with each other on campus. Soon the two camps had developed cultures and rituals of their own. For a short time during the 1960's, the Board of Trustees for the school had voted to dissolve them in order to build a more uniform camaraderie among the students. That experiment had failed miserably once the students and alumni revolted.

The Dirk's wore a patch on the front of their formal academic gowns that featured a dagger making the "I" in the word DIRK. Of the two, they had the reputation of being the more elite and mean. Their members seemed richer and more arrogant than the Targes and their leaders walked around the school like they owned the place.   As one of the current leaders of the Dirks, Lucy Furangle fit perfectly with the long-standing reputation of the clan.

The Targes wore a patch on the front of their academic gowns that was round and that looked just like the ancient Scottish shield called a "targe." A targe is a round shield made of wood with leather stretched across its front. The leather is often dressed up with circles or patterns of nails and at its center is a metal sphere that looked like half a ball. The Targes had the reputation of being comprised of kids from more modest backgrounds. Though there were certainly exceptions, they were also usually the most talented students in class. Unlike the Dirks, the Targes chose their leader through a democratic vote and not from a test of strength and willpower.

For the "First Feast," each student dressed in their formal academic gowns over a shirt and tie for the boys and a dress for the girls. The newbies' gowns were black and long, just like those of the older students, but without the patch that would tell the tale of whether they were Dirks or Targes.

The newbies were told to arrive promptly at 6:00 PM at the Great Hall and sit in the tables at the back of the room. This was part of the plan to let the new kids know where they belonged in the hierarchy of the school. 6:00 became 6:15 without anyone else arriving. Then it was 6:30 and then 6:45. As the time passed, the students looked around the Great Hall as they talked. It was a long room of dark paneled wood. Large ancient beams crossed the ceiling like the ribs of an upturned boat. Candles had been lit around the walls between great heraldic shields and banners. Every ten feet around the room, a small leather pouch was hung from a wooden peg.

By 6:45 the charm had left the room and many of the students were arguing about whether or not they had misunderstood the instructions and if they should leave. After an hour of waiting, a lone bagpiper was heard in the distance. It started low and distant but gradually got closer and closer until it suddenly stopped and the great doors in the back of the hall flew open and gave evidence of the great gathering outside. The piper started again and a group of students marched into the room.

"You will stand when your superiors enter this Hall!" one barked at the newbies.

The other students entered by order of seniority and went to their seats at long tables in front of the room. Then came the staff members of the school followed by the faculty. Finally Miss Witherspoon, the headmistress, entered the room and proceeded to the head table along the front. She arrived at her chair and bowed her head. Everyone followed. Professor Kirk then offered a prayer and as he completed his remarks the older students simultaneously began to sing the Iona Alma Mater.

> Our Iona, born from Scotland's misty shores.
> You stand proud in New Columbia, above all evil's splendid lures.
> Now we join with generations, singing of your loving care.
> Yesterday and tomorrow standing here to sing your praise.
>
> Dear Iona, oh Iona, Scotland longs for its lost seed.
> We will stand, always with you, in your time of triumph or need.
> When the day of reckoning cometh, call on sons and daughters proud,
> Through the winds of change and trouble, you always remain unbowed.

"Everyone please remain standing," Miss Witherspoon announced with a twirl of her right hand above her head. "Dean of the Faculty, Professor Ramos Kirk will now lay the antlers of the white stag in their appropriate place of honor."

Professor Kirk, the only member dressed in a golden gown, unwrapped a pair of deer antlers from the red velvet wrap he had in his arms as he entered the room. He then held them aloft and the older students cheered. The newbies looked at one another, wondering what was happening.

Professor Kirk laid the antlers on the mantel of the fireplace just behind the head table, unintentionally framing Miss Witherspoon's perfectly in place hair. To some of the students' angles of view, it looked much like the headmistress herself was a deer, though one that spent a lot of time on its hair!

Miss Witherspoon then announced the arrival of the mace. The student body president came forward with what looked like a large club and placed it in a small hole in the floor in front of the head table. She bowed to the head table and backed herself down the aisle to her seat.

"Faculty and staff may now be seated," Miss Witherspoon announced as she nodded to the teachers on her right and then those on her left. When the adults had taken their seats and were quiet, she then announced that all members of the Targes and Dirks were to be seated. This left only the newbies standing nervously in the back of the room while Miss Witherspoon smiled at the front.

"My," she observed while turning her head slowly from side to side, "aren't they a precious new group?" She was clearly not expecting an answer from the other students and got what she expected. Jacob felt his cheek's grow red with embarrassment as he looked around the room. Everyone else was looking at the newbies, some smiling, and some scowling at them.

"As is our custom, newbies, you will stand during your First 'First Feast,' or at least until your name is called for the Drawing of the Sporrans." Miss Witherspoon announced as the newbies looked curiously at one another.

Slowly a chorus began to erupt. Hands were pounding on tables and feet stomping as the upper classmen chanted, "stand, stand, stand, stand." After a minute or two of this, Miss Witherspoon raised her hand and the chanting slowed and then stopped. A threatening sense of doom came over the newbies as they stood silently watching the ceremony unfold with them clearly the object of the rituals.

Food service workers from the back entered the room in plain white clothes and brought baskets of bread and bricks of cheese with them for each table. All tables were served except the newbies, who were left standing silently and looking at each other.

Will elbowed Jacob and whispered, "What's going on?"

"Shut up!" Jacob whispered back tersely.

"Excuse me, does a Newbie have something to say?" Dr. Kirk stood and announced. He was looking straight at Jacob who just shook his head and looked down at the table. "Very well, then, I trust we won't have our dinner interrupted again, Miss Witherspoon!" Kirk said as he bowed to her and watched a slice of cheese slip between the Headmistress' lips.

The newbies were all getting hungry and tired from standing. Some of them were starting to get positively angry at having to stand; others just felt sad at being treated so unfairly.

Moments later, a horn blew from outside the window and the door at the back of the room blew open. Jacob jumped. The older children stood and cheered at the sight of two boys and two girls carrying large horns sitting on golden pedestals, one in each hand. As they walked into the room, red liquid sloshed from the openings in the horns and dribbled down their arms. One horn was placed in the middle of each table except where the newbies stood in silence.

Miss Witherspoon stood and announced, "It is now time, ladies and gentlemen, for the drawing of the Sporrans."

A cheer went up around the room.

"Newbies," she continued, "it is now time that you join the fellowship of the Dirks or Targes." As she said each name, the members of that group shouted loudly and projected great enthusiasm by pounding the tables and stomping their feet.

"As Dr. Kirk calls your name," Miss Witherspoon instructed, "you will come forward, bow to the faculty and walk to the sporran calling you to it. The sporran that calls you will know unfailingly where you belong. It will give you a patch for your plain cloak. You will forever then be known as a Dirk or a Targe. Are you ready, newbies?"

There was no answer from the newbies who were busy looking at each other, reading the expressions on one another's faces, and intermittently darting their eyes from sporran to sporran which hung on the walls around the room.

"Newbies! I asked you a question," Miss Witherspoon projected in a tone less familiar and friendly than they had heard from her during their few days at Iona. She repeated, "Are you ready to enter into one of the clans of Iona?"

The newbies all either nodded affirmatively or replied with a "Yes" of varying degrees of confidence and enthusiasm.

"Dr. Kirk, please read the name of the first changling," Miss Witherspoon announced. newbies were unaffiliated on campus until this great banquet night. Then they were considered changlings, but only for a moment. The moment they made their sporran choice, they became newbies again, but then they would be Newbie members of one of the two great clans on campus.

Dr. Kirk stood and pulled a fat book from its stand behind the head table and placed it in front of him. He opened the book that was two feet wide and equally as long. As he did, dust sprang to life and danced about before landing again on the table in front of him.

Kirk looked up at the tables of newbies and announced, "Julie Robinson!" A cheer rose in the room as an impish looking little girl stepped forward and glanced about the room. Everyone's eyes laid upon her as she turned toward the wall to the right of the head table.

"Miss Robinson," Dr. Kirk announced, "I do believe you forgot your bow!"

"Sorry sir," the small girl with dark hair said as she scrambled back to the middle of the room and, just in front of Miss Witherspoon, bent forward and whispered, "Sorry ma'am." Julie then turned back the way she had been going and pulled the second sporran from its hook. She opened it and pulled a patch from its pouch. She stood for a moment silently until calls started to erupt around the room. "Come on!" "What is it?" "Tell us!"

Julie looked up and announced "Dirks!" The Dirks went wild and the chief of the Dirks came forward, pinned the patch upon Julie's cloak and escorted her to one of the Dirk tables where she got a warm welcome and all she could eat.

And so it went from student to student. Virtually every other student picked a Targe badge after a Dirk had been chosen. Most of the boys wanted to be Dirks so they could wear the badge with the dagger, thinking it more cool than one sporting a shield. Jacob, however, because of his encounter with Lucy Furangle of the Dirks, was not so sure that clan was for him.

When Will was called, he recieved a Dirk and was thrilled. Jenny, on the other hand, picked a Targe. Jacob was split and nervous; His two best friends now in two different groups that would compete against one another. Before Jacob's name was called, he looked up just in time to see a large shadow crossing the sky in the window above the head table. Several older students stood and pointed. His heart raced. *Oh no, is that Nibbles?* Jacob tried to clear his mind and make contact but there was too much going on in the room and he was distracted. The shadow passed as quickly as it came and the kids that noticed it sat back down mumbling to those around them but doing nothing.

"Mr. Jacob Boyd," Kirk announced with a grin. He watched Jacob with a special intensity as the boy moved forward toward the table where he bowed and turned. There were only five sporrans left and as much as he tried to feel one of them pulling him toward it, the fact was, he felt nothing. He moved slowly and stalled but still felt nothing. *Eenie, meenie, miney mo* he counted off in his head but without seriously paying attention to its choice. Embarrassed to be standing in front of everyone without being able to make a decision, he just moved toward one and removed it from its hook. Some students cheered. Others watched and waited silently.

The sporran he picked was brown and tattered as were most of those that hung that night. None were very fancy and those that looked the most new went early in the night. He opened its flap and looked inside. There was nothing. He stuck his hand in and turned it sideways toward the candlelight. Nothing. Jacob's heart sank in embarrassment as he looked up at the head table and then around the room at all the students and faculty staring in his direction.

"Well, Mr. Boyd, what is it?" Kirk asked, his arms crossed in his golden robe.

"It's nothing, sir—I mean, *nothing!*"

Jacob turned the sporran upside down to show there was no patch inside. As he did, a gold coin fell out of the sporran and onto the floor. The metal disk hit on its edge and spun. Then it began to slowly turn and roll down the floor toward the head table and then turned across the font of the room. It slowed as students stood and leaned over tables to watch its path. The coin ran out of power immediately in front of Dr. Kirk's place who then came out from behind the table and picked it up. He studied the coin and then announced, "Targe!" clan Targe erupted with excitement as the chieftain, Jonathan Ballardo moved toward Jacob.

Jenny jumped and yelped happily. Will mumbled "darn!" and jabbed the air in disappointment.

Amidst the commotion, Dr. Kirk slipped the coin into his pants pocket under his robe and returned to read the next name in his book.

Gathering at the Gate

It was late and the newbies were sleeping soundly after their large meal at the banquet. Exhausted from the stress and excitement that came with being placed into one of the two great clans, most had no trouble falling asleep. They each now had a new part of their identity that they would carry with them for the rest of their lives. Forever they would think of themselves as being of the Dirk or Targe clan; age would dim but never erase that.

Some of the sleeping young men and women would be awakened first by the commotion in the halls. Others would not awaken until loud pounds shook their doors and caused their hearts to race with fear and anxiety. Julie Robinson would not awaken at all until one of the older girls came into her room and shook her. She had fallen asleep listening to the soothing man's voice on the hypnotic tape she had purchased to learn how to be more assertive. "You are good and people like you. They want to hear from you. You want them to hear you. Speak up and be happy. . . ." The startle she got when she opened her eyes to see a large figure looming over her in a white robe did nothing for her self-confidence.

"Jacob," Will whispered assertively across the room. "Jacob, wake up, I think it's a fire!"

"What? What? A fire?" Jacob answered groggily. By the time he shook his head clear, Will was peeking out the door.

"Get out here, you Newbie puke!" A strong voice called into Will's face.

Will opened the door and Jacob rose from his bed and exited with his friend. Most of the other boys on their hall had already been awakened and were standing at something like frightened attention by their doors casting glances all around to see what was happening.

"Now, boys", an older boy dressed in a gray cloak and pacing down the hall announced, "a gathering of the clans has been called. Put on your robes immediately and assemble at your clan assembly pole. You have two minutes and you don't want to be late!"

The older boys in grey cloaks exited the hall as the newbies scrambled to throw on shoes (often with no socks and some that were mismatched) as well as robes and rush out the door. Boys bounced into each other in the halls and the stairs. Similar events were unfolding in the girls residence hall next door. The nervous newbies made a terrible clamor heading down the stairs and burst through their front doors where they remained, confused and perfectly still.

At one time, like the unfolding of a collective conscience, they all realized they hadn't a clue where their clan's "gathering pole" might be. They had never been told of such a thing. They looked nervously about and mumbled to each other. Finally one saw a torch burning brightly across campus and yelled for everyone to follow him. Not wanting to be the last one, they all pushed and ran as fast as they could across the dark campus. Occasionally, one would trip and fall into another and a half dozen would end up sprawled on the ground, clawing to get back to their feet so as not to get left behind.

When the group from Jacob's dorm arrived at the torch, they discovered it to be held by the chieftain of the Dirks. Will was at his destination, but Jacob was not. The older Dirks started pushing the new Targes away from them and taunting them to find their own gathering spot. Jacob and two dozen others backed away and looked around. Spotting another torch, they all flocked toward it like desperate and lonely moths to a porch light. Over the knoll and across the rocky road, they found the Targe gathering spot as a group of Newbie Dirks scrambled the other direction to find theirs.

Out of breath and with the bottom of their pants damp from the dewey grass, Jacob and the other newbies stood panting and relieved as the older Targes, most of them with hoods pulled up to shadow their faces, looked on silently.

"Welcome Targes!" the chieftain finally broke the night's silence. "You have found your home at the gathering pole." Some of the older boys began to circulate amongst the newbies, silently and gently pushing and prodding them and forming them into a circle as if they were a giant piece of clay. The chieftain entered the circle and laid a targe shield at his feet. "You will now take your oaths of loyalty to the clan and its chieftain," another boy announced.

The newbies were ordered to sit around the targe and place their left hands on it. The chieftain stood in the middle of the shield and looked up through the few clouds that hovered like silver shadows in the dull moonlight above. This began the initiation ceremony for the clan Targe. A similar ceremony unfolded at the Dirks' gathering pole—but such things are so secret that none of them ever spoke to those outside their clan about them, and so they cannot be recounted here.

After several hours of ceremonies, the sharing of secrets, and the taking of strong oaths, a bell rang from the tower on campus. Then two notes answered a single note blown through a bagpipe by a member of the Dirk clan from the Targe piper. The two pipers sent blasts back and forth as if asking questions and then replying to one another while the clans marched in a pincer movement toward the middle of campus where the Great Hall was guarded by two small stone lions that matched the two great lions at the gate.

The two clans marched behind their torchbearer who was closely followed by the clan chief. The older boys and girls, their hoods pulled over their heads, followed next. The newbies followed dutifully behind. Almost no one talked on the march.

Arriving at the Great Hall, the two torchbearers approached one another first. The two clan chiefs then came forward and embraced one another. They turned to the torches and pushed them together, lashing them into one flame with a strap of leather around the handles. The

Chieftains turned and asked their parties to kneel on one knee.

"At times," the leader of the Dirks announced with a pause, "At times we will be two in competition and strife."

"At times," the leader of the Targes interrupted and paused, "At times we will be one together in cooperation and strife."

The two Chieftains turned and exchanged places in front of the other clan's line. They began to march down the road away from the Hall and toward the front gate of Iona. As they did, the members of the clans intermingled again and friends began to talk and joke and welcome one another as if they had been absent for some time. Will found Jacob and Jenny and whispered, "I love this place!" Jacob and Jenny shared that sentiment but their only reply was Jenny sending a punch into Will's arm and exclaiming, "You dang Dirk!"

Arriving at the gate, the two clan Chieftains were handed something wrapped tightly in a towel. Together the leaders walked over to the door of the guardhouse and laid the object on the stoop of the brown metal door. This was the annual tribute the students paid to the security guard for his looking after them and their school. It was only a basket of shortbreads, but it was appreciated. The guard on duty was not at his post this night so the students were alone.

The students formed one mass of cloaked and robed humanity beneath the gate as the two chieftains climbed the two great lions and found their places astride the backs of the great beasts.

"newbies … this is the annual Great Gathering of the clans," one of the Chieftains announced. "We will not come together again like this until next year, that is, unless there is an emergency that requires a gathering."

"In Scotland, the clans gathered to celebrate and to decide upon military strategy when their land was in danger," the other chieftain added. "If circumstances call us to such a moment, we will do so here in this place under the cover of the night. A bell will toll, a lone piper will reply, and a second piper will confirm. That's how you will know to assemble at your clan's gathering pole and then make your way here."

"And, do not be late or you will suffer the same fate as that unworthy boy there!" The chieftain of the dirks pointed over to the fence where the torchbearer walked to illuminate a Newbie dangling awkwardly on the iron fence. He was a Dirk who had taken his time to find matching socks and shoes and comb his hair and straighten his robe and so was late for his clan's gathering. He would not make such a mistake again. His clansmen had hung him up with hooks in his socks, underwear, and shirt. Every morning for a month that boy was the first one up and in the shower in the morning and the first to report for tea in the afternoon.

"newbies ... please come forward and kneel between the two great lions of Iona," the chieftain of clan Dirk ordered. The robed students slowly made their way through the crowd of cloaks and found a place to kneel. Jacob accidentally brushed into Lucy Furangle as he made his way through the crowd. She sent a powerful punch into his back as he passed. It took his breath for a second, but Jacob tried not to flinch and strutted forward pretending he had felt nothing, though his teeth were bared and set tight.

"newbies, you will someday earn your hooded cloaks. Unlike your robes and your clan homes that have been given to you unearned, you will have to prove worthy of your cloaks." The Dirks' chieftain was speaking from beneath his own hood and was standing rather than sitting upon his lion's back. "You have two immediate tasks of character and brains."

"First, you will learn and memorize the great motto of Scotland and of the Iona school," he pointed up at the top of the great black cast iron gate spanning the area between the lions. "Nemo Me Impune Lacessit" he intoned and then repeated it with more force "Nemo Me Impune Lacessit!"

The Targe chieftain then repeated the phrase himself "Nemo Me Impune Lacessit" as he pointed to each word curled in the Iron Gate. Now Jacob could see it. He had noticed what looked like letters before but they made no sense to him. Now he could see the words coming to life. It means 'No one harms me with impunity,' and it is the great motto of Iona and her Scottish homeland. Repeat it now!"

The gathering began repeating the phrase *Nemo Me Impune Lacessit.* The cloaked group sounded together and harmonious. The robed newbies struggled with the words and pronunciation and made a terrible cacophony that sounded more like the chance meeting of out of tune musical instruments than a chorus of human voices.

"Second," the Dirk's chieftain interrupted, "you must memorize and love our Iona's alma mater, the song we sing to her that connects us with that past no longer seen and the future not yet glimpsed." He closed his eyes and recited the words slowly and with obvious affection.

> Our Iona, born from Scotland's misty shores.
> You stand proud in New Columbia, above all evil's splendid lures.
> Now we join with generations, singing of your loving care.
> Yesterday and tomorrow standing here to sing your praise.
>
> Dear Iona, oh Iona, Scotland longs for its lost seed.
> We will stand, always with you, in your time of triumph or need.
> When the day of reckoning cometh, call on sons and daughters proud,
> Through the winds of change and trouble, you always remain unbowed.

When he finished, the older students began slowly singing the song in unison. After the second or third time through, most of the newbies were singing as well. By the fifth time through, all were singing with pride:

> Our Iona, born from Scotland's misty shores.
> You stand proud in New Columbia, above all of evil's splendid lures.
> Now we join with generations, singing of your loving care.
> Yesterday and tomorrow standing here to sing your praise.
>
> Dear Iona, oh Iona, Scotland longs for its lost seed.
> We will stand, always with you, in your time of triumph or need.
> When the day of reckoning cometh, call on sons and daughters proud,
> Through the winds of change and trouble, you always remain unbowed.

With one final warning that they would be tested and retested in the coming days, the newbies were all sent back to their rooms to get a few hours of sleep. As they walked, some talked, but most mumbled the words of the motto or alma mater over and over under their breath trying to keep them fresh in their minds, lest they end up like the boy hanging from his underwear.

Campbell is Dead

The days that followed the great gathering by the gate proceeded, as had the previous few. The students went to class; they exercised and played sports; they studied and talked. The only real difference was the sense of fear and dread that hung over each Newbie at the sight of one of the upper classmen. Would they be stopped randomly and asked to recite the motto of Scotland or the alma mater of Iona? Would they slip up or freeze and end up hanging on the fence, or worse?

Most newbies carried notes in their pockets and quizzed each other relentlessly in their rooms. They tacked the words on the corkboards above their desks. Someone even kept a copy taped to the door on one of the stalls in the second floor girl's bathroom. This was their test and no one wanted to fail!

Of course, some did fail the test. Pants were thrown on the top of lampposts while petrified and embarrassed newbies ran back to their rooms to salvage what they could of their dignity. Some were forced to wear signs on their backs advertising their failure to everyone. On the fourth day after the gathering, Jenny found Will hanging by the straps of his backpack on the gazebo. She helped him down. "Trying to scare the birds away, Scarecrow?" she asked.

Jacob worked hard and memorized them both but no one stopped him for a test. About a week after the gathering, Jacob even started walking toward upper classmen in hopes of getting the chance to prove himself. They always greeted him, but never asked a question. He also noticed that Lucy Furangle, the girl who immediately and sternly put him in his place the first day, had begun ignoring him. It was unsettling, but he mentioned it to no one.

Jacob would visit Mr. Nibbles every day immediately after dinner. They would walk around the campus, occasionally getting strange stares from the kids with bigger and more "manly" looking dogs. The little pug dog seemed to be accepting his place at the kennel down the hill, but Jacob still felt terrible about having him stuck down there and plotted the night when he would sneak down and bring him back to sleep on the bottom of his bed like he did every night at home.

Rumors began circulating around campus that some beast had been seen in the night sky and then reports came on the radio and in the local newspaper of farmers missing livestock. Jacob knew it had to be Mr. Nibbles out getting in touch with his inner dragon, but he never asked him. *I have him cooped up down there like some chicken in a pen, how can I ask him not to have at least a little fun?* He worried, though, as he read the reports and hoped his friend wouldn't be caught.

Because there were always so many other kids around and because the line of communication is much more difficult (and painful) to open between a human and a dragon pug when the beast is in the form of the dog, they barely ever got a chance to work on their connection or to talk. Having made the connection back at home, Jacob felt lonely without it. The newness of it all at Iona, however, kept his mind mostly on other things. Because he was learning about ancient things Celtic and Scottish, he guessed he was learning things that he needed to know relating to his apprenticeship in the secretive Order of the Sporrai.

Once the kids got back from a short Fourth of July holiday, the relative peace and calm of it all began to slowly and in some ways imperceptibly change. Rumors were circulating among the students almost from the minute they got back on campus. Something was afoot in the administration. Miss Witherspoon was not flittering about making nice with parents when they brought their students back to the school. The teachers seemed ill at ease and some strange cars were coming and going near the administration building.

On the evening of July 7th, things took a very bad turn. Mr. Copernicus Campbell, teacher of mathematics and science, turned up at Jacob and Will's door in the early morning hours. He knocked quietly and then stood, holding himself up with the doorjamb. Nothing was right about the scene. Teachers don't show up at student rooms in the middle of the night. Mr. Campbell looked pale and distracted.

"Sir?" Jacob said and hearing no reply, he added, "Sir, can I help you sir?" Jacob opened the door fully. The man wavered slightly to the right and Jacob thought he must be drunk or very sick. "Sir?" Jacob repeated again, "Are you OK?"

"Mr. Boyd," the teacher finally said. "Don't trust what you hear. Things are not what they seem." He staggered slightly forward and added, "Ashland ... Ashland ... go ... True Iona has Remnant's key ...". With those words barely sputtering from his lips, Mr. Campbell fell forward past Jacob and toward Will who was now standing beside his bed.

Will reached for the man but could not make his arms get there in time. Thud. Campbell hit the floor hard. A slight tremor went through the floorboards and into the bottom of their feet. Both boys jumped back at the shock. Then they noticed it. Right in the middle of Mr. Campbell's back was a red arrow with gold fletching. Blood stained his shirt.

Will screamed and fell back onto his bed. Jacob's heart leapt and he swallowed hard. Momentarily, other kids came running down the hall. A few stood frozen in shock. A few others paused to see the situation and then ran down the stairs to pound on Dr. Kirk's door.

Dr. Kirk arrived in a flurry of white, from his hair down to his equally white nightshirt. He pushed the crowd aside to get to Campbell's body, and knelt down. A moment later he stood and pronounced his friend to be dead.

"Well, this is a tragedy, indeed. But, there's nothing more to see tonight, boys. Older students, come, get the newbies back to their beds. Lock your doors tight. All of you ... Lock your doors tight this foul night!" Throughout those five sentences, his eyes locked on Jacob and Will, leaving them feeling accused and uncomfortable.

When the boys had all finally been cajoled back to their rooms, Kirk removed his old black plastic-framed glasses from his face and rubbed his eyes. "Well, boys, what happened here tonight?" he asked.

Will began to sputter nervously, but Jacob interjected the details of Copernicus Campbell's arrival at their door and subsequent fall into the room. "Is that all?" Kirk interjected, as Jacob appeared to be wrapping up his part of the story.

"Well, yes, "Jacob answered as Will attempted to add that the dead man had spoken with them and what he had said. Jacob, however, fearful that he did not know who to trust, cut him off and said, "Well, he looked like he wanted to say something, but that arrow had taken too much out of him."

Kirk looked skeptically at Jacob and then over at Will. Will, still staring at the dead body on the floor, was oblivious.

"Come now boys, let's go down to my apartment where you can spend the night while I get some people in here to take care of our dear friend Mr. Campbell. Grab some clothes so you won't have to come back up in the morning." Kirk was standing at the door waiting for them when he finished his request.

Ramos Kirk took Will and Jacob down to his apartment and put them up in the spare bedroom he used mostly as his library in which he wrote and prepared for classes. Books lined the walls. In the middle of a night like this, however, books were of no interest to two boys who had just witnessed a death. They crawled into the one bed in the room without even a thought that it had been at least five years since the two old friends had shared a bed like this.

"Will, did you notice that arrow in Mr. Campbell's back?" Jacob asked.

"How could I miss it? Do you think I'm blind?"

"I mean, did you notice that it was red with gold-colored fletching?" Jacob fine-tuned his question.

"OK, so it was a pretty, as well as deadly weapon. So what?" Will asked as he closed his eyes and hoped the images of the night would disappear in sleep.

"Who shoots arrows like that?" Jacob asked, his hands clasped behind his head and his eyes fixed on the ceiling.

Will didn't answer. Exhausted, he was already asleep.

Jacob answered his own question. *Bunting Boyle. Bunting Boyle is the only one who has his own special arrows and it was one of them! I know it. But why? Why?* He thought about jumping up and going to tell Dr. Kirk, but then stopped himself as he realized the answer should be obvious to anyone who had been around school. The authorities would figure that out, surely.

And, why would he come to our room? I'm not even good in math and didn't have him for class yet this summer! And what about those words ... "Ashland," "True Iona," "Remnant's key," ... what do they mean? Jacob turned it all over in his head until sleep finally overtook his curiosity.

Bunting Boyle was the teacher of arms and riding at Iona and everything he owned was done in red and gold. The arrow was unmistakably his and sure enough, around campus the next morning, he was clearly regarded as the prime suspect in the murder. In fact, even before morning, campus security had gone to his home down by the stables and placed him under house arrest until the sheriff made it out to interview him.

Creech Rising

The next morning, the school was abuzz with rumors. A general meeting was called to begin immediately after dinner to discuss the situation. There was really no need for such a meeting to tell the students about the murder. By 9:00 AM, not a soul on campus had failed to hear of Campbell's death. Everyone also knew that their teacher had died on Jacob and Will's floor. Some rumors had Jacob or Will mixed up in the murder, but most students seemed to have the facts straight.

By breakfast that morning, Will's nerves had calmed and he decided to take advantage of the situation to become the subject of attention. He walked around the long tables of the cafeteria looking for someone to give him the slightest glimmer of recognition that he could use as an excuse to jump in with his version of the story. His arms would flail at his sides. His eyes would flash. His voice would rise and fall and crack. "I tell you I leaped out of my bed the moment I heard him! I knew something was wrong and was bound to help. I jumped for his falling body, but it was too late. A harrowing thing it was, I tell you! Simply harrowing!" He would end with his head hung in apparent exhaustion and then would move to another audience to hear his story.

Jacob answered questions when kids had them and took their sympathy as they offered it, but he was preoccupied by the mystery of the man's warning that things are not what they seem and the words that were Campbell's last: "Ashland," "True Iona," "Remnant's Key." He had already figured the Ashland part, or, he guessed he had. Ashland, he knew, was the name of the old mansion on the hill through the woods that he had been avoiding looking at for weeks. The first time he had looked at it, upon arriving on campus the first night, it had reached for him like it was attempting to drag him in. Reluctantly, Jacob began plotting a visit to that location he so feared.

The general meeting of the school began just as a hint of darkness descended. Mr. F. Finnius Creech, the Assistant Headmaster, conducted it. Most of his colleagues called him "F" rather than Finnius or Mr. Creech and he was relatively well liked. He was short and soft and seemed kind. He always had a pleasant word for everyone and encouraged them to try their best. He had almost never, however, been in a position of authority. He appeared nervous and very agitated.

"Colleagues and students, I am afraid I have some very bad news," he began. He went on to talk about the murder of Mr. Campbell, though there was no one left to be shocked by that news. And he discussed the fact that Mr. Bunting Boyle had been placed on leave and sent into town to live. Mr. Finnius Creech then added that Boyle would not be missed because his classes in "arms and riding" were outdated and unnecessary anyway. "The arts of warfare may well be the very reason for these troubles," he said. The students looked around at each other in confusion.

"And now, for good news, Miss Witherspoon has decided to take a much needed vacation. She has gone to her sister's in Maine to rest her nerves. The Board of Advisors has asked me to take over until Miss Witherspoon returns."

Heads turned back and forth as students looked at each other inquisitively. Abigail Witherspoon was a constant and steadying presence at the school. She knew almost every student by name and was as dedicated to the mission of the Academy as anyone ever was dedicated to a cause. It was her "little passion, and you are my little people," she had sometimes said. "My little people of the little platoon I belong to."

Mr. Creech continued his speech as soon as all the children turned to give him their full attention again.

"There will be some other changes, boys and girls," the man continued. His confidence seemed to grow as he went. "Yes, other changes that must be made. I assure you Miss Witherspoon has approved them all. Indeed, they have been things she has wanted to get done for a long time but the stress of being overworked had kept her from moving forward with them. They are all changes the Board of Trustees has now asked me to make. I ask you to give me your full cooperation, for these are changes that are being made in your best interest, I assure you." The man worked to show a confidence and strength that would cover his growing lies.

The students grew nervous and the looks on the faces of some of the teachers did not help calm anyone. The teachers looked as confused and worried as any of the students.

"Because of the heinous murder of my dear friend and valued colleague, Copernicus Campbell, we have deemed this campus too dangerous for nighttime activity. Henceforth, there will be no more "gatherings" of the clans at night or any other such activities. Curfew will be at 8:00 PM sharp this summer and, for those of you with us in the Fall, that time will grow earlier with the shortening of the days through the seasons."

Some students mumbled and turned to one another, others just sat silently wondering what would come next and a few were even relieved that no more nighttime raids would occur to shock them out of bed.

"This murder has also taught us the danger of teaching violence on this wonderful, pristine and otherwise peaceful campus. From now on, archery and shooting; swordsmanship and the martial arts will no longer be taught or practiced at our school."

The grumbles of the students grew louder now.

"Silence!" the man at the podium announced, growing still more confident in his manner and speech. "This all, you must keep in mind, is being done for you students, *our precious children!* Miss Witherspoon has personally approved these changes and our governing Board has asked me to make them." He paused, looked around the audience, then back down at his papers.

"What is more, the curriculum, I mean the classes themselves at

Iona, have been outdated for some time. This is the modern world! This is the 21st century! There is no place in our world for the dead arm of the past! We must prepare you to live in this new century, not in the 15th century! We must prepare you for the jobs of tomorrow, not to imitate lives of bigoted dead men! As of today, Latin and Greek will no longer be taught. English literature will be reserved to contemporary approved writers only."

At this, Mr. Ramos Kirk stood and protested loudly from his place against the far wall. "As Dean of the Faculty, I demand you cease this litany of unwarranted changes at once and call a faculty assembly to discuss this!" Around the room, some of the teachers applauded Kirk's motion. Others stood in stony silence.

"Mr. Kirk," Mr. Creech replied, "*you* are not in charge here. *I am.* There will be no such faculty assemblies because I am simply enacting the orders of Miss Witherspoon and the Board of Trustees." He pointed his finger at Kirk and added, "if you no longer wish to live in the *New* Iona, then please, Mr. Kirk, let us help you with your bags!"

A whoosh of air could be heard rushing out of the lungs of shocked students and faculty. Ramos Kirk had been a beloved teacher on campus for decades. Iona was unimaginable without him.

Kirk looked across the room of students and fellow teachers. He turned and walked defiantly out of the room. A few other teachers marched out behind him. Most, however, stayed in their seats and slowly turned their attention back to the stage.

"Now, children, there will be those old people stuck in old ways that will refuse to change. We are to pity them, not make them our enemy. We are to love them until they come around and understand all this is for the greater glory of our beloved Iona and to help you all be the best individuals you can be." Even as he said the words, Finnius Creech was fantasizing about paying Kirk back dearly for his public insubordination.

"These teachers will need to make sacrifices for our *new* Iona, and so will you." Creech cocked his head innocently and bit his lower lip as if in wonder that such terrific kids would be his partners in these changes.

"For too long, we have been rivals on this campus. For too long, divisions have arisen in our ranks and have kept us from reaching the goal of a true extended *family*. I love you all equally and you should all love each other equally. From this moment, there will be no more divisions within our ranks. There will be no more upper classmen and newbies. From now on we will all address one another as 'Ionian Friend'." In a few weeks he would begin to drop "Ionian" from the phrase under the argument that no divisions should be found in the world at all, but that would come later.

Students looked at one another as if this were some kind of joke. He couldn't possibly be serious, most thought. Still others, particularly those who had been at Iona for several years, grew more worried and angry at this smashing of their traditions and the campus culture.

"In this new spirit of harmony and love, I have ordered the gates to be torn down between the lions. The motto wrought in iron above it no longer reflects our new atmosphere of tolerance and care. 'No one harms me with impunity,' is more fit for a military boarding school than a mutual gathering place of friends. One of the lions itself will be shorn of its mantel of privilege and status. The right will still be guarded by the lion, the left, however, will now be guarded by the lioness."

He said it all with such a warm smile and caring manner that many students were conflicted in their emotions. Jacob, even though new to Iona, felt something was not right in all this radical change. He felt uneasy and watched it all as if he were a distant observer of a movie being played on the screen in front of him.

"You, my friends … you, fellow Ionians … *you* are called to be the great founders of our new school. Generations hence will recall your names as the ones who paved the way to what we will become. You are the ones giving us the new order that will last the ages. We teachers and administrators cannot do it for you. You must accept this challenge. You must make the changes necessary for this new order to flourish. And, if you do, if you succeed in changing this culture, you will all go down in history as Iona's greatest generation!"

Some students were beginning to squirm in their seats; others sat straight and proud, now hanging on every word.

"And, one thing more, my collaborators in this new order, we must also abolish that great source of division and exclusivity. We must abandon the old ways of the clans." Many students fidgeted nervously in their seats. The clans Targe and Dirk were part of who they were and what they loved most about Iona. How could they be dissolved?

"There is no place in our modern world for such a divisive thing. We must all be partners and friends, not rivals and class-oriented snobs! clan Dirk and clan Targe will be no more. Let us make a new beginning. Who will step forward as among the greatest of this great generation of students and drop your robe with its class distinctions and its badge of divisiveness? Who will let her's fall from their shoulders into this pile?"

As Creech said it, his voice rose and called out to the crowd with greater strength and confidence than he had shown yet that morning. He ripped his robe from his own back and threw it dramatically off the stage and onto the floor in front of the first row of students. A few, picked earlier by Finnius Creech to be his props, stood on cue and removed their cloaks, throwing them dramatically onto the pile. Then a few more came. Then more. Soon most of the crowd was walking forward and dropping their robes onto the pile. As the moment dragged on, the last group to come forward was doing it more out of resignation than passion and assumed they would get them back after this silly demonstration of unity was over.

"And, now what shall we do with this pile of shame and division?" Creech asked as he opened his arms wide. "What shall we do?"

From the back of the room came a solitary and whispery voice. "Burn them!?" It was one of the newer members of the Dirks and the tone of his voice seemed anything but strong and convicted.

"Burn them? Burn them you say?" Mr. Creech was scratching his check as he spoke. "Well, is that what you all say? Have a little bonfire shall we? With marshmallows melting into a sugary goo from the heat of the burning past? Shall we have a burning, then?"

One after another the selected students in the crowd yelled back, "Burn them!" or "Roast them good!"

"Then, let it be so! The first five who stepped forward to lead us down this path, you now have the honor of taking these filthy garments to the bonfire! Everyone else, go forth across this beautiful campus of ours and destroy all vestiges of Iona's corrupt past! Make the way clear for our new Iona to rise from the ashes of the past!"

With that the students who had been whipped into a frenzy or who were looking for the chance to break something burst through the Great Hall's double doors and they ran across campus. A group went down to the gates where they hit and pulled and pushed until the iron broke and came down. They carried the arch in triumph to the bonfire. Others descended upon the left lion at the gate and pummeled it with rocks and iron bars from the broken gate until its mane was blasted off and its features cut down. Still others ran across campus pulling down banners referring to the Targes and Dirks. It was a scene both frightening and beautiful. Young people taking control of their lives and their society and making things anew.

Not all students took part in the carnage that came that night. There were minor injuries from the antics, but no one was seriously harmed. Some, Jacob included, skulked off to watch and wonder from the sidelines. Conflicted by the scene that unfolded in front of them, they were neither repulsed nor exuberant. They were confused.

Shadows at Ashland

With many of the students dancing and cheering around the bonfire and the teachers either locked away in their rooms or cheering alongside the tribal group, Jacob decided it was as good a time as any to have a closer look at the Ashland mansion. That old mansion had been his dread from the moment he saw it. With the campus gone to chaos, he knew he might just as easily be hurt staying there as by going up the hill where no one else was supposed to be.

He would have asked Will to join him, but Will was having fun throwing things into the bonfire and laughing it up. Jenny was nowhere to be found near the quad. He worried about her and decided to check her room. He opened the door to Jenny's dorm and looked inside. It was now well after dark and he was not supposed to be in the girl's dorm. *Well, the place has gone insane anyway, I guess. All the old rules have been thrown out, it seems.*

He walked carefully up the stairs to the second floor and then down the hall to the fifth door on the right. The door was shut. He knocked. No answer. He knocked again and said, "Jenny, are you in there?"

"Jake, is that you?" came a whispered reply.

"Yes, it's me. Can I come in?"

The door opened slowly, then a hand entered the hallway and yanked Jacob hard into the room.

"What are you doing?" Jacob stammered as he stumbled across the room.

Jenny shut the door tight and turned the lock.

"What are you doing here, Jake?"

"Just coming to see where you were, I didn't see you out there helping burn the place down!" Jacob answered as he sat on the edge of Jenny's roommate's bed.

"Of course not. This is crazy, Jake! Change is one thing, but to burn the place overnight?"

"Yeah, I know. I guess I feel the same way. It's like a movie out there," Jacob replied. Then he asked, "Where's your roommate, the mouse?"

"She's meeting friends and helping to rebuild the school in its new image, I guess."

"Well, instead of holing up in here while Iona burns, do ya want to go explore with me?"

"Sure. Where? And, where's Will?"

"Will's out assisting with the carnage and, after we go check on Mr. Nibbles, we're going out to Ashland," Jacob answered as he stood and headed toward Jenny's door.

"Sure, but what is an 'Ashland'?" Jenny responded without needing an answer, as she was already on her feet heading toward her closet to get a pair of shoes and a flashlight.

"It's that old mansion on the hill behind the stables."

"Cool! Let's do it. That fire will keep everyone busy for a while and we won't be missed."

"And, I figure we can probably see the fire and the shadows moving around it from up on the hill by the mansion anyway, so we can hurry back if we see them heading into the dorms."

Jacob and Jenny stopped by Jacob's room where he picked up his backpack and a flashlight for himself and in a matter of minutes, the pair had skulked silently along the edge of the woods where they wouldn't be seen. They emerged by the stables.

"Oh no … Jenny, look here …" Jacob had made it first around the back of the stables and was standing perfectly still as he looked at the scene in front of him. Instead of a kennel full of barking dogs, he found a series of empty cages.

"Oh, man, this has gone too far, Jacob, who let the dogs out? And, more importantly still, where is Mr. Nibbles?"

Jacob didn't reply at first but walked toward the cages moving his flashlight back and forth across the kennels and the back of the stables.

"I don't know, Jenny. But, I'm sure Mr. Nibbles is alright."

"How can you be sure, he's just a little wee thing of a dog, Jake? He isn't meant to be out on his own!"

"Yep, he's little, but he's stronger than you give him credit for. I'm sure he can take care of himself and will show up by morning. Come on, Jenny, we have other things to take care of."

"Wait just a minute, Jacob," Jenny grabbed her friend by the shoulder and turned him to face her. "You aren't telling me everything, here. I know you and how much you love that dog. What's on your mind and what're we doing out here?"

"Jen, you are always the hardest one to keep a secret from," Jacob began. He then recounted the evening before and how Mr. Campbell showed up with the arrow in his back. Jenny, of course, knew that, as did everyone else on campus. What she didn't know, however, and what Jacob shared, was that he had had a conversation with the soon-to-die math and science teacher.

"So, that's it, another mystery falls upon Master Boyd!" Jenny said with a sneer.

"Stop teasing, Jenny," Jacob responded. "He came to my room for a reason. It wasn't for help. He didn't ask for help. He could have more easily fallen into Dr. Kirk's room but instead he climbed the stairs and came down the hall to mine. That wouldn't just happen like that."

"I suppose not, but, that does remind me that there is a murderer loose and, need I remind you, my friend, that the murderer probably knows by now that Campbell came to *your* room and may have told *you* something he doesn't want anyone to know!"

Jacob had not quite thought of it all that way and hesitated. "Still, it was probably Mr. Boyle who did it, since it was his arrow, that was in Campbell's back, and he's under house arrest—or, by now, hopefully, he's in jail."

"Uhhhh huhhhhh," Jenny responded, clearly unconvinced by Jacob's reasoning. "Come on, then, we're out here now. Let's at least take a look at the old place." Jenny took Jacob by the shoulders and turned him to face Ashland. The mansion loomed in the distance, only half visible above the trees that filled the gap between Iona and the home which once belonged to the founder of the school, a man named Addison Clay. It had been abandoned for nearly a hundred years.

"So, Jake," Jenny said as they waded into the woods, "do you suppose this is all bound up with that little purse of yours?" It was the first time in months that Jenny mentioned his magic sporran. She had been part of his uncovering its early secrets but his relationship with it and its magic had grown and they had agreed not to discuss it since he could no longer share the secrets without endangering her.

Jacob was matter of fact in his reply, "I'm not sure. But, I'm glad you're with me now. And, its not a purse!"

The two weaved through the woods and were glad to emerge into the overgrown gardens surrounding the mansion. The trees cast unwelcoming shadows. They both knew the darkness of the woods could mask unknown enemies. They had seen the movies and read the books about such dangers. Indeed, they both had lived them a year ago when the sporran and the disheveled stranger arrived in their lives. In the moonlit yard surrounding the mansion, however, it was harder for anyone else to hide in the shadows.

The place looked deserted, as Jacob had been told it was. The windows were all dark, but were all in place. It was not run-down, like other abandoned structures they had both seen. Clearly, someone had taken care of the place, including keeping the yard and gardens in relatively good shape.

The two made their way around the right of the house, peering around the corner to make sure no one was in the back. They walked under the great oak tree standing watch over the side, and they emerged behind the house. Two large dark spots called them to the back yard. They approached them cautiously and then, when they came within flashlight distance, they found these two dark shadows were actually tombstones. One was for Addison Clay and one for his wife Lucretia, both of whom died more than a century before. Several smaller stones nearby marked the graves of the children that had died in childhood.

The graves made the night even more eerie for Jacob and Jenny than it had been already. They looked at each other, both wanting to go back to campus but neither willing to say it.

Jacob, it's me.

Jacob heard in his thoughts the voice of the dragon Nibblus Maximus. *It's me. I'm safe but I'm not going back there to those cages.*

Jacob tried to answer, but it was painful and his face contorted with the effort.

"What are you doing?" Jenny asked.

At first, Jacob's concentration was such that he didn't hear Jenny's question, even though she was right next to him.

Master Boyd, I'm fine but not all is well. It's better that I stay free out here for now. Don't try to return your thoughts. She will suspect something.

The word "she" brought Jacob back to the reality of the yard around Ashland as Jenny repeated her question, "Jacob, I said, what are you doing?"

"Oh, sorry, nothing ... just thinking about Mr. Nibbles." He answered honestly.

"See! I knew you were worried about him! Should we call him or go look for him or something?" Jenny asked.

"No. He'll be all right. I know him and he's tough. And, I was just thinking that I bet one of the stable hands took the dogs in for the night to keep them safe from being thrown on the fiery pyre at school."

"Suit yourself. Well, what do we do now that we are here?"

"Let's see if any of the doors or windows are open," Jacob replied. They both approached the house very cautiously, carefully dimming their flashlights lest someone catch a glimpse of their beams.

They approached the door on the rear porch first. The lock was simple and cracked open with slight pressure downward on the handle. Their hearts raced. Jacob pushed the door open slightly and stepped inside. Jenny paused at the threshold and then silently crossed over. Both of them knew they shouldn't be there, let alone late in the evening, but a dull roar from the campus let them know the fire was still going and they would not be missed.

Jenny was looking around the porch at the old furniture and what once passed for houseplants but now resembled unharvested straw sticking out of parched dirt in cracked pots. She didn't notice as Jacob shivered and then froze stiff.

Professor von Niblick had explained to him a year ago that it was "the quickening;" a shot of energy running down one of his arms and his spine. It would come, Niblick explained, whenever he came in the vicinity of someone or something associated with the power of the Sporrai. Here in the dark night, trying to break into a home that wasn't his, the anxiety it caused was more intense than ever.

Jenny turned and started to ask a question when Jacob grabbed her mouth and pulled her into the shadows with him by the door. She started to resist but caught a glimpse of a shadow cutting through the silver glow that the moon had laid on the lawn beside the house. She pushed back even harder into Jacob who himself was pressed hard against the wall.

"Well, I see you didn't waste time," the shadow spoke calmly and quietly.

Jacob and Jenny both thought the voice was talking to them. Their blood ran cold and Jacob felt a bit of nausea bubble in his stomach. The kids remained silent, not answering the shadow but fretting what would happen next. They were expected, so surely they were being ambushed, they both thought.

Bringing some relief to them both, a second voice answered the first. *Maybe we're not caught*, both realized but remained utterly still and silent.

"There are strange spirits about in the land," the second shadow responded, "none of us can afford to have time wasted."

The first shadow fidgeted and then seemed to reach toward the other as if handing the other man something. "Have you found Abigail?"

Abigail? Jacob was turning the name in his head trying to make a connection.

"No. But one thing is for sure. Our girl is not on a vacation and is not with her sister. She has no sister, in fact. I have a hunch, but it will take some efforts to test it."

"Something is also up with the Board. They would never have approved what's happening here," the first man responded.

"Look at Furangle. I suspect he is not who he pretends to be and is behind this in some way," the man with a Scottish brogue replied.

"Never trusted him, myself."

Jacob, I'll get you out of there. Get ready to run and don't look back. Nibblus Maximus knew something was amiss and had connected with Jacob's mind.

A fireball flew across the yard and set a bush in flames behind the house. The dragon had created a diversion. The shadows turned and went away from the house and rushed into the woods from where the flame had come.

Jacob grabbed Jenny and flew out the door and around the house. They didn't stop running until they emerged back on campus and then only slowed themselves to a fast trot that they kept up until they were able to emerge into the safety of the shadow of Jenny's dorm.

Between heavy breaths, they were able to talk some about what happened. Jenny asked Jacob what he thought that ball of flame came from and who the men were. Jacob replied by throwing his arms up and out from his body as if to say, "Got me!" Jacob asked if Jenny knew any Abigails and, of course, neither needed to ask whom "Furangle" was: Lucy Furangle's father. Everyone knew him and his power on the Board of Directors of the school.

Relieved that they had made it back undetected, they agreed to talk about it all in the morning. As they retired to their rooms for the night, the fervor of the bonfire was dying along with its flame and most kids had already gone to bed.

I.O.N.A.

The realization hit Jenny the next morning when she least expected it. She had showered and dressed and was waiting in the library of her dorm for her roommate Elizabeth to come down and head to breakfast. While she waited, she picked up an Iona School yearbook that was sitting on the coffee table. She thumbed through the pictures of girls with their favorite horses or lying under a tree and pictures of boys in fencing gear or athletic uniforms. It was there on the very first page of the yearbook; an introductory letter from Headmistress Abigail Witherspoon.

"ABIGAIL!" she announced while slamming the book.

"What?" another girl in the room asked.

"Oh, sorry, nothing."

Jenny forgot all about waiting for Elizabeth and headed straight out of the dorm and toward the dining hall, hoping to see Jacob on the way.

Jacob was already having breakfast when Jenny arrived. She walked up behind him and whispered in his ear, "It's Miss Witherspoon ... *Abigail* Witherspoon!" She continued walking toward the cafeteria line as if nothing had happened and left Jacob staring after her.

So, its Miss Witherspoon that the shadows were talking about last night. If Jenny's right, that means, the headmistress is not where Mr. Creech said she was but something must have happened to her. What's going on?

Jenny and Jacob didn't find time to be alone and talk about the situation all day. Elizabeth or Will or one of their other friends were always around. The one moment they almost got together, Mr. Creech, the acting Headmaster came over to ask them how they were doing and to thank them for working with him to change the culture of the school.

The day had the same awkward feel as the very first day they arrived. Classes had been changed. Some teachers, including Dr. Kirk, weren't on campus or at least weren't seen. The buzz about the murder of Copernicus Campbell had grown into rumors of all sorts. They blamed everyone from Bunting Boyle to poor innocent Miss Ruth the housekeeper.

A new sign had been placed in front of the Great Hall. It spelled Iona, but with a new twist.

Institute for the

Organization of a

New

America

Some of the kids had started to feel remorse for their destructive behavior the night before, but just as they did, Mr. Creech called a general meeting for 4:00 P.M. Traditional teatime, it seemed, was gone with the other traditions the school had lost in the last twenty-four hours.

The students were nervous and wondering what would happen next. Some wanted to call their parents and go home, but they were allowed no cell phones and the regular phones were not working. Others were thrilled by the excitement of all the changes and the chance to be on the front edge of the revolution of Iona. About half the teachers failed to show up to the meeting. A few other grown-ups were in the room that the students didn't recognize.

Mr. Creech entered the room followed by several other adults dressed in suits. Two men and three women joined him on the stage and sat in plush wingback chairs behind him.

"Ladies and Gentlemen, let me tell you how proud I am of you all," he began. Biting his lower lip and dipping his head, he continued. "You have done me so proud. In just a day, we have cast off so much of the deadening weight of our past! In just twenty-four hours, you have helped us drag our beloved Institute into the 21st century!"

Jacob elbowed Will and whispered, "Did you hear that? He said "institute" and not school or academy!" Will didn't understand the point and shrugged his shoulders.

Mr. Creech stepped back from the podium and pulled a handkerchief from his pocked and dabbed his eyes. "Pardon me," he said, "I'm just so proud of you all and our beloved Miss Witherspoon will be so proud of you as well!" Jacob's suspicions were starting to build, as was his distrust of this man and his ability to tear up over what Jacob took to be nothing worth such strong emotion.

"Some of you have probably noticed that we are changing the signs on campus. We are and will always be Iona! But Iona must now align itself with our new vision. Our vision is not to simply change our little corner of the world, but to change the world itself. We are redeeming our school and we can redeem America! We have the power to transform our society to align with the vision I know you all share with me; A vision of peace and harmony among all people; A vision that aligns with our best hopes, and not our worst fears!"

There was a smattering of applause among the students and the adults on stage applauded with some enthusiasm.

"Boys and girls ..." he paused " ... friends ..." he paused again, "I am but an instrument of your hopes and dreams. I am but the humble servant of your vision for our world."

"As your humble servant, I must read you something now, that brings me great sadness." He pulled a paper from the breast pocket of his jacket and unfolded it. He paused again and then pulled reading glasses from his other pocket. "You will forgive me, won't you, for I have been working so hard in your service that I have gone nearly blind," he said as he dramatically balanced the reading glasses on his nose.

"Dear Mr. Furangle," he started to read.

> "I am writing to you in your capacity as Chairman of the Board of Directors of Iona Academy. I have long enjoyed my time at Iona. But, I have grown tired and the school needs new leadership and innovative ideas. It is time that I leave the school forever and I ask you to accept my letter of resignation.

I wish you and the school all the best as you work to transform
it into an instrument of societal evolution.

Sincerely,

Abigail Witherspoon
Former Headmistress

Gasps rippled around the room as students looked at one another
and started to mumble.

"Ladies and Gentlemen, I know you share my concern for Miss
Witherspoon and will miss her dearly. But we must abide by her wishes—
we owe her that. Mr. Furangle, the Chairman of the Board, has asked me
to take over with a new title befitting our new Iona. He has asked me
to become the new *Director* of our Institute and, humbly and without a
thought that I was worthy of such a responsibility, I have accepted his
offer."

Some students and teachers looked excited at the news. Others had
a look of dread come over them.

"Mr. Furangle," Creech turned and looked at one of the men sitting
on stage. He had a thick head of black hair, slicked back long and tight
on his head. "Thank you for your confidence in me and all you do for our
humble little Iona. Would you like to say anything to our students and
faculty?"

Furangle stood and buttoned his expensive double-breasted black
pin-striped suit. He pulled the sleeves of his jacket and fidgeted with a
thick gold bracelet on his left wrist. The other adults on the stage stood
and enthusiastically clapped as he approached the podium. Most of the
audience followed their lead and stood and clapped.

"Thank you, Mr. Creech," the man began. "Your leadership has been
outstanding, and I see much improvement over the last few days. You are
finally bringing our Iona into the modern world and we all appreciate that
very much. On behalf of the Board of Directors, I ask all of you to give
Mr. Creech your fullest cooperation. And, because this is so important,
Mr. Creech, on behalf of the Board, I want to extend to you all the powers

you need to insure that our experiment achieves its full potential. I urge you to do what is necessary to insure the full cooperation of the students and the faculty."

Furangle stepped back as the adults again applauded him from the stage, but the ovation was muted from the audience. The idea of Mr. Creech being given unlimited powers caught them all by surprise and caused many students and teachers to become anxious about what would happen next.

Mr. Creech returned to the podium with a big smile on his face. "Thank you, Mr. Furangle. I will do my utmost to enact our vision here on our beloved campus."

He nodded at Furangle and then turned to the audience again. "Ladies and Gentlemen, to demonstrate we are real partners in this dream, I will now appoint a student leader to work with me as your liaison." He paused and then asked, "Would Lucy Furangle please come forward?"

The students gasped and some faculty hung their heads.

"Lucy is truly one of our outstanding young leaders here at Iona," he turned and winked at Lucy's father. "Lucy," he said as she approached the podium, her chest stuck out proudly and her chin held high and thrust forward, "I would like you to serve with me as my special student assistant to help watch over this campus and make the changes necessary for a fully modern Iona to come into existence."

Lucy smiled and nodded that she would and then turned toward the crowd. The old divisions within the students had not yet been obliterated and she got applause only from her old clan mates, the Dirks. Jacob looked crossly at Will as he began to applaud but stopped when he saw Jacob's disappointment.

"Sorry buddy, but she isn't as bad as you think," Will whispered.

"Lucy," Mr. Creech said, "our first priority must be the safety of your fellow students. I would ask you, as your first duty, to form a small cohort of guards from among the best and brightest of your colleagues. They will be charged with insuring that rules are not broken and that all students stay safe." Lucy nodded in acceptance.

"And," he continued, "they will help us enforce what I regret must be done." Mr. Creech paused and shuffled some papers. "Until further notice, for your own safety, students, we will have a strict curfew of 6:00 P.M.!" Groans went up all around the room.

"Sorry, children, but remember that there is a murderer that may yet be on the loose and we cannot have you running about in the evenings and falling into his or her clutches!" He was wagging his finger out at the audience. "After dinner, you will each report immediately to your dorms where you will remain until breakfast is served the next morning. Being caught outside your dorms will mean immediate expulsion to the offender and anyone helping the rule breaker, too!"

"Now, Ms. Furangle, you will join the Board and me to discuss your new responsibilities." Mr. Creech nodded at Lucy and then announced, "Dear friends, for the rest of you, I have asked Mr. Mike to prepare a very special meal for you all, including an extra special desert. Go and enjoy!"

The people on stage left the room first as the students started murmuring to themselves. There was considerable concern now raised about what was happening. Some just wanted to get to dinner, and others were hoping to be chosen as one of Lucy's new elite guards, but most seemed uneasy about the turn of events and what would happen next.

Jacob remained silent all the way to the dining hall, despite Will's many attempts to solicit his thoughts. He was trying to take it all in and wondering who the good guys were: Mr. Creech and the Board or the shadowy men behind the old mansion. *Or, was there anyone innocent in all this?* Jacob asked himself.

Trust the Magic

At dinner, all talk was of Mr. Creech and Lucy Furangle. There was no other possible topic, really. With all of the change that had occurred in the last few days, no one was feeling quite secure. Even the most aggressive of the mob from the previous night had started to have second thoughts. Some tried hard not to show concern, but many were uneasy.

Jacob and Jenny didn't have a chance to really talk at dinner. Will sat down on one side of Jacob and one of the older boys from the Targe clan sat on the other before Jenny could make it through the cafeteria line. On the way back, they both tried intentionally to slow down as they walked to let others pass them and head on.

"Jacob, what do you make of this?" Jenny asked.

"I don't know, but I don't like it," he replied. "I think I need to get out to Ashland again. I can't get it out of my mind. Mr. Campbell gave me that clue for a reason and what we heard there last night makes it even more likely the answers lie out there."

"Well, is it really your business? Is it *our* business?" Jenny asked.

"We're here for some reason, aren't we? I didn't want to come here, remember? But I'm here anyway. And, you can't like what is going on here anymore than I do, right?"

Jenny shrugged her shoulders. She thought about saying something like "Maybe its all just an accident, Jake," but thought better of it, at least for now. She said nothing.

"So, something is obviously going on here and I figure I'm supposed to do something besides go to whatever classes are left and then sit in my room for twelve hours a day!"

"Maybe, but how are you going to get out there? You heard what Mr. Creech said about curfews," Jenny said.

"Look, I can't tell you how I'll get there, because I don't know. Just keep your eyes and ears open, especially in case I need you."

"Need me? You aren't going to need me because I'm going with you!" Jenny replied, emphatically.

"Jenny, I don't know what is going to happen, darn it! If I can get you I will. I just don't know what will happen!" Jacob was clearly frustrated at the situation and let it be shown.

The two walked silently until they came to Jenny's dorm.

"Jacob, at least try to get me or let me know what you are doing, okay?"

"Fine. Just keep your eyes and ears open," Jacob said as he turned toward Frazier House and his room inside.

When he entered the dorm, he momentarily thought to stop at Dr. Kirk's apartment but reconsidered when he remembered Kirk had not been seen in the last 24 hours. He guessed he might even have left campus after the altercation at the meeting.

Will had already come back to their room and was down the hall talking with other students when Jacob arrived. The door was open and an envelope was sitting on his desk. Jacob picked it up and looked it over. The outside read only "Mr. Boyd."

He ripped open one end and slid a yellow piece of paper out onto his desk. He unfolded it and read its contents. In big block print, the message read only "Trust the Magic."

He recognized the paper and printing. It was Professor Hammish MacGregor's writing for sure. He remembered it well from the notes on the professor's door in St. Andrews when he was at that royal and ancient Scottish town a year before.

MacGregor, here? But ... Remembering how MacGregor had appeared and disappeared regularly in the first days after he had discovered the sporran, he walked out and looked up and down the hallway. Then he turned and came back to his desk. Glancing out the window as he sat back down, he saw only a man in old jean overalls and denim hat with a pitchfork slung over one shoulder heading back down toward the stables.

Trust the magic. Trust the magic. He turned the phrase over and over in his head. Momentarily a realization came to him. *Of course, the sporran! How could I have been so blind? Why haven't I checked it? Why haven't I used it? What have I been doing?* Jacob wondered why the sporran had not been on his mind much lately and worried if there was something keeping him from letting it enter into his imagination.

Warning from Afar

Jacob walked over to his backpack, which was resting against one of the bottom legs of his bed. He sat down and undid the zipper and removed his books. Before he went any further, he realized he should be more careful and look down the hallway. Seeing no one coming his way, he pulled the door quietly shut.

Safely back in the room, Jacob began to undo the false bottom he had created in the backpack. A few pulls of the string and he was able to pull the cloth up to reveal his magic sporran. Then he uncovered Isildane's ring.

He pulled them out and laid them side-by-side on his bed, taking a minute to stare at the treasure and muse about whether or not he was ready for what might come next. By removing those two items, he was sure, he was agreeing to play a bigger part in the things unfolding around him. It was his choice, he knew, but he also felt that he had no real choice at all. He was there for a reason and it now looked like MacGregor was there, too.

First, he picked up Isildane's golden ring, with its ornate shanks and blood-red stone. He turned it in his hand and then slipped it onto his finger. He remembered being back in the catacombs beneath Edinburgh castle and his finger remembered the burns that came with the fusion of the lion's eye to the ring a year before.

Then, he picked up the sporran and flipped the flap back to show the pouch's pocket. Inside, a small square block lay in the shadows of the bottom. *My enchiridion!*

Jacob turned the little book in his hands. Professor von Niblick had given him the blank book when he left Scotland the year before. He had gotten occasional notes in it from MacGregor and Niblick, but had left it at home. Or, at least he remembered leaving it at home in the top drawer of his desk. Now he wasn't so sure.

He opened the pages and found a new entry dated several days before and from Professor von Niblick. He started to read:

> *Master Boyd,*
>
> *We believe you may be in danger. One of the members of our order has come up missing in America. She knew your identity and was charged with keeping an eye out for you. This may mean you are in danger, too. Stay close to Mr. Nibbles. He will protect you. We are sending help.*

Jacob jumped to his feet, sending books crashing to the floor as the door to his room flew open. "Well, well, a bit jumpy are we?"

"Darn it Will, you scared me!"

"Ahhhh, I see you have your magic purse!"

Jacob jumped on the defensive. "Will, you can't tell anyone, do you hear me? You can't tell anyone about it. Remember, we were in this together from the beginning. Now you have to keep your promises!" Jacob was speaking in emphatic bursts.

"Relax, Dude. Of course I won't tell anyone. Who would believe it anyway?" Will bent down and picked up Jacob's books for him and placed them on his bed by his empty backpack. As he did, Jacob's attention went to his golden ring and he quickly put his right hand into his front pocket and began working the treasure from his finger. *No need for Will to get suspicious about it, too,* he thought.

Jacob slipped the sporran around his waist and tucked the bottom into the top of his pants. He pulled his shirt down over it and worked to smooth down the bulge it made beneath his clothes. The edges of the sporran dug into his belly, but not half as bad as it would the first time he tried to sit down!

Jacob changed the subject and got Will to talk about the changes going on around Iona when a knock came at the door.

"Come in," Will answered.

The knob turned and into the room stepped Lucy Furangle. She was big and her attitude was bigger still. She was followed by two boys that Will recognized instantly as two of the former leaders of the Dirks.

"Hello, Will," Furangle said as she took another step into the room. Obviously ignoring Jacob, she said, "I've been thinking, Will, that we probably need some Newbie help around here with enforcing the security regulations." She approached him, put her left hand solidly on his shoulder and applied slight downward pressure. "Will, welcome to my elite corp of New Guards!" She was not giving him an option or making an offer. His acceptance of this honor and duty was assumed.

Jacob had stayed silent until he finally blurted out, "Why don't you give him a choice?"

Will looked at Jacob but the others completely ignored him. The two goons behind Lucy stepped forward and placed a black armband around Will's left arm. On it were the words "New Guards," in white block letters.

Will said nothing.

"Report to my room at 5:50 PM for instructions on how to make rounds for your floor," Lucy said as she turned and led her party out into the hallway.

Jacob sat down in his chair, the sporran agitating the skin of his belly. He stared at Will. Will himself was starring down at the armband and fingering the letters.

"You aren't actually going to work with *her highness* are you?" Jacob asked, the contempt dripping from his words.

"Well, I don't know, I guess I am, I mean," Will was stammering around uncomfortably.

"For gosh sakes, Will ..." Jacob stopped himself in mid-sentence. It was clear things were not right around the place and Furangle was not the person who should be in charge. He stopped himself, however, as he now half-feared Will for his connection to her. If Will told her what Jacob was about to say, it might be bad, he realized. He changed his sentence and continued with, "well, just remember how long we've been friends and be loyal to me. Promise?"

Will laughed, "Of course I will! Why on Earth would you think I wouldn't?"

"Just promise me," Jacob said and he stepped toward Will and extended his fingers. Will responded with his own fingers and a round of "battle dragons" sealed the promise.

That evening, Jacob had difficulty sleeping. He laid in bed staring at Will's black armband and thinking that no matter how much the new regime had promised to end the old divisions within the students, new ones were developing under their own sanction. It all just seemed to be wrong, but he couldn't figure out exactly how.

As sleep came over him, a dream began to unwind in his mind. A woman lay motionless, almost lifeless on a bed. The bed was plain, a mere mattress on a box springs with an old quilt pulled up tight around her neck. A pitcher of water sat next to a bowl on the nightstand. Jacob approached the head of the bed. Movement caught his eye in the water and he turned. The water shimmered and turned in on itself. He looked deeper into the water and images began to float in the liquid.

Professor Copernicus Campbell's dead face hovered below the surface. His mouth opened, "Ashland ... Ashland ... go ... True Iona has Remnant's Key." They were the same words the real Campbell had spoken as he lay dying on Jacob's floor several nights before. Then dark figures in capes appeared sitting near one another and whispering. Jacob leaned in closer to the water to hear the conversation. Closer and closer he approached. He turned his head away from the bed to get his right ear ever closer to the water and hear the conversation of the robbed people. Closer still ... then ....

Dead cold fingers grabbed him on the back of the neck. He jumped and turned into the face of the woman who was lying lifeless in bed moments before. He recognized the face instantly; it was a sickly-looking Headmistress Abigail Witherspoon. He pulled away as her fingers grabbed at him in desperation. "Find me! Find me! A Scottish Church will help. Save Iona!"

Jacob's hands swung around to knock the old woman's fingers away from him but they met younger hands instead.

"Jacob, Jacob, wake up," Will was trying to get his friend awake. He had just woken up to Jacob's moans and thrashing in his bed.

"Ahhhh. . ." Jacob sat up in bed with Will hovering next to him. Confused for a moment, he came to his senses and said "oh, yes, just a dream ... just a dream ..."

Nibbles Discovered

Members of Furangle's New Guard were stationed around campus on nearly every hall and in each dorm. They were in every class and at nearly every table. Will had to go to training sessions each morning before Jacob even awoke. He would also disappear each afternoon for meetings in Lucy's room. He never spoke much about what happened in those meetings and Jacob really didn't care to hear.

It was after tea had been served and Will had gone on to a meeting in Furangle's room, that Jacob decided he had to go out into the woods and look for Mr. Nibbles. He'd had brief contact with his dragon pug over the last few days and knew he was fine and living in the woods and fields near the campus. With all that was happening and the dream that hung on his mind like drapes filtering everything else he saw and heard, he thought it best to find Mr. Nibbles and consider his options.

Will had left his copy of the New Guard's security plans on his desk and Jacob saw it as his way to sneak off campus and then back on again undetected. Outlined were all the security points, where the student members of Furangle's New Guard were stationed, when they would change shifts, and their instructions.

Jacob checked his sporran, which was securely but uncomfortably tucked into his pants. He reached into his pocket to make sure Isildane's ring was secure, too. Then, with a deep breath, he turned down the stairs and out of Frazier House. He paused for a moment by Dr. Kirk's door but didn't knock. He turned and quietly headed out the main door. On the grounds he walked around the building and into position to walk down toward the stables. It was the path he had decided would get him to the woods near Ashland with the least chance of being seen.

Rounding the corner, a voice came from the shadowy area by the shrubs. "Mr. Boyd? Going somewhere?" Jacob turned to see Mr. Creech leaning on the building, a clipboard in his left hand.

"Oh, Mr. Creech, you startled me. Well …" Jacob stammered. "Just going down to the stables to see the horses."

Creech came forward toward Jacob. Putting his hand on the boy's shoulder, the new Headmaster said, "We are so worried about the safety of all the students with a murderer on the loose, you know." Jacob nodded his head nervously. "Well, see to it that you return before curfew," the headmaster finished, as he removed his hand from Jacob's shoulder.

Jacob nodded and turned to head toward the stables. Crossing directly across the field rather than taking the dirt road, he could see the boy they called "Puddles" playing by himself along the road. Puddles waved and, to be nice to the boy who was almost always treated ill by the other kids at school, Jacob waved back.

Arriving at the stables, Jacob turned to look back toward the campus buildings. He could see students coming and going, but could not see anyone keeping an eye on him or watching the stables. He peeked in the barn where a lone stable hand shoveled out a horse stall. The man's back was toward him. Jacob rushed across the open door and paused on the other side. Before rushing into the woods near the stables, Jacob checked to see if the dogs had been returned; they hadn't. That was a strange relief. With no dogs, there would be no barking as he took off across the last piece of open field before the cover of the trees would protect him again.

One last look back toward campus and Jacob was off running as fast as he could. He ducked under low branches, jumped a log and continued hard going fifty yards into the woods before he stopped, leaned on a tree, and looked back. *No one; I made it.*

A few more yards into the trees and Jacob sat down on a sandstone boulder that was slightly exposed above the mossy ground. He closed his eyes and worked to clear his mind in order to make contact with Nibblus Maximus who he was sure would still be hiding in the woods and keeping an eye on him from afar.

The boy called out with his mind. Nothing. He took another deep breath and tried again. Still nothing but silence met his thoughts. Jacob laid his head in his hands as if that gesture would allow him to concentrate more or amplify his thoughts.

"Jacob … Jacob …"

Yes, it's me. Where are you? Jacob replied in his thoughts.

"Jacob … are you sleeping?"

Huh?

Jacob opened his eyes and peeked. There was no dragon. Instead, it was Jenny who stood in front of him. She looked at him curiously with her right hand resting on her cocked hip.

"What are you doing out here?" Jacob asked as he jumped to his feet.

"More importantly, what are *you* doing? Were you praying or something?" Jenny asked.

Jenny had seen Jacob leaving his dorm and followed him, she explained.

"Jenny, darn it, you shouldn't have followed me!"

"Shouldn't have followed you? Well, I wouldn't have had to if you would have come to get me!"

"I couldn't. It was too risky; too much chance of getting caught."

Cracks suddenly exploded in the tops of the trees up the hill from their position. Both kids jumped; their hearts racing. As leaves and twigs fell around them, the two friends jumped behind a pair of trees. A thud was heard on the ground about twenty yards away and then silence. A meteorite? Plane Crash? Scottish Ninjas dropping from the tops of the trees?

A loud *"Jacob?"* ricocheted around Jacob's mind. His heart sank. Jenny peeked from behind the tree to see a sight that was even more terrifying than the sound of the crashing branches. Sometimes fear causes people to run and sometimes it causes them to fight. And, as in the case with Jenny on this day, sometimes it just causes them to do something stupid.

Jenny jumped out from behind the tree and screamed. She screamed like Jacob had never heard a girl scream before. She screamed like Jacob had never heard anyone scream before. In return, equally caught off guard, the brownish-blue flying lizard-dog screamed in a pitch that caused the leaves of the trees to shake and Jacob's ears to throb.

Jenny turned on her heels and began to run. Jacob jumped in front of her, his skinny chest pushed forward. It was the only way to stop her progress out of the woods where she might be seen and ruin everything. Her torso met his and their arms flew wildly at their sides as the vibrations from the blow cascaded through their bodies. Down the two friends went with Jenny still scrambling forward across Jacob's head, jamming her knee into his right shoulder as she panicked. Jacob held onto her ankle.

"Stop! It's OK! Jenny!"

Jenny twisted like a crocodile in a death roll. Getting her foot free of his grasp, she turned and pulled herself against a small tree that offered her no protection but allowed her to feel some strength behind her. Her breaths came in great gulps and she screamed again. Her scream was met by yet another bellow from the dragon.

Jacob grabbed Jenny's mouth and yelled "Stop it both of you!" The dragon and the girl sat back staring at each other, their chests raising and falling with rapid and deep compressions.

What are you doing? Jacob asked the dragon.

What am I doing? What is she doing here? Nibblus Maximus replied.

Manically, Jenny mumbled "Jacob, Jacob, what are *you* doing? Jacob, what are *we* doing? Jacob, what's going on?"

Jacob took a deep breath, kicked some leaf clutter from around his feet as he thought about what this meant, and then he walked over to the dragon and smacked him playfully on the chest. Jenny's head went back into the tree aghast at what she was witnessing.

"Jenny, don't be afraid."

He began with resignation that this important secret was now out and with his mind swimming about what would happen next. Then his mind began to turn, and pride came over him. A bit of a smile crawled on to his face. At last he felt the swell of someone knowing that *he* had a dragon; that *he* had an extraordinary secret like that.

Don't get too full of yourself, Master Boyd. A voice rebounded in Jacob's head. *You didn't earn your part in this play and don't start thinking you did.*

Jacob did not reply to Nibblus Maximus' humbling advice but instead used his mind to ask, *What should we do now! Do we tell her?*

We can't put the stuffing back into the haggis now … If you trust her, perhaps she can play some part in our story, the dragon replied.

Jacob turned fully to again hear Jenny mumbling as she sat petrified against the tree behind her.

"Jenny," Jacob said, "let me introduce you to Nibblus Maximus."

She just stared and shook.

"Jenny, it's OK. Jenny, he's my friend. He's your friend, too."

Jacob moved toward Jenny and reached for her hand. With hesitation she let herself be pulled to her feet. The dragon turned his fierce jaws away from the two children to reduce Jenny's fear, and then Jacob slowly led her toward the beast, her reluctant feet dragging under shivering knees.

"Nibblus, please let me introduce you to my friend Jenny."

Pleasure to meet you, little lady, the dragon growled in Jacob's head as pleasantly as he could. As he did, his head turned quickly with a smile toward the two. The sudden movement caught Jenny off guard and startled her. She sprang backward out of Jacob's grip and landed the ground.

The dragon rolled his eyes and raised a wrinkled eyebrow at Jacob as it turned again away from the two. *Humans! Human females, especially! ,* the dragon muttered.

Jacob changed tactics and instead began by sitting next to Jenny and explaining that the fierce looking dragon was just the inner side of Mr. Nibbles, the harmless pug.

"Like he was turned inside out but his insides are bigger than his outside. And, his insides happen to be brownish-blue and jelly-like."

He explained as much as he could of where the beast came from and why he was with him. Nibblus Maximus cast glances back at the two every now and then but waited for Jenny to become more comfortable before he made much of a move.

A Deeper Evil Arrives

*J*acob, *the great dragon finally said,* enough of this banter. *The dragon turned slowly.*

Things are worse than you know around here. I've been watching everything very closely and it's more than just the school undergoing change. A dark magic has entered this place, but I cannot find it. The dragon bent his head down toward Jacob as he spoke. I think it's best that I get you out of here, Jacob, for your own protection.

But, can we get Will and Jenny out of here as well? Jacob asked.

I could fly you and Jenny out right now, but I can't come back for Will at this point. We just can't risk him finding out about me and the larger story we share.

Jacob thought for a moment and looked in Jenny's eyes. His mind turned to Will and to the other students on campus. *What about the other kids here. What about Dr. Kirk and the other teachers? Do you think they're in danger?*

Anyone who might stand in the way of the dark magic is in danger, Jacob. You should know that.

Is the danger coming here just because I'm here or is there something more going on? If I leave will the danger leave?

I don't think so, Jacob. I think this is only partly about you being here, but there is something more going on. There are secrets in the shadows of this place that I've not yet been able to drag to the light.

Then, Jacob kicked some leaf litter from the floor of the woods. *Then we stay and find out what is going on.*

Nibblus Maximus did not reply. He was to protect Jacob, but he also craved adventure and appreciated that Jacob was thinking more for the safety of others than for himself.

Jacob, the dragon suddenly said in a whispery mental growl, *someone is coming.*

Jacob turned to look back toward the school through the trees. He shook Jenny out of her silent and stunned stupor and knelt down, taking some cover behind a tree. Nibblus Maximus looked in every direction to see where he might fly out and escape undetected. Seeing no silent escape path through the top of the trees, the dragon closed his eyes and shrank back into Mr. Nibbles. Jacob turned around just in time to see a little curly tail bobbing through the woods.

Jacob and Jenny both knelt behind a tree and watched. Two men were coming up the path about twenty yards from where they were hiding in the woods. Both men paused after they got on the path and under the cover of the trees. They pulled two dark cloaks out from the bags they carried and put them on. Hoods shadowing their faces, they continued up the path in silence and disappeared behind the old Ashland mansion.

Jacob turned to Jenny. "Well, are you with me in this?"

Jenny looked at Jacob and said, "Are you kidding me? I've just been scared to death and am wondering what other secrets you've been keeping!" She paused and with a playful smile announced, "Of course I'm in—there has to be a *reasonable* explanation for all this, right!"

The two started to move their hands together to do "battle dragons," but something about what just happened and the possible dangers ahead made them pull back, wondering if they had somehow outgrown that gesture.

Back on campus, dark colored cars with tinted windows were arriving at the administration offices and Will and the rest of Lucy Furangle's New Guard were getting their orders for the evening and going through training sessions.

In the administration building, a man sat at the desk of Abigail Witherspoon. Into the office walked Mr. Finnius Creech, acting Headmaster. Mr. Creech crossed into the room proud of what he was accomplishing at the school but sank when he saw the man sitting at his desk.

"Sssir …" Mr. Creech stammered. "You? Here? I mean … . Thank you for coming to visit us, sir."

"Do us both a favor and stop your tongue from wagging, Mr. Creech!" said the man in the chair. He cleaned his nails with a long bone handled knife as he spoke. "I like what's happening around here, Mr. Creech."

"Thank you sir, we are doing our best to turn the place around," Mr. Creech stammered with a frightened smile on his face.

"Yes, yes, fine. But we both know what I'm really interested in, Mr. Creech," the man said as he laid the knife on the desk in front of him.

"We do, sir?"

"Let me explain it to you again, Mr. Creech. You can have this school for your little social experiments. I don't care what you do with it or the children here, except one. There's a special child here, Mr. Creech, and we are going to identify him or her, aren't we? I understand a dragon protector has been seen in the area, which gives us more evidence still that a sporran bearer is amongst us. Before you continue your little experiments, I want your staff to uncover the bearer and bring him to me unharmed."

Mr. Creech was now nodding his head rapidly and muttering, "yes sir, yes sir" under his breath.

The man reached into the breast pocket of his black suit and pulled a wad of papers from it. He tossed them across the desk and announced, "As it so happens, Mr. Creech, Iona Academy has had some financial problems recently; some bad investments, some very bad investments, Mr. Creech. Indeed, the bank tells me you are near bankruptcy—and I'm here to bail you out with a loan that will turn the title to this place over to me when it can't be paid off. You will still have your job and you can do with this place what you want. But with these papers, Mr. Creech, we can get rid of the problematic members of the Board of Trustees and any teachers we think might be bad influences around here. Let's start that purge at once, and let it start with that Kirk fellow. Never liked him even when I was a student here and now I don't trust him at all."

"Right away, sir. Never liked him myself," Mr. Creech responded.

"Now, sit down and tell me your plan to detect our little sporran bearer, Mr. Creech," the man said as he invited the head of the school to sit in one of the visitors' chairs in his own office.

"Well, sir, we think we know who it is, sir. There is this Boyd character that seems to be a particular favorite of some of the old grey beards like Kirk. We had other suspects, but have ruled them out. We're pretty sure it's Boyd."

"Then why isn't he here before me now if you are so sure?"

"Well, sir, we aren't *exactly* sure. I mean, the evidence seems to be pointing to him and all … but we don't want to move prematurely, right? I mean, if he isn't the one, we don't want to spook the real bearer do we?" Creech wrung his hands nervously as he spoke.

"Uncharacteristically intelligent, Mr. Creech," the man said as he rose from the seat behind the desk. As he stood, his full height was realized at nearing six foot five inches with a thin frame of mostly bone and little meat. He turned to look out the window into the courtyard of the school and slipped on black sunglasses. "Intelligent, but I'm not a very patient man. I suggest you turn up the heat, Mr. Creech—or when this place goes bankrupt and reverts to me, your little playground will be taken away from you."

"Yes sssir," Creech stammered.

"But then again I assure you that you won't be in any condition to care about this school or anything else if you fail, Mr. Creech."

The man walked round the desk and toward the door. Finnius Creech watched him nervously, hoping not to feel the blade of his knife. "And, if you are going to break these kids and remold them the way we want them, I suggest you do not delay in getting rid of that infernal artwork around the place. It will do us no good to have them dreaming of being another William Wallace or Arthur or George Washington, you know. No room for heroes in our new IONA, Mr. Creech—that includes you, don't forget! No heroes. Get rid of it all and I will send some useful paintings of blocks and triangles and splotches of color down in a few days. They can spend hours looking for meaning in those monstrosities. Keep 'em occupied looking for meaning where there isn't any! Never forget that, Creech!"

The man swept out of the room, leaving Creech dabbing his sweaty forehead and struggling to catch his breath.

Kidnapped

"**D**ear Lucy," Mr. Finnius Creech's voice cracked with tension. "Dear Lucy, please report to my office," the man's voice went into a walkie-talkie.

"Right away sir, just finishing up training, sir," the young leader of the new Guards replied between the crackling of radio static.

Moments later she had dismissed the students with their general orders to keep curfews and an eye out for any trouble makers, particularly those who seemed not to like the changes going on about the place. Most of all, they were to report to her immediately if anything out of the ordinary happened.

Will had been torn throughout the training session about his role in it all. He now became even more conflicted as rumors circulated through the guard that "out of the ordinary" was a code for some fantastical magic about the place. Knowing of his friend's own connection to the fantastic, he wondered if they were concerned with Jacob himself. He even allowed himself to wonder, but just for a second, if Jacob was the "problem" they were looking out for. But he forced that thought out of his head, or at least he tried to—and went to his room to wait his turn to serve as a night guard. Perhaps he could also talk to Jacob and ease his own mind a bit.

Lucy knocked and then walked into Mr. Finnius Creech's office where she found him staring out the window, fiddling nervously with his fingers, and raising his toes up and down with rapidity. Despite her knock, he hadn't heard her enter and her greeting of "Lucy, reporting, Sir!" startled him.

"Oh … yes," he began to stumble but then caught himself and regained his composure. "Yes, thank you for coming so quickly, my dear. Please, sit down."

Lucy took the seat opposite him and wiggled herself to comfort and crossed her legs.

"Lucy, I am afraid things are not going as well as they may seem on the surface."

Lucy's face grew red, as she feared that perhaps she had not been doing a good job.

"No, Lucy, there are spies amongst us and others who would like to undo what we have accomplished. We are going to need to crack down. I have two things for you and your troops. Can I call them troops, dear?" Creech said in a tone meant to convey he wanted to call them "troops" no matter what she thought. Perhaps controlling an army would make him feel more secure.

Lucy leaned forward, eager to have the attention and the obviously important new missions.

"First, here is a list of faculty and staff that I think are a danger to our mission. I want you to put two of your top students on the job of following them at all times and reporting back to me if two or more of them get together." He handed her a crisply folded piece of paper.

"Then, and this is most important, you will understand; we need to decapitate the resistance. Remove the head and the body withers, you know!" Creech brought a hard blow from the side of his hand down onto his desk.

Lucy jerked back.

"I think the head of the resistance is that dastardly little over achiever and generally too-good-for-himself punk Jacob Boyd. What do you think?"

A sinister smile started to emerge on Lucy's face. "Oh, I don't know sir—I mean, yes sir, that sounds about right. He has thought a bit too much of himself since arriving anyway, if you ask me. What should I do with him?"

"I would do this myself, you understand, but I must maintain a certain distance from it all. You understand, don't you?"

"Of course," Lucy said with anticipation.

"Well, you must not let him die. If you need to rough him up a bit, that's fine, but I need him alive."

For the first time, Lucy began to feel a little squeamish. Rounding someone up is one thing—but to mention killing, what did this man think she was?

"Across the back fields you will find a path to the old Ashland mansion. It hasn't been inhabited in years, but I know there are perfectly good jails for bad children out there. Throw him in one of the icehouses and take a pad lock and chain with you to make sure he can't get out."

With those words Mr. Creech flashed back in his mind to a terrible summer he himself spent at his Uncle's farm in West Virginia. There was an icehouse there and his drunken Uncle would punish him by locking him in that dark place for two days at a time. The feeling of being closed in and unable to escape came like a shadow over him again and caused him to shiver with a chill.

"Sir," Lucy said after a long pause.

"Yes, well, now," Mr. Creech said after his mind swung back to the room. "You make sure you take enough manpower to adequately do the job."

"I can handle that skinny punk, myself, sir," Lucy bragged.

"NO! You don't take chances with this one. Do you understand?" Mr. Creech leaned across his desk as he barked the order at her.

"Take at least ten students with you and whatever you do, don't take your eyes off his hands! Keep them away from his waist, in particular, and bind his hands so he can't get them undone while he is in the icehouse."

Lucy took her orders and left the room, ready for such an important mission.

Jacob and Jenny had worked their way back onto campus and to their rooms. Both did what homework they could find the concentration for and eventually went to sleep. Will was awakened at 2:00 AM when it was his turn to go on sentry duty. Thirty minutes later, the door opened again and a group of ten young boys and one girl in hooded sweatshirts quietly entered the room and set upon Jacob.

One gagged him while others held him down and still others tied his feet and arms. Then they wrapped his body tight in a sheet to make it unrecognizable. Within a minute, the gang had their victim out of the room and down the hall. Jacob struggled to no avail.

"Stop!" Will announced as he saw the party heading toward the door. Jacob's ears perked up and he hoped Will was there to help.

One of the hooded group removed her hood and revealed her face as that of Lucy Furangle. "Good work, Will, but this is official business. Carry on and watch our back, if you would."

Jacob squirmed harder and tried to yell through the gag so that Will could hear him. It was no use.

"Oh, yes Sir! I mean, yes Ma'am!" Will replied and turned to watch behind the group as it passed with its victim squirming under the sheet that covered him. The thought of being part of something as exciting as abduction both thrilled and concerned him.

The group carried their victim on their shoulders across the field. *They look like an ancient druid funeral,* Will thought as he peeked around the corner to watch them go.

Jacob calmed down and tried to reach Nibblus Maximus and ask for help. He could imagine the thought of the great dragon descending upon the party with his "brave" abductors fleeing in terror as Nibblus Maximus tossed them into the air like dolls and as Lucy peed her pants in fear.

There was no reply from the dragon, however, and within minutes Jacob felt his body drop onto a hard surface. Voices above him laughed as a door slammed shut and a padlock clicked closed.

Jacob scrambled in a panic to get the sheet off his body and find out where he was. He spun across the floor and wiggled his head until the sheet dropped behind him.

He jumped to his feet, but could see very little. He was in a dark cell, completely round with walls made of stone blocks. That much he could make out. He had heard horses whinny on the way and guessed his captors had carried him past the stables. If that was so, he was sure he must be in one of the three small buildings that he had seen behind the Ashland mansion. He didn't know they were called icehouses or what they were used for, but he remembered them looking like hobbit houses or dwarf dwellings or something. Their walls only protruded a few feet above the ground and their roofs were shaped like a cone, which came to a high point. He was pretty sure he must be in one of them.

He called out in his mind to his dragon protector but got no response. In frustration he kicked the wall and then slid down to a seated position. He was trapped and as if it couldn't get worse, he was in his red checked pajama bottoms and an oversized white t-shirt.

Escape

Moments passed like hours in the dark and cold loneliness of Jacob's cell. He would pull and twist at the ropes until they dug into his wrists and burned. Then he would calm down and try to contact Nibblus Maximus and pray. Soon he would start all over again with the twisting and pulling. The cycle was repeated several times.

Finally, he gave up. It was no use pulling at the ropes. They would never break under his power, he realized. He then tried concentrating on the sporran, which, fortunately for him, he decided to wear tucked under his red checked pajama bottoms when he laid down to sleep that night. It wasn't comfortable, but with all that had been happening, it was his insurance policy and well worth the discomfort.

He believed if he could reach the sporran, he could pull Isildane's sword from it. Isildane's ring was attached to the leather strap around his waist.

It's red jewel, would be most useful in the dark icehouse cell. *Tools made just for such a situation,* he thought, *and completely out of reach,* his mind went on in frustration. Then he had an idea.

The sporran strap was tied loosely about his waist to give it maximum chance to slip around while he slept. If he could just wiggle it down his legs, maybe he could get it off and then open it with his fingers, he hoped. He stood again and sucked his belly in as much as he could. He pushed his legs together as tight as they would go, then spun his hips back and forth. It was no use. The leather strap would not slip down over his hips.

Jacob sat back down again and rolled onto his side; then continued over until the top of his head was on the ground next to the wall and the rest of his weight rested on the tips of his toes. Up he pushed from his feet. Up again. And up again.

Finally he pushed hard and his lower body flew up and smacked uncomfortably against the icehouse wall. He was, upside down and wavering unsteadily. The top of his skull felt like it was splitting under the weight of his body. Mercifully, the strap did come loose and slip down around his hands.

Jacob grabbed the strap with his fingers and let his body fall to the side. For a few moments he lay there allowing the pain to drain from his head while he held tight to the strap. Then he stood and began slowly and carefully pulling the strap through his fingers and moving the sporran from front to back. When the sporran reached his left hip, Jacob felt the ring clasp of the strap and carefully undid it. The soft sound of leather hitting the floor was music to Jacob's ears.

Using his bare feet, Jacob searched the floor for the lump that would be Isildane's ring. Having found it, he kicked it against the wall and then slipped back down the floor until he could grasp it and slip it onto his finger. Then he pulled the leather strap until the sporran reached his fingers and he closed his eyes to ask for Isildane's sword to appear just as it had to help save his life the year before when he was facing the evil in Whipsnade's castle.

The sporran grew heavy as Jacob worked his fingers around the flap and opened it. Inside was a round piece of metal that his fingers recognized as the lion head pommel of the sword. Slipping one foot over the sporran's strap to hold it fast, he stood and as he did, the sword slipped from its scabbard. Even in this prison it felt wonderfully empowering in Jacob's young hands. The two twisting dragons that made up the handle were soft and jelly-like.

Jacob laid the sword down, worked the handle until it was between his feet, and then lowered himself down on his haunches to where the upturned blade could be used as a saw to cut the ropes binding his hands.

He worked his hands back and forth until his shoulders ached and his thighs grew tight. Finally, the blade slipped through the last strand of rope and his hands were free. He jumped to his feet and ripped off the gag from his mouth. He paced to work out the stiffness in his arms and legs before attaching the sporran again to his waist and reaching into its pouch to remove a scabbard, which he attached to the same belt and slipped Isildane's sword into its home.

Jacob removed the ring and looked through the back of the red stone at its center. Like it had done in the caverns beneath Edinburgh, it concentrated the little bit of diffused light in the room and allowed Jacob to see with a red glow. He climbed the stairs and pushed on the door. It was locked tight. He beat on it for several minutes but it did not budge. He sat back down on the floor in despair, trying to contact the dragon with all the brainpower he had. As he did, he looked about the round cell through the red glow of the ring.

The dragon again did not answer the boy's calls. Jacob, however, noticed small graffiti near the floor on the far wall. He crawled over to take a closer look. It was a very basic scratched outline of an antlered deer with what looked like a man following behind on all fours. It all seemed insignificant at first and Jacob went back to wondering, thinking, praying, and trying to contact Nibblus Maximus.

Eventually, he turned the ring again to the small etching on the stone. He had taken the markings above the deer to be nothing but the random cut marks the craftsman made when he smoothed the stone at the quarry. Upon closer examination, though, letters started to come clear. More than just letters, they formed words. He squinted and worked to make them out. It took considerable effort and strained his eyes, but finally he figured out what the words said:

> My heart's in the Highlands, my heart is not here,
> My heart's in the Highlands, a-chasing the deer;
> Chasing the wild-deer, and following the roe—
> My heart's in the Highlands, wherever I go!

A poem? I bet some poor sap like me got locked in here a long time ago and etched this because he was bored. Jacob didn't remember that this was just one stanza from a longer poem by Robert Burns he had heard in Dr. Kirk's class. *Or,* he paused for a minute, *maybe I can go "a-chasing the deer"! Maybe it's a clue left for the next sap imprisoned here. And I'm that sap!*

The man looks like he is "a-chasing" the deer. Maybe I should chase the deer, he thought. *Well, that's fine, then. If I could actually get out of here I would find a deer to chase!* Somehow in dangerous situations like the one Jacob found himself in, it's sometimes enjoyable just to be sarcastic to oneself if no one else happens to be around to listen.

Wait a minute … maybe, just maybe. . . I can chase the deer. He got up on all fours like the etched stick figure and started "chasing" around the wall.

This is stupid, he realized on his second lap. *And it hurts my knees!* He stopped himself and looked at the picture and the words again.

He felt around on the stone. He pushed on the man. He pushed on the deer. Nothing happened. He took the sword from its scabbard and hit the deer with the lion-head pommel. Nothing. Then he noticed the odd shape of the deer's head. It was squarer than would be natural. It was about the same size as the stone in the ring. He lowered the ring carefully to where the head was and gently pushed. He felt the wall catch the stone and hold it. The faint red light was now gone as the stone was attached to the wall. He pulled but it did not budge. He twisted the ring and it turned like a key one half turn to the right and then released. As it did, Jacob heard a series of clicks from inside the wall that sounded like locks coming unsnapped. He stood and pushed the stones, which slowly began to slide away.

The wall removed, a passage beneath the ground came into view. *I don't want my heart to be here either, so I go "a-chasing the deer!"* he thought with more reservations than bravery. Holding Isildane's ring to his eye for light, he entered the passageway and began down the tunnel.

Ten steps in and the door behind him creaked shut. His heart raced and fear again rushed over him. He prayed for a way out and as he looked back he noticed there was a tube attached to the back of the door. He walked back and removed it from its hooks.

The tube was made of metal and was covered in small piles of dirt that had fallen from the ceiling of the tunnel. Both ends were closed with a silver metal cap with small circles of rust dotting them. Holding the ring that gave him light between his teeth, he opened the tube in the darkness. He sat down and poured the contents onto the floor and pulled Isildane's ring again to his eye. In the tube he found a small torch, a striking box for lighting it, and a piece of paper. He lit the torch and stuck it into the dirt next to him while he put Isildane's ring back onto his finger.

Unfolding the paper, he saw it was a map of the tunnels. It showed the way from various rooms in the Ashland mansion to the icehouse. Jacob thought this must have been designed as some kind of escape for people in the house, and he snickered that he would now be using it to escape *into* the house and not *out* of it.

"Well, better get going before you run out of fuel," Jacob said as he picked up the torch and started down the tunnels.

The map showed tunnels to various rooms in the house but the most interesting one, he thought, was marked "Library Bookcase." He passed several bends in the tunnels and continued on to find his preferred route of escape into Ashland.

Occasionally, the walls shook around him and he thought he could hear a faint roar from somewhere above the surface.

Secret Meeting

Nibblus Maximus had gone off to seek counsel and send word to others of the developments at Iona School. He was gone when Jacob was kidnapped and imprisoned, but Jacob's thoughts still hung in the outside air; though fragmented and decaying. The dragon picked up the alarm in Jacob's previous thoughts and roared as he circled the trees and tried in vein to contact his charge.

Separated by many feet of dirt and clay and the walls of the tunnel, the dragon circled above not knowing Jacob was below. With every fruitless circle the dragon got more and more angry. He was angry with himself for leaving when Jacob obviously needed him. He was also angry at whoever was responsible for Jacob's troubles.

He circled low over the trees and then let fly an awful cry of war as he continued like a jet over the buildings of the school. His anger grew so hot that his fire spewed across the lawn setting it aflame to glow like a landing strip at night right up to the oil tanks behind one of the sheds that contained the lawn tractors and other maintenance equipment for the school. As he rose into the air, the tanks and equipment exploded. The fire and noise momentarily gave the beast satisfaction. He banked and landed on the roof of the Spur and Spoon to watch people scramble around campus to put out the fire and gawk at what happened. As he did, he turned his mind back to Jacob and tried to connect or pick up some new clue. His efforts met with no success.

The commotion set loose panic on campus. Several dark cars with tinted windows rushed off the school grounds. Nibblus Maximus swung down close over them listening and feeling for any sign of Jacob in the vehicles. There was none and he left them leave unmolested as he returned to watch the chaos unfold on campus and to search for his friend.

Earlier in the evening, hooded figures had entered the Ashland mansion as darkness fell. No lights appeared to burn in the old house. What was happening inside remained a mystery to all but the hooded participants themselves.

Following the map of the twisting tunnels, Jacob came to a ladder and a shaft running straight up twenty feet. At the top of the shaft, he thought he could detect a slight bit of light. He hesitated. Ashland should be abandoned. *Maybe I should go back and take another tunnel to another room?*

He thought for a minute, but decided to climb up into the library bookcase as he had originally planned. Jacob put the small torch in his left hand and slowly began to climb the cobweb-filled ladder attached to the walls of the shaft. As he climbed, he could hear faint sounds and the flicker of light grew brighter. The shaft narrowed and the walls turned from stone to wood.

He left the torch sticking out of a hole in the stone wall as he pulled himself the last few inches up to where the light was coming through a slit in the wood.

What he saw caused him to startle and nearly fall back down the shaft. The light was coming from small pots of fire sitting on the floor next to three hooded figures seated in a small circle. Jacob looked around the room and saw it was a round library with several doors and windows, each shuttered tightly. Between the doors were shelves filled with books. By the pattern, Jacob could tell he was behind one of the cases and the books beneath his nose told him the same. A chandelier in the shape of a serpent, its mouth agape and pointing downward, hung from the ceiling in the center of the room.

After his initial start, Jacob froze still and resolved to listen, if for only a minute. He could hear the voices plain and strong.

"I tell you there are strange specters haunting the land, Campbell!"

"Kirk, I know you think what is going on is all bad, but sometimes traditions must be remade and new things tried. I tell you there is no reason to think that there is anything more going on here than some good educational reform."

Kirk? Is that Dr. Kirk? Campbell, but Campbell's dead, I saw him die in my own room! Confused, Jacob hung on the ladder with white knuckles.

Just then the group was startled by a crash in the distance. One of the hooded figures got up and peeked through the shutter near Jacob's bookcase. Jacob fell back into the shadows.

"Look, the school is ablaze! Now do you think this is just educational reform, Campbell?"

The figure opened the shutters and an orange glow came through the window. In the mirror opposite the window, Jacob could see the glow of a fire in the distance and something circling in the sky. *Oh, no, Nibbles!* he realized.

Jacob immediately tried again to contact the dragon. Now that he had emerged from under the ground, he was able to connect and tell him he was all right and urge the dragon to take cover and wait to rescue him after he found out what was happening with these hooded figures. He now felt relatively safe in the shaft.

Nibblus Maximus glided to a stop behind the barn, turned himself back into the pug dog and ran back up to the school as fast as his little legs could carry him. He sat amongst the students and administrators watching the guards running to and fro with some yelling things like "where did it go?" and "Who saw that, did you?" Now that he knew Jacob was safe, the dragon hadn't had so much fun since he started a little fire in Chicago a century before and framed Mrs. O'Leary's cow for it.

The hooded figures all agreed this was the final piece of necessary evidence. Educational reformers don't often employ dragons, or fight them either. Something far more sinister was behind the developments at Iona, they now realized.

"Kirk, what about this boy of yours? Boyd is his name, no?" said one.

"Well, I haven't seen anything particularly special about him but he seems to be here for some reason. I can't help but think he is the *reason* this is all happening."

Another hooded figure then entered the room and spoke in a thick Scottish accent. "Your Boyd is my Boyd, dear Kirk."

"Hammish, is that you, old friend?"

The hooded figure pulled the hood back from his face and revealed, to Jacob's shock, Hammish MacGregor. It was the man who had first introduced him to the world of the Sporrai and helped save him at Feddinch House.

"Yes, you old goat it's me. Who else?"

Dr. Kirk pulled his hood back and the two embraced.

"Well, friends, this settles it!" Kirk said. "Hammish doesn't leave St. Andrews except on the gravest business.   There is no grave business for him here unless some magic has been set afire about the place. Isn't that right, my old MacGregor?"

The others stood and pulled their hoods back, revealing Dr. Kirk and Hammish MacGregor were conversing with Copernicus Campbell and Bunting Boyle; A murderer and the murdered!

Call for Help

Campus was a beehive of chaotic activity. The explosion of the oil tanks awakened every student on campus and it seemed they all were out watching the fires. The Aberdeen fire department, which arrived about fifteen minutes after the explosions were heard, battled the flames.

Mr. Nibbles found Jenny in the crowd and snuggled up next to her. "Oh," she said as he startled her, "it's you. I mean, it's my old friend Mr. Nibbles, right? I mean, after what I saw today, I hope you're my friend!" Jenny was whispering in the dog's ear as she finished her sentence. The pug dog just sat watching the remains of his handy work and readying himself to rescue Jacob as soon as the boy was ready to be rescued.

In Ashland mansion, Jacob hung onto the ladder and looked out beyond the shelf of books that hid him. He listened to the four men in hooded robes. Eavesdropping always bothered him, but in this case he knew they were talking about him. Having been kidnapped and left in a prison in the back yard, he felt it prudent to listen and see if these four might have had something to do with it.

"So, Bunting, you murdered my friend Campbell here. What do you have to say for yourself?" Ramos Kirk asked.

"Didn't do a very good job of it, I see," Hammish MacGregor interjected.

"If you want something done right, do it yourself," Campbell said, "but I couldn't stick that arrow in my own back, you know!"

"If I would have wanted to take you out, Campbell, believe me, I could have done it," Boyle responded.

Jacob listened as the men got down to business. As they discussed the situation, it became clear there were two problems that concerned them. The school itself had been taken over by forces hostile to its traditions and who may have done away with their friend, Abigail Witherspoon. But, there was something else afoot, too, which was more mysterious.

"I tell you we need to move that Boyd kid out of here," Bunting Boyle argued.

"Before we do anything, we need to contact Chadwick von Niblick," Kirk interjected. "He knows this Boyd lad better than the rest of us and knows the ancient documents better than anyone alive."

"I wish we could," Hammish MacGregor replied. "I had word two weeks ago that he was on his way to Iona, but have not been able to get hold of him since. I thought he was coming here to the school, but he never arrived. At least not to my knowledge."

"Iona, you say? Well, let's not forget there is *the Iona*, too! I mean, that sacred island after which our school got its name," Ramos Kirk replied. "If so, I wonder what he was doing over there?"

The four thought for a moment and then MacGregor again spoke. "Well, regardless of where our friend von Niblick might be, we have issues right here. von Niblick and I have been thinking something has been amiss for some time within the Sporrai."

Hearing the name of the secret society tapped with the responsibility of protecting the secrets of Isildane and the powers of his treasure sent a burning pain down Jacob's spine and right arm. He winced.

"Yes, Hammish and I have been sensing the same thing," Campbell interjected. "We have, in fact, cut off our contact with the others over the last few months. We think the forces of darkness may have infiltrated the society again and have taken over the imaginations of one or more Keepers."

"We are truly the Remnant now," Kirk added. "We must make the pact now among those of us who have resisted the temptations of the power and lure of the enemy. Let us renew our vows to serve the higher order that created all and gave to us the highest measure of love and the final sacrifice of death."

Jacob watched as the four men then made a movement across their bodies with their right hands and moved forward to kneel in a circle with heads bowed. They mumbled words together that Jacob could not quite make out. Then they each pulled a sword from under their cloaks and held them in front of their faces, the long silver blades reaching toward the ceiling and the serpent headed chandelier above. They then kissed the crosses that the hilts of the swords made in front of their faces. Simultaneously, the men spun their swords that rested in their right hands to the left and down. Now they rested on their hilts and bowed their heads in silence.

Jacob felt uncomfortable watching the solemn ceremony and so bowed his own head and closed his eyes for just a moment. When he opened them again and looked up, the room was empty. A shock rushed through his mind. He wondered if he had imagined it or if he had fallen asleep. *Where did they go?*

Three thousand miles northeast of Iona Academy there is a mystical island where eternity seems to slip more perceptively into reality than anywhere else on Earth. In a tomb in the graveyard outside the ancient abbey, a man came slowly back to himself as if awakening from the dead. His head throbbed and body ached. Slowly he worked his right hand down into his coat pocket and pulled, inch by inch, a small black book from its resting place. In the tight space of the tomb, it was all he could do to inch a pen from his pocket, pull the cap, and open the book. He could not raise his head to see what he was doing and the complete darkness would have kept him from seeing anything anyway. On the page that fell open, the man scratched out the following words:

The man closed the book and attempted to slow his breathing down to be as calm as possible. He could feel his heart slowing. He fought to control the panic and anxiety that he knew would kill him if he let it. His eyes closed and he let his mind go peaceful in contemplation of the end of his journey, which he knew might well arrive soon.

Jacob stood on the ladder stunned and confused. The four were there a moment before but now they were gone. He paused a moment to listen for movement. He heard nothing. A few minutes passed and he stepped up fully behind the bookcase and searched for a way to get through without crawling out on the shelf and knocking books everywhere. He removed Isildane's ring from his finger and looked through the stone, first left and then right.

On the right side he noticed a lever and pulled it. The latch holding the case in place released and let it slide slightly forward into the room. Slowly he was able to inch the right side further into the room and he then stepped quietly passed it and into the library of Ashland mansion. He turned and pushed the case back closed before he looked around.

The pots still had small flames consuming the last bits of fuel. He looked up and saw the chandelier with the snakehead dangling down, its mouth open as if to strike. On the floor where the four had knelt and sworn allegiance just moments before, was the head of a stag in-laid in the wood. Between its great antlers, lighter slivers of wood seemed designed to show some kind of rays beaming from a force beyond. For a moment, Jacob stared at the deer and wondered. So many deer had by now appeared in his life since the sporran arrived the year before that he wondered if they were tied to the deeper story he was now part of.

As he inspected the circle on the floor containing the stag's head, Jacob felt a slight movement of air. Feeling around on the floor, he noted that the air came more from the edges of the circle than the center. *There must be passage beneath the floor and that must be how the four left,* he reasoned. *Still, who could be sure and I am not about to try to find out.*

He turned and looked about for an escape. The rest of the house was dark. He reached back through the bookcase and retrieved the torch that he had left hanging in the tunnel and pulled it through the open shelf. It was barely burning by now, but it was enough to see his way out of the library and into the hall.

Stairs went up to his left, but Jacob was in no mood to explore this house tonight. He made his way to what he figured was the front door and fiddled with the handle until it unlocked. He pulled the door behind him and immediately stamped out the flame of his torch after taking a relieved breath of the night's air.

Free from his prison, he was confused about who to trust and who could not be trusted. One thing was clear to him: it was Lucy Furangle's voice that was with the men who abducted him and threw him into the icehouse. With her and her friends watching the school, it was not safe for him to head back.

In the distance he could see the dull light of remaining fires at the school. He made his way down to the tree line and sat down to think. He was alone and now had no home to return to. It was like the time he got lost in the mall when he was eight. He remembered the terrible feeling very well. He longed for his mother just as much now.

Jacob closed his eyes and opened his imagination to a picture of Nibblus Maximus. *Ok, bud, I need you,* he sent out. Mr. Nibbles heard his friend and turned instantly from Jenny.

"Nibbles, wait, where are you going?" Jenny yelled after him.

The little dog did not turn back but continued across the field and, as the darkness covered his little body, he turned down toward the stables. Jenny watched as long as she could and then turned to go back into her dorm and head to bed.

Jacob whistled when he saw the movement he took to be Mr. Nibbles coming up the path between the two patches of trees. The dog stopped and changed directions toward Jacob's whistle. Jacob opened his arms and the dog jumped into them and licked his face enthusiastically.

Nibblus Maximus, I think you better get me out of here so I can think and we can figure out what to do. It's clearly not safe here for me anymore.

Mr. Nibbles walked out of the trees and began to swell and change form. Jacob walked out, grabbed the dragon around his neck and squeezed his face into the jelly-like flesh. He felt great relief. Jacob climbed onto his back and with a couple of downward thrusts of the dragon's wings the two were airborne and heading south.

Nibblus Maximus kept low, just over the treetops to avoid being seen silhouetted against the night sky. A couple of miles of flight and he tilted forward and bent his wings down to slow their progress. He landed as lightly as he could in the small field that opened amidst the trees. Jacob slipped off and thanked the dragon for the rescue.

As he turned, he could see glowing eyes like small lights at the edge of the woods. He backed into the dragon and drew his sword.
Relax, Bearer. They are friends, the dragon said.

Slowly the eyes approached and showed themselves to be those of the other dogs from the kennels at Iona.

I brought them here when the problems started up there at the school, Jacob. They're fine. We've been living on some pretty fine sheep meat these last few days, you know!

I'm sure you have, Jacob replied. *Think you might be able to start a fire? I'm getting a bit chilly* Jacob asked.

Oh, I am good at that tonight! The dragon replied proudly and made a grunt that Jacob took to be a slight laugh.

The dragon's eyes turned from brown to molten gold and then a small puff of fire flew from its mouth and lit a small stack of grasses and lose branches that the dogs had gathered earlier.

Thanks, Jacob said as he moved over to the flame and warmed his fingers. He then checked his sporran but found nothing. He stuck Isildane's sword into the ground next to him and removed his enchiridion from his pocket. He opened the small book and found a note that caused him to gasp and look worriedly at Nibblus Maximus.

"Nibbs, listen", he said as he began to read the note: "Boyd. Niblick here. Trouble. Entombed on Iona. Send N.M. to help. Have information. Find MacGregor. Fast. Air running out."

The dragon let out a loud cry of anxiety toward the night sky.

I'm sorry. I know you love him. Go to him and save your old master, Jacob urged his friend.

The dragon turned away and dug its right claw into the dirt pensively. *No. My responsibility is now your safety, not the professor's. I can't leave you, Bearer.*

Message in a Collar

*R*ead the note to me again, Jacob, Nibblus Maximus requested. Jacob opened his small black book and read, "Boyd. That is me, you know!" He interjected.

Just read it, the dragon insisted.

Jacob continued reading: "Niblick here. Trouble. Entombed on Iona. Send N. M. to help. Have information. Find MacGregor. Fast. Air running out." Jacob looked up from the text. "Do you think he is here on campus somewhere? It says 'Entombed on Iona,' afterall, and, do you think you are N.M. or is he talking about sending New Mexico?"

No, Jacob, the professor is not here. We spent many years together. I would be able to sense his presence if he was anywhere close to us. No, he is on the island of Iona off Scotland's western shore. I'm sure that is where he is. He wrote he is 'on' Iona, right? People are on islands, they are at schools.

Well, Jacob stopped speaking aloud; *you need to get going, then. That must be 3,000 miles from here. Can you make it?*

Of course I could make it, but I can't go. My duty is to stay with you. Now, let's decide what to do with you.

But, that's it. Don't you see? Jacob interjected. *I'm not safe here and you have to protect me, so take me to Iona where we can try to save our friend and you can be saving me as well.*

Little Bearer, if Professor von Niblick is in trouble, what makes you think you could even survive an encounter with what has trapped him? That is, even if you make it across the ocean!

Look, I'm scared to death, Nibbs! Jacob said as he approached the dragon and put his arm around its neck. *I'm afraid to be here and I'm afraid to go, but I don't see as we have a choice. The professor sent me the note and asks for your help. Shouldn't we be listening to him and do what he seems to want us to do?*

The dragon looked to the sky and took two steps away from Jacob. He bowed his head for a moment and then turned. *Little Bearer, let's move!*

"First, we have to get a message for Jenny and Will. Can you take a note to Jenny?" Jacob asked.

I can make it, but we must move quickly. Iona is many hours flight from here.

Jacob felt his pockets and then had an idea. He took his enchiridion, and wrote a note back to von Niblick. He had no way of knowing the professor would be unable to read it. Then he took a few pages from the back and carefully pulled them from the spine. Guilt washed over him, but it was the only paper he had. And, if it worked like he hoped, it might just prove very useful. Instead of writing on the loose paper, he set it down next to him and turned back to the front of the book and started to write.

Jacob finished his note and picked up the loose papers. He hoped it would work.

Come on, Jacob, we have to move, the dragon interrupted him.

Just a minute. Just a minute, Jacob said while he stared at the blank paper and hoped to see some ink slowly coming to life on the page. He turned the paper into the firelight for a better look. Nothing. Then, slowly an ink spot bled into the paper and dropped down into a "J." Then an "e" and two "n's" and then a "y."

"YES!" Jacob called out and pumped his right arm enthusiastically by his side. He hoped the enchiridion would work with the pages he ripped from its spine and it did.

Jacob folded the note and tucked it into Nibblus Maximus's collar. "Here, friend. Take this to Jenny, please. Then we will leave to try to find the professor." He patted the dragon on the neck and backed away.

Nibblus Maximus moved away from the fire and took a leap into the air, the powerful downward thrust of his wings caused the fire to flame up high and sparks to fly into the air.

Jacob sat back, looked around, and said, "Well, pups, are you enjoying life in the woods?"

Nibblus Maximus circled the school looking for the closest place he could safely land. He settled on hitting the shadowy area near the gazebo and came in low over the trees. He glided to the ground and soon was running around the far end of the gazebo as the little pug.

Nibbles kept to the shadows, as he smelled for danger. Across the field, up the rocky road, passed the library, and he was at the girl's dorm. He pushed with his nose and the door opened enough for him to sneak in. He pushed the door back shut and then wondered what he would do now. He suddenly realized that he had never been to Jenny's room before. *Which one is it?* He walked up the stairs and down the hallway smelling the air for any sign of his friend.

She was behind door 105, he was sure of it. He pushed the door open and walked into the dark room. He put his little front feet up on the bed to the left and looked at the sleeping girl; a small blonde. It wasn't her. He turned to the other bed; sure the sleeping girl must be Jenny. He hopped up into the bed and licked the sleeping girl's face.

She turned and slowly opened her eyes to see two bulging black eyes and smashed face staring back at her only inches away in the dark night.

The girl screamed and flung her arms straight up and under the small intruder. Mr. Nibbles flew across the room and landed hard on the blonde girl's belly, causing her to bounce up and then scream in terror. The little dog let out a terrified yelp of his own and busted out the door and down the hall, rushing into another room and hiding under one of the beds.

"Mr. Nibbles, is that you?" Jenny, having been awoken from her sleep by the screams down the hall, was sitting up in her bed when the dog busted through the cracked-open door. The pug jumped up on Jenny's bed and licked her face. She stroked his head and whispered, "What are ya doing here, little guy?" Oblivious, Jenny's roommate Elizabeth was still fast asleep.

Mr. Nibbles backed off Jenny's chest and onto her bed. He scratched his neck under his collar and Jacob's note and extra paper fell out onto the covers. Jenny reached up to her desk and pulled down the little reading light she used when she wanted to study and Elizabeth was asleep. She shined it on the paper and read:

> *Big trouble. Furangle and her men kidnapped me. Will didn't know it, I am sure. I am OK now, but Iona is not safe for me. Mr. Nibbles and I are going away for a while to take care of a few things. Stay at school and keep an eye on Will, would you? We will need to know what is happening here. If you can, find out why someone would want to kidnap and imprison me. But, don't take any chances. Be careful.*
>
> *Hope to see you soon.*
> *Jake*

"Oh, no, is Jacob OK? Of course, what am I doing? You can't talk! Well, I know you can somehow talk to Jacob so tell him to be careful and I'll do what I can until I hear from him again."

Mr. Nibbles jumped down off the bed and ran over to the window. The commotion was growing in the hallway now and Jenny jumped up and quietly shut the door.

Shaking and mumbling about some giant rat that tried to eat their faces, the girls in room 105 were standing on top of their desks as other girls piled in to see what was going on.

Mr. Nibbles put his small paws up on the window seal. He whimpered and Jenny came over. She looked out the window but saw nothing.

"Do you want me to open it?" The dog licked her hand to confirm his wish and then backed up. She opened the window and the dog took three steps and launched himself up and into the night sky. Jenny panicked and tried to grab him but the dog flew out and began to fall down beyond her reach. As he fell, she could see his outline grow larger and larger until two great wings caught the air and he flew out over the field and toward the woods to the south.

"I'll never get used to that," she mumbled. She closed the window and sat back down for another look at Jacob's note.

Shadows from the Trees

Jacob sat by the fire fiddling with the tassels of his sporran and wondering what would come next. When the magic heated up a year before, he nearly lost his life twice in encounters with the enemy of the Sporrai. As he watched the flames dance in the fire, he relived those moments.

He opened his enchiridion again and began looking back over the letters that Professor von Niblick had sent him during the past year. He looked at his council about avoiding pride and the deadly sins of greed and selfishness. He read again of how the enemy often showed itself in pretty forms and with sugary treats, and not always like the two hideous men he had to encounter in Scotland. He took note at his lessons on prudence and greatness and the glory of sacrifice. He paused at the letter about sacrifice for a moment and wondered if the professor was even now being sacrificed for the higher calling served by the Sporrai. Thinking about the old man who sacrificed his life with Mr. Nibbles for him, he said a prayer and then started back through the lessons again. In the hours ahead, he figured, he might need the lessons more and would have less time to study them again.

Waiting for Nibblus Maximus to return, Jacob kept the fire going by throwing loose twigs and dry grasses into the flames. Occasionally one of the dogs would bring a larger log and lay it within Jacob's reach. As he waited, Jacob scanned the edge of the field, though he had no reason to think anyone would find him or that anything meant him harm from among the trees.

A twig cracked in the distance and the dogs sat up at attention. A german shepherd named Tucker growled and then a collie named Pumpkin followed. The rest now stood and Jacob spun around. He had been around fires enough during camping trips with his father that he knew the disadvantage he was in; being near the fire cut his ability to see into the darkness as it also lit him like a torch no one could miss. He backed up slightly, trying to get out of the direct firelight and pulled his blade from its sheath. The light caught the shank of the blade and danced on it's surface.

At the edge of the trees, a stirring began. Jacob could see shadows, but nothing more. The dogs growled and circled around the boy. If he could have faded into the ground right then, he would have. The fright of an unknown danger took over his mind and he backed up again. Out of the edge of the trees now, he could see the shadows moving into the grass. He called out to Nibblus Maximus but heard nothing in reply. He prayed to see his friend's wings beat above the far trees and descend to his side.

"Master Boyd," one of the shadows called out.

Jacob did not reply. *Just because they know my name*, he thought, *doesn't mean they are friends.*

"Master Boyd, I say, is that you?" Jacob didn't know what to do. He called out to Nibblus Maximus again as the shadows came closer. He could see that there were three.

"Jacob, Jacob Boyd, that is you, isn't it son?" came the voice of another of the shadows. Now they were within fifty feet and he could begin to see them as less shadows and more like large walking blankets with no distinguishing features. Feeling trapped, he finally answered.

"Yes, it's me. What do you want?"

"We mean you no harm, Sporran Bearer."

Jacob was silent but clenched and unclenched the handle of the sword nervously. He kept it close to his leg so it was not to be easily seen.

They were twenty feet away and still no sign of Nibblus Maximus. Jacob called out through his mind once more and begged for him to return swiftly.

Count to three and hit the deck! Jacob heard the order rocket through his mind. Startled, he didn't even wait until a two count, but fell hard to the ground. A second later a large whoosh of air rushed over him, sending hot ashes flying out of the fire in all directions. The three dark blankets dropped to the ground as two wings thrust violently over their heads. Jacob looked up to see Nibblus Maximus bank back up and to the left of the fallen men. He then banked again back toward Jacob and landed with a couple of running steps. Small embers flown from the fire burned a hundred little fires in the field around them.

I've got your back, Jacob, the dragon said.

"We serve the Order of the Sporrai," one of the blankets yelled out.

"Nibblus Maximus, if that is you," another of the downed figures yelled, 'why, I nursed you as a pup, beast!"

The dragon dipped his head down and his eyes squinted into the dark, trying to catch the look of the man speaking from the ground.

"We are getting up now. Slowly, slowly we move. We mean no harm," one of the men announced as they sat up to their knees and then stood. Jacob moved slightly to his left and closer to the dragon.

"Nibbles, that is you, isn't it?" the man asked.

Do you know these men, Nibbs? Jacob asked, fear pulsating through him.

I don't know, stand back.

Their arms outstretched, they took slow steps toward the dragon and the boy. The dogs growled and settled into pouncing positions. They were ready to fight. Jacob nervously squeezed the handle of his sword. When they entered the firelight, Nibblus Maximus recognized them and let out a belch of fire. The men ducked, one hitting the ground on all fours, as the fire disappeared above their heads. The sudden belch of flame scared Jacob as much as it did the strange men and he fell backwards over the claws of the dragon's back right foot.

"Nibbles!" one of the men yelled in an angry voice.

Who are they? Jacob asked.

Don't worry, I'm playing with them, they mean no harm, Jacob.

Then, why? What? Jacob's thoughts were confused.

"Nibbles, so help me, boy! I am starting to regret all the days I spent playing with you many years ago!" The man straightened himself and moved close. Jacob recognized him. It was Hammish MacGregor, Jacob realized with great relief. Professor MacGregor had saved his life in St. Andrews a year ago and, except for Professor von Niblick, he was the only other "Keeper" Jacob had knowingly encountered. He trusted him as much as he trusted anyone.

"Master Boyd, I do hope you might remember me," the man said in his deep Scottish brogue. He had a long beard and hair coming up in every conceivable direction on his head. Jacob remembered well this disheveled look. The two others walked close behind MacGregor and as they entered more clearly into the firelight, Jacob recognized them as Dr. Ramos Kirk and Copernicus Campbell.

"So, I guess he does have a touch of the eternal magic about him, MacGregor," Kirk said as he looked at Jacob.

Nibblus Maximus continued to sense Jacob's discomfort and sent him a soothing message. *Don't worry, Jacob, they are friends. I was playing with them, but they are friends and of the Order of the Sporrai.* Jacob hadn't noticed it until then, but he was experiencing that twinge of electrical pain down his neck and into his right arm, which was holding the sword of Isildane. It was the quickening and Jacob knew it well.

"Well, Nibblus, that low pass you made at us up there on your way to the academy, surely wasn't an accident and Master Boyd being way out here in the fields, certainly can't be a coincidence. Why are we all gathered here?" MacGregor was speaking as he undid his cloak in the fire-warmed air and let it slip from his shoulders. Beneath, he wore an old pair of over alls and a flannel work shirt. Jacob recognized the clothes as being those of the man he saw walking toward the stables after he found the note on his desk that said, "Trust the magic."

Jacob, show him your enchiridion. The dragon sent the message to Jacob's mind. *Show him the note from von Niblick.*

Jacob sheathed the sword of Isildane and pulled the small black book with gold letters from his pocket. He opened it to the page with the note from von Niblick and stepped toward MacGregor.

"He wants me to show this to you," Jacob said.

"Well, then, we have a gift for you, too, right Campbell?" MacGregor nodded at his friend as he took the tiny book from Jacob's hands.

Copernicus stepped forward and said, "You might find these a bit more warming and appropriate for the out-of-doors, son." He then handed Jacob a pair of jeans and a sweatshirt to go over his pajamas. "Thank you, sir," Jacob said and immediately began to slip them on.

MacGregor turned the page into the firelight where he could read it more easily. A grave countenance came over the professor's face. His eyes drooped in sadness and he passed the book to his colleagues.

"Nibblus, are you going to try to find and rescue our friend?" MacGregor asked.

The dragon let out a call into the night that confirmed his intentions. "But, what about *him*, then? He is your charge and you can't take him with you," Kirk now stood forward and interjected.

"Sir, I know he is to protect me, but, you see," Jacob interjected nervously, "I'm not safe here anymore either. I was kidnapped tonight and thrown into a dungeon or something up at Ashland."

"Ashland? Tonight?" Capernicus Campbell interjected. "What did you see up there, then?"

"Oh … nothing really, sir …" Jacob stammered. "I mean, I saw the four of you up in the library but nothing else."

"Us in the library? Nibblus!" MacGregor yelled at the dragon.

"He didn't have anything to do with me being there." Jacob was coming to his friend's defense. "You see, I was kidnapped from my bed tonight by a group of people and they threw me down into some dungeon. I only saw you because I was able to escape through some tunnels."

"Well, never mind that now, I guess. Obviously, you know that Bunting Boyle did not kill old Campbell here, that is one secret out," Kirk said.

"Sorry if I scared you there, Jacob," Campbell said as he came over and put his arm on Jacob's shoulder. "We had to create a diversion, you know, and we thought that was a good way to test you to see if you really were this chosen one MacGregor and von Niblick have told us about. I see you dare bare the sword of Isildane," Campbell moved Jacob over toward the firelight and bent down to look at the handle of his sword. "Magnificent, purely magnificent! No ordinary craftsman could forge such a weapon, you know. How lucky I have been to have lived to see its return."

"Here, sir, you can take a closer look," Jacob offered as he reached to unsheathe the ancient weapon.

"No!" Campbell said as he backed away. "No, Jacob. Such a power and burden has been given to you and I could not bear to have it even for a moment. You must never allow another to handle that weapon, or its sheath for that matter. Didn't von Niblick explain that to you?"

"Sorry, sir. No sir. He did not tell me I had to be the only one. Sorry."

MacGregor stepped toward the dragon and said, "Nibblus Maximus, you cannot take this boy on this long flight and into danger upon your bare back. Let's you, Campbell and I go try to rig something up at the stable. Shall we? Kirk can keep Master Boyd safe here with the dogs while we are gone." MacGregor then turned to Ramos Kirk, "I suspect he has some questions and you might have some things to fill him in on, before we get back. Come on Copernicus, we have little time if they are going to get to our friend von Niblick before it's too late."

I'll be back as soon as I can, Jacob. Be ready for my return, Nibblus Maximus said and then stepped away from the three men and the boy before he launched himself into the air and headed back toward the Iona Academy's stables. Campbell and MacGregor turned and headed toward the woods that separated them from the school.

Remnant Unmasked

Dr. Kirk and Jacob stood watching the dragon's inky shadow pass away in the night sky. "Wise men know what wicked things are written in the sky," Kirk mumbled.

"Sir?" Jacob asked.

"Oh, nothing. Come over here. Let us sit and talk while we wait."

The dogs gathered around Jacob and Kirk and watched the tree lines. An older female collie named "Pumpkin" came over to him and laid her body along his right leg where she could be petted. With his strokes of the dog's fur, Jacob began to relax for the first time in hours.

"Do you mind if I light my pipe, Jacob?" Kirk asked.

Jacob shook his head no.

"It's a nasty habit you know, and you should never, ever start. Now, yes I occasionally do smoke my pipe but nothing else, and you know that friend of yours, von Niblick, has a special leaf that he has produced that really isn't too bad for you, in moderation, you see. Now that terrible stuff people put in those paper tubes or directly in their mouths, just revolting!"

Kirk took a burning stick from the fire and put it into the bowl of a white pipe carved into a claw cupping an egg. Jacob was fascinated by what he could see of the intricate design of the pipe. Kirk breathed an air through it's stem and then stopped.

"You know, this is very selfish of me." Jacob just looked at him without knowing how to respond because he hadn't a clue what he meant. "Our good friend von Niblick is in some box or something somewhere without enough air to breath and here I am abusing the privilege. Well, not me!" He tapped the tobacco out of his pipe and onto the ground before replacing the pipe in his cloak pocket.

Jacob became deeply concerned again at the thought of von Niblick being short of air and time running out. Seeing his expression change as the boy turned to look into the fire, Kirk offered, "Perhaps we should say a prayer for our friend? Would you like to speak for us?"

Jacob shook his head no.

"Well, I am not much for offering mine for public scrutiny either, so perhaps we should offer our own silently, then." Both closed their eyes.

After a moment, Kirk interrupted the silence. "Son, I am very pleased to be able to serve with you like this. It's a privilege and an honor."

"But, I haven't done anything but get kidnapped!" Jacob answered.

"Someday, you will understand your role and what you have done. You are a Sporran Bearer. That, I am sure, von Niblick told you. Not only are you a Bearer, but you wear the ring of Isildane there on your finger and his sword hangs about your waist. Do you not know how special that is?"

"No, I don't, really," Jacob answered.

"Well, son, I guess it is time to learn more. Your life has just been put in great danger up at the school and none of us were around to help. And, now you are about to embark on a very dangerous mission. I guess it's time for you to learn more about what's going on ... there are stranger things afoot than are dreamt of by most today."

Jacob turned and looked at Kirk, who had removed his plastic framed glasses and held them in one hand while he pulled a pocket watch with the other.

"What time is it, Dr. Kirk?" Jacob asked

"What? Oh," Kirk had simply pulled the watch out from habit and hadn't even looked at it. "Nearly midnight, son."

"Where to begin? Where to begin?" Kirk muttered to himself.

"Son, you are a Bearer in the order of the Sporrai, that much I know you know. MacGregor and von Niblick and more of us are Keepers serving the same order. Our order is ancient, Jacob, and exists to pass on the knowledge and wisdom and sense of wonder that once animated more of us than now we can count as allies in this fallen world of ours."

"The sporrans come to us from Isildane who himself was but the instrument of the power beyond space and time. The great expert on that history is von Niblick himself and because we must believe he is alive, I will leave it to him to instruct you on the ancient tales," Kirk told Jacob. He barely looked up from the fire or his shoelaces, Jacob could not tell which.

"But, Jacob, the Sporrai is not what it was, either. There is a dark force in this universe of ours that feeds on greed and gluttony and hate and is twisted by self-interest. Son, that force has grown stronger and the means at its disposal have grown more tentacles than we once imagined possible."

"But the Sporrai," Jacob interjected as he felt he needed to say something and not just sit there. "Surely the Sporrai is strong and you, I mean," he paused and tentatively added, "I mean *we* can defeat them."

Kirk smiled and reached down to tie his black leather ankle-high shoe. "*We* is right, son. I am glad to hear you accept your role in this with us. But, we are not strong. The Sporrai is not strong anymore. Over the years, members of the order have lost their faith and their way. They have lost the knowledge of our ancient fathers and have lost a faith in the eternal goodness. 'The best lack all convictions, while the worst are full of passionate intensity,' as my old friend Yeats has said."

"But, not in the Sporrai!" Jacob asserted. "How could members of the Order lose their way? How? We can all see the power, can't we?"

"Jacob, evil grows in all kinds of soils. Even in the Sporrai, we are but men and women of flesh and blood, you know. We all suffer from the sins of humanity and the temptations of living for one's self and ignoring what we don't see. So, don't be surprised that even in the Sporrai and with people who have been blessed by so much, that you have those who fall."

Jacob poked the fire and tried to understand and remember.

"Evil has entered the Sporrai from two directions. First, some have just lost their way and their understanding. They are just lost to us and most believe in nothing, so they are of little danger to the secrets we keep and the treasure we defend. There are others, however, who have not gone blind like these, but who have had their eyes turned. Most of them have turned inwards on themselves, Jacob. Almost like their eyes cannot see anything but their own blood coursing through their flesh. These are a danger because they see nothing but what keeps that blood pumping through their veins and the money going into their pockets and their trinkets glittering. These are the ones who would sell the true treasure or their friends for just a few more dollars or few more days of life."

Jacob grew concerned at this news. *How can I trust you, Kirk,* he thought, *if corruption even has entered the Sporrai?*

"I know this is a lot to soak in," Kirk talked as if he could read the boy's mind. "But, I assure you that it is true and you will need to keep this very much in mind. Trust MacGregor, von Niblick, Campbell, Boyle, and me. We are of the remaining part that has stayed true to the ancient ways and the truth that gave the world these powers. We are the Remnant, Jacob. We serve the truest core of the ancient Sporrai, but we are but a remnant, a small band holding on to truth while the world rushes the other way." Kirk was looking over at Jacob now and pulled a fountain pen from the upper right breast pocket of his suit vest.

"Here, Jacob, I want you to have this." Kirk passed his pen over to the boy who took it cautiously even as he protested that he could not accept the gift. "Jacob, it has no magic powers, but it was my father's and he gave it to me the day I finished reading the last of Sir Walter Scott's *Waverly* novels. Wonderful but seldom read books, those are. How the world would be better off if more people pulled their imaginations from that stone of Scott's. But," he stopped himself, "there is no time for such lamentations."

"It's just an old fountain pen, Jacob. It works most of the time and fairly well. I have had no sons and would like to pass it along on another important night to a boy I am proud of. This is an important night and I would like you to have it."

"Thank you, sir," Jacob replied as he fingered the pen. It was smooth and fat, but the firelight did not provide enough light to inspect it well. "I will remember you and remember this night and pass it along someday, too."

"You are a good boy, Jacob. I do think von Niblick and MacGregor are right about you," Kirk said as he patted Jacob lightly on his left knee. "You know there is an ancient prophesy, Jacob, that a remnant will return someday. It is said that a remnant will come, a remnant of Jacob, and it will lean again on Truth rather than falsehood," Kirk offered.

At hearing his name associated with a prophecy, Jacob's stomach turned and a chill went down his back. He shivered.

"Cold?" Kirk asked.

"No sir," Jacob replied.

Kirk stoked the fire. He then broke a stick and put the pieces in the fire near Jacob. "Whether you are the Jacob of whom the prophet spoke, I cannot say, but what is sure is that we are but a remnant now and must fight for the good, the beautiful, and the true, until others come back to the way and will join us. Remember the numbers 10 and 21 and the name Isaiah."

Jacob did not react, but listened and played nervously with the stick he was poking into the red coals beneath the flame. He turned the name and numbers over in his head. He remembered being number 10 in baseball two years before and knew a kid named Isaiah once.

"Jacob, you have already made choices that have put you here with me tonight and I am glad for them. You will have to make other choices now, each of which can lead you into further danger or away to safety or even into the icy cold hands of the enemy. None of us can make those decisions for you."

"The path of the remnant is never easy, Jacob. That is our lot in life; to suffer for the truth and to do so without losing our faith and giving in to our selfish desires. We are a remnant. On the ultimate winning side of course, we must believe that you know. But we are a remnant, just a small remnant of a once great order."

As Kirk paused, Jacob took the chance to interject, "But how am I to know right from wrong and who are friends and who are not?"

"Ah, yes, the ancient question of the philosophers and of young men and women of every age. First, your question is excellent for you must never doubt the difference between right and wrong. That is a line that will always be drawn for us, whether we wish it to be seen or not. The Author drew that line in his imagination long before we awoke to wonder about it. As for us seeing it, now, that is a difficult chain to untangle, young man, a difficult chain indeed."

A deep and steady beat in the air started to become barely perceptible to the dogs. They sat up, unnoticed by the professor and the boy. Pumpkin, the collie lying against Jacob, suddenly startled and jumped to her feet. Jacob and Kirk turned and looked to the sky. An inky black spot was moving fast and low over the trees.

"Just sit still lad and keep hold of that sword, most often it is wickedness that approaches from the darkened sky."

The spot grew larger until they could make out clearly that it was wings rising and lowering from the sides. Jacob greeted the thought of Nibblus Maximus returning with conflicting emotions. He knew he was safe with him arriving, but he also knew that the sooner he arrived back, the sooner he would be on a hazardous mission to rescue von Niblick.

The wing beats brought the dragon closer to the fire as it left the treetops and entered the low sky above the field. As if they were at an airport waiting for a friend's plane to land, Kirk and Jacob stood silently and waited for the landing gear to descend and then touch down on the ground.

Jacob felt a smack hard into his back and he flew forward toward the ground. Kirk's body dropped hard onto him and crushed the air from the boy's lungs. Jacob felt like a rib had been broken. The dragon came down with its claws outstretched and made a tearing pass at the two on the ground. The talons cut into Kirk's back and he tensed and grunted with pain. His face smashed to the side in the dirt, he stretched his left eye upward in time to see the beast bank in the firelight. The light confirmed for Jacob that this was not Nibblus Maximus.

"Not Nibs, roll on your back and lift your sword, Bearer!" Kirk exclaimed as he rolled off Jacob and onto his back, fertilizing the ground with the blood seeping through his cloak.

Both lay still by the fire with their swords extended into the air. "Don't let the sword fall. Call Nibbs now!" Kirk ordered. As the dragon banked for another pass, Jacob opened his mind and called out to the dragon pug. He heard a loud call of anxiety from the distance but nothing more.

The beast finished his turn and began a fast descent toward the two victims who were lying on their backs below.

"When I give the signal, cut my way with that blade and I will cut yours, we will slice him like we had a giant pair of scissors," Kirk ordered. "Now, hold, hold, hold," Kirk whispered. The dragon descended with long sharp talons reflecting the firelight. Jacob could not take his eye off those talons.

"And, NOW!" Kirk ordered. Jacob waved his sword to the left and Kirk waved his hard to the right. Before they heard any hint of the tink of metal on metal, the two felt their blades cutting into flesh. Blood splattered on them as the dragon called out into the dark night in pain and rose again.

"Grand work, son. We gave that beast the nail clipping it needed!" Kirk exclaimed. Jacob didn't have the composure to offer a response.

Near the edge of the woods, just above the tree line, they heard another cry. *Nibbles, please let it be you!* Jacob cried out in his thoughts. A second inky spot was approaching quickly in the night sky. The first rose and banked away from the approaching spot, flew for a couple hundred yards away and then turned and came fast back toward the firelight. As the second spot approached, Jacob could feel Nibblus Maximus's presence.

Having a spot of fun without me, are we Bearer?

The first dragon was turning and heading back, one bloody claw dangling from the last bit of cartilage that had not been severed by the slicing motion of the two swords. As he turned, Nibblus Maximus was able to drive headlong into the other dragon's chest. The force of the blow sent the dragon tumbling backward, blood spurting from its toe and air being forced from its lungs. Nibblus Maximus did not give his enemy a chance to recover but pushed back again with his mighty wings and propelled himself into the beast once more. He swung his own hind leg at the dragon's wound as he simultaneously bit into it's neck.

The combatants tumbled to the ground fifty yards from where Kirk and Jacob watched. Hitting the field, the dragons were flung apart. Nibblus Maximus sprung up and ready in his place. The other dragon rose and snorted, then turned and limped several hops in the other direction and awkwardly took flight. All could hear the agony of the wounds in the beast's bleating calls. Nibblus Maximus did not follow, but backed up, warily watching the inky spot in the sky disappear over the trees to the south. Jacob and Professor Kirk rushed up to the dragon pug and enthusiastically congratulated him on his victory.

Thanks, Jacob expressed, *but couldn't you have arrived just a little bit sooner?* The dragon did not answer.

The three turned and walked back toward the dimming fire as they heard MacGregor and Campbell entering the field. They were carrying something between them as they walked.

"Having a little sparring practice I see, Nibbs!" MacGregor asserted as he approached the fire. "Jacob, here is a little something you are going to thank us for profusely about 1,000 miles from now when you are tired and flying 5,000 feet above the Atlantic on this guy's back."

In the firelight, Jacob could see they were carrying a saddle. "We had to take two horse saddles and splice them together to get something big enough for your ride," Campbell offered.

"Come on big fella, lie down here and let's get this on you. He needs to get out of here before 'Old Three Toes' out there comes back with one of his friends," Ramos Kirk said as he patted the dragon on his right flank. Nibblus Maximus snorted and laid himself flat upon the ground. The three men set to work stretching the saddle over his back and strapping it on.

"Your turn, Bearer," MacGregor finally said.

Jacob had watched silently while they worked, growing ever more nervous about the flight. He stood and stared, not knowing what to do.

"Well, don't you like what we've done?" Campbell asked.

"No, sir, I mean, it's not that, sir." Jacob was too embarrassed to say it was nothing but fear that kept him from moving.

Jacob, it's going to be fine. You are not safe here anyway and will bring dangers to everyone unless you leave. And, von Niblick, we can pray, is still waiting for us. We must move fast. The dragon had turned to look Jacob strongly in the eye as he sent his message.

I know, Jacob replied and stepped forward.

"Here, you'll need my cloak," Kirk offered.

"And have mine, too, it will get very cold up there, son," Copernicus Campbell added.

They bundled Jacob in the two cloaks and then boosted him up into the saddle. They explained how the saddle would work to allow him to lie down, face first, where he could sleep when he got tired or when the wind bit his face with too much chill. His feet were strapped tightly into the stirrups with leather straps. Long straps of cloth with buckles were wrapped under the beast's belly and up around Jacob.

"Here, pull this strap down with you when you lay down, Master Boyd," MacGregor instructed. "It will bind you tight."

Jacob's stomach felt like a deep well with no water. Nausea began to weaken his legs. A bead of cold sweat formed on his forehead and he leaned forward.

"Son, take this, son," Copernicus Campbell was handing Jacob a small hunk of a kind of bread.

"What is it," he asked.

"Just a wee hunk of bread, son." Campbell answerd.

"Campbell, that is not what I think it is …" Kirk asked.

"Ah, well, let's just call it an old family recipe, shall we? Now, take this, it will help you with the flight."

"Yes, Jacob, do take it," Kirk interjected as he finished tying the straps around Jacob's left leg.

Jacob reached out and took the chunk from Campbell's hand. He smelled it and then took a small bite, then another. With each swallow he felt more calm and steady. MacGregor reached a flask up to Jacob's lips and said, "go on, have a drink, too." Jacob drank a large gulp from the tea and MacGregor handed him a full bottle for the flight. Campbell then added a larger hunk of bread to Jacob's pack.

"Jacob, you're going to be fine, you know. Trust in the Truth behind the Sporrai and you will be fine," MacGregor said as he stroked his long beard down flat.

"Fare ye well, Bearer," said Campbell.

"I might just want that pen back someday, Jacob, so you better take good care and bring it back with you," Kirk said as he patted Jacob on his left thigh.

"Yes sir. And, please, do take care of Jenny and Will, won't you?" Jacob asked.

"We will, son, we will," Campbell answered for the three.

MacGregor was now standing in front of the dragon and speaking to him. "Remember, he is the Bearer who has assembled Isildane's ring and now carries the great one's sword. Don't take any chances with him. If you must choose between Niblick's life and his, remember you are sworn to protect Master Boyd at any cost."

Nibblus Maximus snorted and raised his head.

Let's go, Jacob, the dragon spoke in Jacob's mind.

The three men backed away as Jacob shut his eyes and said a prayer. Two steps forward and three beats of his wings and the two were airborne. Jacob opened his eyes and looked down. They were just above the tree line and he pinched his eyes shut tight again. The two flew north toward the Iona Academy, but banked east just before clearing the trees. Jacob could see spots of light from the lampposts of the school, but little more. They flew off toward the brighter lights of the cities in the distance that would lead them to the coast.

Bearer, this will be a very long flight. I suggest you eat some more of that bread and put your head down for a while.

PART II

BOOK OF KELLS

Room Search

Though he had barely been breathing at all, the oxygen was quickly running out in the prison that was designed to become his tomb. Each breath became more painful as the air ran thin. The man felt himself slipping away from life as his body resisted.

Deep in his imagination, more active and vivid than he had ever experienced a vision before, Professor von Niblick saw the bottom of the box he was in turn to soft grass. Ahead he saw the round paving stones of a path. He walked toward the stones effortlessly and turned. Behind him was pain and struggle; before him was the final path away from the suffering. A smile crept over his lips as his imagination allowed him to step onto the first stone of the path. One foot followed the other as everything around him faded slowly from color to black and white and then began to disappear completely as he gave himself over. His steps then began to grow heavier and more difficult. Confused, he struggled on.

High over the Atlantic, Jacob had a vision of von Niblick gasping for air and knew they were nearly too late. He swung his arm down at his side in frustration and cried out for the dragon to move faster. The movement of his swinging arm unbuckled the antler tip latch of his sporran. A mighty wind swept over the sea. It rose up from the water and toward them in the sky. When it hit, the wind pushed Jacob up and back. The cold air rushed in his face and stabbed his ribs with icy picks. The sporran had flung open and the great wind rushed into the pouch.

Von Niblick heard a voice come whispering around him like a breath.

"It is not yet your time, Keeper," he heard as a rush of fresh air fluttered his beard and rushed into his nostrils. "Not yet your time," he heard as the path faded and his eyes opened to see the inside of the box that held him captive. His body jerked violently, as if new life had entered a lifeless form. He was almost sad to be alive, for he had caught a glimpse of life beyond the struggle and he was pained now by its loss.

Above the Atlantic, Jacob lowered his head once more to rest on the dragon's back. He pulled the cloaks down tight around him. Nibblus Maximus envisioned his old master again, lying helplessly in a box covered in dirt. But his eyes soon caught sight of the fog being chased from the sea by the light of a new morning. Then the outline of land could be seen in the distance and a desperate hope rekindled.

In her dorm room, morning light was coming in through the dull blue curtains between the two desks. Jenny stirred awake as she heard movement in the hallway. Because of the commotion the night before, most of the girls were still sleeping soundly in their beds as breakfast time approached.

"Yes, who is it?" Jenny replied to the knock on her door.

Another knock, but no answer. Jenny got up and flattened her hair down with her hands and smoothed her pajama shorts. She slipped Jacob's note beneath her pillow. "I'm coming."

Elizabeth barely stirred, but opened her eyes and watched Jenny walk to the door. She cracked the door open and peeked into the hallway where she saw Lucy Furangle and two boys.

"Yes?" Jenny asked.

"You boys wait out here," Lucy said to her guards, "I can handle this." She then pushed on the door and Jenny gave way without a struggle. Lucy walked in silently but with her eyes searching the room.

"Yes, Lucy, can we help you?" Jenny asked. She turned to the boys who were looking into the room with perverse curiosity. "Do you two mind?" Jenny said as she shut the door in their faces.

Lucy walked over to the window, trying to observe everything she could. "It seems that last evening there were some disturbances on the hall. Did you two see or hear anything out of the ordinary last night?" Lucy asked.

"Disturbances? What kind of disturbances?" Elizabeth asked as she sat up in her bed. Jenny said nothing.

"And, you, Jennifer?" Lucy asked.

"My name isn't Jennifer, it's just Jenny, and nothing particularly disturbed me last night. What happened?" She was annoyed enough that the little deception was easy to pull off.

"It seems we had an infestation last evening. Some sort of giant jumping rat attacked some girls down the hall."

"Whaaat?" Elizabeth asked and then shrieked and climbed fully under her covers and held them down tight. "I hate mice!"

"Whatever," Lucy dismissed the girl under the covers. "Any news on this, Jennifer?"

"It's Jenny and no, I didn't see any rats last night."

"Well, what do you know of your friend Jacob Boyd?" Lucy was studying Jenny's face intensely as she asked.

"I know he is thirteen, a boy, lives on Longbranch Drive, plays baseball, is mediocre in school, sometimes wears a really ugly blue shirt with …"

Lucy cut her off angrily. "Funny! I mean, do you know where your friend might be this morning?"

Jenny tried to be calm and remain forceful. Having been called Jennifer twice in the last two minutes made it all the easier as she felt an annoyed anger growing in her belly. She would feel guilty about it later, but not now. "Is this a trick question? My guess is that he's at breakfast asking the server for an extra sausage link."

"You think you're a funny girl, don't you?" Lucy walked toward Jenny. Jenny backed up a half a step before she realized she was backing away from the bully. "I'll have you know that your friend Jacob disappeared last night while your friend Will was on guard duty. Will reports Boyd was not in his bed when he got off duty and he never came home. No one in the boy's dorm seems to know anything."

Jenny tried to create an inquisitive and concerned look on her face.

"You know what I think, Jennifer? I think he had something to do with that giant rat that visited last night."

Jenny ignored Lucy's slight against her name this time. "What do you think? Do you think he turned himself into a giant rat in order to sneak into the girl's dorm?"

"I'm not sure what I think, Jennifer, but I do hope you'll do your duty and report to me or Mr. Creech immediately if you hear from him." Lucy walked passed Jenny and opened the door. "Oh," she added, "Mr. Creech would like to see you in his office this morning after breakfast." She closed the door behind her and disappeared down the hall.

Elizabeth was mumbling nervously under the covers and peeking one eye out near her pillow.

"Would you stop that? There are no rats," Jenny said with annoyance.

"But, how do you know?" Elizabeth asked as she pulled her whole head out from under the covers.

"Because I do, that's why," Jenny said as she walked toward the window.

"You see," Elizabeth offered, "it's not that I'm really afraid of rats, but my mother, you know, well, she was attacked like once by some little mouse or something and has never been the same and then … " Elizabeth went on with her story, while Jenny stood by the window paying her no attention. She was looking off into the morning air and worrying about Jacob.

Jenny spent the morning in a stress-filled daze as she showered, got dressed, and prepared for breakfast. She read Jacob's note over several times when Elizabeth left the room to brush her teeth and retrieve the retainers that she left soaking in the bathroom over night. After putting on a pair of khaki shorts, Jenny tucked the note into her back pocket and headed to breakfast.

In town, two local farmers and a bartender were at the police station swearing they had seen a flying saucer in the sky during the night. "I tell you it was the same saucer that's been abducting my sheep" one of the farmers insisted aggressively.

"Come on now, Hank," the police officer interjected, "what would aliens want with your sheep?"

While the three swore out affidavits of what they saw, a reporter arrived to take their story. The next morning, headlines would blare: "Sheep Stealing Aliens May be in Area."

Jenny walked into the cafeteria for breakfast and Will rushed up to her. "Jenny, Jenny, have you seen Jacob? He disappeared sometime in the night and I don't know where he is." Will was obviously exasperated.

Will had long been a close friend, but he was also part of the Dirks and was on Lucy Furangle's staff. She had to be careful how she responded. "Yes, I know, Lucy visited me this morning to see if I had seen him. I haven't."

Will was holding onto Jenny's shoulders and looking her strongly and desperately in the eye. "What do you think has happened to him, then? Do you suppose it is that *thing* he has? Do you suppose that old purse of his or someone having to do with it has finally done him in? We should've destroyed that thing the moment it arrived last year. Should've burned it or buried it or something; Carried it to the very cracks of Mount Doom!" Will was speaking loudly and frantically.

"Will!" Jenny was stern. "Keep your mouth shut about that stuff. We don't know what's happened to him, but he knows more than we do about all that and it's none of our business to question his decisions on it, much less to discuss it in public. Now, let's not speak of that again, you hear? We could put him in danger by even mentioning it."

"Mentioning what?" came a man's voice over Jenny's shoulder.

Jenny saw the strange look in Will's eyes and turned. It was Mr. Creech, new headmaster of the school.

"Sir?" Jenny said as she stalled for time and an answer.

"You said something about danger and not mentioning something, didn't you?"

"Oh, well, yes," Jenny answered as she stepped dexterously in front of Will to keep him from saying anything. "Yes, well, you see, Will was saying how that Boyd boy must have gotten himself lost or something and didn't come home last night and might be in danger, you see, so I told him, for our own well-being, you see, that we shouldn't *mention* him being in *danger* because it would only make us worry that much more." Jenny looked anxiously into the man's eyes for evidence he was buying it.

"Yes, well, in any regard you both will let Lucy or me know immediately when your friend is found, won't you?"

Will poked his head out from behind Jenny and said, "Yes sir!"

"And, Jenny, I do so look forward to our little meeting after breakfast. Dear little Lucy did mention it to you, didn't she?"

"Yes sir, she did. I'll come to your office as soon as the first bell rings to end breakfast," Jenny said with some dejection in her voice.

"Now, run along and have something to eat, little ones," Mr. Creech said with a smile. He stood in his place to watch them walk up to the counter, retrieve trays, and start down the line.

While Will and Jenny nervously picked at their breakfast, two teams of Furangles' guards were searching their rooms, each accompanied by a new member of the school's staff who had arrived within the last day. Miss Ruth, the tall, lanky, freckled cleaning lady was being detained in the library of Frazier House, being asked questions about anything she may have noticed out of the ordinary in the last few days and if she had seen Professor Kirk or Jacob Boyd.

"Take anything suspicious, Mr. Creech said, anything suspicious, guards," a gruff man in a dark black suit barked at the rest as they searched every corner of Jacob and Will's room. A similar scene was unfolding in Jenny's room.

The Painting

When the bell rang calling students to leave the cafeteria and head to their first sessions of the morning, Jenny told Will to be careful and assertively ordered him not to speak about what he knew of Jacob's *private* life.

"What does she think I am, an idiot?" Will mumbled to himself as he exited the door and turned right, heading to class. Jenny went straight toward the administration building and her meeting with the Headmaster.

"Jenny Sawyer, ma'am, I'm here to see Mr. Creech," she told the receptionist on the first floor of the administration building.

"Sure Sweetheart, he's expecting you—go on back."

Jenny walked passed the receptionist's desk and turned right into the open doorway of what had been Miss Witherspoon's office. The pictures of the famous students of her ancestor Dr. John Witherspoon had been removed. A piece of modern art had been put in their place above the desk; stark red and black streaks of paint chaotically merging on the canvas. As she studied the painting, she began to see what she took to be eyes emerging from the darkness of what might have been a head, if the twisted form was humanoid. She shivered.

Mr. Creech looked up from his papers.

"Well, Ms. Sawyer, how good of you to come. Please sit down."

Jenny stepped forward into the room and passed a conference table on the left and a wall of bookshelves on her right. On the table were a large stack of blueprints and drafting tools and plans. She paid them little attention.

Jenny sat quietly as Mr. Creech put his papers down and leaned over his desk to rest on his forearms. "Ms. Sawyer—well, why don't I just call you Jenny?" he began. "Jenny, we have a problem, you know. Your friend Jacob obviously must have disregarded the curfew last night and has gone off and gotten himself into trouble. Is he the kind of kid that gets into trouble a lot, Jenny?"

"No, sir; Jacob is about the most good and genuine kid I've ever met. He doesn't break rules easily, you can bet on that!"

"Well, that is an admirable defense, Jenny—but why would he break curfew and disappear like this? Can you tell me that?"

"No, sir." Jenny shook her head.

"Have you seen him in the last day?"

"No, sir." Jenny was starting to get more nervous and she feared it showed in her demeanor. She was worrying now that Mr. Creech would keep probing and she would either have to tell him the truth that she had *heard* from him or she would lie. She didn't look forward to having to make that decision.

"Mr. Creech," the receptionist's sweet voice came through the doorway, "you wanted me to tell you the moment *he* arrived. The guard at the gate says he just passed onto campus."

Creech became agitated and dismissed Jenny with, "Well, we can talk more later, but you be sure to come and tell us if you see Mr. Boyd."

Jenny rose and couldn't help but take one last look at the painting above the desk. It was the most disturbing image she had ever remembered seeing: unnatural and utterly without beauty of any form. It was cold and dark. It reminded her of death and to look at it gave her the slight feeling of choking on sooty smoke. Behind the blackness of the form she thought she could make something out, barely a flicker, but something there; eyes, perhaps. She would regret looking at it, for the image now had found a seat in her imagination.

She turned down the hall to the left out of the Headmaster's door and walked toward the front exit. As she passed the receptionist's desk and turned to the right, the two great doors opened before her. Men in black held the door and she could see a large black car parked in front. A tall man with jet black and slicked-down hair was taking big strides away from the car and toward the open door. A woman exited the car behind him, wearing a deeply red and supremely tight dress that ended at the bottom in dark hose, which in turn melted effortlessly down into black heels with red accents.

The man was Furangle. Jenny recognized him easily. But, she couldn't imagine this elegant and stunningly attractive woman was the mother of the beast Lucy. They came down the entryway without acknowledging her and turned. Jenny held back and waited for them to pass. Something in their attitude and their look made Jenny feel disgusted. When they had passed and the two men at the door had followed, allowing the doors to close behind them, Jenny walked out into the fresher air of the morning outside.

Mr. Furangle and the woman walked into Mr. Creech's office without hesitating at the door. The woman pulled the door shut and the two bodyguards placed themselves flanking the door in the hallway. The woman leaned on the conference table fingering the pencils and rulers that rested upon the blueprints. Furangle stood behind one of the office chairs across the desk from Mr. Creech and leaned on its back.

"Creech, where's the Boyd kid? I want to interrogate him myself."

"Um, well, sir, we have a slight little problem." Mr. Creech was squirming in his chair. Furangle's eyebrows rose ominously and the woman snapped the pencil she was twirling in her fingers. "You see, we got him and we got him good last night. We took him from his room all fine. He didn't know what hit him. Then we took him to the icehouse up by that old ruin of a house beyond the stables out there." Mr. Creech was pointing out the window. "We threw him in, you know, and bolted the door tight. We put him in bound tight, too."

"Yes, so what's the problem?" Furangle asked.

"Well, he isn't there."

"He isn't there?" the woman interjected with annoyance.

"Do you mind?" Furangle said to the woman. "I can hear the little man. Then where is he, Creech?"

"Sorry, sir. We don't know, sir. "

"You don't know? You don't know where he is? I leave you with the simple task of taking one of your own students: *Your* student, Creech. I didn't ask you to go kidnap some kid from his parents across the country. I didn't ask you to find someone who had been lost. All I asked was for you to hold onto one of your own students. That's all. You can't even do that and you expect me to leave you here in charge of this school so you can conduct your little educational experiments?"

"I'm sorry, sir, he must not be a normal boy, you see, or he must have had help. There must be a conspiracy around the place, sir." Mr. Creech had shrunken even more and was miserably trying to placate Furangle.

"Save me your sniveling, Creech." Furangle turned and looked at the woman leaning on the table behind him.

"But we're searching his room now and we're also searching the room of his best friend, a girl named Sawyer who I just spoke with before you arrived."

"Well, at least that is *something*. Bring me whatever they find, instantly," Furangle ordered. "Now, Lilith, darling," Furangle walked over to the woman and patted her hand. "Lilith, I want to leave you here to take care of this little issue for me." The woman smiled, slid up on the table, and crossed her legs.

Mr. Creech was getting more nervous by the moment and interjected, "But I can handle this."

"Obviously you can handle nothing, Creech. You just do your little leveling experiments on the educational program around here. Of that, I do not care. But Lilith will now be in charge of this Boyd situation. Is that clear?" Furangle leaned on the chair.

"If that is what you want, sir, yes, it's clear and I will be sure to do whatever I can to help Ms. " He paused, realizing he didn't know the woman's last name. "Ms. Lilith with her task," he finished with the only part of her name he knew.

The Book of Kells

165

"Just stay out of my way, little man," the woman uncrossed her legs and stood up on the black and red heels she had been dangling off her toes just moments before. "And, my name is Frost—*Dr.* Frost to you."

Lilith Frost, yes, Mr. Creech had heard of her somewhere before. Perhaps in a glamour magazine, he thought, or perhaps she is a renowned scientist he had read of in his journals. He couldn't remember, but he did remember having heard of a "Dr. Lilith Frost" somewhere.

Frost walked over toward Creech, who grew tenser with her every step. "Sit down, Mr. Creech," she said with a forceful voice that dripped with sweetness like thick honey. The man slunk down into his chair dutifully. "Mr. Creech, I *so* admire what you are doing here to reform this school and improve these children and our world. And I urge you to continue your efforts and plans." She was now behind his desk and leaning on its top. Creech nodded as he stared, lost in her deep black eyes.

"I won't get in your way. Please try to stay out of mine and we will have a wonderful *relationship*," she said. She put a hand on his shoulder and pushed herself up. She turned and stepped slightly away from the desk and toward Furangle who stood and watched the show humorlessly.

"Now, I will need the best room you have in a dirty country place like this," she said with some vinegar infusing in the honey of her voice. "And I will need a place to work, not an office like this, of course, as *charming* as it is. No, I need some place to work that is, well—more *up to date*, you see?"

"What she means," Furangle interjected, "is that she needs a comfortable room to sleep and dress but a cold, clean, sterile place to work."

"Sterile?" Mr. Creech asked. "You mean like an operating room?"

"Perfect!" she announced as she turned back toward him, her dark hair flowing to the left slightly slower than her head.

"Well, we don't have one of those, you see—no need to operate out here—but we have science labs. And in fact there are plans over there on the table to build more—right, Mr. Furangle?"

"Never mind. I don't have time to wait. I will have my own mobile labs brought in until we can knock down some of these old ruins you call buildings and put some modern, up-to-date and useful facilities in," she said dismissively. "Now, where can I lay down and think, darling?" she said sweetly to Mr. Creech.

Creech rose up from his chair and led them out of the room. "Oh, Mr. Furangle, I should've thanked you for the painting. Very modern and quite stunning," he said as he glanced over his shoulder at the black and red painting of long splotches. He paused. His eyes narrowed. *Was something different?* He squinted more. *It couldn't be. Could it?*

Columba's Bay

The morning light was rising in the east as Jacob began to come back to consciousness. The dragon pug turned slightly north, allowing the sun's light to peek into the cracks of Jacob's eyes.

Jacob turned his head back west for a moment to avoid the temporary pain of the new light. The right side of his face was resting on the soft flesh of Nibblus Maximus's neck as his eyes opened completely. Below he could see the white caps of the waves reflecting the sun's light golden rays. He had barely been awake during the journey but had not remembered dreaming at all. He startled to realize where he was. He felt ill.

His start got the dragon's attention. *Welcome back to the world, little Bearer! Campbell's bread and MacGregor's tea, pretty powerful mix that. Prepare yourself for landing Jacob. We are almost there.*

Jacob lifted his head and looked over the dragon. He could see the larger white caps of waves breaking on the rocks, then the white sand and black rocks of the beach and beyond them lush green fields. As they got closer he noted the small white dots in the grassy fields were sheep having a breakfast of that same grass they were decorating. It was a beautiful site, but it was scary too.

He found himself thinking about Ian again, the boy who was once wrapped up in the sporran magic with him last year but who had failed the test and from whose life the magic had slipped away. *He's probably safely in bed right now having nice dreams and soon will have a good breakfast with his family. Sometimes I wish this was over and I could be him rather than me. How I would like to be sharing oatmeal and orange juice with Dad right now.*

He closed his eyes. He opened them again to see a puffin flying along their side. "Well, hello, little fellow." Seeing the black and white bird with the puffy cheeks and orange bill lightened his heart and made him glad again. He imagined the little guy with spectacles waddling around. He giggled. His giggle ended as Nibblus Maximus suddenly tucked his head and the two dropped.

"Ahhhh," Jacob yelled as his stomach leapt up into his throat and then dropped again, "What are you doing?"

Sorry boy, just needed to get below those circling sea birds up there who were crowding our airspace. Where is the air traffic control system when you need it?

Is that Iona down there? Jacob asked.

That's it. We are now above Columba's Bay on its south corner. Though I wish we could land and I could rest, I think we better circle the Island and see if I can pick up some clue as to where the professor might be. We will come back here to land among the rocks in the south. There are fewer people down there and less chance of getting caught than to the north.

It's so small, Jacob remarked.

It is small in geographical size, maybe, but don't underestimate the power of that little place. I have been here many times and never get over the spirit of it. The eternal seems to seep into the temporal world of ours down there in a way I have seldom seen in my travels. It is about three and a half miles long and just over a mile wide at its widest, Jacob. That is good for us, as there will be more of a chance of finding the professor than if we were on the mainland. Now, let me concentrate to see if I can pick up a thought from Professor von Niblick.

OK.

Nibblus Maximus turned slightly left to head up the western side of the Island, passed the "Bay at the Back of the Ocean" and then moved to their left slightly again to pass the bulge of land just above the bay, then back right as the island grew narrow again toward its northern tip.

See the even smaller island there to the north, Jacob? That is the island of Staffa. It is an even tinier island but has a most important history. Fingal's Cave is there--a massive sea cave and has been used as sanctuary for seamen and Vikings and smugglers during storms. But for us it is no place for shelter in a storm. It is, shall we say, "occupied territory." There are forces in this world that would not dare to step foot on the sacred ground of Iona, but must sulk and stare jealously at the island from afar. Most could come and go unmolested, but if we were to venture there, a battle would surely be joined— not a battle we would welcome.

Jacob said nothing in reply but watched below and shuddered at the sight of that little island to their left as they crossed the northern tip of Iona and headed south. Jacob could see the mainland of Scotland down to his left, but he preferred to watch the seabirds flying in formation and then occasionally diving toward the sea.

Again at the south of the island, the dragon banked right over Columba's Bay and announced that Jacob should hold on tight. *It's all rocks down there, Bearer, you don't want to fall out on those! Hold strong!*

Take it easy, please, Jacob replied. His stomach felt like there was a couple of fast caterpillars chasing each other around inside.

I am going to slow us down by skimming the water before we hit the rocks. Feet up, boy! Feet up!

Jacob was so tense with his jaw clenched and face smashed into the dragon's neck that he could barely understand Nibblus Maximus'words. He peeked open his left eye to see how close they were to landing on the ground. There was no ground beneath them. Water, water, water, everywhere and they were only a few feet above it.

"Ahhhhh," Jacob yelled out and sent the word flying over and over incoherently through his mental bridge: *water, water, water!*

The dragon's front feet skimmed the top of the bay. Up from the surface came a large spray into Jacob's face. He spat the sea water from his mouth and yelled again, "ahhhh ... we are going to ..."

Before another word could escape his lips, another spray flew up, part of it going up his nose and more meeting no resistance until it hit the back of his open throat. Jacob gagged and spit and snorted.

Two more foot drags and Jacob felt the sudden jerk that meant they had hit dry land. The dragon took several running steps upon the dark volcanic rock and let his back end drop hard to the ground. His front followed in utter exhaustion. Jacob opened his eyes and saw a large worm-like strand of saltwater snot dripping from his face toward the rocks below.

We made it old boy! We made it! Jacob was patting the dragon on the side of the neck as he bent upright and stretched his back. *More salt in that landing than I would care for, but we made it!* He bent back down and kissed the dragon's neck.

You can land yourself next time, Bearer, the dragon said with annoyance in his voice. *Now, please get off so I can stretch myself and rest my back.*

Jacob pulled the cloaks from his back and dropped them on the rocks below. He then unstrapped his waist and legs and kicked his right leg up over the saddle and slipped off the left side.

He had not stood on his own legs in many hours and, having been tightly strapped in, they were asleep. They buckled upon contact with the rocks. He wobbled left, then right, and then fell into a crack between two rocks. Nibblus Maximus gave a guffaw and added *well, Jacob, looks like you better leave the landings to me!*

Funny! Jacob responded as he stretched his back against a rock and rubbed some blood and life back into his legs before he would try to stand again.

Jacob looked over at his friend and couldn't recognize the expression he saw. The dragon pug looked older and more worn, like an old sweatshirt put on one last time. *Are you OK, Nibbs?*

I will be fine, Jacob. I am not as young as I used to be and trans-Atlantic flights are never easy. He was too kind to mention that carrying and extra hundred plus pounds of squirming pre-teen had added to the toll he paid. *But, we don't have time for our own troubles, we must go and find the professor before it's too late.* The dragon started to rise to his feet again, but they buckled under his weight. Jacob saw the exhaustion and pain written on the beast's face.

Come on, friend; just rest a minute while I take that saddle off your back. Jacob stood and steadied his legs. Then he walked over and started to unstrap the saddle from the dragon's back. When he got it unstrapped, he walked backwards pulling hard until it slipped off and onto the rocks. *What do I do with it now?*

The dragon turned his head and looked around the beach. *I am too weak to drag it away and you don't have the strength to get it far. Just stick it between some rocks there where at least it will be inconspicuous. If someone steals it, well, I guess I will just hold you by your belt in my teeth for the three thousand mile flight back!* Nibbs had not lost his sense of humor in his tired state, but Jacob did not find it a funny thought at all.

Now what? Jacob asked as he finished shoving the last bit of the saddle and cloaks as far beneath the rounded top of the rocks as he could manage.

Now we rescue the professor!

But you're in no condition now. You need to rest, Jacob replied.

We have not the luxury, Bearer! A friend is in grave danger and we are here to help, not to rest.

Still, Jacob could see the exhaustion in the dragon's eyes. *Nibbs, I think we're going to look a bit conspicuous walking into town, a boy and his dragon, don't you think? Maybe "Mr. Nibbles" will be a bit less likely to cause a scene?*

Bearer, you couldn't be more right, but changing back and forth will probably do me in and my little pug legs on these rocks will slow us down.

Well, friend. You keep calling me "Bearer" and this old sporran isn't very heavy, so I suppose I had better start bearing some of the load myself. Besides, you carried me here; the least I can do is carry you. Come on, just for a little while.

Nibblus Maximus knew he was in no condition to argue and slowly started to shrink, like a big balloon with a small pinprick. He kept his deflation under control until he got to be about the size of a small Shetland pony and then, like a dam had broken, he shrunk to the point that he disappeared completely!

"Nibbs," Jacob was yelling in a panic, "where are you? Where did you go? Nibbs!"

Jacob jumped from stone to stone over to where his friend had stood just a moment before. He remembered the dragon telling him about how special Iona was and how the eternal seemed to seep into our reality more closely than in other places. That thought encouraged his mind's eye to imagine Nibbles disappearing into another dimension. "Nibbs!" he yelled again as he jumped to the rock immediately next to where his friend sat a moment before. He was near panic by now. *Not alone. Not here. Not now!*

But his concern disappeared like steam in the air. Jacob laughed and went down on one knee to keep from falling over from the stress. Mr. Nibbles was lying in a crack between the two rocks he was straddling when he was larger.

"Thank you, pal," Jacob whispered and smiled at his friend and servant who was already fast asleep. "I'm not sure how to get us to the abbey and grave yard, but I know it's not in the ocean, so let's head through these rocks and see what we find." Jacob was talking to himself more than to the sleeping dog.

He bent over and picked up his friend as carefully as possible and turned to walk up off the rocky shore and toward the green grasses to the north. Mr. Nibble's little smashed face lay in the crook of Jacob's left arm where he would soon start to drool ever so slightly.

MAGIC PAPER

D r. Lilith Frost was hanging clothes in the closet of her new room on the second floor of The Spur and Spoon. A knock came to the door and she gruffly offered, "Yes?"

"It's Lucy, Dr. Frost, Lucy Furangle."

The woman slinked toward the door. "Oh, Lucy, dearest. How are you?"

"I'm fine, Dr. Frost. How are you?"

"Oh, you can see I am fabulous, just fabulous, dear!" The woman, full of pride, turned herself to show off her perfect form in her equally perfectly fitted dress. "Come on, now, help me put these things away. They aren't nearly enough for me to do my proper work with, but they will have to do until I can get back to my own closets and servants, you know."

Lucy stood to help but could not figure out what to put where, so she fumbled a bit and moved the cases around on the floor before the woman interrupted.

"Let us forget this for now, what news do you have for me Lucy?"

"Well, Dr. Frost, my father told me to come right over and find you and …"

"Yes, dear," the woman interrupted, "I know why you are here, but what do you have to say?"

"Well, we've searched the rooms of the accused collaborators, Boyd and Sawyer, and have found little of interest. In Boyd's room we found this curiosity," she picked up her backpack and unzipped it. Inside was another crumpled and empty backpack, which she picked up and held out in front of her.

"Is that some kind of joke?" the woman testily reacted.

"Well, no, Dr. Frost, I know it looks like just a backpack and I guess it is a backpack, so it looks like one," Lucy responded defensively and full of nervous tension. "I mean, it is a backpack, but look in here, it must have been hiding something, see?" Lucy was holding it open and showing inside where a false bottom was covering a secret compartment.

"What did you find in there?" the woman asked as she leaned eagerly forward toward the girl.

"Nothing. Sorry. Boyd must have hidden whatever was in there, I guess, or maybe he has it with him?"

"With him? What do you mean *with* him? Didn't you search him before you *lost* him?"

"Well, you see, he was asleep when we abducted him. He didn't have anything on but pajamas so surely he didn't have anything valuable with him."

"Frustrations upon frustrations! Has your father not taught you anything? The level of incompetence in this place is appalling." The woman mumbled to herself as she walked over to the window and looked out. When she spoke again, she had gained control of her emotions. "Lucy, dear, run along now and bring Boyd's girlfriend to me would you?"

"Sure. At once." Lucy couldn't get out of the room fast enough.

"Oh," Dr. Frost caught Lucy just as the girl's hand grabbed the cold metal of the doorknob. "And, make nice to that girl. Make her your friend and give her no indication that anything is wrong."

"But I don't like her," Lucy instinctively responded.

"Well, at least you have that virtue about you. It is something to build on, you know, not liking people is where many of us start. You have some promise after all. Now, work on your lying skills by working to make her *believe* you like her. Understand? I want you to watch for any sign of the Boyd kid contacting her and for anything suspicious. Report back to me twice a day. No other job or security need will come before this one—is that clear, dear Lucy?"

The Book of Kells

175

"Yes, ma'am. I'll do just that, then," Lucy responded, eager to please the woman she had come to admire as head of her father's "Security in Science" department.

As Lucy turned to leave, the woman interrupted her once more. "And, Lucy, dear, there is an annoying little kid playing out there in the rocks outside my window. Have him go away, please. He is quite annoying and stupid-looking!"

"Gladly—I was planning to do that for you anyway. I find him intolerably annoying, too."

Classes were in a shambles on campus, what with the change in curriculum that had occurred since Mr. Creech took over from Miss Witherspoon. Some of the faculty had left or been sent away. Some kids knew where to go and what classes to attend. Others didn't really know where to go, so they met in the gymnasium to be separated by the substitute teachers into groups for activities. Jenny bet that the substitutes would not miss just one person not being at the gym, so she snuck back to her room and locked herself in.

As she sat thinking about all that had happened, she noticed things seemed different in the room. She looked around and noticed some things slightly out of place and the covers to her bed had been pulled out and only haphazardly replaced. She realized her room had been searched. She peeked out the window and saw no one near, so she slowly pulled her blinds shut enough to mask her movement, should anyone be watching. She sat and wondered who might have been there.

Then she pulled from her back pocket the paper she had been given by Mr. Nibbles the night before. She laid it out on the desk and glanced back up at the door to again make sure that the latch had been pulled over and locked. She looked down and read the note Jacob had scribbled on the paper.

Jenny wondered where Jacob could be and hoped he was OK. *Why did he send me more paper than just the note?* she wondered. She turned the small stack of papers over in her hands and then looked back again to his note. She then turned the page over. To her surprise, the next page was not blank. She pushed back and dropped the paper onto the desk. *I know there was not another note on this paper this morning! I know it! It's been in my pocket all day.* She stared at it, but could not see the new note because the page with the original note had flopped back over as she dropped it.

Jenny took a pencil from her top drawer and slipped the lead tip beneath the top sheet containing Jacob's original note. She pulled it up and it fell back to the left. Her eyes had not deceived her. On the next sheet of paper there was writing that matched that of the first page. She leaned forward but kept a safe distance. One more nervous glance up at the latch of the door to ensure it was locked and her eyes settled again on the page. She began to read.

> Jenny,
>   I know you are thinking this note was not here when you read it last night. You are right. It wasn't. Took me awhile to get used to it as well. Here is the bottom line for now: This paper is some kind of magic paper. It is from something called an enchiridion that Professor von Niblick gave me. Whatever you do, keep it very secret. Even though I am now on the Island of [scratched out text] … well, let me just say I am far away (in case someone finds this besides you), we can communicate using it. Whatever I write on my pages will show up on your pages and disappear from mine. Whatever you write should disappear on your pages and show up in my book.
>   I don't know how long I will be gone or what will happen. But, I know there are very bad things happening at Iona. From what I am told, you should be very careful around Mr. Finnius Creech, Lucifer Angle – I mean, Lucy Furangle, of course, and anyone connected with the Furangles and those that may arrive at the school. I am not sure what is happening, but we are pretty sure it is bound up with this thing I carry. They were after me for a reason and now they will probably be after you and Will to get to me. I'm sorry for that.

THE BOOK OF KELLS

If you can, while always protecting yourself and looking out for Will, try to find out what is happening. Once I am done here, I will be back to try to help, or at least to get you and Will out of there. If things get bad before I get back, though, don't be a heroine, just call your folks or mine and get you and Will home safe.

Update me as you can, but take no chances of this falling into the wrong hands. Virtual battle dragons your way.

Jacob

Jenny sat back and thought for a moment. She was glad to have more contact with Jacob, but felt a bit uneasy about *magic* paper and what might be happening around her. It all had a corroding effect on what she had proudly considered to be her very rational mind. Though she had now come to expect the irrational and odd in life, it still was a new sensation to actually *believe* in it. She decided to try to write back to her friend using the enchiridion paper. She opened the bundle of papers to the next page, picked up the pencil she had used to open it a few moments before, and then began to write.

Jacob:

Got your note. I hope you are right and this does work. I wish I knew where you were. I would feel better if I did, but understand that we can't risk people knowing if you may be in danger.

Things are nuts here. Mr. Creech called me in and asked about you today. Fortunately, he didn't ask the right questions, so I told him nothing. You're right. They are interested in you and are probably after you. Lucy Furangle's dad was on campus this morning with a very pretty woman that couldn't possibly be her mother—or anyone's mother for that matter! They came in like they owned the place and went into Mr. Creech's office just as I left. Creepy group, that. And, they have bodyguards now. Jacob, didn't we learn from Plato or one of those old guys that dictatorships start when the bodyguards arrive?

Jenny sat back and watched the paper. She sat for a few minutes and stared. Slowly, the lead markings began to fade, just as Jacob said they would. Soon they were gone. The page was blank. She picked up the edge of the paper and turned it over to see if it had faded through onto the next sheet. Nothing.

"This is just not right!" Jenny mumbled to herself just as a knock came to the door and sent a startled rush of adrenaline through her limbs. Her heart raced. She froze, utterly silent.

The knock came again. This time she knew she had to answer because someone had already searched her room and had a key. They would find her no matter where she hid.

"Yes, who is it?"

"It's your friend," the girl choked on the words, for she had really never been capable of friendship. "Your friend Lucy!"

What the heck? Jenny wondered. *What is she doing here? My friend, indeed, the old bat!*

"OK. Um … I am feeling kind of nauseated," *doesn't everyone around you,* she thought to herself as she continued, "just a minute and I'll get to the door."

Though she had a master key of her own, being student head of security, Lucy Furangle waited in the hall for Jenny to come to the door and open it. Before she did, Jenny grabbed the paper from Jacob's enchiridion and slipped it securely into the back pocket of her khaki shorts. She pulled her shirt down over the top of the pocket for added security.

When she opened the door, Lucy sported a big smile that Jenny instantly interpreted to be fake. She might have been good at many things, but acting was not to be one of Ms. Furangle's talents.

"I'm sorry to hear you're sick, let me come in and comfort you," Lucy said, while suppressing her reflex to gag at the very thought. Jenny tried to slow her down and politely send her away, but couldn't think of what to say quickly enough to stop the bull from moving into the barn.

"Now, you just lay down and I'll sit here with you and we can chat a bit until you feel better," Lucy said. She sat down on Elizabeth's bed and pointed Jenny to her own. Jenny looked down at her bed and realized with a bit of panic that she had not thought to mess it up to make it look like she had been lying in it.

"Go on now, just lay down until you feel better."

Jenny walked to her bed, nervously wondering what was going on and what Furangle really wanted with her. She laid down stiff and uncomfortably looking at the ceiling, trying to avoid eye contact with her "comforter" sitting on the bed across the room.

"You didn't show up to classes this morning, so I knew something must be wrong and came right over to see if I could help," Lucy explained. "I was worried about you because you always have had a perfect attendance record and are one of those fine students we can all count on to be where she is supposed to be."

"Yes, thank you for your concern, but I just wasn't up to it this morning. Must have been something I had for breakfast, you know. But, I'm feeling a bit better now, so you can ..." Jenny was trying to dismiss her now so she could go back to figuring out what to do, but it was no use. Lucy interrupted her sentence.

"Fine, then, let's head out for a little fresh air, shall we? Though I much prefer the air of closed spaces myself, I'm told that most prefer the open air and it's good for you when you're ill. Let's you and me give it a try, friend. I really hope to help you feel better, you know." Lucy was already standing as she finished.

Reluctantly, Jenny agreed to get up and, though she faked a slight pain in her belly as she did, she made no other reference to her "illness." She knew now that Furangle was going to sit in the room with her until they left.

As the two walked out of the girl's dorm, Lucy began gently interrogating Jenny about Jacob.

"As head of student security, you know, I really must make disappearing students part of my business, you know," she kept interjected whenever she felt Jenny get annoyed by her questions.

Finally, Jenny just started telling her *everything* about Jacob—everything *but* about the sporran or dragon pugs and such. She just started gushing out information from the time she met him in Kindergarten to the time they built a zip line through his back yard down to her's and how they didn't realize fishing line would not be strong enough to hold them. The stories made her wonder about Jacob and worry about him even more, but they kept Lucy's mouth shut as she listened and tried to find any clues amidst Jenny's babble. Having worn her out through a loop around the school and sitting together at lunch, Jenny changed the subject.

"Lucy, as head of security, you must know everything that's going on around here, don't you?"

"Of course, it's my job, you know—to know what goes on around here. My daddy and Mr. Creech tell me everything."

Jenny nodded her head in understanding and then asked, "What can you tell me about all these trucks and dozers and stuff that just came in? Are we planning to rebuild the whole school or something?"

Lucy hesitated but the chance to be a know-it-all was something she could not possibly resist. "Of course *we* are rebuilding the place. Who would want to stay in these old buildings when we can have new ones of glass and steel? They are unsafe, these old buildings, you know. The wood is a firetrap and the old bricks are crumbling from the inside. They aren't efficient, you know. *We* need efficiency." She emphasized the "we" as if she were intimately involved in the planning of everything important at the school. "*We* are going to pave over all that useless grass and knock down those nasty trees and replace them with nice and flat and safe concrete, you know. Those nasty mud puddles will become flat and smooth with the new road. Then the new buildings will come."

"What kind of buildings?" Jenny asked.

"Well, if you must know, *we* are building some new science labs first. It's not enough to talk about changing the world, you know, that's what Daddy says. We must be part of the solutions to today's problems and that means experiments and science, not dusty old books ... you're smart enough to know that, of course. I'm surprised Daddy let this place rot as long as he did."

"What kind of experiments?" Jenny asked as she took a sip of orange juice.

"I'm head of security you know, not science. So, I'm not sure, but I *am* sure that it is very important work that will change the world. After all, we have now brought Dr. Lilith Frost onto campus and she is one of the world's foremost scientists doing wonderful things to improve people."

"Improve people? What kind of improvement?" Jenny interjected.

"Oh, you know what I mean. Manipulating our genes and such to fix diseases and wrong bad attitudes and things like that. All very exciting and very good, you know. I was in her office a few years ago when she designed a rat that was not afraid of cats and was ten times as strong as a normal rat and could run for hours at top speed and could eat anything it wanted without gaining weight."

"Why would anyone want a rat like that?" Jenny asked.

"Oh, I don't know, I'm sure it is just early experiments to see what is possible with us humans, that's all. Anyhow, she doesn't care about rats and things, just about changing the world. We are going to be at the heart of some very exciting changes, you know. Do you want to meet her?"

"Oh, I don't know ... she sounds very busy, Lucy," Jenny stammered.

"No, she'll want to meet you, too, I think. Let's go over to meet her now before my next shift starts."

Lucy was already up ordering one of her toadies from another table to come and clear their trays for them. Before Jenny could find an excuse to stop it, they were walking across campus toward the Spur and Spoon.

The little boy the kids dismissed as "puddles" was sitting on the side of the road playing in the rocks in front of their destination.

"Didn't I tell you to get out of here?" Lucy yelled at the little kid, who was the son of one of the grounds keepers for the school.

The little boy looked directly at Jenny, not Lucy, as Furangle yelled at him.

Jenny felt bad for the boy and wanted nothing more than to yell back at Lucy and tell him it was OK and he was not hurting anyone. But, she knew if she stood up to Lucy now, she would instantly be back on the outside of things and in a more difficult place from which to figure out what was going on. Instead of interjecting, she slowed down to get a step behind Lucy. As they passed close to the little boy, she winked at him and dropped a dollar that was in her pocket onto the ground. She hoped it would make him feel a bit better and know everyone wasn't as mean as Lucy and some of the other kids on campus who treated him poorly.

"Personally, I am most looking forward to the new road and the end of those puddles. Let that kid stay home where he belongs and out of our sight!" Lucy offered to Jenny.

They entered the Spur and Spoon together and went upstairs to Dr. Frost's room where Lucy knocked.

"George, that better be you!" the woman inside barked.

Lucy turned to Jenny and faked a smile. "No, it's Lucy again, Dr. Frost," she announced.

Frost flung the door open with an attitude of exasperation. Before she could speak, however, she saw Lucy was not alone and stopped herself. A new demeanor came over her and she smiled a difficult smile. "And, who do we have here?"

Jenny recognized the woman as being the one arriving with Mr. Furangle earlier that morning. She took a half step backward.

"This is Jenny, Dr. Frost," Lucy announced with a rise of her eyebrows, "Jenny Sawyer, you know."

"Oh, come in, darlings," the woman beckoned with a flip of her long black hair.

The Tree Speaks

The two girls entered Lilith Frost's room. She motioned them to sit in the two wicker chairs that were by the window.

"Well," the woman said as she leaned against the edge of the tall bed, "it's always good to meet one of your little friends Lucy. Now who did you say this was?"

Lucy was momentarily stumped by the question. She knew Dr. Frost knew who Jenny was.

"I'm Jenny, Dr. Frost—Jenny Sawyer."

"Oh, of course, I've heard some about you. You're friends with the poor boy that's been kidnapped," the woman said, cocking her head to the left slightly and smiling.

Jenny jumped in, "No. I mean, I'm sure he wasn't kidnapped. Lost, maybe? Run away? I don't know, but I really don't want to think of him being kidnapped."

"So he runs away a lot, perhaps?" the woman straightened her neck and pushed her chin forward toward Jenny.

"No. He doesn't run away."

"When was the last time you saw him, dear?" the woman re-crossed her ankles, letting one red toe of her pumps stick into the air.

"Oh, at dinner last night, I suppose."

Lucy sat silently watching Dr. Frost work her face into contortions of compassion and sympathy.

"Well, dear, since you were very close friends, we wouldn't want you to be back having to go to school with the other kids. I'm sure, I mean, that you could not concentrate with this on your mind and with all the other kids asking you pesky questions about him all the time. So, I tell you what we will do," the woman sat back on the bed and crossed her legs in the other direction. "You will work with my team now, where we can keep you company and so we can be ready to help your friend as soon as we get any word about him. How does that sound?"

Jenny shrugged her shoulders and mumbled, "OK, I guess, but I don't want to be a burden. Maybe I can just go back to my room and lie down a while. I haven't been feeling so good."

"I don't think that is a good idea, sweetie," the woman stood again and turned. "Here—you can lie down on the bed right here while Lucy and I go tend to some business. "

"Oh, I couldn't Dr. Frost, my room is just across campus," Jenny stood and interjected.

"Your room is a potential crime scene waiting to happen, Jennifer." The woman gave only the slightest pause of confusion as she elongated and changed Jenny's name. "As the best friend of the little boy that was kidnapped, you might well be next in line, you know," the woman's eyes had widened ominously and Jenny felt herself leaning back away from the slender wall of red finery that now stood too close for her comfort.

"Lucy, come with me. Jennifer dear one, do lie down for a while here. I will be back soon and then you and I can talk about the business we will do together … it's a very exciting time in the scientific world, you know. At least in *my* scientific world."

Jenny watched the woman put her hand on Lucy and escort her out of the room. She wanted to run or find something to say that would get her out of the room, but she could think of nothing.

"Do lie down and rest, dear, but don't try on any of my clothes, please. They would just not do for you at all. Not at all!"

The old wooden door painted light blue to match the walls of the room slowly pulled shut and the latch snapped into place. In the hallway, Dr. Frost said to Lucy, "Now, you sit down stairs and wait for me to return. Whatever you do, make sure Miss Sawyer does not try to leave my room. Is that clear?"

THE BOOK OF KELLS

185

"Yes, ma'am," Lucy snapped back like a soldier taking orders.

Inside the room, Jenny stood nervously and tried to hear what was being said on the other side of the door. She knelt down to peek through the keyhole of the old brass lock. No light could be seen through the notch. Then, she saw movement in the shadows of the lock. She gave a start as a veil of light then appeared through the hole. Footsteps told her the two had walked away and the new light was evidence that Dr. Frost had taken the key from the lock's receiver. She waited for the two to descend the stairs and then reached to gently try the handle. The door was locked and she was trapped in the room of Dr. Lilith Frost.

Lucy took up a spot in the drawing room where she could sit and see the stairs. From the stoop outside, Dr. Frost motioned to the driver of her car. He stood smoking a cigarette in the shade of a high cut pine at the corner of the house.

"Comt du! I need to get the labs functional. Are they all here yet?" She was walking toward the car as the driver started toward her, his cigarette dropping casually into the pine needles at his feet.

"Yes, Ma'am, the last one arrived about an hour ago."

Jenny watched out the window as the black car drove out of the drive and down the dirt road passed the stables and back up to the end of campus where the gymnasium was. It went by the tennis court and then disappeared out of her sight. She looked down after the car disappeared and saw the little boy nicknamed "puddles" dust himself off as he turned and headed toward the small wood-framed house he lived in on the edge of the campus woods.

The bed was high and plush in the guest room of The Spur and Spoon. A deep purple and gold blanket was folded at its foot. Jenny ran her hand over it as she walked down the edge of the bed thinking about her predicament and what could be done. At the bottom, each corner of the wooden footboard turned gradually into a lion's back and then ended in a lion's head with bared teeth. Jenny rubbed her hand slowly up over the wood onto the lion's head on the right bottom corner of the bed. She rubbed her fingers carefully into the folds of the wood that made the beast's face. She bent down to look more closely at the carved animal and felt herself drawn to the area around its right eye. She looked deeply into the shadows around the eye and slipped her left pointer nail into the creases.

Tap, tap, tap, tap.

Jenny jumped and straightened instinctively at the sound of something tapping on the window behind her. She turned. She could see nothing but a slight breeze blowing the great oak's leaves and branches. She stalked over toward the window, being careful to stay to the right side where she had some protection from being seen. She peeked out around the curtain. She could see nothing out of the ordinary.

Tap, tap, tap.

The sound was coming from behind the curtain. She leaned over further and peeked again. She was just in time to see a small hand withdraw from the outside seal on the window.

Jenny jumped and let out a small whimper, as she tried to capture her breath and her wits. *A squirrel. Must have been a squirrel's paw. Sure. That's it! I didn't notice, but it must have been hairy with squirrel claws. It must have been the glass that made it look bigger.* She approached the window again, her nerves on edge. She pushed her brown hair back from her face where it had fallen as she jumped. As she got to the window, she saw movement going back down a large branch toward the tree's mighty trunk. The leaves shielded whatever it might have been and so Jenny was able to reassure herself that it was just a squirrel.

She flipped the latch on the window and opened it. Warm summer air brushed her face. "Hello little squirrel," she called out in a volume half way between a whisper and a normal speaking voice. "You startled me, you know. Oh," she giggled, "did you think I was a giant nut?"

"Friend of the Bearer," a deep but slight voice came back from within the branches of the tree.

Jenny's eyes jerked from branch to branch. Then she turned with a start, now assuming the voice must have come from within the room. Nothing was there.

"Do not be afraid, friend of Master Boyd," the voice returned. This time there was no question but that it was coming from outside the window. She turned again and took a half step back.

"Hello?" Her voice cracked with fear.

"Don't be afraid, Bearer Friend. You have seen me before and I have served. Remember the woods that treacherous night more than a year ago? I was with you and helped you escape with the lad called Will."

Jenny remembered that terrifying night very well. She had laid in bed occasionally during nights since then seeing the face of that stranger as he raised his hands up and down and was somehow turning the lights on and off in Jacob's empty home. Occasionally over the last year she would get a shiver when she passed the woods between her house and Jacob's and remembered being thrown to the ground and protected by an unseen man who had covered them with a cloak and made them lie painfully still while the evil man searched for them.

"Who are you?" Jenny's voice quavered. She backed far from the open window. There was no response, or at least none she could hear. When the silence greeted her, she realized she had backed so far away from the window that anything that might be in the tree could not have heard her. She shuffled toward the window warily and asked again, "Who are you?"

"They call me Angus," the voice came back again. "But my name is of little importance here. You must trust me. You are in danger and I have been sent to help."

Jenny said nothing but searched the tree with her eyes, trying hard to see the man belonging to the voice. The leaves were thick and moving gently in the breeze. They kept her from being able to pick up anything out of the ordinary within its branches.

"You must trust me, Miss Sawyer. You must come. Jacob has trusted me and you must as well."

Jenny was confused but she knew two things for sure and another one she felt pretty good about. First, she knew that this Dr. Frost had all the makings of a villain. Second, she was sure that only the one that helped Will and her that night a year ago could have known he had done so. And she felt pretty good that if someone was bringing Jacob's name into it, they probably were on the right side of what was happening. For a moment she thought about writing in the little pages from Jacob's enchiridion notebook, but then thought the risk of losing it or having it seen or taken by the person outside the window was too great. She knew she had to make this call on her own.

"You really don't have time to be indecisive, young one," the voice urged. "Look up above the window and you will see that I have buckled a good stout line above it for you."

Jenny looked up and turned her head several different ways until at last she saw the long, thin line running off the roof and down through the tree toward the ground. It was almost transparent and blended nearly completely into the foliage of the tree—almost perfect camouflage.

"Just above the window is a handle. Come on, now. Just hang on and slide down and out of there."

Jenny stood frozen and considering her options. She looked up at the handle and down at the ground. She looked again into the tree trying to find this person bidding her to fly.

Seeing her hesitation, Angus knew he had to do something to get Jenny to move. "Lass, that witch is going to make a meat pie of you when she gets back you know! She eats little girls like you!"

The claim was so preposterous Jenny was not sure what to make of it. *Sure, this Lilith Frost seemed evil, but being evil doesn't make her a cannibal.* Though she didn't think she was likely to be eaten, she did look down at her legs and pinched her thigh as if she was checking to see what grade of meat she would make. She leaned out the window and reached up to test the handle on the escape zip line.

Figuring she needed one more push, Angus took a stone from the pocket of his waistcoat, took careful aim, and fired it as straight as he could up toward the window. It flew toward Jenny's head, flying just passed her right ear, and hit a water glass on the table beside the bed behind her.

Jenny jumped at the sound and her heart raced. She didn't even turn to see what might have made the noise, but feared it was Dr. Frost unlocking the door. Up on the window seal she went, crunched into a tight ball. Through the open window, she straightened up and grabbed the handles above her head. Then, Jenny froze again.

THE BOOK OF KELLS

"A cadger's curse this is! " the man said in exasperation.

Angus then reached up to the rope and shook it wildly. The vibrations ran up the line toward Jenny's hands. Just before she felt them, she saw the waves rising toward her. Her eyes widened like saucers just before her hands started shaking. The vibrations let the handle loose from its clip and it started down the rope. Jenny held tight. Her body started to stretch and open into the warm afternoon air. Before she knew it, that infernal power of gravity had stretched her to the point that her toes could hold the window no more and her legs flew out and under her floating body.

"Ahhhh …" she yelled as she zipped down toward the ground.

"Shut your haggis hole, lass!" the man spit as the girl flew past him.

Jenny did a double take at the small man sitting on a branch as she flew by. She flew out the other end of the tree and crashed into the ground behind the stone wall that surrounded the Spur and Spoon.

"Just lie there, lass, just lie there. Don't move," the man was whispering to himself as he watched the windows of the bed and breakfast. With no sign Lucy Furangle had heard Jenny's cry, he dropped to the ground and ran to the wall. He looked over the wall to see Jenny picking small twigs and leaves from her hair and spitting moss from her lips.

Angus jumped over the short stone wall and sat hard on the ground near Jenny's feet. "A fine run, lass, but ya need to work on stickin' the landin'!"

Jenny back-peddled a few inches, more as if attempting to show she was ready to run than actually trying to get away from the little man. She looked at him, from his little brown boots up to his blue waistcoat that sat tightly over a white ruffled shirt and then up to his pale, clean-shaven face and finally up to his brown unkempt hair.

"I wish we had time for a chat, Miss Sawyer, but I'm afraid we don't. They'll come searching for ya soon and behind this wall will probably be the first place that wee witch Furangle will look," Angus said as he stood and peered over the wall and back toward campus.

"Come. Follow me, if you please." The small man came up to about Jenny's chest when she stood next to him. They hunched over as they ran near the wall, then sprinted across the pasture where the horses were turned loose most mornings, then down by the stables. As they dodged from the cover of one bull dozer to another, Jenny ran her hand along the edge of one of the front blades. She felt the power asleep in its potential where the men had parked them and headed to lunch. The two continued into the woods beyond.

"Where are we going?" Jenny asked as they entered the protection of the trees.

Angus slowed and then stopped. He leaned his right forearm on a tree and looked at the ground as he caught his breath. Jenny leaned back on another tree about three feet behind the small man. After a pause, he looked up and answered, "The mansion." He then started a quick walk through the trees and Jenny followed close behind.

Remnant Opens

Without speaking, the small man and the girl walked through the woods until they reached the edge of the trees where the grounds around the old Ashland mansion ran up to the house. Angus took a whistle from his pocket and blew it three times, making a squawk that startled Jenny. The window blind in one of the second story windows moved up and down three times and Angus announced, "that be our signal, lass, let's fly like the stag and the roe."

Angus started out across the grass. Jenny held back for a second and then sprinted after him. Angus's short legs forced him to take more strides than Jenny, but still the man was quick and Jenny worked to keep up with him. As they approached the door, still running hard, Angus let himself crash into the hedge to the left of the front door to stop himself. Jenny stumbled but grabbed a branch and swung around it like it was a pole and then banged her back onto the brick wall of the house.

Angus emerged from the bush, brushing the small twigs and green needles from his clothing. "Let's move, lass," he said as the front door slowly creaked open. Up and in the door he dashed. Jenny followed up the steps but looked up at the man holding the door for her as her left foot hit the top stair. It took her only a fraction of a second to recognize the man's face. There, looking out into the afternoon sun was Copernicus Campbell—the man Jenny knew had been murdered a couple of days before and who died in Jacob and Will's room. The terrified girl screamed at the gentlemanly ghost. She changed her momentum instantly and flew her body back off the porch, her arms and legs flailing wildly in the air as she descended into the hedge. The stiff branches of the hedge let her sink partly but not enough for her kicking feet to hit the ground and gain traction for an escape.

To the screaming girl, the specter announced, "Hush yourself young lady or you'll blow everything." Then he jumped down beside her. Jenny looked the other way and kicked wildly. "Miss Sawyer, if you don't mind, I am trying to unhook you—or would you rather hang there like a pig on a spit for the night?"

Jenny felt the hands of the ghost reach over to her—one hand on the back of her belt and another lifting at the bottom of her ribcage. She felt herself levitate up and out of the bush, then descend again to the porch. With the ghost behind her, she rushed the only way she had to escape. Into the house she flew, slamming the door behind her and leaving Campbell out on the steps. She hit the area rug in the entryway of the house. It slipped on the smooth wooden floor. Her feet shot forward and she went down hard on her back. Opening her eyes, she was looking into the business end of a pair of brown leather boots.

"Miss Sawyer, do you mind cooperating, please?"

Jenny looked up and saw the face of Dr. Ramos Kirk who was looking down at her sternly. The door opened and the ghostly figure announced, "What a week! I die one day and get the door slammed on me the next! Have you no respect for the dead, girl?" The man then laughed.

"Leave her alone, Campbell," Dr. Kirk ordered as he bent down and brushed Jenny's hair from her face. "You see, Miss Sawyer, old Campbell here is no spectral force. He did not die that night in Jacob's and Will's room. That was just a diversion. He is fine and so are you. Come on now," Kirk pushed his black-framed glasses back on his nose and then reached down to help Jenny to her feet. "Get this young lady some tea and a biscuit or something," he announced.

The men took Jenny into the study where Jacob had seen them meeting a few days before. They sat in a circle on chairs near the empty fireplace. Dr. Kirk sat next to Jenny on her left. The small man named Angus sat on her right. Copernicus Campbell sat next to Dr. Kirk and Hammish MacGregor completed the circle. The snakehead chandelier hung from the ceiling between them. Jenny looked around nervously at the dark old wood paneling and antique furnishings as she sipped tea from a blue and white china cup.

"Miss Sawyer," Dr. Kirk began, "you know us all now, I believe, except perhaps Hammish."

"She knows me, though we have never met," Hammish MacGregor interjected as he bowed slightly in his chair. Jenny did recognize him as the man who arrived in her hometown a year ago when the sporran entered Jacob's life and strange things started to occur. "It is my sincere pleasure to now make your proper acquaintance, young friend of The Bearer," he finished with another bow of his head.

"Evil floats on the air of the school, you know, Miss Sawyer," Kirk began again. "Your friend Mr. Boyd is long far from here now and there is nothing more we can do for him from here. However, we must now work with what we have and with the situation we are in."

Jenny had seen enough on campus recently to feel what the man meant; even if she didn't quite understand all that he had in his mind. She looked at her tea, but it didn't seem appropriate to take a drink now as the weight of the moment had descended upon the group. She sat her cup down on the chess table next to her. She felt a little light-headed.

The men took turns telling Jenny parts of what they had discovered and what they believed was unfolding on campus. They were sure Abigail Witherspoon did not leave the school voluntarily, as Mr. Creech had claimed, but had been abducted and was being held somewhere nearby. They were also sure that Mr. Creech was up to no good but was not bold enough to be the ultimate driving force behind the changes on campus. They were very troubled by Dr. Lilith Frost's arrival. They had discovered she was a somewhat famous scientist who was doing experiments in genetic engineering and the cloning of animals. A few years before, she had famously engineered a housefly with dozens of eyeballs that grew from nearly every joint of its body. She had also engineered a race of super rats that were not afraid of cats, fought ferociously, and could exist on very little food. "Ratmo," she called the first of these creatures. Jenny had already heard that story from Lucy.

"Most unnatural! Most unnatural!" Ramos Kirk kept muttering as he shook his head in disgust.

They explained how they would be there to help, but also that Headmaster Creech, Mr. Furangle, and Lucy all knew them to be an enemy of what they were planning and would be watching for them, particularly now that they had left the campus without explanation. There was a chance, however, that they would not know Hammish MacGregor, as he had not been a member of the campus community.

While they developed a plan to counter the situation, they asked Jenny to join the fight and go back to campus where she could spy on what was happening.

"Miss Sawyer," Kirk brought the moment to a head, "what we are saying is that we now need you to join us. We need you and Jacob needs you, young lady. Iona herself needs you, too, and I suppose the students need you to serve, too."

"It seems," Jenny said, "pretty much everyone needs me then?"

"Ah, yes, now that is an interesting insight, young lady. We are all called to our destiny and much depends on us following it," Kirk said as he reached a hand over and patted Jenny lightly on her left knee.

"What about Will?" Jenny asked.

"Yes, little Mr. Renrut, yes, we have been discussing his rather precarious situation," Copernicus Campbell began to answer. "It seems he has a foot in each camp, which is the most dangerous place of all. He's a good boy, you know. But he has been chosen by evil for particular temptations and he is serving Furangle and her crew now. He doesn't know the nature of what is happening, of that we can be sure. But he does have ties to them and cannot be fully trusted right now by us. And, on the other hand …"

"Never mind that, Copernicus," Hammish MacGregor cut him off. "What he is saying is that poor Will thinks he can have it both ways— be good and also be around fundamentally misguided people. We have decided to take Will out of the way, Jenny, for his own good, you see."

"Take him out of the way?" Jenny bolted up in her chair and in an agitated voice declared, "What does that mean?" Her mind had conjured instant visions of abduction and murder.

"Calm now, good friend," Kirk touched her knee again and motioned for her to sit back. He could tell the nature of her fears for her friend. "We have decided that Campbell will use one of his little potions, you see, to help Master Will get some safe sleep for a few days in the infirmary."

"You won't hurt him?" Jenny asked with great concern.

"No, lass. Frankly, I am not sure old Campbell has the *stuff* anymore for a truly dangerous potion. Do you old man?" MacGregor answered. A hint of sarcasm tipped his tongue.

"I could bloody well do away with you!" Campbell reacted in a prideful huff that made Jenny smile.

Jenny thought about Jacob and the sporran and what he had written magically on the pages she had in her pocket. She wasn't sure what to think or who to trust, but she was pretty sure that Jacob trusted these men and she was even more sure that Furangle and Lilith Frost and their group were up to no good. She reached for her tea and sipped it as she thought through the situation. The men sat quietly and let her think. After what seemed like many minutes but probably was no more than a few dozen seconds, Jenny came to an important realization. *What am I thinking about? I'm sure Jacob trusts them and what else can I do? I'm in a strange old house with these guys and no way to escape anyway, so what am I supposed to do?*

"Well, seeing as you have me at a distinct disadvantage here and Mr. Angus rescued me from Dr. Frost, I suppose I have no good choice but to join you gents in your fun." Jenny sat down her tea, trying her very best to appear brave and as "adultly British" as she could muster.

"That's a friend of the wee Bearer if I have ever heard one," MacGregor stood with excitement. He laughed happily.

Jenny smiled at the praise. "So what are we going to do next?"

"You are going back to work for Lilith Frost," MacGregor announced.

Jenny's heart sank and her head grew confused. *Work for Dr. Frost? Whose side are they on anyway?*

MacGregor laughed at the look on Jenny's face. "No worries, lass, we'll be watching ya. We must get ya back on campus and without them knowing you were gone. If they suspect you, the plan will be up. We will be in touch soon."

Without pause, the men moved Jenny up and out of Ashland mansion. Angus led her on a dead run down through the woods, up past the stables and toward the Spurr and Spoon. As they ran, the black car containing Dr. Frost started up the road from her new labs by the gymnasium at the far end of campus. Dust rose from behind the wheels as the car snaked its way around the school. Angus looked up and saw the car on the move.

"We have little time. Faster, faster, friend of the Bearer!"

The two picked up their pace as much as either of them could stand. The car kept moving. Jenny looked up and saw the car and her adrenaline pushed her harder. She was near panicked as she ran and watched the car spitting up a cloud of dust behind it. Suddenly and quite unexpectedly the car stopped. Jenny couldn't make out what was happening but put her head down to run harder up the hill toward the house.

"What is going on?" Lilith Frost spit from the back seat of the car as she slammed down a folder full of charts and graphs.

"A small child, a small child is in the way," the driver announced in an apologetic tone.

"Well, move him out of the way, then!" she ordered.

The driver blew his horn. Jenny and Angus heard it and looked up. Then they put their heads down again and continued toward the house, becoming more fatigued with each footfall. Jenny felt herself wishing she had followed through with her New Year's resolution to get into better shape.

"Get out of the way," the driver yelled.

Puddles just sat in the road, seeming oblivious to the driver's yelling and blowing of his horn. Finally, the driver got out.

"Son, can't you hear?" He walked toward the human obstruction. The boy ignored him completely and continued stacking small pebbles on top of one another in the shape of a small pyramid in the bed of a dry mud puddle.

"Son?" the man repeated. The boy looked up and smiled. "You can't play in the road, kid!" The boy got up and slowly walked off the road and started across the field. He said nothing.

By the time the driver got back into the car and started moving again, Angus had Jenny strapped to the end of the zip line. He started to struggle back toward the woods pulling the rope and elevating her toward the window of Lilith Frost's room. Though she was nervous and a bit motion sick by the time she floated up past the tree and hit the window seal with her foot, she was able to get her balance and throw herself into the room.

The crash of her body on the floor snapped Lucy out of the nap she was taking while on duty downstairs. Startled, she jumped up and ran the stairs two at a time. Jenny heard her coming and dove for the bed. Lucy grabbed the door handle and pushed. To her relief, the door was still locked. She descended the stairs again relieved that Jenny had to be still securely locked away in Dr. Frost's room. When she reached the bottom of the stair, Dr. Frost was just stepping into the doorway.

Infirmary

The metal key scratched into the lock and then clanked onto the metal tumblers. It snapped open. Jenny was lying on her side on Dr. Frost's bed, her eyes only barely cracked as if she had actually been sleeping. She stretched as the lean, dark woman slinked into the room followed by the significantly less lean and less dark girl who had served as her watchman. The perfume hit Jenny's nose like slight needles being injected into her nostrils; not unpleasant, but forceful.

The woman cocked her head. "I hope you got some rest," the woman said in silky tones.

Jenny sat up and replied, "I'm feeling much better now." She hoped Dr. Frost would let it drop and not ask more directly about her "rest," of which she had none at all.

"Good!" Dr. Frost said and then sat down on the edge of the bed next to Jenny. She put her hand on the girl's knee. Uncomfortable, Jenny looked down at the woman's hand. Her hands were long and lean and smooth. Her fingers were tipped with intensely red nails that matched perfectly the woman's shoes and dress. The color did not match the temperature of her hand, however. It was cold and though it was on Jenny's skin, it felt somehow distant. The woman's fingers depressed only slightly into Jenny's flesh and then retreated after Jenny looked down at them nervously. "I am ready for you to come to work for me now, dear Jennifer."

Lucy stood in the doorway smiling meanly at Jenny as her name was botched again. Jenny was annoyed but said nothing. She was confused by all that had happened in the last few hours and more than anything she wanted time by herself to think. Well, she really wanted to know Jacob was all right and to have him there to talk it over with. But she knew that was impossible and she was too rational to hope for what was impossible.

"Lucy dear," Dr. Frost said as she looked across the room.

"Yes, Dr. Frost," Lucy answered, expecting to get a good assignment this time and eager to please.

"Lucy, take Jennifer here, would you, down to Trailer Number 2."

"Yes ma'am, and then what can I do?" Lucy stood a little straighter and stepped into the room.

"Oh, nothing. Just do your rounds or something," Dr. Frost turned back to Jenny and pulled her up off the bed to move her along. Lucy looked dejected.

On the walk down the road that snaked across campus, Lucy barely spoke. She had hoped for a better assignment and the chance to work more closely with Dr. Frost and her experiments. Now Jenny seemed to have moved from prisoner to special assistant and Lucy was confused. For that matter, Jenny was just as confused. Her eyes darted around the field for any glimpse of the little man named Angus.

The area behind the gym on the north side of campus had been turned into a small industrial village. Trailers of various sizes, all clad in silver aluminum, had been planted in the tennis courts and in the grass around the gym. Until the trees were cut down and earth ground flat beyond the stables, these trailers would be the place Dr. Frost would be conducting her experiments and the new business of the school would be transacted.

When the two girls arrived at the trailer with the number 2 on the door, Lucy turned back toward campus, dejected. Jenny took a deep breath and stepped up the three metal stairs leading to the door. She knocked; half hoping there would be no answer. There was not. She stood silently wondering whether she dared to walk away. She turned and looked around campus. She heard young voices coming from the gymnasium nearby. *Sounds like they are cheering a basketball game*, she thought.

"Can I help you?" a man's voice startled her. She turned to see a middle aged young man with dark hair, glasses upon a chain around his neck, and wearing a white lab coat.

"Oh, yes, please. I am Jenny Sawyer, sir. Dr. Frost sent me down to help."

The man looked at a clipboard he had in his hand and said, "I don't have a Jenny on the work list."

Just then the phone inside the trailer rang. As the man turned to answer it, Jenny assured him, "well, then that is fine, it must have been a mistake." She turned and stepped down the stairs. She was relieved. She could hear the man mumbling on the phone as she stepped into the grass and started to walk away.

"Young lady," the man called out. "Did you say your name was Jennifer?"

Jenny rolled her eyes and kicked the grass. She turned. "Some call me Jennifer, I guess," she said, "but Jenny is my real name."

"I just got the call to expect you. Come on in, then."

Jenny hesitated but then walked back up the steps and followed the man into trailer number 2. The door shut behind her and automatically locked. Jenny looked down at the bolt of the door lock to confirm what she heard. The man seemed almost uninterested in Jenny, and barely even bothered to look at her as he talked.

"Not sure what I'm to do with you," the man mumbled as he studied his clipboard.

Jenny looked around the trailer. It was some kind of command center or organizing room. A half a dozen computer monitors were on desktops. There was only one chair, however. The walls were covered with posters, most of them anatomy posters of human bodies or animal bodies. Various charts and graphs dotted the walls. Clipboards, like the one the man was staring at hung from hooks by the closed door leading to a back room. A wall of filing cabinets formed the front wall to the right of the door.

THE BOOK OF KELLS

The man grumbled as he fumbled with his clipboard. "What am I to do with a girl? I have important things to do. What does she think I *do* down here, anyway? The place doesn't run on its own."

He turned to Jenny and said, "Well, why don't you run an errand or two for me, then."

The man fumbled with some files on his desk and pulled one from the stack. He handed it to Jenny without even looking at her. "Here," he mumbled. Then he pulled another file and this time turned toward her and said, "Jennifer, dear, please take this first file, the grey one, to Trailer number 4 and the second one, the manila one, over to the infirmary and give it to the new nurse. No one else gets it but the new nurse, whatever her name is, which I can't remember. They can't expect me to remember everything you know. But no one gets this file except the new nurse—is that clear, Jennifer?"

Jenny wanted to roll her eyes and correct him again on her name, *but why bother*, she thought. "Yes, I understand perfectly. Grey one to Trailer Number 4, manila one to the new nurse and only the new nurse at the infirmary."

"Yes, dear—then why don't you just come back in the morning and by then I'll know what to do with you. Run along, then." The man did not seem to need Jenny to respond, but went back to work immediately.

Jenny left trailer number 2 and walked down toward trailer number 4. They all looked the same—cold silver aluminum siding with no windows and each sat upon its own set of wheels, as if they had just arrived or were planning to leave at any moment. As she walked she could hear the cheers of the other students in the gym. But now she could hear something else as well. Though she couldn't place the sounds, she thought they sounded like some kind of animals howling or baying or roaring or barking or chattering … or something. It was a most unusual sound that gave her a most unusual sensation, and not a pleasant one.

Jenny walked up to the door of trailer number 4 and knocked. At first there was no answer, but her knock seemed to disturb something inside and she heard the bizarre sound again. This time she thought it might actually be coming from inside the trailer itself. She backed up a step and knocked again, mostly to test her theory. She was right; the animal noises grew louder after her knock. She listened, almost in disgust.

The door opened abruptly. It startled her and the files fell from her nerve-stricken fingers.

The woman answering the door was wearing a lab coat and holding a clipboard just like the man in trailer number 2. She made no move to bend down and help. Jenny mumbled, "sorry," and bent to pick up the files. As she did, she noted the label on the grey file said, "Gryphon Failure Number 34." She handed it to the woman and explained that she was delivering it from trailer number 2. Without a thank you, the woman took the file and shut the door. The sound of the door shutting sent off the cacophony inside.

Jenny stood for a second thinking about the label on the file. *"Gryphon Failure Number 34", what could that mean? Surely they aren't experimenting on a Gryphon, as in the mythological creature? But, there's no boy named Gryphon at school. What are they up to?* She thought about how government agencies and military operations used code names and figured that must be the answer.

As Jenny turned toward the infirmary on the older part of campus that had not been taken over by silver trailers, she looked down at the file she was holding. The label on this manila folder said, "IAN NELSON—Results of Blood Work." *Well, I don't remember any Ian on campus, but at least that sounds like a person's name and blood work is something a nurse deals with, so that sounds fine.*

Jenny thought through it all as she walked. She said hello to the occasional student and to one of the new teachers who had been brought to campus. As she passed the headmaster's office, Mr. Finnius Creech opened a window and called out to her.

"Jennifer dear, come here please," he called.

Jenny was not pleased to hear the man call her 'name,' but she went over dutifully to the window.

"Jennifer, dear, have you had any sign of our lost boy, Jacob Boyd?"

"No, sir. I haven't seen him."

"This is most disturbing, Jennifer, you know. Most disturbing. You realize that we will have to contact his parents if he does not show up soon, and he will be in a lot of trouble."

"Yes sir, I guess so."

As the new Headmaster spoke, Jenny's eyes glanced away from him. She was attracted by a reflection at the far end of his office. She squinted slightly to make it out. It was black and red and seemed to be moving, growing maybe. She stared and then remembered the hideous painting Mr. Creech had hung in the office. *It can't be, can it? It didn't look quite like that when I saw it. It looks bigger, somehow, stranger. Maybe just the reflection, maybe. . .* She was no longer paying any attention to what Mr. Creech was saying. She just wanted away from that vision.

"Mr. Creech, sorry, I have to deliver this file to the infirmary, you know. I'm working for Dr. Frost now."

The man shot up at the sound of Dr. Frost's name and smacked his head on the windowpane. "Oh, yes, by all means, then, carry on."

As Jenny ran off, the headmaster yelled out, "Be sure to tell me if Mr. Boyd returns!" He was rubbing the back of his head.

Jenny paid no attention but kept running toward the infirmary and didn't stop until she got to the door. She entered the infirmary but saw no one. She walked in, poking her head around the corner. There, lying on a cot and looking as pale as she had ever seen a person, was her friend Will.

"Will!" she exclaimed and then rushed in to her friend's side.

"Oh, mother, is that you, mother?" Will cried out.

"Will, it's *me, Jenny!*"

"Jenny? Jenny? Jenny, the pony from Camp Trenton? I didn't know you could talk, old girl! Oh, if only I had known! The conversations we could have had over those sugar cubes and apples!"

"Will! No. *Jenny*—your *friend* Jenny. You know, Jenny and Jacob from the subdivision next to yours?"

"I'm afraid your friend has a very bad fever," came a woman's voice from the doorway behind her. "He's been spouting nonsense for the last hour."

Jenny turned and looked. She didn't recognize the woman but figured she must be the new nurse. She handed her the file folder and asked, "Will he be OK?"

"Yes, I'm sure he'll be fine. I'm ready to give him an ice bath here in a minute to cool him down. I'll take care of him. Now, go on your way and come back and see your friend tomorrow."

"OK, Will—you be good now and I'll come see you tomorrow."

"Thanks for visiting again, pony," Will called back. "Next time I'll feed you a carrot or a sugar cube. Mom, do we have any sugar cubes?"

Jenny and the nurse both laughed. "Let me check the cupboard, dear!" the nurse said and giggled.

Jenny stopped under a tree in Miss Charlotte's Garden where she was shielded from being seen by most passers by. She remembered the men from Ashland mansion telling her they would get Will out of the way and she assumed this is what they meant. She hoped he would be all right and said a prayer for him. She pulled the loose papers from her back pocket and pulled the stump of a pencil she had stowed there as well and scribbled down the story of what had happened during the day. She wrote about the searching of her room; of Dr. Frost; of Angus and Kirk and the rest and them letting her into the secrets a bit more; of the strange noises; of the file folders; and of course, she wrote of Will's illness. She hoped Jacob would get her note in his enchiridion notebook and would soon reply with news of his own.

When she was finally done with the letter, she went up to the cafeteria for dinner and then went to her room with Elizabeth to catch up on what was happening on the rest of campus.

Niblick Rescued

Jacob carried Mr. Nibbles north toward the village. Occasionally he whispered to the sleeping dog lying in the crook of his arms or said a prayer for Chadwick von Niblick, who was lying somewhere near death on the island. By the stone buildings ahead in the distance, Jacob could tell they were approaching the village of Baile Mor, the only community on the island.

The dog's eyes suddenly opened and life came back into his legs. He kicked at Jacob's right arm. The pug's claw caught Jacob's skin and scratched. "Ouch," Jacob exclaimed as he dropped the dog to the ground. Before he could ask him what he had done that for, the dog was excitedly smelling the ground and running off along the stone wall that ran on their left side.

"Nibbles!" Jacob called out.

The adrenaline was running so high in the dog that he did not even hear Jacob's call. The pug ran along the wall, smelling as he went and turned into a gate that opened up into a series of ruined medieval buildings. This was the ancient Augustinian nunnery first occupied more than eight hundred years ago by prioress Bethoc, sister of Reginald MacDonald of Islay. Some believe it was the ancient home, also, of the last remnant to escape Atlantis before it disappeared forever beneath the waves. Jacob knew none of this, but it was clear to his eyes that no buildings still stood. None looked out defiant and strong against changing times. Nothing was left but partially ruined walls and manicured grass squares that once were rooms.

Jacob hurried into the gate, but the dog was now gone. "Nibbles!" he called. There was no answer. Jacob closed his eyes and called out through his mind, *Nibbles, where are you?* No reply. The boy opened his eyes and began to jog down the path that weaved between the ruins of the Nunnery. "Nibbles!" he would call out as loud as he could but not loud enough, he hoped, to call attention to himself. Tourists walked the grounds, taking photos and hoisting small children up to peer over the ruined walls. He tried to be as inconspicuous as possible as he searched for the little dog.

A flash of yellow caught his attention ahead on the right. It was a blonde woman in a yellow t-shirt and white pants running (more like stumbling quickly) toward him. She looked over her shoulder occasionally but didn't speak. As she got closer to Jacob, he could see the look on her face and he knew what she was running from.

Jacob ran in the direction of the woman, who nearly crushed him as she panicked wildly down the path. He dodged left just in time and then made the turn where he first saw the yellow streak of a woman emerge from behind the ruined wall. He saw what he feared.

The beast was neither dog nor dragon. It stood much larger than Mr. Nibble's tiny form, but it was not as big as Nibblus Maximus. It's front legs, though, were huge and ended in great claws that were tearing at the ground. Large globs of turf were flying into the air. For a second, Jacob hung his head and let himself wonder how he was going to explain it. Then he remembered their mission—*von Niblick! He must be under that ground!*

Jacob raced over to where the half-dragon-half pug was working. He tried to jump in and help, but those claws where long and were tearing with abandon into the turf. *I could only slow him down,* he thought. *Or, one of those claws will slow me down permanently!*

Jacob looked around but saw no tourists nearby. He walked around the beast, watching him work but staying out of the way.

The right claw came crashing down and a mighty roar went up into the heavens. The beast had either hit the hard stone foundation of the island, which everywhere lies only a short distance beneath the grass or he had hit the top slab of a tomb. He hopped back and stuck his broken claw into his mouth.

Are you OK, Nibbs? Jacob asked.

The beast shook the pain from his paw but did not answer. He went back to work, scratching more cautiously this time at the surrounding soil.

Jacob was walking by the edge of the grass square upon which the dragon-pug was doing its damage. Of no use up there anyway, he jumped down into the next level. An ancient stone retaining wall kept the ground about five feet above his head. The dragon-pug was that far above him.

This must have been some kind of basement, Jacob thought. He brushed his hands along the stones of the wall and wondered about the medieval hands that carved them. As he rubbed the stones and wondered about von Niblick, he felt the quickening: the pain came through his fingers, shot up into his arm and ended in a pinch in his neck. He jumped back. A clod of black dirt dropped on his head with a thud. "Nibbs! Watch it!" he shouted. He brushed the remains of the dirt from his head and shoulders and then peeked up over the wall. He saw no tourists attracted by his yell. He breathed a sigh of relief and slunk back down the wall.

Jacob looked at the stones that had given him the shock. He looked around them at the other stones and compared them all. They all looked the same—a mix of grey and red – just like all the other walls on the island. He drew his finger around the stones and then noticed the difference. The stones that gave him the shock were not as tightly encased in mortar as the others. *These look like they've been moved,* he thought.

Jacob took a deep breath, ignoring the particles of black dirt and green grass that fell like rain around him. He reached for a stone. He felt the electric pulse. This time he was expecting it and gritted his teeth. He held the stone until the pain passed and then bettered his grip and pulled. He pulled again in the other direction and the stone let lose of its own grip in the wall and slid out. He looked around to see if he was being watched before he pulled the stone fully out and dropped it to the ground. Behind the stone was utter blackness.

Excited, Jacob took Isildane's ring from his finger, bent down, and held it to his eye. The red gem threw beams of light into the hole enough for Jacob to see that the wall beneath the sod was hollow and in the space there seemed to be something unnaturally square.

Jacob grabbed the stone next to the one he had removed and with both hands he pulled it free. Then he pulled the one below it and the one below the first hole. Now, he could see the square clearly. It was the bottom of a wooden box. Jacob mustered his courage and reached for the wood plank. His finger tips gently brushed it; the sensation that returned was anything but gentle, however. A shock like sticking your finger in an electric plug ran up his arm and sent him reeling back and collapsing on the ground. He paid no attention to the pain, however, because in that sensation he knew what was behind that wood plank.

Nibblus, he's down here! I found another way into the tomb! Jacob yelled through his mind as he sat back up in the grass. The dragon pug leaned his big head over the end of the wall. Jacob pointed to the hole. The beast stretched his neck down to see and gave out a cry of excitement.

Keep working! The dragon communicated back as his head disappeared above the wall. Jacob jumped to the wall and continued pulling stones. The half-dragon-half-dog leapt off the wall and before he landed on Jacob's level, he had returned to being little Mr. Nibbles again.

Jacob worked as quickly as he could. Stones cut and squared many centuries ago now were falling with ease and Mr. Nibbles was excitedly dodging them as he jumped at the wall, trying to see into the growing hole.

When Jacob felt the hole was big enough to slip the box out, he reached up and began to pull. The box barely budged. He pushed it to the left and then tried to pull. Nothing. He pushed it to the right and then pulled again. It moved slightly. He took the ring of Isildane from his finger and used it to scan the inside of the hole. He could see the rough edge of a rock still holding the wooden box in place. He pulled the rock out of the wall and let it fall. Reaching once again into the cool hole, Jacob grasped the bottom edges of the box and pulled hard. It began to slip out toward the light.

As the box emerged, Jacob felt the thrill of accomplishment, but a creepiness also came over him. The box was a coffin and in it could either be a dead man, or a barely alive Professor von Niblick. It was freaky to think of the alternatives. As the box slipped out beyond the tipping point where the bottom weighed more than the top still in the hole, it began to slip from Jacob's grip. He could not hold the weight of the box and its contents.

The bottom of the box crashed into the ground. The top came out of the hole and began to fall toward Jacob. The boy dove out of the way. The coffin crashed into the green ground where Jacob had just stood. Mr. Nibbles jumped at the box, frantically scratching at it. But the box was now upside down and Jacob knew he didn't have the strength to turn it over to open the lid. He didn't need to. Mr. Nibbles—frantic and furious at his inability to break into the box with his scratches—again let his head swell and his left paw grow to three and then ten and then twenty times its pug size. One crashing blow shattered the bottom panel of the box.

Jacob rushed over and began peeling back the broken shards of board and tossing them to the side. When the wood was away, a lump was left on the ground. It did not move and was covered in the white silk lining of the coffin. Jacob was afraid to touch it. *Who knows what's beneath that cloth? Who knows what condition it's in*, he thought.

Mr. Nibbles, however, didn't hesitate. He grabbed the white cloth with his teeth and began to pull it off, working backwards with his little legs. The silk pulled away and revealed the lifeless body of a man, his long grey beard clearly visible from beneath his face down body.

Mr. Nibbles and Jacob both moved in on the man. Jacob pulled him over, using the man's shoulder as a handle.

"Professor von Niblick! Professor von Niblick!" Jacob yelled at the lifeless face. Mr. Nibbles licked the man's cheek and whimpered. Remembering a move he had seen on TV movies before, Jacob slapped the lifeless body, but only lightly; too lightly, he realized. The dog barked in the man's face and Jacob again yelled "Professor! Professor!" his voice then tapered off to a mere whisper. "Please, Professor, be alive. I'm sorry it took us so long to get here. Please be alive!"

He was losing hope by the second. Jacob flipped von Niblick's hand over, pulled the sleeve of his tweed coat up to expose his wrist and fumbled for a pulse.

"Not even cold and ya be stealing me watch, Bearer?"

Jacob jumped back.

The man's eyes opened and he smiled; then coughed violently and gasped for air in great breaths.

"Professor! You're alive!" Jacob called down to the man.

The dog leaped up and down next to the head of professor Chadwick von Niblick and then licked the man's face. The professor smiled between coughs and finally said, "Jacob, lift me and prop me up against the wall so I can catch my breath."

Jacob came around the professor and put his hands underneath the man's armpits. He lifted and then turned the man around. The professor bent his knees and pushed back with his heels in the ground. When he reached the wall, Jacob stepped aside and the professor leaned back against the stones. He took long and slow draws of air and closed his eyes. Jacob could read the pain on his face.

"Do you need a hospital?" Jacob asked.

The man shook his head to indicate "no," but did not open his eyes.

For more than half an hour, the three sat against the wall silently as von Niblick collected himself. Finally, the professor broke the silence with, "Well, then, I'm as good as I'm going to get for awhile. We'd better get moving before we get caught and have to explain these stones and the broken coffin and all."

"And don't forget the big hole up there," Jacob was pointing to the top of the wall and the higher level of ground. "Old Nibbles thought he could tunnel down to you and made kind of a big mess!"

"Let's go, then," von Niblick said as he pushed himself up. "To the abbey, boys, that's the place we'll be safest. Come on."

"What about this mess?" Jacob asked.

"This mess? Well, let's let the archeologists deal with it. They will have a fine time 'discovering' a new tomb then, won't they? Or, maybe the alien hunters will come to find a new landing spot for UFO's where Nibbs dug his hole," the professor replied. "Or, maybe even a dragon myth will be started! Imagine that!" He led the other two up out of the lower ground and then out of the ruins of the ancient nunnery and toward the abbey church.

The Welsh Sanctuary

Von Niblick and Jacob snuck into the abbey church without being seen, or so they believed. von Niblick made a quick scan of the interior of the abbey and pointed Jacob to the four stained glass windows with their images of four saints: Margaret of Scotland, Columba, Bridget, and Patrick.

"Iona is a sacred island, Jacob, but we can still meet danger everywhere but in here and in the small chapel of Oran in the cemetery nearby," Professor von Niblick explained. "This is hallowed ground and no force would dare attack us within the sanctuary. That does not mean there are not spies even here, so let us talk quickly, carefully and quietly."

Jacob was so happy to have saved the professor's life that he just stared into the man's eyes and puffed himself up with pride.

"Jacob, more than just saving me, I am glad you are here for another reason. Quickly, let me see that ring of yours. You do have it, don't you?"

"Of course," Jacob answered as he slipped the ring of Isildane off his right hand and cautiously presented it to von Niblick while keeping it well concealed between them in the pew. From beneath his long coat, the professor pulled a large fold of leather. He laid it on his lap and unfolded it. The large swath of leather turned out to be nothing more than a way to protect and carry what was within.

As von Niblick pulled back the last flap, Jacob could see a much older and stiffer piece of leather, which was wrought with gold. "This is the long-lost cover of the *Book of Kells*. Ever heard of it, Master Boyd?"

Jacob shook his head and answered, "No."

"Oh, Master Boyd, you have so much to learn; so very, very much to learn. What do they teach you in those American schools, anyway? Well, never mind about that now. The *Book of Kells* is the most beautiful book ever created by the hands of man. It is an illuminated manuscript of the greatest story ever told. Its pages, all made of vellum, which is thin leather, are rich in beautiful drawings of animals, people, and symbols. Columban monks here produced it on the Isle of Iona more than a thousand years ago. After repeated attacks by vikings and other enemies, the monks moved the book to the abbey at Kells in Ireland. There the Vikings attacked again and again. The monks heroically defended the book for two centuries. Then, in 1006, just over one thousand years ago, the book was stolen. Three months later it was found and returned to the abbey but it had been buried and was damaged. Most importantly, there were pages missing as was the cover. This is that cover, Jacob. It has not been seen but by a few unrecorded souls for more than a thousand years. The jewels that once adorned the cover are gone, as you can see."

"Now, if I don't miss my guess, the gem that completed your ring also fits into this cover. Now, let's see here." The two looked down upon the ancient flap of leather. There were four indentations, roughly of the same size. In the middle of the four oval indentations were two long and narrow indentations. One ran horizontally; another vertically. Together they connected in the center of the front cover and separated the four stones into four corners.

von Niblick took Isildane's ring and pushed it down into several of the holes and then removed them without result. He took his right index finger and moved it around the indentations to clean them of the sediments of ages past. He blew into the holes as a final method to clean them of dust. He tried again. This time a smile crossed his face as he twisted the ring into a hole that seemed to better fit the shape of the gem. He twisted clockwise and then lifted. The ring came up from the ancient leather, but the gem did not. Once again, Jacob's ring looked like it did more than a year ago and before he found the red stone to complete it in the catacombs in Edinburgh. Jacob felt a shiver cross his shoulders and he grew worried. von Niblick, sensing Jacob's concern, patted him on the knee and said, "no worries, lad, your ring will be complete again here in a quick bit." von Niblick lowered the ring again and twisted in the opposite direction. The red gemstone again left one of its ancient homes and re-entered its place within the gold work of the ring.

"Just as I suspected, Master Boyd." von Niblick looked around the chapel again before continuing. "You see, Jacob, the gems on the cover were all very powerful parts of the ancient treasures returned by Isildane. Just like that sporran of yours and the sword you now carry, and the ring you wear. It was decided long ago that the treasures were too powerful and valuable to be kept together and had to be separated, for the good of the order that protected them and of the wider world. The gems once decorated the *Book of Kells*. It is written that when the treasures again are needed, they will be found. But, Jacob, prophecy is not clear on *who* will find them—friends of the power that guided Isildane on his quest, or its enemies. We must insure the right conclusion to that prophecy."

"What about the story that you said was held under that cover?" Jacob asked. "You said it was part of a great story. Is it the story of Isildane?"

"Oh, no, Jacob." von Niblick answered. "It held the greatest story ever told in the history of man. That is surely true. But Isildane and what he did is but a reflection of the greater story this cover once held and the Columban monks once copied."

Jacob looked a bit confused but remained silent.

"But while we rest, I should tell you about how we got here today— or at least how *I* got here today. You got here through a story of your own, I presume, and to that next."

Jacob nodded his head but said nothing. He glanced from his own ring to the cover of the *Book of Kells* as von Niblick wrapped it back up to protect it from any prying eyes.

"You will remember that rubbing you did of the tomb from Tron Kirk last year, won't you?"

"Of course," Jacob responded. He had often daydreamed about being back in that shop in Edinburgh. He often re-imagined the moment when the mysterious symbols began showing up on his black construction paper. He saw the lion and the deer slip again onto the paper while he rubbed the colored wax stick over the slab of stone. "I have yours that we exchanged. It's hanging in my room at home."

"Yes, well, I have continued to work on the symbols that you uncovered and connecting them with the ancient prophecies and the stories I have translated from Sporrai history. The stag that emerged from behind the knight, upon very close inspection, was made up of much smaller symbols that included animals and initials right out of the *Book of Kells*. I put the clues together and believed it must be showing the location of the lost cover of the book. The leather from the hide of the stag was used to create the original, I knew that. Looking at the hide outline on the rubbing and seeing the tiny symbols used to create it, helped me understand that it would be found where it was expected; that is, where it was created, right here on Iona."

"I wrapped up your rubbing, packed a bag, and had Gladys Lafoon make me a lunch. Then I headed out on my way here. Unfortunately, in the shadows of Cowgate Street, someone was lurking and waiting for me to leave. They followed me to my motorcycle and then jumped me. Must have been an iron bar or something like it that smashed into the back of my skull."

"When I awoke, I was in one of the sporrai sanctuaries in Wales. They told me I had been found unconscious in an alley in Edinburgh, but I had my doubts. I would later discover I had been unconscious for days and when I came to and wanted to move on, my 'friends' would not let me leave, no matter how much I protested about the urgency of my getting here to Iona. You see, Jacob, I think they are not my friends anymore at all. There has been a poison that has seeped into the Sporrai and I am no longer sure where it is safe or who can be trusted. We are a remnant, Jacob, nothing more than a remnant now." von Niblick looked sad and solemn as he spoke.

"After several days of gaining my strength, I made a break to get out of the sanctuary. Fortunately, I am old and served there once. I know where the secret doors are and late one night after the nurses had made their last rounds for the evening, I made my plans take flight."

"I made it out of my room undetected—though they had me in one of those infernal hospital gowns with no back, you know! How those got into a sporrai sanctuary I'll never know! That was my first order of business, Jacob, getting some real clothes to cover my naked back end. Not that I'm ashamed of my nakedness, you see, but it would be mighty hard to sneak out of anywhere while I looked as I did. I found some where I knew I would, in the locker room attached to the baths. Fortunately, a gent about my size had been taking in the baths and, well, let's just say he probably had plenty of room to hang his towel in his locker when he came out. Though I bet he clung to that towel tightly! No worries, though, Lad, I have already made amends for my *appropriation* of his goods and sent him enough money to cover his loss and then some."

"I nearly was caught in that locker room, though, when another man came out of the steam room just as I was about to dress. Thinking fast, I grabbed two towels and wrapped my hair in one and this old beard of mine in another. Why, I must have looked like some fat Egyptian pharaoh with my hair all done up and beard twisted in a towel, but it kept the man from recognizing me, at least. I kept my head down and moved out of there just as soon as I could tie my new shoes.

"Next, I knew the secret passageways behind the western walls but had to make my way into the dining hall to get to the hidden door next to the fireplace. Middle cherub on the left, you know, remember always to check the middle one first if there are three—we have been unimaginative that way. I snuck down the hall keeping close to the walls and pausing wherever I could find a safe corner along the way. When I reached the door of the dining hall, I paused again. Something just started to eat at me. Have you ever had that feeling? That feeling that wells up in your mind, but you feel in your gut as if something were taking little bites of your belly and you couldn't stop them until you could figure something out?"

A bit confused, but very interested in the professor continuing his story, Jacob nodded his head.

"Aye, I figured ya did. Well, I had that feeling and it told me it was not leaving until I figured out more about what was going on. Me, imagine it, me, the translator of ancient Sporrai texts, having to sneak around one of the Sporrai sanctuaries! So I took a quick look into the dining hall and saw no one was there, as one might expect of a dining hall in the early hours of the morning. I made my way over to the fireplace and manipulated the old cherub, which obviously had not been moved in some time, and entered the passageways behind the walls. Up I went on the old metal ladder that was bolted into the wall and then up to the conference rooms and studies. I'd guessed that if there were any meetings taking place at that hour, it would be up at that level."

"Sure enough, as I approached the wall of the old Scott Reading Room, I heard voices. At first, they were difficult to uncover. Then, I approached the back wall of the fireplace. Fortunately, it was a warm summer night in Wales and no fire was burning. I was able, then, to slide a block out of the back of the fireplace ever so slowly and carefully and just enough to stick my ear in the crack. I could not risk moving the block enough to see who was in the room, but I recognized a voice or two, I do believe."

"I listened as long as I thought I could, Jacob, but eventually someone would come check on me in my room and I knew I had to be out of the house before they did. What I heard is why you are here, Master Boyd. I would not have used the enchiridion to summon you or Nibbs just to save my life. I have lived long and would gladly pass on and to better things, but I didn't have that choice. I needed to get this information to you and to get you out of that school you were attending."

"You see, what I discovered is that the Welsh sanctuary has become the headquarters in Europe for a conspiracy within the Sporrai. Some of the Order have simply lost their faith and their way and, as such, have become the dupes of the more sinister element. In every part of the world, Jacob, there are those who are weak of faith and who would put their trust in that paper in their pocket books more than the great power. They are easy marks for the evil that would manipulate them."

Jacob squirmed in his seat and glanced from Niblick's face down to the ancient leather cover in the man's lap. He said nothing but his interest was piqued and that sense of nervous cold started to come over his limbs again.

"I have a good idea it is a man named Furangle that is behind this."

Jacob's butt lifted off the seat as he eagerly interrupted. "Sir, Furangle, yes, that is the name of the guy at Iona Academy – Furangle! He has a daughter named Lucy Furangle who is now in charge of security," Jacob said with incredulity.

"Lucy Furangle, you don't say," the professor then crushed the names together with a visible shiver. "Lucy Furangle; Lucifer Angle," he pronounced, "It must be him for there is no other who would name their daughter such a sickening name as that. Just inviting evil, he is!" von Niblick paused for a moment as he looked down at the floor, then shook himself out of his world of thought and turned again to Jacob.

"Yes, it must be Furangle, then. What is his role at Iona, Jacob?"

"Well, sir, he's chairman of the board and seems to be pulling the strings. The old headmistress has resigned and Mr. Furangle seems to have picked Mr. Finnius Creech to become the new headmaster," Jacob answered.

"The headmistress resigned? Abigail Witherspoon? Impossible, I tell ya! She would never leave her post. She is one of us, you know, and a good, trusted soul. She cannot be one of them and cannot have resigned. I just don't believe it possible. Tell me more, then—quickly."

Jacob walked von Niblick through the changes at Iona, including his kidnapping and his conversations with Ramos Kirk and the others.

"What are they up to? What are they up to?" von Niblick mumbled to himself. I'll try to contact Kirk or MacGregor later, but we will have to leave that problem to them for now. We have our own problems, Jacob."

"It seems," the professor went back to his story, "those who are twisted within the Sporrai, have cracked some of the ancient codes and have discovered some of the hidden clues that were created long ago when our forefathers decided that the treasures of Isildane were to be broken up and hidden around the world to keep them out of the hands of the 'new men' who were coming along with their wishes to use the powers to rework the world or make a profit. What is more troubling still, lad, is that it looks like they have a Bearer in their power now."

"Remember in Edinburgh when I explained the ancient prophecies to you and how our fathers predicted that there would come an imposter in the form of a Keeper and so they made it impossible for any Keeper to enter the most sacred places?"

Jacob nodded his head for he would never forget that feeling he had when he realized he would have to go alone into the catacombs beneath the Edinburgh streets to look for *Lia Fail,* the Stone of Destiny. He had to go because no Keeper was permitted to enter.

"Well, it looks like they have a Bearer that they are squeezing for information or that they have corrupted. I don't know who it is or how this has happened, but it is the most troubling development since the first signs started pointing us to the rift opening within the Sporrai. Have you met any other Bearers, Jacob?"

"Not that I know of, besides, Ian, I mean. But you know him because you helped him with his little kelpie problem," Jacob whispered back.

"Of course, but it cannot be Ian, for the magic has slipped out of Ian's life as his mind has lost the memory of what has happened and his imagination has lost the understanding that came with the sporran he inherited. He failed his tests, so I can't believe it's him. He couldn't tell them much, right?" The man spoke to convince himself more than to ask a question.

"Then there are others like me, Professor?"

"Not exactly like you, Jacob. There are other sporrans, twelve to be exact, though they are not all carried at one time. But, you also bear a ring that has not been worn in centuries; so, no, there are none quite like you. You probably have come into contact with other Bearers from time to time. One rainy day when you were out with your parents and a car went by that drew you to watching it head down the street and out of sight for some unknown reason. Or, perhaps one day in town there was a certain girl who captured your imagination, though you don't know why, and you thought about her and pictured her on and off through the day. Could always be just a touch of infatuation, of course—but it could also be that she carried with her something cut from the same stag as your sporran. Remember, most who encounter the magic have no idea what has happened to them. Only the lucky few … or perhaps I should say that only the *unlucky* few are given the power to comprehend what is happening around them or to know that they are part of anything special at all. Your old friend Ian was given that power, but failed his tests and now should remember nothing of what happened."

"But, if you know so much, why don't you know who are Bearers now and who these people might have control over?" Jacob asked.

"There are protections within the Order, Jacob—just as there are in life, I suppose. If any of us knew all, we would all be tempted with using that power for selfish ends, or even using it for what we think are good ends. None can be trusted with such omniscience and power—not even you and me."

As they spoke, the occasional worshiper or tour group walked around the edge of the abbey. Jacob and von Niblick paid them little attention. von Niblick was beginning to explain how he had found the cover of the *Book of Kells* but was soon afterwards ambused and left to die in the coffin when a man entered the abbey.

A deep voice arose from behind them. "Well, what do we have here?"

Jacob and von Niblick both turned with a start. Jacob felt a shiver cross down his back and he winced. Seeing the reaction, the man smiled a wicked smile.

"So, Niblick, I see they let you out of Wales, did they? And, you found a little friend to play with, too. How quaint. Just worshiping, I suppose?" The man stood with his head slightly cocked to the right, his hands resting on the silver tip of a black walking stick.

"Good to see you, too, Mortimer, though I didn't think your kind ventured into abbeys and such very often."

"Just historical curiosity that brings me here, nothing more. Who is your little friend?" Jacob stood still and tried hard to look confident and strong as the man glared at him.

"A boy on study holiday from America. I promised his father last year that I would have him back for another visit and am taking him through the Hebrides," von Niblick answered.

Unconvinced, the man nodded slowly.

"We were just taking a wee rest before heading back out on the Pilgrim's Trail, you know," the professor saw a chance to cut off the conversation and took it. "I suppose we should be getting along. If we want to see the island before the ferry heads back tonight, we had better get going, Wilmore." von Niblick was looking at Jacob, but Jacob was momentarily stunned that von Niblick had just referred to him as 'Wilmore.' "Come now, lad," von Niblick was nudging Jacob down the row. "Well, I suppose we will see you around, Mortimer," the professor shot back over his shoulder.

"I'm sure you will. Good luck on your trek, Wilmore!" Jacob didn't immediately turn, but he soon realized he was supposed to pretend he was Wilmore and respond when his name was called. He turned and gave a small wave but said nothing. The two walked down the stone aisle toward the door and exited without looking back.

"Jacob, you are not safe here with me anymore. Not outside the abbey. If Mortimer suspects anything he might come after us, but we couldn't stay in there near him and have him question us."

Jacob instinctively reached for his sporran and felt it beneath his shirt. It gave him a feeling of some comfort.

"Call out to Nibbles and locate him. Get yourself back down Pilgrim's Trail to the beach and get him to fly you to the Island of Mull. He will know where to take you."

Jacob just stood looking at the professor. "But what about you?"

"What happens to me is of no concern right now. You have your enchiridion with you?"

"Yes."

"Then we will be in contact that way. For now, go!" the professor forcefully ordered the boy and then pushed him in the direction of the other buildings near the abbey.

"But," Jacob stammered as a tear welled in his eye. He could tell something was terribly wrong in the professor's voice and there was a hint of fear he had never seen in the man's eyes. von Niblick turned away from Jacob and watched the door of the abbey for the man with the black walking stick to emerge again.

Jacob called out to Mr. Nibbles in his mind, but as he did, a terrible pain came down into his brain like a dropping garage door. He stumbled back as his eyes went slightly blurry.

CRIES IN THE NIGHT

Jenny spent a disturbed evening trying to make sense out of what was happening. Occasionally she would let herself drift into a state of denying it was all real. Those moments would not last long as reality would creep back into Jenny's imagination. She would know it was somehow true, even if she could not make out the complete shape or details of the truth she was living in. She remembered nights lying awake as a little girl trying to convince herself that the scary shapes were but shadows from her toys. She wished she could be home and thought much about her parents and her neighborhood and her own safe bed overlooking Longbranch Drive.

She didn't sleep well. About one o'clock in the morning, she awoke as clear-headed as if it were mid day. She looked over and saw her roommate was sleeping soundly, cuddling her pink teddy bear under her chin. Jenny turned off her bed and walked to the window. The night was dark, but there were spotlights around the entrances to buildings. That was not unusual. But there were other lights, too; they came from her left and over by the gymnasium where the new silver trailers had been placed.

Jenny opened the window and hung out into the night air. Lights were moving back and forth in the trees beyond the tennis courts. She felt that disquieting feeling creep over her. It was that feeling she remembered from when she was younger and something strange would happen after she had gone to bed; an odd sound in the kitchen, a door slam in the basement, a neighbor's dog suddenly barking, a shadow in her toy box that looked curiously like a monkey wielding an automatic revolver.

She kept her courage and listened. Machinery was running off behind the gym. She could guess it now. The lights were from equipment or trucks or other vehicles moving back and forth in the area near the gym, the tennis courts, and the new trailers. She wondered what they were doing in the middle of the night. The steady humming of the machines was then punctuated by a loud animal scream coming from the same direction. It was shrill and seemed to emanate from pain.

Jenny jumped back, static electricity attracting her hair to the curtains. Her heart raced. She quickly shut the window, locked it, pulled the curtain, and slid nervously back under her covers. She looked over enviously at Elizabeth's teddy bear. She bundled her blanket and squeezed it tight to her chest and neck. Eventually her mind would slow and she would drift off to sleep. Until then, that horrible animal scream replayed itself in her mind and she puzzled on what could be happening. She wished Jacob was still on campus.

The students had begun to settle into a new routine at Iona Academy. They had new classes and new teachers. They had less athletics and no martial arts. They had new computers in every classroom. The vestiges of the old orders of Dirks and Targes were being systematically dismantled. A couple of Targes had been caught sneaking out in the night to steal away some of the banners on campus to protect them from being destroyed, but most students seemed to be accepting the new order with a quiet resolve.

After breakfast, Jenny headed directly toward Trailer #2, though she wanted to visit Will. As she walked down the rocky road toward the trailers, the little boy nicknamed puddles was sitting by the road.

"Good morning," Jenny said and smiled at him. The boy didn't look up from his rocks. Jenny hesitated and considered saying more, but moved on.

"Good morning," Puddles answered quietly as she passed.

Jenny turned. Puddles hadn't looked up. She smiled and turned to head on her way.

"Do you like animals?"

Jenny stopped and turned again. Puddles was still not looking up from the rocks sitting in front of his crossed legs.

"Do I like animals?" Jenny repeated his question. "Sure, I like animals very much."

"The dogs and most of the horses are safe. Hidden beyond the trees," the boy said.

Jenny looked around the area to see if anyone was looking. Then she knelt down and said, "What do you know about them?"

The boy didn't answer. Jenny waited a minute and then said, "Well, I hope they will stay safe." She then got up to head on her way.

"But," the boy stopped her again, "the other animals are not safe."

"The other animals? What other animals?" Jenny asked as she knelt.

The boy did not answer but stood and said, "I have to go home now." Before turning away he added, "I'd like to see the lion. If you see him, tell him hello." He dropped the rocks from his hand and ran across the field toward the small white house where he lived with his father on the edge of Iona Academy.

Jenny watched him go. *A lion?* she wondered.

Jenny was given menial tasks in Trailer #2. She shredded some old papers. She copied down some numbers from a computer screen onto charts. She made copies of papers she didn't care to try to understand. Through the day, however, she thought of the scream in the night and of the machines and of Puddles. When she was dismissed for lunch, she didn't go straight to the cafeteria, but instead she walked behind the trailers, by the tennis courts, and up to the older tree-lined campus road that would lead her back to the cafeteria.

Behind the trailers, she saw what the machines had been working on long into the night. Trees were pushed down and the ground scarred deep beyond the tennis courts. If she hadn't seen the lights the night before or the machines lined up nearby, Jenny would have guessed she was looking at a fresh crater made by a dropped bomb. She wondered if they were building a pond. She walked along the edge and up toward the road.

After lunch, Jenny walked to the infirmary to visit Will. He was sleeping soundly when she arrived, however, so she left him a note but did not wake him. On her way back to Trailer #2, she looked around as best she could for any sign of the men she had met in Ashland mansion or the small little man who helped her escape the Spur and Spoon and then return to it. There was no sign of them and little Puddles wasn't around either. She would have welcomed a word with him and asking about the animals he mentioned, especially the lion. His strange words intrigued her.

The black and red painting above his desk had changed daily but so gradually that Mr. Creech hadn't realized it. The blacks had swirled away from the reds. The smoky curls had retracted into solids. The reds were moving out toward the ends of the frame starting to form a background. The blacks were concentrating toward the center and were forming the vague outline of something new.

"Have you found the Boyd kid yet?" the voice was shouting into the other end of the phone.

"Well, no sir," Mr. Creech answered nervously. "We are very sure he is not to be found here on campus or in the area. Something must have happened to him, maybe an accident in the woods somewhere, I suppose, or maybe he has made it home." Mr. Creech was speaking quickly and without breathing.

"I didn't put you there for 'maybes', Mr. Creech," the voice shouted back. The man continued, "What about Frost, has she been able to make any advance yet in the experiments?"

"Well, sir, I don't know that, sir," Mr. Creech responded. "I know she is working hard. The lab trailers are all up and operational. The patient has arrived and so have the animals. We are keeping them down in the pens where the student's pets used to be—whatever might have happened to them I can't say."

"And," the man interrupted, "how may I ask do you plan to keep them a secret if they are down at the pens where students will likely go to check on their pets?"

"All taken care of, sir. You see, sir." Mr. Creech was proudly now preparing to brag on his plans. "We have told the students that all the pets are fine and getting the best of care. We are just keeping them in protective custody during the transition and while all the machines and such are on campus. We have placed large tents all around the cages with thick canvas walls tied down tight. "

"Well, see to it that they don't get curious! I'm only leaving those kids there at the school at all, you will do well to remember, because *you* want to do your own silly little educational experiments on them and because it provides some cover for our real project." The voice continued its aggressive tone, "If *anything* goes wrong, just one little puke kid gets down there and discovers our animals *or anything*, those kids are gone and Dr. Frost gets full control of that little academy. Is that clear?"

"Nothing will go wrong, sir!" Mr. Creech responded.

"That was not the question, the question was, 'is that clear?'"

Mr. Creech felt frustrated, frightened, and humiliated but he answered with only a slight hesitation, "It is."

"Now, how is my darling little Lucy?" the man asked.

"She's quite fine, sir. She's doing a fine job as student head of security and you will be proud of how just yesterday she busted three former Targes who decided to bring out their old badges and wear them to dinner. I tell you she moved her people into place and took them out before they could even cause a scene for the others."

"I suggest, then, Mr. Creech, that you have three good examples there to share with the other students and teach them all some needed lessons."

Mr. Creech smiled and nodded his head as he replied, "a fine idea." As he did, a bit more black paint wisped over toward the center of the painting; floating from backdrop to foreground.

Outside the Abbey

Through blurry vision, Jacob could see the door of the abbey open and the man exit and calmly slip a black felt hat onto his head. He tried again to send the message to Nibbles but again the wall of pain came down through his skull and kept him from reaching out. Fear overtook him as he watched the man named Mortimer approach von Niblick. Jacob stumbled back behind one of the buildings and shook his head to try to clear it. He tried to concentrate anew, but kept finding himself peeking around the corner watching the men who seemed to be in a heated conversation.

Jacob pressed his head back against the wall hard and he felt a twinge of pain in the back of his skull. For a second he marveled at the sensation and felt liberated. Then the wall of pain returned. *The new pain,* he thought, *drove out the old pain. Maybe that's it, if I can cause myself pain, maybe it will drive out that pain that is blocking me from getting to Nibbles; if for just a moment.*

Jacob turned again for a quick peek at the two men who were still standing opposite one another in front of the abbey. Then he turned back around and bounced the back of his head into the wall. The slight pain did drive out the wall he felt in his skull, but only for a shadow of a second. Knowing he had to cause himself even more pain if he was to break down the wall, he pulled up his right sleeve, took a deep breath, and smashed the back of his elbow onto a rough part of a stone block. The pain was slightly slower getting to his brain, but it was more powerful and the scraped layer of skin insured it would stay longer. As some drops of blood dripped down his arm, Jacob seized the moment to send a mental picture before the wall again came crashing down in his skull.

Bearer, I'm over here, behind the cross. Jacob could now hear Mr. Nibble's thoughts but could not see him. *Just clear your mind and be calm. Someone has cast a spell to block your thoughts from getting to me. Just be calm. We have a crack in it now, let's keep it open. I am behind the great cross. Just try to be calm and clear your mind. I will make my way over there to you as soon as I can, but am a bit stuck out here.* The little dog was crouched behind the stone base of the great Celtic cross that stood just yards from the entrance of the abbey.

Jacob searched the shadow behind the cross, but could see no sign of the dog. He didn't know if he was to fear only Mortimer, or if there were others waiting. He took his right hand bearing the ring of Isildane and opened the flap of his sporran. He felt it grow heavy. He reached in and found the gelatinous dragon handle of his sporran blade. He looked around and, seeing no on-lookers, he pulled it quickly from its home and brought it to rest again at his side. By this time, he could hear the professor and the man called Mortimer yelling at one another, though he could not make out the words.

Jacob, it is time we made a move. I can't sneak out from behind this cross unseen. So I'll make a scene. As Jacob watched across the green grassy yard, he saw the little brown ball of fur emerge from behind the cross and head directly at Mortimer and the professor. Being able to see his friend at that moment gave Jacob a fleeting second of peace, which was quickly shattered as the dog ran directly up to the men and started to growl and bark angrily at them. *What is he doing?* Jacob wondered.

von Niblick was first to pay attention to Mr. Nibbles and yelled at him angrily, "Get out of here you mutt!" As he did, he swung his left arm down at the dog and Mr. Nibbles went tumbling over himself and then ran off yelping down toward the village. Jacob stood in shock as he had just witnessed the professor intentionally hurt his old friend and Jacob's protector.

"Now," the professor was saying to the man, "I told you the boy knows nothing. I am just doing a favor for his father."

"I saw him wince when I entered the abbey. He is a Bearer, isn't he? You haven't taught him to conceal his emotions and control himself yet, and that will be the downfall of you both, Nibblick! So, the rumors are correct, aren't they? You have found a Bearer who you think is the chosen one, haven't you? Too bad for you all that stuff is just rubbish. There was no Isildane and no such power to rise again and help in the time of need. There is just power and never was anything else. Maybe I will spare you, just for the pleasure of you being around to see our ultimate triumph over your backward ways, Nibblick." The man made a feint to walk away then turned quickly, his walking staff now turned to a long silver blade.

Jacob could see the man raise the blade as he turned toward the professor and then lunge forward. "Nooooo!" Jacob yelled involuntarily as he started out across the grass, his fear temporarily subdued. von Niblick stumbled backward as the man pulled the sword hilt back. Hearing Jacob, the man turned and smiled like a hungry cat spying easy prey. A bit of blood dripped from Mortimer's blade.

He became distracted by something behind Jacob. The boy didn't turn but kept running toward his fallen friend and mentor. Behind him, a dragon emerged from the shadows and roared.

I'm getting you out of here, Nibblus announced.

Jacob fell on his knees next to von Niblick and bent over him. The man was making a gurgling sound but then whispered, "*Book of Kells*, get the cover out of here," and opened his coat. Jacob grabbed the ancient leather cover, slightly damp with von Niblick's blood, and looked into the man's knowing eyes.

The dragon made a run over the head of Mortimer, who backed off slightly. While the man was off-balance, the dragon yelled into Jacob's mind to be ready and he would pick him up. As he swooped in after Jacob, however, the boy turned and shoved the cover for the book into the closing talons of Nibblus Maximus. *Get it out of here, I'm staying*, Jacob yelled back defiantly as the dragon looked down in confusion.

"Jacob, no, go!" von Niblick uttered. Jacob ignored him and rolled over and up onto his feet, his sword clutched in both hands. He took a defensive posture.

The man laughed and said, "Now, laddie, you know I don't mean you any harm, don't you? I'm sure you are a wonderfully talented lad with a great future and I can help that. This is not between you and me but between the future and the past; the dead arm of the past that just got punctured." He looked down at von Niblick.

Jacob said nothing but stood ready for what he assumed would be a fight, if a short lived one. He knew it was likely the man would cut into him like he had von Niblick. But he was not going to leave his friend alone to die.

The man started making an arch with his sword. It spun in his hand and then came to rest at his side. "Just leave him, lad. Come with me and you can keep your dragon, of course, and then you and I can work together to do great things for the world, lad. What is your name?"

I'm coming back, get von Niblick up, Jacob heard in his mind. He bent down and, without taking his eye off Mortimer, began to lift von Niblick. "Come on, Professor, you have to help me, I'm not strong enough," Jacob whispered in desperation. *Please give me strength,* he pleaded silently as he lifted. von Niblick had enough life to help pull his feet under himself and Jacob lifted. The dragon had dropped the cover of the *Book of Kells* discretely on the opposite side of the hill called Dun I and was quickly bearing down on the scene in front of the abbey.

Concentrating on Jacob, the man did not see the soft blue hues of the dragon as it descended in the sunlight. Jacob struggled against the urge to look up and back, so he would not give the dragon's position away. He listened to the dragon's count in his head. *Three, two, one, now Jacob, jump!*

Show Trial

"Tell Mr. Dave to give the kids an extra sugary dessert tonight at dinner," Mr. Creech said into the phone. "And get word out that everyone is to assemble in the Great Hall tonight at 7:00 PM."

Finnius Creech hung up the phone and stood. He smiled, proud of what he was about to do, as he leaned on the window frame and looked out across the lawn. Students moved from one classroom building to another as he watched. They seemed oblivious to what was about to unfold in their lives.

Looking to his left as he peered out his open window, Mr. Creech could see the front door to the library. The door opened and out started what looked like a parade of walking art. The paintings all had legs; very human legs. Some had heads, depending on the size of their frames. The old artwork from the library walls was being taken away. Students had been given the task of removing them all. The very large black and white drawing of Don Quixote on his horse Rosanante was taken out first. For a generation that skinny Spanish knight and his horse had stood like a welcoming committee to students entering the library. It was rumored that his lance, pointing straight up, was a guide to a secret room above the second floor. The rumor had circulated so long that no one on campus now knew if anyone had ever discovered it. Then there were the battle scenes of Culloden and Bonockburn and of that ancient Celt warrior-king looking to the sky and seeing the St. Andrews cross being made by clouds against the deep blue sky. Then the busts of Robert the Bruce and William Wallace came out together. They were followed by some of America's founding fathers with George Washington leading the way for those other powdered wigs. They were all being taken to a storage room in the horse barn and would be replaced by artwork that the new administration found more suitable for the young people they were trying to create. Mostly, those would be twisted metal sculptures and abstract paintings students could stare at in wonder of what they might be and what the artist had in mind.

Mr. Creech yelled out to the parade, "Get them all, kids, get them all! No need for that old stuff in our *new* Iona! Out with the old, you know! Always out with the old!" Most of the students in the parade of obsolete artwork could not hear their schoolmaster and just continued on toward the stables. Creech closed the window and brushed his hands together as if he was casting off some dust. The new headmaster said to himself, "Yes, no need for that old stuff around here. No need for heroes in *my* Iona!"

At lunch, there was tension in the air. Every table seemed alive with conversations about what was happening on campus. The announcement of a special evening meeting in the Great Hall seemed full of possibilities. The more optimistic kids were wondering if Miss Witherspoon might be returning or if there might be a surprise dance or one of the old feasts that used to be held once a month. The more pessimistic kids thought the school itself might be shutting down or something more terrible had happened to their former headmistress. Others wondered if they were finally going to find out what kinds of classes and clubs and activities were going to be implemented when the dust all settled from the changes. There were a few older students that were keeping to themselves and looking regularly over at Jenny. Jenny, however, didn't take any note of them.

Jenny left lunch earlier than most of her classmates. They had more time to relax as there was not much to do right then at Iona. There were not yet enough new teachers on campus to replace the ones that left or were fired, so classes and activities were going in shifts with the "down time" of the students being spent in the gym. Most of the boys played basketball. A few of the girls shot hoops on the side or played hopscotch. Others of the girls just sat in the stands talking and giggling or reading until their numbers were called and they could go to class or activity. Unlike most of the students, Jenny had a job to report back to.

Jenny wondered what was happening around them. She didn't dare mention her uneasiness to others. She knew any mention might force to the surface a passing mention of the Remnant, or of Ashland or the small man that helped her escape the Spur and Spoon. She resolved to keep it all to herself. Enveloped in a fog of confusion, she walked absent-mindedly toward the silver trailers.

As she walked, she noticed small movements around her. A pop in the grass to her right, then one to her left. She stopped walking and looked up from the ground. Jenny saw nothing out of the ordinary. She looked left. Nothing. She looked right just in time for a small pebble to hit against her cheek. The rock stung slightly, but scared her more than it hurt. Her hand shot to her cheek. "Ow," she exclaimed.

Jenny still saw nothing and continued to turn in circles looking for the cause of the flying pebble. She stepped forward again, trying to make it seem like nothing had happened. If there was someone playing a trick on her, Jenny was determined not to let them be gratified in the success. Another pebble hit off her right arm. She spun just in time to see movement behind a nearby oak tree. Without hesitating, she rushed at the tree. A small figure jumped out from behind the trunk.

"Puddles!" Jenny exclaimed. "What are you doing throwing rocks at me? I thought we were friends." The part about being friends she said mostly out of pity for the little guy, while the other part was meant to scold.

"I didn't mean to hurt you. I hope I didn't hurt you," the little boy said without making eye contact with the older girl.

"I'm OK, but why did you do that?" Jenny asked.

"I needed to ask you something," the boy replied, now looking around to see if anyone was watching. "Come behind the tree with me."

The oak tree offered very little cover, but it was fat enough at the base to shield them from the windows of most campus buildings.

"What's going on, Puddles? I mean, well," Jenny bent down to look into the boy's eyes more directly. "Do you have a name you want to be called besides Puddles?" she asked with a cock of her head. "You must have another name."

"It's OK, everyone calls me 'Puddles' around here. I don't mind, really."

But Jenny could tell that the boy did mind and so asked him again, "No, really, what is the name your parents call you?"

"Well, Dad sometimes calls me just 'boy' and, well, Mom died a few years ago so she doesn't call me 'Angel' anymore. But at my school they call me Derek."

Jenny was moved by the boy's loss of his mother. "Well, then I'll call you Derek, if you'd like me to," Jenny offered. Her eyebrows rose slightly and she grinned after saying it to show the boy she really did care.

"Alright."

"Now, Derek, what's wrong?"

"Oh, well, you see," the boy was stammering and looking at his feet shuffle between the exposed roots of the tree. "I don't know *your* name—would you tell me *your* name?" he asked as he looked up through the tops of his eyes.

"Of course," Jenny smiled and a little giggle escaped her throat. "I'm Jenny."

"Jenny, they aren't bad boys are they?" Puddles shot the question at her as if it were a rocket that had been lit inside him and was finally let free of its launcher.

"Bad boys? Who are you talking about Derek?"

"The boys that Mr. Creech is going to put on trial! You know, the ones that got caught putting their old badges on. Oh, I did love to watch you all go into that big place down there at night in those robes." Puddles was pointing to the Great Hall.

"What kind of trial, Derek? What boys?" Jenny asked.

"He's going to make an example out of them. That's what I hear. Old

Mr. Creech is going to scare them good and then do something with them so they won't ever set foot here again! I heard him talking about it."

"I don't know what's going on, Derek. But, let's both keep our eyes out and keep in touch, OK?"

"OK," Puddles answered. "But, are they bad boys?"

"No, I'm sure it is not bad to play at the way things used to be, Puddles—I mean," she caught herself, "Derek. I'm sure they are good boys, but this place is just confused right now. That's all. Just confused." *We're all confused*, she thought. "Do you know anything else going on?"

"Well, I know those paintings are all being put into the stables, in an empty stall that used to belong to an old horse called 'Modesty's Mother' that hasn't been around, Dad says, for a generation. I know there are new paintings coming. I know that the animals are in great danger. Do you, Jenny, know anything about the animals yet?"

"I don't Derek, I don't. Tell me again about the animals."

"You heard them cry, haven't you? I hear them cry in the night. I hate these people and what they're doing," Puddles said emphatically as he kicked the tree, trying to show his toughness.

"What are they doing to them, Derek?"

The rest of the students were now exiting the cafeteria and many were moving in their direction.

"Gotta go," the boy said. "I bet you miss your friend, don't you? He was nice to have around," Puddles said as he turned and started to bolt down the road toward his home at the edge of the woods.

"But, what do you know of Jacob?" Jenny shouted after the boy. It was no use, he was moving on now and that was that. Jenny wondered if he feared the other kids or just didn't want to deal with their teasing.

During the afternoon, Jenny started snooping around more in trailer #2. She went through some paperwork and looked at some files when she was left alone. She didn't discover much in her work. Or, perhaps it should be said that she didn't think she found much from her efforts. She did find references to lions and birds and mythical creatures, all with numbers after them, almost as if they had been criminals posing for a mug shot.

At 7:00 PM, all students were called together in what was once called "The Great Hall." Now it went by the name "multi-purpose room" and its dark old wood was in the process of being replaced by wall-to-wall grey carpeting and wall paper of blue with small gold designs. The students all looked around in wonder as they entered. A few of the oldest students were seen wiping a tear or two away at the sight of the room they had loved as the place of the great feasts. The tables were pushed to the edge and temporary grey chairs were formed in lines in the center of the room.

The students talked anxiously about the changes and about what to expect that night. They knew they were to be there, but didn't know why. After they had been seated and were relatively in order, Mr. Finnius Creech marched in the back door and to the front of the room. A group of other administrators and a few of the faculty followed the new head master. They all wore suits. Behind them, three students were led in with Lucy Furangle and some of her guards surrounding them. Jonathan Ballardo, the former head of the Targes, when there was such groups, was first. Then came Erika Christy and George McDonald. They were all older students and members of clan Targe.

The students all looked at one another and wondered what was going to happen.

"Citizens of Iona," Mr. Creech began using his lecture voice, "we have made great strides these past few weeks. Great strides. We have replaced the old divisions with a new harmony. We have removed the old art of war and replaced it with the new images of comfort and compassion. We have done away with the martial arts and replaced them with science and skill-building that will be useful to the new world order. We have come far; dragging this place into the modern world with us!"

"But there have been set-backs. There have been those who have resisted our new project. These three here, for example, have held out. They have clung to the dead arm of the past, reaching through the ages as it does to strangle our creativity and hold us back. 'Their crime?' you ask. Their crime was in the clinging itself, for anyone who clings to the dead past cannot be tolerated among us. They have hidden their old badges of inequality and brought them out to separate themselves from our new covenant."

The three kids shook their head and looked confused. Surely it was not a crime just to keep our old badges and talk about the way things used to be, they thought. The students in the crowd just sat in wonderment.

"Children," Mr. Creech continued, "all of this we have done for you. It is all for you that we work to improve this school. It is for you that we bring about this change. Even for you," the man said as he pointed toward the three boys. "That is what makes this trial so difficult for me," he bit his lower lip and looked down. "It is always so difficult to see young people giving away their lives to the denizens of the cemeteries and the inky monsters of musty books."

"You have been charged, young ones, now how do you plead?"

The three looked at each other and out at the crowd. Finally, Jonathan Ballardo said, "What should we say?"

"Say you're guilty," Lucy Furangle yelled out.

"Guilty?" Erika said. "Guilty of what? Of remembering? Of keeping a few scraps of cloth? Come on!"

Jenny was watching from her seat and shifted to the front edge with anticipation. She had very little contact with Erika, but could tell she liked her spunk very much. She thought she would probably go up to the girl and congratulate her for being so strong when this was over. She hoped they might become friends.

"Exactly guilty of that. Do any of you deny it?" Mr. Creech asked as he walked away from the three and stared toward the far wall. None of the three offered a response. "Hearing no denial, you are found guilty."

The crowd of students mumbled at the ominous word.

"Lucy, take these three to their rooms. For the next week you three will be segregated in your rooms. You will not leave your rooms for any reason but to use the restroom. Meals will be brought to you. Your roommates will be moved to other rooms so you will have no contact with them. Perhaps during the next seven days you will find that you like the new way of doing things and will join the rest of us as new citizens of the new Iona. Take them away, Lucy!"

THE BOOK OF KELLS

239

"Now, as for the rest of you, if you have any left over badges or other items from that old academy of ours, you can turn them in to Lucy or one of her guards with no questions asked. But, do it within the next twenty-four hours or you will suffer the same or a worse fate as these misguided young people." He thrust his arm out straight toward the three convicts.

The students watched their three colleagues being walked out through the back door. Jenny was particularly drawn to watch Erika. As she did, Jenny saw the girl's left hand move and concentrated on it. She strained to see what she thought was Erika giving a slight and subtle 'thumbs up' sign to some of the students watching. She wondered what it meant. *Could there be a wider conspiracy? Or, was she just trying to show she would be OK?* Jenny wondered.

The Black House

Jacob yelled "Now! Up!" into the professor's growingly ashen face. At the same time he jumped as best he could while trying to support von Niblick's weight. von Niblick straightened up and gave what effort he could to raise his feet off the ground. The left front claws of Nibblus Maximus caught around Jacob's left arm. The dragon's right front claws missed von Niblick's arm, but caught just enough of his coat to puncture it and close together. He lifted the man as if he were wearing a harness. The dragon barely got the two out of Mortimer's reach as they passed over. The tip of his upraised blade caught the heel of Jacob's left shoe. Mortimer split the salty air of Iona with curses as he watched the dragon carry the Keeper and the Bearer off to safety.

Nibblus Maximus flew down behind the hill of Dun I and gently let the two down before coasting to a stop a few yards away. *Jacob, are you all right?*

Yes, I think so.

As Jacob caught his breath and brushed himself off, a woman tourist came bounding around the corner of Dun I calling out, "Here sheepy, sheepy. I know there have to be sheepies somewhere around here. Here sheepy, sheepy."

As the woman looked up, she noticed Jacob and began to offer a hello and ask if he had seen any sheep. But, her eyes caught movement behind Jacob before she could finish her thought. It was large and blue movement and was not the sky or the sea.

She screamed.

Startled, Jacob screamed in return.

The woman's hand went to her mouth as horror colored her eyes. She swooned, stumbled, and fell unconscious against the hillside, her yellow visor cocked awkwardly toward the sky. (In fifteen minutes her husband would find her and shake her awake. She would babble about how horrible she looks in the color blue and she would insist they never again go looking for sheep.)

Nibblus Maximus closed his eyes and sighed. *Time to move on, boys. . . big nosed tourists coming in on the right, evil Sporrai Keeper coming in from the left. Jacob, help get the professor on his stomach. Then get up on my back and hang on with everything you've got.*

The professor was now docile and did not say a word. He made every effort to help roll himself onto his stomach. As he did, the dragon walked over and securely sunk both sets of front claws into the back of his coat. Jacob crawled onto the dragon's back and reached low around his neck. The dragon rocked back and forth as he struggled to get into the air with all the added weight. They banked left and then right. They wobbled. Then the dragon got enough air under his wings to flatten out and move north toward the sea.

Jacob did not look back for the man or to see if anyone else was watching. He just buried his head into the dragon's soft flesh and asked, *Where are we going?*

To the Island sometimes known as Carnglass. There is a safehouse there that we must hope has not lost its bearing. We should find shelter there and be able to help our friend heal.

Jacob closed his eyes, said a prayer, and hung onto the dragon with everything he had. They were soon over the water and then turning to head south. It took nearly an hour of struggled flight for the dragon to get the wounded professor and Jacob to their destination and it took such effort that he could barely communicate with Jacob as he flew. Approaching the rocky shore, Jacob opened his eyes when he felt the water spray up into his face. The dragon was approaching the beach too quickly to land and Jacob called to him to slow down.

Just hold until I tell you, Bearer!

Nibblus Maximus turned near the ruins of small homes up the beach and as gently as he could set the unconscious professor down near the one cottage whose roof still appeared intact. He then turned back out to sea, flew about fifty yards, and then turned back again toward land. He dropped his feet gingerly into the water, which sprayed up into Jacob's face and caused him to sputter and spit and struggle to see. Slowing down quickly as the beach approached, they hit in a few feet of water and Nibblus Maximus stumbled the last few yards toward shore.

As Jacob dismounted, the dragon collapsed in exhaustion. Jacob patted his head and thanked him for working so hard to get them there.

The dragon struggled to communicate. *There; take the professor in that house. I don't have anything left to give right now.* The dragon's face fell flat onto the beach and his eyes closed. Over the next few minutes, he would slowly deflate, like an old balloon with a slow leak, until he was no bigger than his normal pug size.

Jacob walked up to the ruins of the old homes. They were single room dwellings that had stood against the rains and salty air since the days of the Vikings. Most of them were now nothing more than stone walls with occasional wooden doors lying off their hinges and rotting. One house was different. Its thatch roof was held on by ropes anchored to small boulders that hung like Stone Age Christmas decorations around the side of the cottage.

Jacob approached the hut cautiously. Taking a large salty breath, he knocked at the door. There was no answer. He knocked and then paused again. There was no reply. He looked at the door and noticed that there was a place for a padlock, but none held the door shut. He pulled the metal plate from around the hook of the lock and slowly pushed it open. Light had already been coming in through a hole in the roof and now was entering through the door. He stepped in and announced himself several times. He was nervous that someone was inside the home or would come along and catch him where he was not supposed to be; perhaps taking him for a thief.

Locals would call this a "black house." Dating back as far as the Vikings, these homes got their name because they have no proper chimney to evacuate the smoke. The peat fires were built right in the middle of the room, the smoke rising up and out the hole built into the thatch roof. Not all the smoke would escape, however, and the decades of residue built up on the stone walls, the thatch roof, and the beams turned them all ebony. To the left of the door was a table, some cabinets, and some cooking utensils. To the right was the strangest bed Jacob had ever seen. An old-fashioned cotters closet bed, it was built of boards all the way up to the ceiling to keep out the drafts. Only a narrow slit was left through which the occupant of the bed could roll onto his mattress. A curtain hung down over the opening to keep the air out and provide some privacy.

Jacob looked curiously at the big box bed and wondered what might be behind the curtain. He angled toward the bed. He pulled his sword and cautiously lifted it toward the curtain. Slowly he placed its blade under the curtain and then, with his heart jumping into his throat, he pulled it up. To his great relief, there was nothing in the bed but some blankets and a pillow.

Jacob retreated from the room and returned to von Niblick. Mr. Nibbles was up licking the professor's face and the injured man was stirring slightly to consciousness.

"Professor, I'm going to drag you into this house now and get you out of the wind." Jacob was not sure he could drag the man, but he knew he needed to try. He also knew Nibblus Maximus would never get through the small door to help, so he was on his own.

Jacob reached under von Niblick's arms and started pulling him backwards, the back of the boy's legs beginning to burn before he got across the threshold and the tendons in his back stretching as far as they could go. To get the man up into the cotter's bed, he had to lift and turn each part of the man's body separately starting at his chest and arms. It was a difficult and uncomfortable endeavor. He stood and stretched once the deed was done and before reaching into the bed again to check the man's breathing and straighten his clothes. Nibbles looked on from the door as Jacob carefully pulled open the slit in the side of the professor's bloody shirt. There was too much dried blood for him to see the nature and size of the wound.

"Nibbles, would you go get this wet?" Jacob tossed a handkerchief he had pulled from the professor's jacket pocket. The pug dog picked it up and scampered out the door and down to the ocean's edge. When he returned, Jacob took the wet rag and began to clean the blackened blood clots from the wound. The professor's skin felt hot and he moaned as Jacob gingerly wiped.

"I don't know what to do! I'm not a doctor," Jacob muttered in frustration. When he got it cleaned, Jacob took the bloody kerchief and tossed it outside the cottage door. He then searched the cabinets for medicine and among the cans of food he found some balm that seemed to be for dogs or sheep, as those were the pictures on the jar's lid. *It's better than nothing*, he reasoned and spread some of the yellow jelly on the professor's wound. He finished his first medical procedure by cutting into strips a white sheet he found at the bottom of the bed. He placed them over the wound.

"Professor, if you can hear me, please get better," Jacob said as he closed his eyes over his mentor and friend.

Night was coming and Jacob could feel the temperature dropping. Along one wall of the cottage was a pile of dark brown blocks stacked like wood. He picked one up and held it to his nose. *It must be peat for the fire*, he guessed. He had read about how the Scots dug the peat bogs into blocks to be dried and burned like wood. He stacked a few logs in the pit in the middle of the floor and then went outside to pick up some of the driftwood he had seen on the ground in front of the cottage.

"Nibbles, how about sharing a bit of that inner fire with us?" Jacob said as he held the wood out in front of him. The pug dog began to swell. When he was fully again into his dragon form, he said, *hold it steady boy, steady.* Jacob saw the dragon draw a large breath and then felt the heat against his face just before he saw it fly through the air. The flame engulfed the tips of the wood branches in Jacob's hands. *Thanks, bud*, the boy said as he moved back into the cottage and stuck the flaming branches under the peat blocks. They soon caught fire.

We're going to need fresh water, Nibbles. Can you look around and see if you can find some for us while I tend the fire to get it going strong? There was a well up from the stone ruins that Nibbles found in short order and he and Jacob brought a bucket of fresh water back to the cabin before nightfall. Jacob was frightened and wasn't sure what to do, but it did not hit him with full force until later that night when he finally stopped working to share with Nibbles a can of beans he found in the cabinet.

Until he settled down for bed, Jacob checked the professor regularly, talked to him, and wet the man's lips with water. He made his bed that night on the floor next to the cotter's bed, pulling some blankets up over him and keeping one on the floor beneath him. He laid his sword down beside his body and touched his sporran periodically for reassurance. Mr. Nibbles curled up into the warm shelter made by the crook of Jacob's bent knees.

Though he had pushed the door tightly shut and latched it from the inside, the door would not keep out all intruders this night. The moon was casting a light silver glow upon the surface of the calm ocean. Far from land, the silver on the surface began gathering itself and moving. As it moved silently over the surface of the depths, the silver grew until it took the form of a figure, fast moving and sleek. It was long and flowing, this silvery figure, like long ribbons billowing behind a kite.

The figure rose off the water's surface as it approached land and became translucent in the cool night air. It moved over the beach and toward the small cottage. It paused for only a second at the sight of the bloody kerchief beside the door, then moved up the outer wall, across the roof, and down into the cottage. Around the room it floated and watched the three as they slept. It brought itself to a stop as if it stood upon wispy feet. If fate had allowed Jacob's eyes to open that night, he would have seen a woman in silvery-white smiling down upon him.

The figure moved toward the professor and then entered his bed. It enveloped his body and moved in and out of his wounds. She kissed him gently upon the forehead and then backed out into the cottage again. She looked at Jacob as if she had longed to see the boy and wished to speak to him. Instead, she leaned down and brushed his hair back from his face.

Twisting in the air, the apparition rose up and out of the hole in the roof
of the cottage.

Lion's Ear

As Jenny walked with the crowd out of the Great Hall, a couple of older students jostled her. At first she thought it was just too many people trying to get through too small a space. She was pushed again. She looked crossly back at the boy who did it, but he did not return her glance. Then she was pushed from another direction. "Hey, what's going on?" she finally said as she spun to face the girl behind her.

"Why, whatever do you mean?" the girl responded.

Jenny didn't say anything but turned back around to continue out the door. Her adrenaline was pumping and she hoped there would not be a larger confrontation.

The boy that pushed her first approached her again and said, "If you think you're special because you're working for *that woman* and these new people—you aren't!"

"I don't," Jenny started to respond but was cut off.

"Yeah," one of the girls said, "you better watch yourself around here 'cause not all of us are happy with what's going on. Maybe you should've just run away with your boyfriend."

"But," Jenny started to object to Jacob being called her boyfriend, to them saying he had run off and to the assumption that she was happily working for Dr. Frost. But the others peeled away from her too quickly and exited the building. Jenny was angry and confused. She found her roommate just outside the door and they walked home together under what was a darkening evening sky.

The next morning, Jenny awoke and dressed for work. Her roommate slept in for another half an hour before she had to rise for breakfast and her new chemistry class.

About half the school was up and at breakfast by the time Jenny arrived. Among those who were, Jenny recognized the kids who had given her a hard time the night before. She broke eye contact with them nearly as soon as she made it. She was afraid of causing them to become even more agitated with her and perhaps encouraging them to pick a fight. As she walked down the line with her tray, she again thought through who the kids were. None of them had been troublemakers before, she marveled. *Why now?*

She sat with some old Targe friends and ate her breakfast of scrambled eggs and sausage. She didn't feel like getting up to get toast, but Ben, a nice boy from Massachusetts who said little but smiled much brought her a piece on his second run from the toaster. She chatted about happenings at the school and listened to the others talk about the budding romances at Iona. At 8:45, she excused herself to start her walk to the silver trailers for a morning of work.

Jenny stepped out of the cafeteria and onto the red brick porch.

"So," came a voice from around the corner of the building. Jenny turned and saw the girl she had encountered the night before. She heard footsteps coming from behind her and she turned slightly to see it was the other kids who gave her a hard time the previous night.

"Yes? It's Emma, isn't it?" Jenny asked.

The girl barely acknowledged what Jenny said. But she lifted her head in a way that told Jenny she was right about her name.

"So," a voice came from behind her. "You're the girl who's helping them conduct their evil experiments, huh?"

"What?" Jenny said as she squinted her eyes and turned slightly so she could see the boy behind her but without losing sight of Emma. She didn't know what would come next, but feared being blindsided.

"We've been watching you. We know you're Dr. Frost's little assistant."

Jenny wanted to say something but she wasn't sure what. She said nothing.

"Not all of us are as happy about all these changes as you are, Newbie. This school was our school long before you came here and now you are helping Creech and Frost enact their plan at *our* Iona. We didn't ask you to come here or your boyfriend to run away and cause the security crack-down, either."

Jenny wanted to object that she didn't like the changes going on either, but she was anything but sure that was a good idea. But, she certainly couldn't let the kids think Jacob was her boyfriend.

"He's not my boyfriend … wherever he is." She added the last part to head off any questions about his whereabouts.

"It's about time to choose sides, Ms. Sawyer. That is your name, right?"

Jenny pushed her head back, trying to look as tough and unruffled as possible.

The boy continued, "The time is coming when you will either need to be on *their* side and be driven out of here, or be on the side of the old and true Iona."

"What's going to happen?" Jenny asked. She backed slowly up toward the edge of the porch to put some distance between her and the other three.

"That, you don't need to know," Emma said.

"For now, do what you want, but you better not say anything about us to anyone, is that clear?" The second boy, who had said nothing to that point, stepped toward her ominously but remained silent. Jenny recognized both boys as some of the oldest students on campus, but really couldn't remember their names.

"And be thinking about whose side you're on," Emma said as she brushed up against Jenny's left side as she moved passed her. All three students jumped off the brick porch.

Jenny stood and watched them go, then took a deep breath and stepped off the porch herself. She was feeling particularly lonely after the encounter and decided to visit Will before reporting to work. She arrived at the infirmary and the nurse immediately waved her in.

Will was sitting up eating some oatmeal for breakfast when he saw Jenny peek from behind the privacy curtain that hung around his bed. "Morning Jenny!" he exclaimed with some excitement in his voice.

Jenny smiled. "Boy, you're seeming better."

"Much better, thanks. The doctor says I need to stay here for a couple more days to make sure I have my strength back, but I can probably go outside for while this afternoon, he thought."

"That's great. I hope you get out of here soon. Without you or Jake, it's kind of lonely out there."

The two chatted for just a few minutes before Jenny had to excuse herself to get to work.

"Come back this afternoon, if you can, Jenny. Maybe you can wheel me out into the sun for awhile?"

"Wheel you out? Not a chance; maybe *you* can wheel *me* out!" Jenny joked.

Jenny took the path behind the new trailers and by the tennis courts. She was curious to see what was new with the hole that was being dug. She still figured it was to be a pond. She was surprised to see that the hole had not gotten any bigger. In fact, it looked like it might be shallower than it was the day before. The edges went down maybe six feet, she guessed. At the bottom, there was a flat layer of dirt that seemed to have been added back and smoothed over. She walked around the edge as she moved toward trailer #2. As she did, Jenny noticed something of dull gold protruding from the new bottom of the hole. It was small and triangular. She bent down to look more closely. It was ten feet from her: down six feet and out four.

"See!"

Jenny jumped at the sound. Her heart raced as her legs straightened and pushed her back up. She turned. "Puddles!" she exclaimed. "You scared me to death!"

"Sorry friend," the little boy said. "But, you see the lion? You see what they did to the lion? I told you! Isn't it awful! Aren't they awful?"

"Lion? What are you talking about?" Jenny asked.

"There! You see it!"

"I see a lot of dirt and a little patch of gold-yellow. That's all I see."

"It's its ear, friend. They cut off its head! Isn't it terrible? Its head is down there under that dirt."

"What? A lion's head?" Jenny asked with amazement. "How do you know?"

"I watched them dump it there this morning before most of the campus woke up. They do their experiments in those trailers at night. You've heard them, haven't you? Those terrible cries in the night?"

Jenny had heard those sounds but she didn't answer. She looked around to see if anyone was watching. "What else do you know?" she asked.

"Trailer # 3 is where they keep the animals. There are more down by the stables. And trailer # 4 and 5 is where they do stuff. What do you think they did with that lion's body, Jenny?"

"Wow! I don't know. Maybe they ate it?" *Oh no*, the thought then crossed her mind, *what if they fed it to us in the cafeteria? Oh, gross!*

"I have a key," the boy said as he dug into the pocket of his dirty jeans.

"What?"

"I have a key to all the trailers." He pulled it from his pocket and held it out high in the air. "See, one of those guys dropped it yesterday when I was watching them. I picked it up. I wanted to help the animals. Will you help?"

"Put that *down*," Jenny said as she looked around to see if they were being watched. "How can *I* help?"

"Maybe you could let them out? Maybe you could find out what these people are doing with the animals? I trust you, Jenny. I know you're not really one of them and I know you're good and I know you're friends with Jacob. And, you've been nice to me. Most students here aren't nice to me." The boy handed the key to Jenny who involuntarily let it push into the palm of her hand. "Here," he said.

"Well, I don't know, but I have to get to work," Jenny said.

"They are always all gone at dinner time, you know. All the workers go to dinner at 5:00 and the next group doesn't come to work until 8:00. You could do something then."

Jenny patted Puddles on the back and said, "Thank you, Derek. If there is something we can do, I will—but I can't promise, OK?"

Hebridean Sea Trout

Jacob awoke the next morning to groans and moaning. He jumped to his feet and sent Mr. Nibbles springing into the air and back against the bottom boards of the cotter's bed. After Jacob got over the shock, he thought to himself that von Niblick's moans were a good sign. They demonstrated more life in him than the man had shown since the encounter with Mortimer.

Jacob took the towel he had been using the night before, dipped it in the pale of water, and then squeezed water between the professor's dry lips. The man swallowed and his eyes opened sleepily. Jacob smiled. Mr. Nibbles jumped up into the bed, crawled up by his old master's head and licked his face. von Niblick's mouth moved ever so slightly to form a hint of a smile and then his eyes closed again. Jacob picked up Mr. Nibbles and set him back on the floor.

What are we going to do? Jacob asked silently as he slid down the boards of the cotter's bed and onto his own blankets on the floor.

I tell you what I am going to do, Mr. Nibbles answered. *Well, first I am going to tell you what I am not going to do. I am not eating more of those beans for breakfast! What I am going to do is go and get us something decent to eat. You fire up the peat again while I am gone so you can cook when I return.*

Please don't bring back a sheep, Nibbs. I don't know what to do with a sheep! Jacob replied.

The hunter can't always choose his prey, my boy, the pug replied.

Be careful and hurry back, in case that Mortimer guy was able to follow us or someone else on this island has seen our smoke, OK? Jacob stood and walked to open the door. He turned to let the dog out, only to see the blur of a half pug-half dragon stretched long and lean exiting the smoke hole in the thatch roof of the cottage. Jacob shook his head and then heard a roar that reverberated in his bones. *Be back soon, Bearer.*

As the morning went along, the professor started to show more signs of life. Jacob was too hungry to wait for the dragon to return from the hunt, but boiled some water in a black cauldron and made some tea from the can he found in the cabinet. He stirred in some sugar and squeezed some of it between the professor's lips.

With a moment to relax and think, he remembered his enchiridion that he had sat on the table the night before but hadn't had the energy to remember to check. He opened its pages and found a note from Jenny. His heart was instantly lightened to have news from Iona Academy and particularly from Jenny.

Jacob read of the developments at the school. He was relieved that Jenny now knew about the Remnant of the Sporrai. He knew that Kirk and MacGregor and the rest would take care of her. He was concerned about Dr. Frost and the new trailers and the strange animal sounds. He hoped Will would be OK and was sure, from what Jenny said, that the Remnant had intentionally made him sick in order to get him away from Furangle's crew and save him during the dangers ahead. He responded with a note of his own.

Jenny,
Thanks for your note. I can't tell you much about where I am. Frankly, I don't know where I am right now, but if I did I still couldn't tell you in case this note fell into the wrong hands there at school. But, one thing you need to know is that I know Ian Nelson. You said you had delivered a report on him but that doesn't make sense. I knew Ian last year when I was in Scotland. He is from Oxford, England and had a

Hearing a commotion outside, Jacob put down the small black notebook and grabbed his sword. He opened the door slowly. *Just me, Bearer, just me*, the dragon had returned with a big wiggling fish in his mouth.

"Well, that's not a sheep, that's for sure!" Jacob approached the dragon, who dropped the silver fish onto the ground and began to shrink back into his compact form once more. Jacob picked up the fish by its gills and then wondered what he should do. Fortunately, he had seen his father clean a fish once or twice on fishing trips, so he at least could give it a try, he thought.

Looking around the beach, he spotted a log sitting up on its flat end. *Perfect*, he thought. He laid the fish on the log and pulled his sword. With dramatic flair conducted mostly to entertain Mr. Nibbles, Jacob swung and then rose the sword above his head, twisted again, and then brought the blade down hard through the fish's neck. Its pointed silver head fell onto the rocks.

Jacob looked down, proud of the fine cut he made and said, "Sorry to have to do that, but thanks for being you, little fish. We will eat and be thankful for your life."

Jacob then retrieved a knife from the cottage and cleaned the fish, washing the carcass and his tools in the cold surf. He sat in a small chair by the peat fire and held a griddle over the flames with the white fish meat sizzling ever so slightly. The mix of smoky peat and oily fish made a delightful smell that filled the room. His mind began wondering back home. What were his parents doing right at that moment, he wondered. He worried that they might find out he was not at the school and would worry about him. He didn't want them to worry. He continued thinking, then, about Jenny and Will and Iona. As he stared at the white fish changing color and texture slowly as it cooked, he heard a raspy voice rise up behind him.

"Is that Hebredian sea trout I smell?"

Jacob turned with a start. "Professor! How are you feeling?"

Professor von Niblick had rolled onto his side and was looking through the slit in the curtain and scratching the base of his gray beard. "I've seen ten thousand better mornings than this, that is true. But," he coughed and then continued, "the smell of fresh sea trout on the salty air of the Hebrides surely lifts the spirits. Don't you agree?"

"Yes, sir—I guess it does."

The man rolled his head back again and looked up at the thatch roof. Jacob put the trout, which he thought was probably done, down next to the fire and poured another cup of tea and took it to von Niblick. Jacob helped him lift his head with one hand and put the cup to his lips with the other. The professor took as much as he could and nodded his eyes with thanks. Jacob laid his head back down, cut some of the fish away from the rest with a fork and brought it on a plate to the professor. He fed him little bites of the fish, punctuated by sips of the tea. By late morning, the professor had gone back to rest. He eventually awoke feeling much better.

Nibblus Maximus went out for more fish for lunch and as the professor gained strength, he and Jacob began to talk about what had already happened and what had to happen next.

An Alliance Forms

Jenny did her filing work, but was distracted most of the morning. She looked over the records she had to file to see if she could understand any of them. She couldn't make out much more than a name here or there. There were lots of numbers and formulas and graphs and charts. There were lots of Latin names and scientific terms. When she was handed a paper to file under the name "Ian Nelson," however, she took special note. She moved slowly, very slowly, toward the file drawer that she knew held the files with people's names. She moved so slowly that it was almost painful.

Her delay paid off when the doctor working in the trailer with her stood, stretched, and announced he was going out to get another cup of coffee. As the door shut behind him, she yanked the drawer open and raced her fingers back to the 'N' section. *Nelson, Ian Nelson,* she said to herself, *now, why is an old friend of Jacob's here from England?* She pulled the file and opened it on top of the other files in the drawer. She kept the paper she was to file in her left hand and held it poised to drop in the file the instant someone came to the door.

The file was nearly a half an inch thick and had numerous paperclips attaching sections of papers to one another in groups. On the inside left side of the folder there was a paper stapled on four corners. **"The Case of Ian Nelson—General Orders"** was its title and it was dated about five months earlier. She was scared enough that she felt her breath catch and then come in short, quick bursts. She glanced at the door again before starting to read.

IAN NELSON
SB 27856
<u>Picked up May 1</u>: Oxford, England
<u>Blood type</u>: O
<u>Height</u>: 5' 3"
<u>Weight</u>: 102
<u>Class Estimate</u>: Novice

<u>Preliminary Interview Result</u>: Subject seems to retain little knowledge of his time close to the power. He has told stories of being in Scotland and of the other boy whom he has identified as a "Jacob." There is reason to believe that Jacob is an American and is probably still within the circle of the Sporrai. This Jacob should be located as soon as possible.

<u>Suitability Evaluation</u>: Nelson is a good subject for a mental sweep. Good intelligence should still be discoverable in his fresh condition. Evaluators believe he is a good candidate for memory reprocessing and capture.

<u>Instructions</u>: Begin Experiment Series 2357 with preliminary treatments in early May, transfer to America in June, then begin final mental sweeps and memory reprocessing in 30 days after arrival in America. Carefully record every image and memory recovered from the probes. Even what seems like the most insignificant thought might be of interest to our employer—leave nothing out of your reports.

Jenny felt her legs become tingly and weak as she read. Jacob's friend by the same name was from Oxford, he had told her that. The Jacob mentioned must be her Jacob. She leaned her forearm against the filing cabinet to steady herself. She thought she might be ill. After glancing at the door and straining her ears to hear any evidence of someone approaching the trailer, she looked back down at the file.

Inside, she read the first page that was a report dated in January, more than a month before the instruction sheet she had just read:

The Nelson boy does fit the description we found in the notebook that belonged to Old Crow. I have been watching him for several days now. I do not believe the magic is still with him, but he seems to have been close to it recently. If the Old Crow was right about him, this boy should also still retain some of the old knowledge of the other boy Crow was tracking.

Give me the order and I will pick him up and deliver him to one of the safe houses.

Meanwhile, I will keep up my surveillance of the Nelson family.

GSP

Jenny began to turn the page when she heard footfalls on the steps. In a panic, she began to push the drawer. Before it noisily snapped shut, she got hold of her senses and grabbed it, letting it more quietly slip into place as she spun around and leaned on the next filing cabinet. As the trailer's door opened, she smiled a nervous smile and leaned back further to show just how relaxed and innocent she was.

The young doctor walked back in with his coffee but said nothing. As he turned to sit back down at his computer, Jenny started to move away from the cabinet. The cabinet grabbed her and pulled her back. *Crap! I shut my shirt in the drawer!* The nerves in her chest tightened again. She knew she couldn't stand there long without causing suspicion and she knew she couldn't just pop the drawer back open without causing the doctor to turn to see what she was doing in. Slowly, very slowly, she reached her left hand over to the drawer and slid the latch as quietly as she could to the left. She thought she remembered that the drawer caught slightly on the bottom as it opened, so she lifted it as best she could as she pulled. The drawer moved quietly out of its locked position and released her shirt.

Jenny realized that she had not taken a breath, just as the doctor said, "Girl!" He didn't wait for a reply and she didn't offer one. He lifted a file behind his head and said, "Deliver this to trailer #4, and then go off to class, or whatever you kids do around here." Jenny stepped forward and took the file. Her breath was still caught in her chest and she could say nothing.

She turned out the door and pulled it very tight behind her. The air rushed out of her chest like the steam from a hot kettle. She leaned back against the trailer to calm herself and stiffen her legs before she stepped down the stairs. Her thoughts oscillated between fear for herself almost getting caught and for Ian. Though she didn't know the boy, she felt pity for him and wished she could help. She reasoned that he must have been kidnapped and was being experimented on somewhere at Iona Academy.

Jenny walked back toward trailer #4. Without looking down at it for fear of causing suspicion if she was seen, she wondered what was in the file she carried. Her mind wandered off its leash as she let herself consider that it might be an order to kill Ian or kill one of the animals or do some other terrible thing. She shook her head to try to get the ideas to drop out. They didn't. She looked around. There was hardly anyone out near the trailers and tennis courts. Students were in class or at activities. She could see a group playing soccer over in the corner of one of the fields. The workers were mostly at work in their trailers, she guessed. She turned a corner behind trailer #2 and bent down. She laid the folder beside her foot and pretended to be tying her shoe. As she did, she flipped the file open. To her relief, there was just a single sheet of paper inside with a series of numbers and graphs. She was only carrying data and was glad of it.

Jenny stood and continued toward trailer #4. As she passed #3, she remembered the lion's head and Puddles telling her that the animals were kept in this one. She put her hand on the silver aluminum side of the trailer and let it flow back as she walked. It reminded her of passing her hand through a cold brook and watching the waves it created. *If only life was that safe and things fell back in place that quickly in life,* she thought. She thought of the animals inside and hoped they were not being mistreated. She had always loved animals, almost all animals. Of course, like most girls, she didn't much care for snakes or rats, though the occasional mouse might seem cute—if it was on TV and not anywhere near her. *If they kidnapped and were experimenting on a boy, what must these people be doing to animals?* she considered. *The animals!* she exclaimed to herself in a derogatory tone; she did not mean the furry beasts inside.

She could hear slight rustling inside, but she knew from her work in trailer #2 that they were well-insulated modular units that kept the sound very much within their walls. She didn't expect to hear much. That thought, though, disturbed her even more as she wondered what must go on at night when the cries can be heard so easily across campus.

Jenny knocked on trailer #4's door and waited. There was no response. As she waited, she noticed that there was a small box beside the door. It had slots that looked like they covered a speaker and there was a small button like a doorbell. The trailer that she worked in didn't have such a system, but she had seen them before. She pushed the button and waited.

"Yes," came a woman's voice through the box.

"I'm delivering a file from Dr." she paused, realizing again that she still didn't know the man's name she worked for, "well, from the Dr. in trailer #2."

There was no reply through the box, but soon the door opened half way and a woman in a lab coat stuck her hand out and grabbed the file. Without a thank you or any polite gesture at all, the woman slammed the door shut. As the door closed, Jenny caught a glimpse of the inside. There were tables and tubes and machines that made it look like the operating rooms she had seen on commercials for TV shows she didn't watch.

Jenny didn't go to class that afternoon. She knew she would just be given busy work, anyway, as that was all they had done since the old faculty had left and the changes occurred. It was becoming clear to all of the students that they were no longer the most important people at the school. What was happening in those trailers had trumped them. Though, Mr. Creech would regularly remind them that "a full complement of new teachers, trained in the new ways, would be on their way soon." Instead of wasting her time with busy work, she went out under a tree, the tree where she first met the little Weeling named Angus. The tree was about as far away from the trailers as she could get and not leave campus, she thought. Though, if she could leave campus, she would have.

She sat down in the soft grass under the shady tree and leaned back against the trunk and pulled the extra papers from Jacob's enchiridion and a pen from her pocket. She wrote to Jacob about what was happening. She spent some time recounting what she had learned about Ian and asked him for a description of the English boy, in case she ran into him on campus. She mentioned the lion's head, which seemed positively bizarre to say. *Would he even believe there was a headless lion on campus?*, she wondered. She ended the letter with an uncharacteristic sentiment for a girl who prided herself on her ability to reason through things and to not give in to irrational fears. "Jacob, please come back soon and then let's get out of here forever!"

A branch snapped and leaves rustled overheard. Jenny's heart raced. She sprang forward, landing on hands and knees and turning her neck abruptly. Landis had flown up off the stone wall, had grabbed a branch and had fallen on the ground next to her before Jenny knew what was going on. Emma and Nolus followed him over the wall. Jenny cowered back. She was outnumbered and far away, now, from the sanctuary of other students and Iona staff. She was cornered.

"What do you want? Leave me alone!" She was attempting to appear fearless and a dangerous quarry not worth the price of tangling with.

"Relax, short stuff," Emma said to her as she got down on one knee. Emma was at Iona mostly because it was a chance to practice volleyball all summer without the distractions of her home life. She was tall and muscular. Jenny would look at her thigh as she bent down and note that there were more muscles flexing in that bend than she thought she had in her entire body. Her silky red hair was back in a ponytail and she wore a burgundy tank top with golden "Lady Trojans" across her chest.

Landis had stubbed his toe on a root when he landed and he was rubbing it through his shoe. Landis was a senior at Iona and had been on campus for six years. He started as a summer camp student, like Jenny, Will, and Jacob, but was sent there year-round when he entered the ninth grade. His parents told him it was good for him and better than any schools near his home in New York. Landis never was able to shake the feeling, however, that his parents just didn't want him around. He had come to love Iona, though, and the faculty and students were as much his family now as were his parents some 500 miles away.

Nolus pulled himself up next to the tree and began carving a stick. Nolus Evans was about the quietist boy in school. He said little, but never seemed uninterested. He was shorter than both Emma and Landis, but was muscular and had a mop of silver-white hair that nearly glowed at night. He had been at Iona for just two years, but quickly came to love the school and consider it home. Like Landis, his parents had sent him to Iona without much consultation and they divorced soon afterward. His father was now remarried and had moved to New Mexico. His mother was still at home, but was preoccupied by the problems of his twin sisters who always seemed in trouble for something. He guessed she would send them away if any place would have them. Since they wouldn't, it was him who left.

Jenny was preparing to run, or for the beating that would come if she failed in the attempt. Then, she saw the pages of the enchiridion sitting among the roots of the trees. *No!* She looked up at the others, batting her eyes from each one and then back to the pages. Her mistake was clear. She had called attention to the pages. Nolus reached for them. Jenny dove and hit the dirt in front. It was too late. Nolus had the pages and was looking at them. Jenny knew he must have been reading the note to Jacob. Now everything was ruined. She would be in unknown danger and with the ability of them to communicate with Jacob, he might even be in danger now, too.

Nolus looked at the pages. He turned them over. Then handed them to Jenny with, "Here are your sheets of paper." Jenny grabbed them and looked. Mercifully, the words she had written had already disappeared. They had faded away to Jacob just as Nolus picked them up. He knew nothing but that she had carried some paper with her to the tree. Relief washed over her but then she remembered the danger she was in herself. She slipped the pages back into her pocket.

Noting the fright on her face, Emma again attempted to sooth her fears. "Look, Jenny, we aren't here to hurt you or anything. We just want to talk."

Jenny didn't answer, but scooted back in the only direction one of them had not yet cut off.

"Look, Jenny," Landis said, "I know we tried to scare you earlier. We thought you were an enemy, then. But, Emma ran into Dr. Kirk today down at the bakery in town. She had gone with Mr. Dave to pick up some pastries for breakfast and Dr. Kirk was there."

"Anyway," Emma interrupted. She was annoyed at her story being told by someone else, particularly Landis who always was trying to run everything. "I saw Dr. Kirk and told him what we knew was happening on campus. I told him how we were going to drive you out of here so you couldn't help Dr. Frosty-butt with whatever she is up to. He must really like you, girl, cause I thought he was going to tear my head off!"

Jenny felt good that Dr. Kirk cared that much about her.

"Anyway, he rose up out of his seat and ordered me to sit down. He then told me that you were only working for Frost because you were ordered to and that he knew you were not a friend of this new regime at Iona but would work with us to defend the old ways. Is that true?"

The three searched her face intensely. She considered how to answer. She couldn't be sure that these kids were fully of "The Remnant" that she had been introduced to. But, if they knew Dr. Kirk and he had told them that, they must at least be allies, she reasoned. *It's worth the risk.*

"Yes, I guess it's true," Jenny said. "I have talked to Dr. Kirk and like things a lot better the way they were when we arrived around here and Headmistress Witherspoon was here."

"Well, good, then," Landis said. "Dr. Kirk told Emma that we should talk to you about what's going on and see what we can do to know more. We're going to meet with him tonight. After dark we'll meet out at the Ashland mansion."

Jenny stalled to try to process what was happening and how much she could safely tell them. Landis knew by the look on Emma's face that he had gone too far, too fast. He didn't want to scare Jenny into silence.

"Actually, let me tell you what we know and what we think. That might be better." Landis looked over at Emma as if to show how he was fixing the situation without her help. "We think a couple of things are happening, here, Jenny. First, this Finnius Creech character is just a front man for some other people. He doesn't seem smart enough to be running this thing himself, does he? Well, he's trying to experiment on our school and our education here and make it something new and different. But, that all has nothing to do with these trailers and Dr. Frost and all these scientists. We know about the exotic animals being brought onto campus and about our dogs having run away or having been killed or whatever happened to them. We think Dr. Frost is doing experiments on the animals like she has done before. Before they shut down the Internet on campus, we found out that she had been thrown out of all her University labs because of unethical practices. She was doing really bizarre things. We think she is here to do experiments that others won't let her do in their labs or on their campuses. It's not us, but just a safe place for whatever freakishness she is up to."

It all seemed right to Jenny and she nodded. The urgent feeling of wanting to contribute and appear to have information herself got to her and she blurted out, "yes, and we found a head of a lion down in the new pond. Puddles showed me."

"Just the head?" Nolus interrupted.

Jenny nodded.

"Even if they killed the poor beast," Emma said, "why would they cut its head off? That doesn't make any sense." Everyone knew she was right, but none of them said anything.

"OK, look," Emma said as she took charge, "its too risky to stay here together. Let's meet tonight at 10:00 P.M. Down by the stables. We can go from there together to meet Dr. Kirk."

"A password. We need a password," Nolus interrupted.

"A password? What for?" Landis asked with incredulity.

"A password so we know who we are in the dark," Nolus answered.

"If you don't know who you are in the dark, a password won't help you," Emma interjected. Her eyebrows were raised up toward her red hair and the sarcasm clung and then dripped off her final words.

Nolus said nothing with his mouth, but his eyes told Emma exactly what he thought of that comment.

"How about we use the name of my lost friend, 'Jacob'?" Jenny blurted out.

"'Jacob' it is," Emma agreed. "We will each say, 'is that you, Jacob?', when we see someone approaching or hear something in the dark."

"And we can answer," Jenny said, "'yes, it's Jacob, Jacob Boyd.'"

"Deal!" Nolus announced.

"Now, let's go, guys. Jenny, it's a pleasure to know you are a friend of Dr. Kirk and of the old Iona we all love."

Landis, Emma, and Nolus all put their hands together and looked at Jenny. She leaned her hand in. The three others then said the now forbidden ancient motto of Scotland and the old school, "Nemo me impune lacissit!" Next time, Jenny would know what to expect and would recite it with them. This time she followed theirs with her own recitation, a split second behind theirs and under her breath. *No one harms* us *with impunity*, she translated.

Retrieving the Cover

"**D**raw me up lad, and draw those blankets around to support my back."

von Niblick was struggling to raise himself to a seated position. Jacob took the extra blankets from the bottom of the crofter's bed and pushed them behind the professor with his left hand as he helped lift him with his right.

"Thank you, Lad. Now, bring me the cover for the *Book of Kells* and then sit down here beside me."

Jacob felt embarrassed. He knew they had left the cover on the Island of Iona when they escaped Mortimer. Maybe he should have gone back for it, but he knew it would be dangerous and von Niblick needed his care. He worried about it since they left, but he had decided it was both easier and probably necessary that he stay with the professor. In this moment, however, he instantly felt it was the wrong decision.

"Well, professor," Jacob started hesitantly. "Remember that Nibblus Maximus took the cover and dropped it on the other side of the hill on Iona before he came back to save us. In my fear of you dying and us trying to escape the Island, then, I guess I didn't think to pick it up and I didn't think it right to go back."

"Not here? Lost? Out of my way, lad, out of my. . ." von Niblick was agitated and pushed Jacob up from the bed as he spoke. Then a deep and ugly series of coughs came up from his lungs and convulsed his body. He dropped back down onto the pillows, his eyes shut.

"I'm sorry, Professor, I did what I thought I needed to in order to save you, and save me, too."

"I must go and retrieve it. The cover cannot be lost to the enemy," the professor mumbled.

"Sir, you are in no condition even to get out of bed. I'll go back and find it."

The professor shook his head from side to side indicating he did not approve. But, the man also knew that Jacob was right. He was in no condition to go back to Iona and even if he got there, he knew he did not have the strength to fight off Mortimer. The man lay silently and considered the options. Then he spoke to the boy who sat pensive by his side.

"Jacob, you are too valuable to the cause to be risked."

"But ..." Jacob started to interject. He had a growing feeling that he should act in some way to retrieve the cover.

"Listen to me, lad," von Niblick stopped him. "I don't have the strength to fight you, too."

Jacob mumbled, "sorry," and fumbled with the tassels of the sporran hung from the belt at his waist.

The man made another attempt to get up but failed. "Jacob, listen carefully. I am afraid we have no choice. You will need to go and let us pray the cover is still where the old dragon left it. Go and retrieve it, if you can. No matter if you find it or not, return here immediately. If it is not there, we will then have to act to alert the Remnant to begin the search. Or," he paused, "we will act directly to *neutralize* whoever's hands have found its ancient leather."

"Yes, sir," Jacob reacted as he pulled up the blankets around von Niblick's neck. "Can I do anything for you before I leave?"

"I'm spewin' feathers, here; some more of that tea, perhaps? Sit it on the chair here by my bedside so I can reach it, if you would be so kind." The man closed his eyes again and asked, "Jacob, do you think you can make it there and back, just you and that troublesome dragon pug of yours?"

"Yes, sir. I can."

"I do believe you can, at that," the professor said and smiled. His smile, however, masked the fears that were churning inside: fears for Jacob; fears for what might have happened to the cover; fears for what would happen next if he didn't survive and his knowledge was lost before he could pass it along.

"Wee Bearer," the man said, as if he had now changed his mind and had more to share. "There are three sets of kings buried on Iona. They are the kings of three people's bound up most directly with Isildane's treasure. They are in three tombs. The *Tumulus Regum Scotiae* holds the remains of 48 kings of Scotland. The *Tumulus Regum Hiberniae* holds the remains of four Irish kings. The *Tumulus Regum Norwegiae* holds eight Norwegian kings. These were once glorious tombs, you know, but they have been hacked at by Vikings and knocked at by treasure seekers and the salty winds of centuries until there is little left above ground but stone slabs."

von Niblick asked for a swig of tea and then leaned his head back again. "Lad, we don't have time to share much with you today, for the cover must be retrieved. But, you should know this: those tombs are in the Reilig Odhrain, do you know what that is?"

Jacob said "no" and tried to understand the words the man said and wondered how they were spelled.

"Well, son, that is the cemetery on Iona – Reilig Odhrain." The professor chuckled and coughed. "Funny, you know, Jacob. I was buried alive there not but a few days ago and now I am remembering that the place got its name because of a man named Odhrain who was buried alive there on the orders of St. Columba himself. Ironic, isn't it?" He chuckled and coughed again.

Jacob didn't find his friend being buried alive or that some man 1,500 years ago had been buried alive there to be funny at all.

"He was buried alive in an attempt to secure the walls of the church from ever falling," von Niblick continued. "The old bugger was dug up three days later. He was still alive and started spouting non-sense about the afterlife and so Columba had him buried again! No need to rebury me, you know, old Jacob, because I still got it right!" The professor reached out from under the covers and feebly squeezed Jacob's arm.

Jacob found the man's tale quite odd and wondered if it was the professor's fever talking.

"And that reminds me, Jacob, you know Margaret is not buried there anymore. Did you know that? No. Her head isn't either. They kept her head in a silver box, you know. She travelled around quite a bit for hundreds of years in that beautiful silver box."

Jacob backed away slightly not knowing what to think. von Niblick's left hand dropped from Jacob's arm where it had been resting.

"Some even say her hair stayed lovely and blond on that chopped off head of hers for hundreds of years. Right up until that infernal little rebellion over in France … animals … they did something with that lovely head, you know, and it has not been seen since."

Jacob thought he better step in and see if he could get to the bottom of what the professor actually wanted him to know. Tombs were one thing, carrying around a head was quite something he didn't need to hear about right then, he suspected.

"Sir," Jacob said. "Sir, is there something else I'm supposed to know or do while I'm on Iona, then?"

"Ah, lad, forgive a feeble old man, won't ya? Of course, just, if things go well and you have the cover, return here immediately. Hopefully, by the time you return, I will be in better shape and we will be off to the mainland and safety."

"I understand," Jacob interjected, "but what if it's not there?"

"Not there!" von Niblick was agitated again. "It *must* be there, we must believe that. But," he paused and took several deep breaths, "we must also prepare for the alternative." The professor took a deep breath.

"Jacob; I believe we have to gamble here. I am going to guess that if Mortimer has found the cover, he will rush off Iona immediately. He will go to a sanctuary where he can study it and plan his next move. Or, if he is in the service of some higher and darker power, he will take it away to them to claim his reward and get further orders. So, if you do not find the cover, let's make an effort to get to the tomb of the Norwegian kings—the *Tumulus Regum Norwegiae*."

THE BOOK OF KELLS

Jacob's mind ran back to the "Tomb of Six Keepers" beneath Edinburgh Castle; his heart fluttered, his arms tensed. He did not welcome entering another tomb.

"I regret that I cannot tell you what to do there, but perhaps the treasures and weapons you bear will open some secrets to you that I have not been able to decipher. I did not get time to study the cover before I was struck and buried, but I have reason to believe that cover of the greatest book ever written, has a bigger role to play than simply covering its pages. Somehow I think that cover will lead its bearer to greater treasures and important places."

"Like a map?" Jacob interjected and then instantly regretted interfering with the professor's story.

"Aye," the professor nodded. "The four jewels and the cross that once adorned the cover, including the jewel you bear, must somehow connect the dots. I can't say how or what the meaning is. It is all lost in a fog of time and myth thicker than the early morning fogs of these islands. And, that reminds me, lad. Reach into my breast pocket here and take that slip out."

Jacob pulled the covers down from the professor's neck and reached two fingers into the outer breast pocket of his coat. There he found a folded piece of paper and removed it. Jacob unfolded the note. It looked like a poem. Across the top was scrawled 'Jacob?' and what looked like a title read simply 'chapel P.' He didn't have time to read it before the professor intervened again.

"Perhaps that will prove helpful, I do not know," he said with a cough. "Now, Jacob, off with you and that infernal dragon, too. I have no more strength to give this morning. Be strong and stay true, Bearer."

Professor von Niblick shut his eyes and his head rolled toward the wall. He had no more energy to hold it straight.

Jacob whispered a good wish to the professor and stood. He looked at the paper in his hand and read it silently.

Chapel P

Pieces broken
Whole no More
Questing knight
Who opens the door

Can ask of Meaning
Of past in crumbles
If he dares
Perhaps he stumbles
Kings surround
The precious treasure
Memory awakened
To take his measure

To be felt, not touched
To be asked, not rushed
Truth will be found
With a silent sound

Makes Andrew's mark
Upon the floor
Opens his eyes
And fears no more

How can this help me pick up the cover? He wondered. *Good grief, I don't have time for a puzzle now. Maybe when I get together with Jenny again we can figure it out.* Jacob refolded the piece of paper and slipped it into his right front pocket.

He filled the professor's cup of tea again and replaced the blanket up around his neck. He checked the sword belt to insure the sporran and sheath were in place and secure around his waist. He took a couple of bites of sea trout, being careful to leave some for the professor and gulped some tea.

Within minutes, he was airborne. From the back of Nibblus Maximus, Jacob looked back over the island and saw in the distance a grand old house. The house was large and dark and ominous as it loomed above the heather spotted with grey rocks; an old house of fear. He wondered if anyone still lived there and hoped that if they did, they would not find the professor in the small cottage along the beach. He turned his head and looked out to sea where he knew Iona awaited him, as did an unknown fate.

As they approached the northern tip of Iona, the dragon took a wide swing away from Fingal's Cave. Though it was obvious to Jacob that they were not taking the quickest possible route in, he said nothing of it.

Nibblus Maximus warned Jacob again of the potential dangers ahead. The dragon made his charge promise not to take unnecessary chances if they got separated, and to follow Professor von Niblick's orders exactly. As they came to the island and the dragon felt sure he had found an approach that was safe from prying eyes, they began their descent through the light clouds that hung above the sea.

Mercifully, an engine malfunction on one of the ferries that brought tourists to the island had kept most of the new tourists on the mainland that morning. They were able to sputter through the surf and to a relatively soft landing among the rocky shoreline of the northern tip of the island just before the island's highest point—the hill called 'Dun I.'

Jacob jumped immediately from the dragon's back and was rushing across the rocky terrain as the dragon was shrinking back into pug form. He bolted over rocks toward where the dragon said he had dropped the cover. He slipped on several rocks as he leapt from one smooth wet landing pad to another. But in a moment he was at the spot and there, tucked between two grey stones was a patch of brown leather. He smiled as he approached it and he sent a message back to Mr. Nibbles. *Got it! It's right where you left it.*

Jacob knelt down next to the patch of leather. His sword sheath caught on a stone as he bent and he had to readjust it before continuing. He reached for the soft old leather wrap that contained the much more ancient leather cover of *The Book of the Kells*. He was filled with great anticipation. As his fingers closed around it, however, a sharp pain rushed through his fingers, up his arm and then dug like a dagger down into the right side of his neck. The pain was strong, but it would not let him drop the cover to get relief. With a grimace on his face, he pulled the cover from its crevice and fell back.

Jacob sat with his eyes pinched shut and his teeth set tight as he endured the pain. When it subsided, he felt some pride in having persevered and a confidence that having done so had strengthened him. He unwrapped the cover. He turned it in his hands. The leather was musty and as old as anything he had ever touched. It was plain and besides its age, relatively unexceptional in appearance. Its ancient jewels and adornments had been taken away long ago. He pulled it over to compare it with the leather of his sporran—an exact match. He realized with great excitement that this was indeed of the same ancient hide cut by Isildane.

He opened it in his lap and examined the inside. It was softer and whiter than the outside. He marveled that the stitching still held up after some time being buried and then being lost or hidden for centuries.

Jacob, we do not have time for you to play archeologist out here in the open like this, the dragon-pug scolded the boy. *We must get back to Cairnglass and the professor now that we have what we came here for.* The dog had come up behind Jacob and was now making its way the last few feet to where the boy sat.

Jacob had gained a new confidence and strength, however. He thought he could actually feel his small muscles strain under his skin with new power. The cover, as plain as it was, held a fascination for him as strong as any of the treasures of Isildane he carried. His fingers rolled slowly over the insides of the open cover. He felt his fingertips tingle as they moved. He noticed a trail of bluish light that seemed to follow his fingers across the surface. He studied the light carefully and watched its hypnotic dance behind his fingers.

As the blue light moved across the page, Jacob gradually came to perceive something underneath. It was like looking into a stream of water and noticing a pretty colored rock in the stream's bed. It was neither clearly visible nor completely obscured. He moved his fingers slowly to the right and then to the left. He moved them up and then drew them toward him. Gradually he came to believe he was seeing something important in the light of his finger trails. Though Mr. Nibbles was nudging him with his pug nose and attempting to contact him, Jacob was enthralled by the light trails.

"Just a minute!" he finally barked back at Mr. Nibbles. As he turned toward the dog, he was drawn to the pug's paws. He noticed how each toe fixed itself close to the next one and together they formed a complete pad. *Yes, that's it!*

Jacob took his entire right hand and laid it flat on the far left end of the inside of the cover of the *Book of Kells*. He pressed it as flat as he could get it and then slowly moved his hand to the right. Just as he suspected, the hand cut a big swath of blue light on the inside of the leather cover. His heart jumped. The expanded light that came from the connection of his hand to the ancient leather unveiled its secrets to him. He could see a map. The lines and drawings and symbols were unmistakable. "A map!" he exclaimed.

Excitedly, he moved his hands more quickly to try to uncover the entire map. As he exposed one section, however, the glow would disappear on the last and it would be lost. He could only see about an eighth of the map at any time. Then he passed over the edge of the cover. In the blue light of his passing hands he could see the stitching of the outer edge of the cover come undone. As his hand slipped completely from the leather, he could see the stitching being replaced. He passed his hand back again and watched the stitches come undone in the blue light and then close up again with the passing away of that light.

Jacob nearly burst with pride as he thought about showing the professor what he had discovered. He wrapped the ancient cover back into the soft leather folds of its protective sheath. He clutched the package under his left arm and reached over to scratch Mr. Nibbles on his head.

"The professor will be very interested in this, boy! Now, let's get out of here," Jacob said aloud as he rubbed the dog's head.

Mr. Nibbles turned and the two started back down the beach. From there they would take flight back to von Niblick. But, Jacob's moment of triumph was not to last even a moment longer.

"Is our friend dead yet?" came a man's oily voice from above them on the side of the hill of Dun I.

Danger at the Stables

They each made their way through the dark, having slid on kitten feet down their halls and out of doors. Each rub of leaves in the trees and each snapped little twig beneath their feet echoed in their ears like thunder and spiked their breath with fear.

When an animal cry went up from the trailers, Emma nearly collapsed in panic. She was near the gazebo in the field and sat down upon its only step to get control of her nerves once more. She tightened the hair in her ponytail and saw a shadow passing along the dirt road running down to the stables. She hoped it was one of the others, but held steady and silent for a moment to let it pass beyond sight of her, just in case.

Jenny was behind Emma, though neither of them knew it. As she approached the gazebo, Emma suddenly stood up from her step. To Jenny, the tall, thin shadow looked like a spectral force rising from the floor of the gazebo itself. She wanted to scream but somehow kept control of herself. "J-J-J-Jacob?" she stammered the password. The shadowy force in front of her hung absolutely silent and unmoving. Emma knew she heard something behind her, but was that "Jacob" she heard? Was it the password? She didn't move.

"J-J-J-Jacob?" Jenny repeated.

"Jacob? Yes, it's Jacob. Jacob Boyd," Emma responded.

Jenny recognized Emma's voice and the password was right. "Its me, Jenny," she announced.

Emma took a deep breath. Her shoulders visibly relaxed and her head fell forward in the shadows cast from the dim lights outside the field. Jenny jogged up to her and they embraced. They had barely gotten to know each other, but common danger has a funny way of accelerating relationships.

"Why didn't we just agree to leave the dorms together?" Jenny asked.

Emma just patted the younger girl on the shoulder and nodded her head toward the stables.

The stables were down a slight hill from the field where the gazebo stood. Nolus and Landis had seen each other emerge from their dorm and had made their way up passed the Spur and Spoon and then down into the horse field and up to the stables.

They were waiting quietly for the girls when they saw a single being approaching. It seemed to walk with a slight limp. Without saying a word, both boys pulled themselves up as close against the stable wall as possible to hide their silhouette. They froze and listened for the password. The shadow, however, continued silently toward them. All the boys heard was the crunch of displacing the sandstone rocks on the road. As it came near, the being walked within the illumination of the light hanging above the stable door. It became very clear very quickly that this man was not Emma or Jenny.

He had a dark fedora hat that shadowed his eyes and the rest of his face except his chin. He wore a dark coat that was mis-buttoned slightly and so puffed out on the right side of his chest. He leaned on a short walking stick, his fingers on his right hand curling down over its brass saddle horn handle. The boys froze with fear. Landis thought about Emma and Jenny and hoped they would not come bounding down the road while this man was there.

Nolus looked at Landis and shrugged his shoulders. Landis began considering their options. He thought maybe a diversion would work. Maybe he could fire a rock over into the woods and the man would go over to investigate and then he and Nolus could bust up the hill and try to find Jenny and Emma before they got to the stables.

"Are you just going to sit there, boys?"

The man's words broke the stillness of the night and rent it in half. There was now a "before" world hanging next to an "after" world with the difference being created by the power of the man's voice upon their minds. The boys did not move as the old world of secrecy disintegrated into the darkness and the new world of being caught settled fully upon them.

"Come now, boys, we haven't all night." The man lifted the tip of his fedora and tilted his head back. The boys recognized him as their former teacher Ramos Kirk.

"Dr. Kirk!" Nolus bounded up from his seat, brushing the back of his pants which were now wet from sitting in the damp grass. Landis followed more cautiously.

Kirk was not eager for an embrace of small talk. Rather, he gruffly asked, "Where are the girls?"

"We're not sure," Landis answered.

"Not sure? Didn't you accompany them through this dark night?"

The boys shook their heads slightly but did not verbalize an answer.

"Young men these days," the man said sadly as he turned out to look into the dark field. "Come on, get out of this light, then," he said as he led them back around the stable.

As the man and two boys turned the stable corner, a small voice in the dark said, "what took you so long?"

Dr. Kirk startled only slightly, but Nolus jumped back into Landis's chest and they both fell into the waterspout on the corner of the barn. Nolus let out a whimper and Landis exclaimed a startled mixture of letters.

"Jacob? Jacob is that you?"

Both girls giggled slightly at their feat. They had seen the boys' encounter under the stable lights and so made their way out behind hay bales and the watering trough and got in place before they returned to the shadows themselves.

Dr. Kirk was not amused. "There is time for levity, I assure you. But this is not one of those times, young ladies. There is serious evil afoot and you will do well to keep a seriousness about your countenances until this trouble has passed or until your parents arrive to take you home."

Both girls looked down and Nolus, behind Dr. Kirk's back, stuck out his tongue at Emma. Landis gave him a half-power punch to the chest.

Chapel Oran

Jacob froze. Mr. Nibbles snarled and turned. Above them and walking slowly in their direction was the man who had attacked Professor von Niblick.

"Dead or not, I should have known he would send you back here to explore his old curiosities and mysteries he cannot possibly comprehend. He is like that, you know, always endangering the lives of young men less educated and prepared than him. He has always been that way, you know. Always."

Jacob froze, confused about what to do. Then he involuntarily fidgeted with the cover under his arm. It was a grave mistake.

The man's eyes flashed.

"Well, I see he didn't send you back for idle searches among the rocks of this place. He sent you back for something he lost. Well, it wasn't his to begin with, you know. So, it won't be a problem for you to return without it." The man kept walking at a steady but unhurried pace.

Jacob, be ready to bolt for the sea, Nibblus Maximus communicated in a tone of great urgency.

Jacob took a step back and then another.

"Son, what is your name?" the man asked.

Jacob did not answer.

Mr. Nibbles, however, answered the man by making his head swell very quickly and then just as quickly he let a ball of fire fly from his throat. Jacob felt the hot air as the flame passed his head.

The man dropped back and down as the flame blew toward his face.

Jacob didn't need an order from the dragon to know what to do. He turned and ran as fast as his legs would take him over the rocky ground toward the sea. He thought Mr. Nibbles would swell and swoop down, picking him up as he ran and delivering him to safety. What happened, however, was a very different matter.

Jacob, I'm coming, put your arms out and keep running, Nibblus Maximus shouted into Jacob's skull.

Jacob stuck his arms out at his side to give maximum targets for the dragon's claws. He kept his legs moving as quickly as he could as he lept from rock to rock. He was almost at the sea and was ready for the dragon to grab him. He gritted his teeth as he anticipated the potential of a slightly misplaced claw digging into the flesh of his arm.

Suddenly a spray of salty ocean water exploded high into the air in front of him. Jacob startled and stopped. As the last of the spray of water fell back to its Atlantic home, Jacob found himself looking out at a most hideous sight.

A large green serpent shook its head and spit excess water out of its mouth. It looked in Jacob's direction and let out a call that vibrated in Jacob's chest. The serpent then turned its head away. To its right appeared a small ferryboat. People on board were screaming at the hideous sight. The monster stretched out its body to propel itself toward the small craft.

Nibblus Maximus buzzed Jacob's head but did not pick him up. Instead, the dragon flew over the sea to engage the menace bearing down on the innocent people on the boat. Jacob stood, confused and frightened.

Keep running! The dragon called back to Jacob. *Make for the chapel in the graveyard. It is holy ground. Hide as best you can. I will get there as soon as I do away with this overgrown worm!*

Mortimer smiled and waved an order to the sea serpent, which was coiling itself tight near the ferry. Jacob turned his head and looked at the man. He paused, took a nervous deep breath, and ran as fast as he could back up toward the right side of Dun I and on a path toward the tombs at Reilig Odhrain and the chapel.

The man in the long trench coat stopped. He had expected the dragon would not leave his charge but would keep him nearby on the beach. He planned for the encounter to unfold there together where the serpent might be of assistance. He was momentarily stunned by Jacob's sudden change of direction. It was just the kind of head start the boy needed. But, it would not provide him much time. His legs and arms pumped fast and hard. As he ran, Jacob kept wondering what he could possibly do against this man once he was caught. He hoped the dragon might finish off the serpent quickly and be at the chapel soon after he arrived.

Up the dark grey pathway Jacob went as fast as his legs would carry him. He ran through the gate into the walled graveyard of Reilig Odhrain and then sprinted to the small chapel near the far corner. Without turning to see how closely Mortimer had been able to follow him, he sprang under the Norman archway of the chapel entrance and pushed the door open. He slammed it shut just as fast. He struggled to catch his breath.

There was almost nothing in the small building. It had walls of stone painted white, a small alter in front, a few benches and little else. On the south wall he saw a slight recess and went over to it. It was a different color than the rest of the room. The bare stones in the center made him think it was a bricked-up old fireplace. Several arches rose above the exposed stones and formed a three-part pattern that reminded Jacob of a fleur-de-lis or perhaps of a shadow of a large hulking man with bulging shoulders. He pulled a bench over to offer what little protection it could and lay down behind it.

Jacob was not lying in an old fireplace, however, but in a medieval tomb recess. Though it must have once been quite beautiful, the stonework had broken down over the centuries and was now simply unspectacular. On one side, however, Jacob could see what he thought resembled an animal carved out of the stone. His attention was drawn toward it. *Could it possibly be?* He wondered. *Could it be a dragon pug? Really?* He felt the outlines of the animal whose shape had gradually been eaten away by the salt air as if it were merely a carving in soap. As he did, Jacob felt a slight tingle.

He rested his hand on a stone ledge just beneath the carving. The ledge moved. He pulled his hand back and heard a latch crack open. He feared it was Mortimer at the door and he flung his body back down behind the bench and into the corner of the tomb recess.

A slight breeze of cool, stale air over his left ear was the only warning he had before the stone floor suddenly gave way beneath him.

Chapel Perilous

Jacob rolled down a ramp and was spit out before he could regain control. He landed hard on his right shoulder and hip. Without a slight hesitation, he jumped to his feet and reached into the air. He jumped. He couldn't reach the ceiling above him. He looked around in the dark, frightened and confused. In front of him was a dark wall of stone. He turned. He saw where the light was coming from that allowed him to see.

Jacob stood, stunned. His face was bathed from a golden glow hovering twenty feet in front of him. He took a step back. He looked left and then right into the shadows. He could see nothing looking back at him, but that gave him little comfort. He stood silent, looking on at the golden glow. At it's base was a large rectangular stone. He remembered the Lia Fail and wondered if this might be the true Stone of Destiny. Hovering above the stone were small pieces floating like dirt particles in a stirred glass of water.

Jacob shifted his feet and his left foot slipped off a slight ledge. He picked it up and something dripped off. Cautiously, he touched the ooze on the back of his shoe and brought it to his nose. The smell sent his imagination back into the catacombs beneath Edinburgh Castle where he was more than a year earlier. He remembered the trench fires that lit his and Ian's way through the passages. Jacob reached into his pocket and removed a small package of water-resistant matches, which he had found in the old cottage. He struck a match and cautiously dropped it into the trench. Fire crept slowly in two directions away from him, casting light up on the walls as it went.

Jacob jumped back from the trench light. Behind him he could now see a skull nailed to the wall with a spike entering each eye socket. At the end of each black spike was a black fist. In the dark ooze in the trench below, he could see various vertebrae and other bones partially sunk. Sickened and scared, he turned away and dropped his head. He wiped a cold bead of sweat from his forehead and then looked up to see the flame crawling around the edge of the walls. Jacob thought he must be back in a set of catacombs like the ones he had been in the year before.

He soon noticed he was wrong.

The flame showed he was now in one room about the same size as the chapel on the surface above him. As the light reached the far wall, it became clear that he was standing in some kind of subterranean chapel or church. Pillars formed an inner area surrounding the glowing particles that hung in the air. To the far walls and beyond the trench fires were a series of stone boxes, long and narrow. Jacob walked over to the right and noticed they were tombs with effigies of the deceased carved into the lids of the sarcophagi.

As he looked up on the right wall, he noticed letters etched into the stone. Though it took him a moment to make them out, they read "REGUM NORWEGIE" Was *that one of the phrases the professor mentioned to me?* He was not sure. He remembered there were two other phrases. He went to the wall in the front where he found "REGUM SCOTIAE" and then hurried between those tombs over to the left and found on that third wall "REGUM HIBERNIAE."

Yes, these are the words. These are the tombs. The Norwegian kings are over there, I bet facing their homeland. The Scottish kings are up front there in the center. And, here, here are the Irish kings. Jacob looked down at the faces carved in stone on the four boxes at his feet. Then he looked up on the wall again and noticed a Celtic knot, intricately carved into its face below the letters. He walked to the front wall and saw twelve sarcophagi on the floor and then counted thirty-six small rectangle doors carved from the stone wall. *Did the professor say there were forty-eight Scottish kings buried on Iona?*

Below REGUM SCOTIAE was written "Nemo me impune lacessit." *Yep, that I recognize for sure!* He remembered back to the safer times at Iona Academy. They already seemed so long ago. He wondered if kids were still getting hung on the fence for not remembering that ancient motto of Scotland or if that tradition had also been banned. He thought again of Jenny and sent a hope her way. "I'll write when I can get control of my situation, Jen," he mumbled.

He moved back to his right and there counted eight stone boxes containing Norway's kings. "Well, Professor, I've found your tombs, whether I'll ever get out and tell you about them or not," he said to himself.

Jacob walked back to the place he had first landed, trying not to look at the skull nailed to the wall behind him, or the bones now partly being burned in the black ooze. He looked back up at the ceiling, but could make out no door. He looked around for something on which to stand. Tombs surrounded the inner chapel in the floors and walls. The center aisle led to a table with a cross sitting on it at the far end. He could see it through the glow of floating particles.

Seeing the great stone glowing in the middle, Jacob wondered if it was safe to approach and try to pull it over to where he stood. He thought he might be able to stand on it and reach a latch or handle or something in the ceiling that would open the trap door that had swallowed him.

He moved in close and slow, watching the particles dance in the air above the great stone slab. He wondered what was generating the light. Slowly he reached for the ring handle on the right end of the stone. He watched as his hand was bathed in light. His skin appeared somehow more healthy and alive. Jacob marveled. Then he felt a squeeze; then a pull. He tried to pull away, but the light or something in the light had grabbed his hand and was squeezing tight.

"Ahhhh," he gasped in pain and fright. He pulled again and the force let go. He flew backward onto his back; a throbbing pain ran up his arm and into his neck. He laid on his back recovering. He looked up at the ceiling. As he did, he realized that even if he could escape now, it was likely Mortimer was up in the chapel or just outside the doors waiting for him. *Maybe I'm safer with dead kings than with a live Mortimer,* he thought.

As he sat up, Jacob noticed that the inner area of this underground chapel had a drop stone façade coming down about two feet from the roof. The columns ran just on the inside of the stone slabs and they ran around the entire inner area. There was writing on the face of the slabs and he stood to see it better. It was in Latin or some such language he did not understand. He walked around trying to read it. There were five sections set apart by four symbols—a goat, a lion, an eagle, and a man. The professor had said something about those four, he was sure, when discussing the *Book of the Kells* in the abbey a few days before. He patted the leather cover he had pushed into the top of the back of his pants and under his sword belt.

Five sections! Book of Kells! Wait a minute! Jacob reached into his pocket and removed the folded piece of paper Professor von Niblick had given him. There were five sections to the poem on the page. There were no symbols, but the sections seemed to match up with those on the stones.

He noticed that right in the title was another clue that the poem might just be related to this place he found himself in. "chapel P" he read with excitement. *I am surely in a chapel.* "Pieces Broken!" *There, right in front of me,* he realized, *right in front of me are pieces broken and floating on the air.* His excitement was growing. He read on.

"Who opens the door," *well, I guess I opened the door, but am I a* "Questing knight?" *In my dreams!* "Kings surround," *sure kings are everywhere surrounding this place! Dead ones!* Jacob wasn't sure if he was glad they were dead right then or not. He read on through the rest of the poem, now sure he was in the place mentioned in its words. Then he came to the last line, "And fears no more." *Fears no more! Fears no more! That's what I need. Do I ever need it,* he lamented as he looked into the shadows again to insure there was no one watching behind him. He turned and saw he was only being watched by the skull spiked to the wall. He read the poem over again in full. Then a second time more slowly still.

THE BOOK OF KELLS

289

Chapel P

Pieces broken
Whole no more
Questing knight
Who opens the door

Can ask of meaning
Of past in crumbles
If he dares
Perhaps he stumbles

Kings surround
The precious treasure
Memory awakened
To take his measure

To be felt, not touched
To be asked, not rushed
Truth will be found
With a silent sound

Makes Andrew's mark
Upon the floor
Opens his eyes
And fears no more

Well, he thought. *I am most in need of fearing no more, so maybe I can start there. But, that is the end. Who starts at the end?* Then Jacob remembered hearing the saying "and the first shall be last and the last shall be first." It was good enough for him. He wanted to lose the feeling of fear that sat in his chest like an anchor. He wanted that more than about anything at the moment. He wanted it more than anything except, perhaps, to know he would find a way out and be home with his parents again to have a nice supper and talk before giving them a hug and then curling into a warm and safe bed of his own on Longbranch Drive.

THE IONA CONSPIRACY

OK, let's start backwards, then, he decided. "Make Andrew's mark/ Upon the floor/ Opens his eyes/ and fears no more." He said it over in his head several times. *Andrew's mark, Andrew's mark ... St. Andrew ... it must be St. Andrew and his mark must be the mark of the St. Andrew's Cross, the flag of Scotland ... Make the mark on the floor.* Jacob pulled his sword from its sheath. He didn't know why he hadn't done it the second he hit the floor, but he hadn't and now realized he wouldn't have been ready if he was in danger. *Stupid,* he said of himself.

Jacob took the tip of the blade of Isildane and placed it on the dirt floor up to his right. He began pulling it toward him and to the left. Slowly and gently he moved it, barely removing the layer of loose dust and dirt from the path he was tracing. Then a peculiar thing happened. The sword was stopped in its path. Later he wondered why he didn't force the blade through when it met resistance. He didn't know but was very glad he was more patient.

He bent down to see what was obstructing the blade and noticed a lump across the path. He blew the dirt from it and as the dust resettled along the path, Jacob noticed a line of string. He blew further down and saw the string ran back toward the wall behind him. He guessed it continued in the other direction toward the wall to the left of him as well. He puzzled for a moment and then stood. He walked to the wall to his right and crouched. He looked at the string like a golfer lining up the winning putt on the 18th green. He took his sword and laid it parallel to the ground and then flung it, hilt first, at the string.

The beard that hangs from the lion's chin caught the string and moved it back, just like Jacob himself would have done if he hadn't stopped. As the string moved, Jacob saw dust particles rise into the air in four directions. Two rose in the direction of the side tombs and two ran into the corners of the wall behind him. The "X" was clear.

A sound came from the wall in front of him. Quicker than he could recognize, two objects flew from the side walls, one crossing directly in front of his face. They met with a great crash in the center of the wall behind where he stood a moment before. Shards of the dry and brittle skull flew into the air and then bounced and quivered to rest on the stone floor. Jacob's heart jumped and his pulse raced as he sunk down by the trench fire and stared at the black fists on the back end of the spikes that were meant to skewer him.

Jacob closed his eyes and said a prayer of thanks. He opened them again and looked at the pieces of skull that had come to rest on the floor around him. "I guess you were even more stupid than me, old chap!" It was the first time since his arrival that he had thought about those dry bones actually being a real person. *A treasure hunter? Just a boy like me who fell through the trap door? Member of the Sporrai or of its enemy?*

Movement on the floor caught his eye and dissolved his imagination. The strings were coming tight once more and were being camouflaged by the dirt and dust that was falling back onto them. The trap had been reset.

Jacob wanted out more than ever. He closed his eyes and tried to contact Nibblus Maximus. To his continuing frustration, he couldn't penetrate the walls and ground with his mind. He then thought of the poor people on the ferryboat and realized it was probably better that the dragon protect them from the sea serpent, anyway. He hoped his little Nibbles would be all right and might even be able to get rid of Mortimer before he got out. He looked up again at the ceiling and reminded himself that he had no way home unless something else happened. He knew it would either work to discover more about the place or sit and make this his tomb. He resolved to get back to work.

Jacob read the poem again and thought about starting from the top this time but could see the pieces broken and figured he was the one who opened the door so he was already passed that. And, not having to fear, as it said in the last line, made him want to give it another shot. He mumbled the last stanza over and over again. "Make Andrew's mark. I did that and nearly got killed, darn it. Wait, no fear, opens his eyes, Andrew's mark." Something was coming to him now, he marveled.

Close your eyes in sleep, maybe, or prayer. Upon the floor. Those dead kings are on the floor with their eyes closed, I guess. Maybe something to do with them? Andrew's mark. If it is the "X" cross of St. Andrew, well, I remember the story of how he was crucified on an "X" as a sign of humility.

He thought he wasn't worthy of being killed the same way his Lord was. Well, if Andrew's mark is a sign of humility, then how do we show humility? He looked around at the kings and it came to him. He had seen it a hundred times in movies and read of it in books. *No one approaches kings but on their knees; a sign of humility. Of course, that must be it!*

Jacob carefully stepped forward and knelt down in front of the glowing stone and floating pieces. "OK," he said aloud, "I am humble and am on the floor. See? Not proud. Andrew's Mark. I am not worthy and so am showing it." Jacob was peering up through the tops of his eyes as his head was bowed.

Movement in the front of the chapel suddenly caught his eye and sent a shot of panic through his body. Emerging in the shadows was the figure of a man.

Suddenly Jacob remembered the phrase the professor taught him to say the year before when he was sent into the catacombs in Edinburgh. "I serve the Order of the Sporrai. I serve the Order of the Sporrai," he repeated but did not move. As the man emerged from behind the glowing center of the chapel, Jacob could see it was a king. He wore partial armor covered by long flowing robes of red and gold. He wore a crown atop his head of wavy hair. He carried a shield in his left hand and a sword in his right. A rampant lion was on his shield. "I serve the Order of the Sporrai!" Jacob repeated at the man again without moving his body.

The king walked to the edge of the graves of the Norwegian kings and stood, not ten feet from where Jacob knelt in sublimation.

"Sir," Jacob said in a quivering voice, "I mean, Your Majesty, Sir, I serve the Order of the Sporrai." Jacob was breathing heavily and hoping beyond hope that this man would be friendly.

The king motioned for Jacob to rise. Jacob stood unsteadily. Neither made a sound. The man looked Jacob over from head to foot. His eyes paused as they passed over the sporran around Jacob's waist. The king then raised his eyes into Jacob's before searching him again with his gaze. Jacob stood silently looking into the man's eyes. He felt like he was being watched from some distant place, not merely from across the room. The sight of Isildane's sword in Jacob's right hand caused a visible change over the man's countenance. He bowed slightly and stepped back toward the shadows. He remained silent and unmoving.

Jacob had no idea how much time had passed before he finally decided to act again. He read through the poem again and this time hit upon the stanza that read, "Kings surround/ The precious treasure/ Memory awakened/ To take his measure." *Kings around the glowing center, which is probably the treasure,* Jacob figured. *Memory awakened? Maybe that is referring to the big guy standing over there. After all, when he was staring at me, maybe he was taking my measure.* He remembered hearing the phrase somewhere before.

If I'm right about that, Jacob figured, *this other stanza about not being touched probably referred to the glowing area that zapped me earlier. Clearly, it shouldn't have been touched but what does it mean for it to be 'felt'? And what about this "Truth will be found with silent sound?" Well, I am being silent, so maybe the truth will come. If it does, I hope it doesn't look like* him, Jacob said to himself as he looked over at the king who still stood silently in the shadows.

Jacob read the last remaining stanza that he had not thought he had figured out. "Can ask of meaning/Of past in crumbles/If he dares, Perhaps he stumbles." He turned it over in his mind again and again. Finally, he came to guess "past in crumbles" might just refer to the particles floating in the glowing center. *It certainly looks like crumbles of something,* he thought. *"Can ask of meaning,"* he read. *Ask of who? Of that guy? Of the glowing force? Of one of the other dead kings? Oh, um, wait a minute. What is this part about my possibly stumbling if I dared? I don't like that line.* Jacob looked down at the ground and the slightly submerged string of death he had uncovered. *Surely I don't want to stumble onto that and get stapled to the wall!*

Jacob looked at the entire poem yet again and read aloud, "Pieces broken, Whole no more/Questing knight/Who opens the door/Can ask of meaning/Of past in crumbles/If he dares/Perhaps he stumbles."

OK, he thought, *I can ask, it seems, about the broken pieces that were once whole in some distant past and what they mean. I am not getting out without taking the risk, it seems. Heck, I can't even move with him over there now. So, here goes.*

Jacob ran what he might say over in his mind several times. He finally began to speak in a low and unsteady voice. "Sir, um, Lord, what is the meaning of these pieces that are broken?"

The man stepped forward toward Jacob and the boy's heart raced and his mind ran over what seemed to be his great mistake. The man took only a couple of steps out of the shadow, however, and knelt before the glowing elements hanging in the middle of the chapel. He looked over at Jacob and motioned for the boy to follow his lead. As Jacob's knee landed upon the ground, the suspended pieces began to move. They spun around each other like they were caught in a vortex—Jacob wondered if some door had been opened in the ground beneath them and some airy force had been let into the room with such tremendous power that it had caused the small tornado. He hoped it might be a way home.

As they spun, the elements began collecting in groups in the air. Soon there was not one great vortex but two. Then Jacob could make out three distinct collections of the spinning pieces. Soon pieces started adhering to one another and building themselves as if by the hands of an invisible craftsman. There was no sound. There was no clanking of metal pieces, though it was becoming clear to Jacob that most of the pieces were metal and glowed gold. He didn't know if the elements were gold themselves, however, or just appeared that way from the glowing gold light that still surrounded them.

Jacob marveled at what appeared to be many invisible hands working the pieces back into their former substance. They were taking shape. There were two long and large elements and one small one in the middle. As they continued to be worked, Jacob noted the one on his left taking the form of a sword. The one to the right was longer and thinner. *Perhaps a lance*, he thought. The one in the middle was complete before the other two. It was a cup. When they had completed their transformations and the circling wind inside the glowing area had completely stopped, there was a sword suspended on the left, a lance hanging in the air on the right, and a cup on a short stem with wide base hanging in the middle.

The cup held his imagination strong in its glory. *The Grail!* He announced to himself with excitement. *The Holy Grail! Could it be?*

Particularly since the previous year when Professor von Niblick told him that Arthur and Merlin were indeed true characters and were bound up in the Order of the Sporrai that now held him, Jacob had read much of the legends of the great king and his knights. *The Grail, if this is the grail, yes, this, of course, I am in the chapel Perilous! chapel P, of course!* Jacob looked down to confirm that von Niblick had indeed written "chapel P." on top of his translated poem. He struggled to remember the legend but could only remember that the questing knight was to ask the meaning of the broken pieces of the past. They would be reconstituted and their meaning would be revealed, perhaps immediately, perhaps later. Then other good things would happen, he was pretty sure of that. There was something about wounds being healed; he had a vague recollection of that. Still, "Perilous" in the name of the place he was now in with at least one dead king standing nearby did not make him feel much safer at all; excited, but not safer.

The Grail! The Grail! The excitement got the best of him and he stood and moved toward the suspended cup. He did not notice the king's head bow further as he did. If Jacob would have seen the man's gesture, he might have known of his impropriety. He moved closer and reached for the cup. As he did, just like had already happened to him once, but more powerfully still, a great power peeled through his skin, up his arm and exploded between his shoulder blades. He dropped back to the ground rolling with pain.

When he again recovered, he remembered the stanza of the poem that read, "To be felt, not touched/To be asked, not rushed/Truth will be found/ With silent sound."

Stupid! Stupid! Jacob berated himself. *Well, I've stumbled and the warning was right there in front of me!* "To be felt, not touched," he read over several times. Jacob got back up and knelt again like the king. He then said, "OK, I'm humbled again and making the mark of Andrew in humility here. Now, I wish to know the meaning of these pieces. I mean, I wish to *feel* the meaning of these pieces, if I can." Jacob peeked out of his right eye at the king and then at the glowing objects.

The cup began to turn. The red liquid in the cup did not spill from its container as it moved. Jacob marveled at that. It was defying the basic laws of science as Jacob knew them. The boy's eyes focused on the red, the deep, deep red of the liquid. He became melancholy. Gradually the red liquid took over his imagination. He came only to see red and he knew it was good. But in that knowing, he also could feel he was getting a warning to beware of false reds. *True reds? False reds?* He didn't understand those feelings at all.

In the red of the great cup, Jacob was shown many things. He saw ancient happenings and modern ones. He came to understand, he thought, at least some of the meaning of these broken objects that had just been reworked whole again before his eyes. He came to know that they were broken because the world was broken and could no longer understand what once united the good and the great. He understood he was being able to see his world through ancient eyes.

Much of what he saw, Jacob never told anyone. He felt it was a gift he was not to share. He saw a great stag. He saw the lance piercing its side and he wept. He saw blood drip down the rectangular stone before him. He saw Isildane and marveled at him wielding the sword that now hung from his own belt. He saw the sword itself being forged by a lone craftsman on an isolated mountain crag. He saw Isildane earn its hilt and pommel in great battles. He saw Isildane carrying a great skin and saw nearly invisible hands guiding him as he cut from it the treasures of the sporrai.

He saw the man break the knife that did the cutting and cast its pieces into the depths of the sea. He saw kings being crowned upon the stone and kings being carried on shoulders and barges to their burial grounds. He saw monks at work on a great book of color and beauty. He saw others at work on a large piece of leather. Some would work a map and words into its soft interior. Others then set jewels and a silver cross into its more beautiful and smoother side. Jacob recognized it at once as the cover of the *Book of Kells*; the very leather he carried under his belt.

He saw all this and more. He came to understand much. More important to him than understanding, however, is that he came to gather strong pictures in his mind that would serve him well in the times ahead.

Finally, he felt fatigued and his mind wondered to Jenny and Will and Iona Academy and the modern Remnant of Kirk, MacGregor and the rest. As he did, he was given a vision of terrible things. He saw fire and death. He saw hideous creatures comprised of unnatural body parts. He saw Abigail Witherspoon as he had once in a dream days ago—old and sickly and in bed. He saw scientists experimenting with terrible instruments. He heard cries in the night.

Finally, he saw Ian, his old friend. They were walking along the street together in St. Andrews and talking of having a scone. Then Ian was being lured away from him. Then the boy who once was part of his adventures was being yelled at and threatened. Jacob saw him strapped to a wall with wires going into him and machines all around him beeping and zipping. He saw Jenny nearby talking to a small figure in white.

Then the red came back to him. This time it was not good; Jacob could feel the evil. Black entered the red and spun within it. The black infected the red throughout and then came back together. The black began to lift out of the red and a face began to fade in. It was the leathery stranger from Feddinch House. It was Whipsnade. It was Mortimer. It was evil with a thousand names. Exhausted, Jacob finally fell forward on his face and lost consciousness. As he did, his knee tripped the string and two more black bolts flew through the air and crashed like a clap of thunder into the wall behind him. Jacob heard nothing.

WITHERSPOON

Dr. Kirk led Jenny, Emma, Nolus and Landis behind the stable. They went beside the old dog kennels, which were now covered in large blue tarps and nailed tight to the ground. The metal doors were exposed and locked, but nothing else. The cages rattled as they went by. Things were alive in those old kennels, but there was no dog bark or even any kind of noise they could recognize. There was just the rattling of things hitting up against the fences as they walked by. Kirk did not hesitate or even acknowledge the noises and the kids had no choice but to keep going after his lead.

They made their way stealthily over to the edge of the cut path that led to the old Ashland mansion. Then the four of them picked their way up the right side of the path, staying as close to the trees as possible, but not actually entering the woods where it was darker and more dangerous and where twigs waited everywhere to be snapped loudly beneath their feet.

When they arrived at the yard around the mansion, the five of them made a dash for the house, as much as Dr. Kirk ever "dashed," anyway. Much slower than the kids could run, his walking stick thrust back and forth at them as an ominous warning not to try to get ahead of him.

Nolus looked over at Jenny at just the wrong time. Dr. Kirk's arm thrust back and the tip of his stick jabbed between Nolus' ribs. The unsuspecting boy buckled and gasped. Jenny giggled, but only under her breath.

The door was opened and shut almost instantaneously upon their arrival on the porch. Though the house was completely dark on the outside and seemed utterly abandoned, it was warm and light inside. No one mentioned this anomaly at first, but Landis would later inspect the windows and discover there were some sort of plastic boxes built around them that kept all light from getting to the outside. To anyone watching from Iona Academy, the house seemed as cold and dark as it had been in two decades. But to the Remnant, it was a safe house almost right in the middle of all the troubles unfolding on campus.

Dr. Kirk took off his coat and hung it on a peg behind the door. The kids looked around and marveled at the beautiful old woodwork and staircase. Though it all could have used more upkeep, the floors, walls, and staircase were all made of matching caramel colored wood that was bathed in warm light from the oil lamps. Hammish MacGregor scratched his long grey beard as he inspected the children. He introduced himself to the kids as Dr. Kirk slipped off down the hall.

"Come this way, team," MacGregor said. He led the four into the library where Jenny had first been introduced to the Remnant.

The girls and Landis all focused on the men standing at a desk in the far corner of the room. Nolus looked up and saw the snake-headed chandelier hanging above the middle of the room and wondered about it, then looked around for other such oddities, as he followed slightly behind the others into the room.

"Well, Dr. Kirk, this is your team, is it?" Copernicus Campbell asked as he straightened up at the desk.

"It's the best we got, I fear," said Dr. Kirk who was now entering the library from behind them. He was carrying a tray of cookies and coffee cups of milk. "Nothing like a ginger snap dipped in milk to calm the nerves on a night like this, young ones."

Campbell moved toward the tray saying, "Don't mind if I do."

"For the kids, Campbell, not for you," Dr. Kirk said as he moved between his old friend and the tray and then walked him back toward the desk in the far right corner of the room.

"Sorry we can't have a fire to dry out the back of your britches, boys!"

Dr. Campbell said as the kids moved toward the cookies. Landis and Nolus turned slightly in embarrassment.

"What did you do to 'em?" MacGregor asked in Dr. Kirk's direction. "Scare the water out of 'em did ya?"

"Water?" Nolus then realized this old bearded man was accusing him of peeing his pants and he would have none of that. "I mean, no!" he stumbled.

"Not water, you say?" MacGregor replied with a cock of his head.

"No. I mean, yes. Yes. It was water, but not what you meant." Nolus tried to fix his answer.

"No? What did I mean?" MacGregor asked.

"Leave him alone, Hammish. They were sitting in the dewy grass by the stables," Dr. Kirk stopped his friend from teasing the boys. Jenny and Emma both laughed sheepishly.

"Enough of this," came a woman's voice from the dark corner by the desk. She stood and lit a candle near her.

"Headmistress Witherspoon!" Emma exclaimed and ran over to her side.

"Yes, it's me, dear," the woman said as she squeezed Emma's shoulders and smiled knowingly at her. Tears began to form in the girl's eyes. She had worked in Miss Witherspoon's office the last year and had gotten to know her very well. More than anything else among the changes at Iona, she had been desperately worried about what had happened to the woman she considered to be an extra grandmother. Emma buried her head into the top of Miss Witherspoon's blue dress.

The other children greeted the former headmistress. She had not remembered Jenny's face from the girl's short time on campus. But she knew who she was expecting that night and welcomed her by name.

Dr. Kirk took charge with, "Sporrai, we do not have much time!"

"Aye," MacGregor replied.

"We must get these youngsters back to campus before they are missed and while they still have time to get some sleep," Dr. Kirk said.

"Back? Do we have to go back?" Jenny asked. The other kids perked up attentively. All of them felt safer with the teachers they had come to love and admire in this old drafty house, than they did back on campus with the new rules and new people and new programs and Furangle's guards.

"We aren't yet ready, dear. We couldn't sustain a fight when they would come looking for you all. No, you have to go back but not for long." Miss Witherspoon was holding Emma around the shoulder. "If you choose to join in our efforts to liberate Iona, it won't be long until we have things under control again."

The boys puffed out their chests as if reacting to a challenge. Emma smiled. Jenny masked her concern with a half-smile of her own.

The group all sat down in stuffed chairs and love seats. Nolus nibbled at ginger snap cookies non-stop. He had always had a sweet tooth and nothing set it afire like being nervous. His appetite for cookies became positively veracious. The others were a bit embarrassed that he would eat as many as he did, but Dr. Kirk and the others didn't seem to mind.

"First, the quick background," Witherspoon said as she crossed her legs.

Dr. Kirk moved toward a small decanter on a table with small crystal glasses and poured a drink.

"I didn't leave Iona. That blasted Finnius Creech poisoned me. I never trusted him," Witherspoon said as she uncrossed her legs. "He came with all the degrees and recommendations and the board wouldn't listen to me. I never wanted him. Never trusted him. But the board wanted *new* ideas, *new* energy, and a *new* mission for the school and so we hired him. The little worm was nothing but trouble from the beginning!"

"Abbey," MacGregor interjected, "perhaps we can rehash the school's administrative politics at some other time?"

"Yes, well, anyway, the worm poisoned me and then they hid me up on the second floor of the infirmary. I didn't know where I was or what was going on for days. Then one day a little angel came into my room. Strange little angel, if I do say so." She shook her head. "He talked at me as if I were a horse, I remember that."

A horse? Jenny's mind ran back to the day she had visited Will and he had talked as if she were a horse.

"Anyway, thinking I was a horse, he unhooked me from all the tubes they used to keep drugs going into me to keep me in a coma. I guess he thought they were my reins or ropes or something and my bed was my stall. I groggily remember that angel standing over me saying 'Awe, little horsey, horsey, need to be able to run free the horsey should be!' Anyway, he left and said he would come back to visit me the next day after he visited with another horsey. As the drugs gradually wore off, I came to my senses, figured out where I was, and that night made my way out of the infirmary. Good Dr. Kirk, here, always so good to me, found me stumbling in the woods in that hideous flowered hospital gown they had me in! I'm glad you are a gentleman of another age, good Dr. Kirk!"

"Maybe your age of chivalry is not dead, like your man Burke once claimed," Campbell offered in Dr. Kirk's direction. Kirk did not reply.

"Miss Witherspoon," Jenny interjected, "I wonder if your angel could have been my friend Will? Do you remember him?" Miss Witherspoon shook her head negatively. "Well, he is new like Jacob and me and he is in the infirmary now. Dr. Campbell drugged him and he is there."

"Campbell!" Witherspoon exclaimed. Her eyes were boring holes directly into Campbell's face and he could almost feel the heat. "You poisoned a student?"

Campbell looked over unhappily at Jenny then defended himself. "We had no choice, Abbey. We thought he would get in the way or spout off and endanger Master Boyd and our plans. He knows too much about Master Boyd and unlike Miss Sawyer, he doesn't seem to understand when to keep his mouth shut. Its just a mild form of equestrian delirium, that's all."

"I want him out of there, then, at first opportunity, is that clear?" Headmistress Witherspoon ordered. Turning toward Jenny, she added "Sounds like, my dear, he may have been my angel, indeed!"

Dr. Kirk then briefed the students on the existence of 'The Remnant,' though he did not mention anything about the greater mysteries of the Sporrai. He just told them about their group that aimed to retake Iona and stop whatever evil was afoot in their little community.

"Now, kids, tell us everything you know about what is happening at my beloved Iona," the woman requested of them.

They took turns telling the Remnant members of the changes on campus. They briefed them on the show trial and the new regulations that had eliminated all old traditions and courses. They told them of the removal of all the old paintings and lots of the old books that had been taken out and put in the stables. Jenny told them of what she knew from her time working in trailer #2. When she told them about the file she had uncovered for Ian Nelson, Professor MacGregor dropped the glass he was holding. It shattered on the floor.

"There is no time to lose, Abigail! We must act and act now!" MacGregor was on the edge of fury as he spoke. "The boy Ian must be saved and we *certainly* cannot let them tap into his deep memories! Everything could be lost!" He was standing now. Shards of glass were grinding into the hardwood floor beneath his right foot. The entire mood of the room changed dramatically with this new information. It was as if an ancient king had just gotten word that the barbarians had breeched the gate.

"Here, Horsey, Horsey ..."

Bunting Boyle, the old teacher of weapons and the martial arts, stepped into the library of Ashland mansion with heavy feet. He had been listening to the conversation since he arrived in the doorway and hadn't wanted to interrupt. He could hold himself back no longer.

"We must act and we must act NOW!" he aserted. "I told you we were letting them get too entrenched down there. That evil must be stamped out, I tell you, and we must do it now! We should have struck back the day that witch arrived! We are not just playing with little educational reforms here, we are talking about them playing with the very stuff of life down there—and if they do have this former Bearer, this Ian kid, nothing is safe. The danger will grow from this little point of ground but it will not be contained. It will seep into the culture and into science and into books until no one has the desire to stand in their way—not even the Remnant!" Boyle was easily the biggest man in the room, with a barrel chest and closely cropped hair. He lectured from behind the loveseat on which Landis and Nolus sat.

"Bunting," Hammish MacGregor interrupted in his Scottish brogue. "We must strike, you are right there; but not in anger and emotion. We are a small group and must plot our counterpunch carefully; very carefully."

"You are often too careful and too slow, friend," Bunting replied.

"We are at a point where we must act, we all know that," Abigail Witherspoon said very calmly and slowly. "We must gather as much information as we can and then must be ready to act. First, we need to get these kids back into their beds before they are missed. It's bad enough having them snoop around looking for Jacob. Now that I'm gone, too, they will become more suspicious and maybe will even crack down again on the kids."

Jenny was fiddling in her seat and felt the key Puddles had given her bulging slightly in her front pocket. Like water breaking through a dam, she suddenly blurted out, "I have a key!"

The room became silent as everyone stared at Jenny inquisitively.

"You have a key?" Copernicus Campbell broke the silence. "A key to what?"

Jenny wondered what possessed her to blurt that out, but answered without hesitation. "The little boy who plays in the road. You all know him. The kid the students call 'Puddles,' though his real name is Derek. He gave it to me. He said it was a key that opened the doors on the trailers."

"Have you tried it?" Miss Witherspoon asked.

Jenny pulled the key from her pocket and shook her head. "I just got it earlier today, actually."

"That's it," Bunting Boyle interrupted. "Now it's clear that we are to act. We have a key. We can get in and get the information we need and then liberate this place from the evil crawling like maggots through what remains of the corpse that was once mighty Iona!"

Dr. Kirk was fiddling with his walking stick and looking at his shoes. "He may be right, Abbey. He may be right. If they have this Ian child and they are experimenting on him in some way, not only may we be needed to save the Order, but we can't forget the child himself. We must not forget our responsibility to the person here while considering the greater good beyond."

"There will be no need to have this debate, Dr. Kirk," Miss Witherspoon interjected, "if we do not get these youngsters back to their dorm rooms before they are discovered missing. The whole project will be in jeopardy if they are caught. Kirk, Campbell, Boyle, go back to your planning with the maps and leave me to get these children out of here."

As the men went back to the desk with the maps of Iona laid out on it in the corner, Abigail Witherspoon stood and motioned for the children to follow her. She walked out to the front door. "Do you think you can make it back onto campus without being seen?" They all nodded, but not with any degree of confidence.

"Then go back to campus with this mission. First, do not get caught. Second, say your prayers and write a note to be mailed to your parents telling them you love them. Third, keep your eyes and ears open tomorrow for any information we could use. Fourth, Jenny, you lay low and if you can get out of spending much time with the scientists or Dr. Frost, do it. That is too dangerous now, I fear. The rest of you, go about your routine and just be alert. If you don't hear from any of us tomorrow during the day, meet us here again tomorrow night. Now, God bless each one of you." Miss Witherspoon kissed them each on the head and hugged them to her tightly.

Through the dark and keeping in the shadows close to the trees, the four raced down the hill. They continued up passed the barn, across the field, and with a hesitation to look for anyone on the lookout, they burst toward their dorms. Up their stairs they rushed and were in their own rooms in less than five minutes from their start. Jenny's roommate was fast asleep and Jenny was very relieved not to have to try and explain where she had been in the middle of the night. She hoped the others were equally as lucky. The stress had paid its toll and it was not long before she was asleep and the images from the evening slipped out of her consciousness.

The next day, the four children, kept apart from one another as much as possible. Jenny didn't realize that would be the plan until she sidled up to Emma at breakfast and was promptly sent away. She got the picture of what was happening after Emma smiled and then stomped off with her nose in the air. For a moment before that, however, she thought Emma was being positively nasty to her.

The environment around campus was tense. Rumors were circulating among the students that more of them were to be sent home and others were to be put in detention. The group that was in charge of removing the artwork was given lists of more books to be removed from the library and from the common areas of the dormitories. They were to drop them off in a cart that would be taken to the stables until the first anniversary of "New Iona" when a great bonfire would be built to consume all the remaining elements of the past.

Another group was given the task of covering the great stone Celtic cross that sat in the middle of the quad with a bed sheet. "I don't approve, I don't approve, you understand," Miss Ruth told them as she gave them a sheet. The students paid no attention to her but rushed off to their job. The cross only survived the destruction of the first night of the revolution because it had sunken over the years several feet into the ground and the students themselves could not budge it. Mr. Creech vowed it would be uprooted and destroyed as soon as the construction teams no longer needed the heavy equipment.

After breakfast, Jenny went back to her room to write Jacob on a sheet of his enchiridion paper.

Jake:
Good news. Miss Witherspoon is OK. She is with your friends "The Remnant" at Frazier House. They are readying, it seems, for some kind of counter move against Creech and his crew. I probably shouldn't say more now, in case this is found.
Please be careful and come as soon as you can with that beast of yours.

Jenny

When she was done, she looked out the window and thought about what was happening. She watched the kids hauling books out of buildings and throwing them into a cart that had been pulled up in front of the library. She was sad as she watched the books tossed by the boys, but couldn't quite understand her feelings. She watched as Lucy Furangle marched across campus looking like she owned the place. Members of her New Guard flanked her. Finnius Creech came out to check on the progress of the new projects he had given out and two men dressed all in black accompanied him. They had short-cropped hair and had muscles that bulged through the thin cloth of their black clothes.

Jenny turned around to her desk and removed the key Puddles had given her. She had moved it into the blue shorts she put on after showering. She looked at it and put it down on the desk. She put the tip of her right index finger in the hole and spun it around on the desktop. She watched it go around and around and lost herself in the image of the spinning key. She let her eyes unfocus and refocus as she tried to watch the shadow of the key that hung slightly behind the spinning edge. *Didn't Jacob say something about how Copernicus Campbell—before he "died"—had said something about a key? Hmm. Probably just a coincidence, I guess.*

As Miss Witherspoon suggested, Jenny took out a pen and paper and wrote a note to her mother and father. With everything going on, students had the suspicion that Creech was looking at their mail and censoring anything that might alert the outside world that anything was out of the ordinary on campus. She wasn't sure, but couldn't take the chance. She wrote a simple letter telling her parents that she loved them and that the weather was nice and asked lots and lots of questions about their work and about the garden and about her "Munga" and Pap. As she wrote, she kept thinking of poor Ian and what might be happening to him. Though she had never met the boy, she felt sorry for him. And, she wondered about Will. Finally, she couldn't take being shut up in her room any more. The night seemed never to want to come and liberate her from the room. She grabbed a chocolate bar from her drawer and headed to the infirmary.

On her way, she picked up two books that the boys had dropped on their way to the cart. She turned them each over and looked at their titles. One was called *The Bruce—King of All Scotland* and the other was called *Hero Tales of American History* and was written by a guy whose name she recognized as a former President, Theodore Roosevelt. Though

she wanted to keep them safe from the fire, she knew they were not hers
to keep.

When she arrived at the infirmary, the nurse on duty was not at the
front desk. She waited a moment and then cautiously walked back to
where Will's bed was kept. So as not to disturb the other sick students,
she whispered, "Will, it's Jenny. You awake?" There was no answer from
behind the curtain. She said it again. Nothing. She pulled the curtain
back. Her heart raced as she looked upon an empty bed. She turned and
saw the nurse returning from the ladies room down the hall. "Ma'am, has
Will been moved?"

"What are you doing here, girl? You should have awaited my return
so I could sign you in. This is irregular!"

"Yes, ma'am. Sorry. Have you moved Will?"

"Will? You mean that boy from over there?" the nurse pointed to
the empty bed.

"Yes, Will Renrut. He's a friend of mine."

"Well, then, you're a stronger woman than I. That boy is as looney
as a bat. Always carrying on about the horses and calling me 'Old Grey,'!
Would you like to be called 'Old Grey'? Do you think I like it?"

"Well, no, ma'am, I'm sure you don't. But—"

"Yes, well, so, I have really sick patients to take care of and not just
creepy kids who insult me to keep track of," the nurse said as she walked
away.

"Excuse me," Jenny raised her voice to stop the lady who was walking
away and fixing her grey hair back up into a bun. The woman turned.
"Are you saying you don't know where Will is?"

"That's what I just said, little girl! He was here this morning. Now,
if I find him, I'll be sure to tell him that some other horse came to see him
today. Sign in and sign back out so I know you were here." The woman
continued on her way toward the cart of medical equipment against the
far wall.

Jenny looked for Will as best she could without incurring the wrath
of "Old Grey." She looked down the hall. She peeked in the broom closet
and the men's room. She looked for movement under the door of the

locked doctor's office. She stood up, her hand on her hip. She bit her lip as she looked down the hall and wondered what could have become of Will. Gradually her eyes began to focus on the painting at the end of the hall. The painting was of a woman on a pretty grey dappled mare. She looked like she was on a foxhunt, like those that took place every year in the fields and woods around Iona. *Grey Mare! A horse! Of course he's gone to visit the horses!*

Jenny turned and burst out the door. She leapt from the top stair and landed on the sidewalk. She looked around for any sign of him and, seeing none, started off across the field toward the stables.

"Miss Sawyer!"

Jenny startled. Her legs stopped short and her arms flung forward then back quickly to maintain her balance. She looked over into the face of Finnius Creech.

"I hear you were under the weather today and didn't report to work."

Knowing she shouldn't be running outside if she was supposed to be sick she answered, "I'm feeling much better now."

"Well, good. Then I suggest you report to your trailer for work."

Jenny's mind raced to Will and where he might be and what would happen to him now if he was out and she couldn't look for him. She decided she had no choice but to relent and said, "On my way, sir!"

Jenny turned and started walking toward trailer #2. As she did, she stretched on her tippy toes to try to look over the rise and down to where the stables rested in the bottom. On the third stretch, she caught sight of a ghostly white figure walking in front of the red stables. She stretched to another look and saw what was unmistakably a hospital gown blowing open in the breeze. Blushing, she quickly averted her eyes toward the ground between her feet. *Oh my gosh, he escaped without his pants!*

Jenny looked back and Mr. Creech was still nearby. She knew she couldn't risk heading to the stables after being ordered to report to work. And, she didn't want Will to go back to the infirmary where the nurse obviously didn't much care for him. She saw Puddles playing in the road fifty yards ahead. She picked up her speed and waved her arm in hopes of getting his attention. Puddles waved back and Jenny motioned him over.

"Can you do me a favor, Derek?" Jenny whispered.

"Of course, because you're going to save the animals," Puddles replied.

"OK. Well, my friend Will is not quite 'right' if you know what I mean. He's down by the stables in a hospital gown, mooning the whole campus! Can you go get him and take him up to that old house up there on the hill? Just tell whoever answers the door that you and he are friends of mine, and that I hope they will take care of him for me."

"I can do it!" Puddles said with eagerness. He started to jog down the road.

"Oh, " Jenny called after the boy. "You might find it useful to act like a horse!" Puddles looked puzzled but turned and kept jogging toward where Will was crossing into the stables calling out "Here horsey, horsey! Here horsey, horsey!"

Head or Tails?

Jenny reported to work and hoped Puddles would be able to take care of Will and get him up to Frazier House where he would be safe. She also hoped she would not get in trouble for sending them up to the house, but she didn't know what else to do. She took every opportunity to step outside and look around from the trailer's steps. She never saw any sign of Puddles or Will that afternoon.

The doctor gave her projects stapling papers and punching numbers into the computer. She did it all slowly because she was so distracted. Every time she passed the filing cabinet, she stared at the drawer with the file for Ian Nelson in it. She didn't know enough to really imagine him and what he might be going through. But that would soon change and so would she.

When the time came for the doctor to go home with the rest of the scientists that worked the day shift, Jenny's work was not done. The doctor asked her to stay and finish entering the data into the computer before she left for dinner.

"The next crew will not be in for a while, so just pull the door shut and make sure it's locked when you leave. Leave the computer running and calculating like we always do. I'll see you in the morning," the man said to her as he was removing his lab coat.

Jenny was nervous. She knew this meant that she would soon be the only person in the trailers until the next shift came. She thought so hard about the key in her right front pocket that she imagined for a moment that she could feel it glowing warm against the skin of her upper thigh. Her anxiety was so high that her fingers grew weak as she typed the numbers into the computer. She finished entering the numbers in about fifteen minutes and then sat back taking deep breaths.

I was given this key for a reason. Miss Witherspoon said to gather what information we could. I'm going to have to risk it. What if I get caught? What if someone is in there when I open the door? Dang it. Oh, I know, I can take a folder with me and if I get caught, I'll say that I was given orders to drop the folder off before I left. I might get uncovered tomorrow when doctor what's his name comes back, but, heck, by then the world could turn upside down with our meeting at Ashland tonight.

Jenny grabbed one of the data folders she had been entering and walked outside. She looked left and then right. She watched as students were heading to dinner and the last of the daytime shift scientists were leaving Iona in their cars. She turned out of trailer #2 and thought for a second about trying trailer #1—but it was Dr. Lilith Frost's own personal work place. Jenny didn't have the courage. She turned back toward the other three trailers overlooking the big ditch where her and Puddles had seen the lion's head.

She walked passed the end of Trailer #2 and was startled when Puddles stepped out to greet her.

"Puddles!" Darn you scared me!

"Sorry, Jenny," the boy said meekly. "I just wanted to tell you that I got your friend up to the old house. The old headmistress from the Academy took me in. It was nice to see her. She is much nicer than old Creech!"

"Yes, she is," Jenny answered. "Derek, you can be trusted, can't you?"

"That's just what she asked me. Of course I can. You're my friend and you're going to save the animals."

Jenny was puzzled. "Thanks. You go on home now, OK. I don't want you to get into any trouble. I am going to see if this key works."

"Good! I knew you would use it! My dad will be looking for me, so, I'll see you tomorrow. Thank you, Jenny. We all thank you."

Jenny found the little boy so curious and what he said about her so odd. Still, she said nothing except, "Thank you, Derek."

Puddles went off toward his home on the edge of Iona's woods where he lived with his father who worked on the maintenance crew on campus. Jenny turned to trailer # 3 and cautiously approached the door. She thought about looking around to see if anyone was watching but realized that if they were they would see her standing at the door and looking suspicious which would be just as dangerous. She would slip in as quickly as possible.

Jenny slipped the key into the lock and turned it. The lock snapped open effortlessly and she slipped quickly into the trailer. To her relief, no one stood there to greet her, though movement was all around. From floor to ceiling, the trailer was covered with cages, though each had a light blue cloth covering its front and keeping the animals from seeing her. The exception was a tank full of snakes that formed the front end of the trailer. She stepped quickly away from the glass and shivered. *Gross! There must be dozens of them! Yuck!*

She took a pencil from the small desk and lifted one of the cloths. Behind it was a monkey that jumped at the front of the cage and made a horribly loud scream. Jenny dropped it back, her heart racing and her hand over her mouth to stifle her own instinct to scream. She took deep breaths to calm down. She vowed to try only one more. She walked to the other wall and repeated the lifting of the veil. In the chosen cage was a large red bird, its head tucked into its wing. It did not react and she was relieved. *So this is where they keep the animals, at least the small ones.*

She snapped the door closed and moved on to trailer # 4. The key worked equally well and she slipped quickly inside. The inside of this trailer was much different. Rather than cages, there was a medical table along the right wall as she looked toward the back. Above the table were shelves and peg boards full of medical equipment and instruments for performing surgery. Along the left were medical monitors and computer screens. Along the back was a light blue curtain drawn tight.

Jenny looked at the monitors, watching the lines move up and down and listening to the machines beep. She watched another that looked like it was measuring the power left in a battery. She gave some attention to a flat screen monitor hanging in the middle. It was showing something that she could not make out. She squinted at it. The picture was dark, as if the camera was filming with too little light. As she thought about it, she figured it was probably monitoring what was behind the curtain in the back and if the curtain was pulled, better light for the camera would flood in.

She stared at the monitor another minute. She could see long things that looked like hoses or wires going into something that looked like a fuzzy stump. There were other things in the picture, but they were too shadowy to make out at all. *Well, we've come this far, let's take a look,* she thought.

Jenny walked over to the curtain and pulled it slightly back. Still too dark, she realized. She pulled the curtain back further. At first she still couldn't quite make out what she was looking at. She stared and studied. Then she backed up and bent over as nausea overcame her. She thought she just might puke. *Now I know where the rest of that lion went!* She wiped a cold sweat off her forehead and sat back on the floor, as her legs grew weak.

Behind the curtain was a glass wall. Behind it were two glass cylinders. In the left cylinder was golden fur waving in a clear liquid. A tail curled in the bottom of the cylinder; the mane waved above it. Four paws dangled from lifeless legs. Tubes and wires formed a kind of medical crown and then ran through the headless neck into the torso of the deposed king of the jungle.

To the right was a cylinder of similar liquid. It contained an extremely large head of a bird of prey. Its beak was as big as Jenny's hand. The feathers moved gently among the bubbles. A metal arm came out from the wall and held the head by the neck. Tubes and wires ran up into the neck. She guessed these wires and hoses were keeping the flesh of the beasts alive.

Jenny stared at the motionless parts of animals in utter confusion and with a big open pit in her stomach. When she regained her composure, she stood and slowly approached the glass wall. As she did, she leaned on the operating table. She was not expecting it to be on wheels and it slid against the wall, causing a bang that startled her anew. She looked up just as one of the lion's paws ended a contraction. Her eyes shot over to see the bird's eye now having opened and by all indications, it was looking at her. *Oh, please, no!*

She grabbed the curtain and slammed it shut. She looked up at the monitor, as the light faded and the picture became dark again. But now even through the grainy screen, she knew a paw moved that could rip her in two and an eye looked around above a beak that could tear her flesh from bone. *Does a bodiless bird tell any tales?* That eye would grow and become even more ominous as it hung back in her imagination to rise up unasked again and again in the dark nights of her future.

As she got control of herself, she noticed two buttons below the monitor. One was labeled "Experiments: Trailer 4" and the other was labeled "Experiments: Trailer 5." The button for trailer #4 was glowing green. She knew the monitor was showing what was happening with the experiments in the trailer she was in. She pushed the button for #5, hoping it might get her a good view of what was happening there without actually having to break in and risk getting caught anew. The screen flashed and changed.

The quality of the picture was better than it had been, but was still suffering from low light. Jenny cocked her head slightly to get a better angle as she examined the screen. She could make out tubes and wires and medical monitoring equipment. They were around a bed of some sort, though angled severely up so that it resembled a board leaning against a wall. As she looked at the lump on the board, there was movement in the picture. At first it looked like a ball. As it came to a rest, however, she realized she was looking at a head. It looked like the face of a boy about her age. She jumped back slightly, prayed there was a body attached to the head, and burst out the door.

Mercifully, the students were at dinner, teachers were either on their way home or at dinner with the students, and the scientists had all left for the day with the night shift not expected for another hour or so. She ran over to the back of the gym, where she leaned against the wall to catch her breath and make sense of what she had learned. She slipped down, her hands on her knees. Her mind ran quick and confused.

Oh, man! Oh, man! Dead birds, dead lions. No, wait, they aren't dead. Headless live lions. Bodiless live birds. A boy's head strapped to a table being experimented on. Oh, I hope he has a body with his head! He must have a body with his head! Animals in cages. Snakes ... lots of snakes. This is not Iona! What are they doing?

She glanced at trailer #5 and thought about going in to try to help the boy. She quickly thought better of it. *He could be really sick. They could be helping him. Yeah, sure they are! Helping him! Or, it could be just a head. What would I do with a boy's head?* The possibilities were sickening. *No, but I'm not going on like nothing is happening, either. I can't do it anymore. Maybe I can help. This is hideous, what they're doing.*

She stood and took a deep breath. Then she started running. She jogged at first, but after she started her descent toward the stables, she opened it up into a dead sprint. She turned up through the path between the patches of woods and soon arrived at the door of the Ashland mansion. Her chest was rising and falling quickly as she tried to catch her breath. She rubbed her aching thighs before coming up the steps to the door of the house.

MISSION CYCLOPES

Jenny didn't even need to knock. Little Angus was serving his time in the watchtower of the house and sounded the alarm. Hammish MacGregor was waiting at the door and pulled her inside the moment she arrived. She stumbled across the floor several feet, saw the area rug that tripped her up on her last visit, and sidestepped it artfully.

"What brings ya in such a huff, Lassie?" MacGregor said.

Jenny was still catching her breath. "Awful, just awful!" she announced.

"Oh, now, is it really all that?" Copernicus Campbell said as he entered the room.

"Come, Jenny, into the library ya go and tell us all about it. Copernicus, do get the wee one some lemonade. It was a long run for her up that hill."

MacGregor put his arm around her and walked Jenny into the library. She sat in the seat she had taken on her previous visit and gradually the other members of the house assembled. Jenny waited, but was nearly ready to burst before they had gathered and MacGregor said, "Now, Jenny, what is this terrible news you have for us?"

His words were like the pulling of the drain plug to Jenny's mouth. Her words came fast and furious. All remained silent as they listened to her tale of headless lions and bodiless birds and cages full of animals. They listened with particular attention as she told them of seeing the boy in trailer #5 that she guessed was Ian Nelson. Though she was scared, revolted, and a bit exhausted, she felt particularly good about being able to share the news with the group. She felt vital and important.

"Neoterists!" Dr. Kirk suddenly announced. "Neoterists!" he repeated, this time standing and moving to the center of the group. He positioned himself to be standing between the antlers of the wood-inlaid stag head on the floor in front of the cold fireplace.

"I think I know what you are going to say, Kirk, but go ahead and say it plain and strong," Abigail Witherspoon said.

"Neoterists and Gnostics—they are! I tell you! Neoterists and Gnostics!" Kirk pounded his walking stick in a way Jenny thought was far too hard to be good for the beautiful wood floor.

"Yes, Kirk, everyone is a Neoterist or a Gnostic to you. What's going on in that gothic mind of yours?" Copernicus Campbell interjected.

"Are you blind, here? Can you not see what they are doing? They are attempting to reach into the past with their science. They are attempting to reach into the realm of myth with their probes and wires and chemical formulas." Kirk was swinging his walking stick now back and forth as he lectured the others. "The bodiless bird! The headless lion! Put them together, people!"

"A gryphon!" the little man named Angus offered as he slapped his left hand down onto his thigh.

"Yes, a gryphon. They are creating a gryphon! The sight and cunning of a bird of prey! The power of a lion! They are reaching into myth with their science and attempting to bring the power into our world! Neoterists and Gnostics!" Kirk created another divot in the wood floor as he brought the tip of his stick crashing down.

"Great Caesar's ghost!" Abigail Witherspoon exclaimed. "What else could they have done? Miss Sawyer, you say the head and body were not attached, right?"

"Yes, Ma'am, I mean, no they were not attached." Jenny shook her head.

"*That* one might not have been attached, but maybe that one was not the first. There might be more. And, those other animals—who knows what kinds of beasts they are attempting to engineer? Or, what kind of army of beasts they have *already* engineered!" Kirk was now leaning on his staff and looked down his nose at the rest.

"Campbell, you are uncharacteristically quiet," Abigail Witherspoon observed.

"Seems a bit too fantastical to me. Not sure what I'm to make of all this."

"I will tell you what to make of it. These Neoterists are engineering ungodly creatures to do their bidding. And, people like this, with power in their eyes and money on their minds will not stop there. They will not stop there because they cannot stop themselves. They will go on to experimenting on *people* to create a 'better' race or a 'better' warrior or a 'better' scientist. Just think about it. Why else are they here? There are two hundred helpless kids down there ripe for chemical re-creation."

"They already have one," Jenny interjected. She was trying to get the group to remember poor Ian and his situation.

"Jenny, we know what they are up to with poor Ian. I don't think he is part of those experiments. He is too valuable to them to be beheaded, at least for now," Hammish MacGregor answered. "You see, Jenny, Ian is a former Bearer. A sporran came into his life for a time. It did what it was supposed to do and he kept it safe. When he proved unworthy of keeping it for longer, it faded out of his life. The memory of his time with the sporran faded with the colors reflecting the magic having faded most quickly. He retains, however, his normal memories from that time and there are residual pictures sunk into the deepest part of his mind that still contain the secrets he once knew. They are never wiped fully clean, you see."

Jenny watched him quietly.

"So, you see Miss Sawyer, what they are attempting is to use their science and perhaps their modern psychological methods to get into the deepest and most primal parts of young Nelson's mind. It is there they hope to uncover what he knew that might help them track down who he was in contact with within the Sporrai."

"You mean Jacob, don't you? They're searching for Jacob, aren't they?" Jenny gulped.

"Yes, Jacob for sure. But also me and the others that watched him," MacGregor answered. "They are after whatever knowledge will help them in their quest for power."

As soon as Jenny had started unwinding her story, Bunting Boyle went to the desk in the corner where he pulled a map from the drawer. He was listening, but was also working hard drawing lines on the map and moving small objects around in different locations.

"We have no time to waste," Dr. Kirk slammed his walking staff again into the floor. "We must liberate the school. We must liberate the Nelson boy! We must crush the Neoterist Queen herself and send her creatures out of this world to where they belong. We should do it now!"

"All that, huh, Kirk?" Copernicus Campbell asked. Without pausing for an answer he added, "and all that from just us few?"

"Kirk is right, Copernicus. We cannot wait. At any moment they might break into Nelson's inner mind and then our task will be much harder. Now we have them centered here and occupied with their experiments and ruining my school, let's not forget!" Abigail stood at the end of her speech and added, "We fight! Now, we need a plan. Where is Bunting?"

"Way ahead of ya mum!" Bunting stood up from his position of being hunched over his map. "I've been waiting for you all to stop jabbing and get down to business."

As they all moved toward Bunting and his map, Miss Witherspoon pulled Jenny aside. "Jenny, your friend Will is upstairs resting. Why don't you go up and get him. If he is feeling up to it, have him dress and come down to us. We will need all the hands we can get during the hours ahead."

The members of the Remnant had decided they had no choice but to move and move quickly. Copernicus Campbell was the only holdout. He argued for patience and more time to understand what was going on. In the end, though, he agreed to follow the Headmistress's lead and do his part. The plan that Bunting Boyle had developed relied upon surprise and what he called "the old ways of stalking the stag." They would spread their resources in a wide circle around Iona, what he called a "tinchel." They would gradually move in toward the center, creating a perimeter from which they could launch their forays into the campus and back out again. If things went wrong, they could descend upon the problem spot from multiple directions at once. To make the plan work, however, they would need more than just the eight of them.

Jenny's first job was to rush back onto campus and get hold of Emma, Landis and Nolus. She was to find them and bring them back to the stable where they would rendezvous that evening under the cover of darkness. Miss Witherspoon gave her a strong hug and sent her on her way.

Bunting Boyle took MacGregor with him to sneak back into his home at the other end of campus and retrieve more arms and supplies, including walkie-talkies so they could communicate around the line. Angus the Weeling was given the post of watching the school from the watchtower. Having spent most of his life tending to his duty in the catacombs beneath Edinburgh, Angus had developed extremely sharp vision in low light. Indeed, he preferred the night to the bright parts of the day.

Because he had been part of Lucy Furangle's guard, Will knew where they kept their equipment and the schedule for changing the guards. He knew in particular that Jimmy Stalwart—who was to come on duty at 10:00 PM—never showed up on time. It was almost a guarantee that the meeting place for the New Guard would be unmanned from 10:00 P.M. until at least a quarter past. Will's job was to get onto campus and in place where he could see the guard leave her post on the hour. He could then rush into the small office, sabotage the monitoring equipment, and borrow what he could find that might be of use.

Each had their job to do and was sent, in turn, to execute the first stages of the plan. Jenny arrived in her room to find Elizabeth listening to music and doing a crossword puzzle. Jenny wanted to warn her of what was to come, but knew she couldn't. She just said, "Don't wait up for me. And, well, I'll see you later." She stuffed a couple of granola bars into her backpack and put on long pants and a sweatshirt. In just a few minutes she was heading up the stairs to find Emma. A few minutes later they were pelting Landis's window with pinecones and small rocks. Opening the window while one of the missiles was on its way, Landis caught a cone to the left ear.

The two boys and two girls were on their way back down to the stables when they encountered Will on his way to his position. They exchanged greetings and Jenny reached over and did "battle dragons" with her old friend in the dark as they parted.

"For Jacob, do it for Jacob," she whispered as they broke up.

Just as Will had predicted, Jimmy was late for his post and the office was wide open. Will entered on his haunches and then bent over the computer monitors where he proceeded to snip wire after wire. The screens fizzled and went blank. He had stuck a plank in the Cyclopes' eye and the enemy was blind. Will looked around the office just long enough to find a walkie-talkie and sneak back out the door. He lay down in the bushes as he heard Jimmy coming. When the door closed, he busted across the field and into the trees. Fortunately, Jimmy assumed the computers and monitors had just been turned off. He didn't assume foul play and didn't immediately come looking for an intruder.

By 10:30 everyone was back at the stables and all first missions where completed successfully. "That was the easy part, team. That was the easy part," Bunting Boyle said.

Furies Unleashed

Jacob had no idea how long he was unconscious on the floor of the subterranean chapel. When his eyes opened there were numerous great men that had emerged from their graves and were watching him with intensity. Jacob shook his head, wondering if he was still asleep and perhaps dreaming it all. He struggled to his knees and then, when the kings did not move, he pushed up to his feet. Again he had the feeling he was being watched by eyes from the far beyond and he squinted to try to see back.

The sword, lance, and cup had again been broken into tiny pieces that were floating on the air above the great stone. On a small table next to him was a biscuit and a drink. Famished, he took the bread and the drink and consumed them with abandon. Then the kings began to move. Jacob backed up toward the trench fire behind him. They assembled and began to cling to one another and climb. It was a bizarre and haunting thing to see. Kings in long robes and armor of various styles were climbing on top of one another as if they were boys again. Then they stopped. Jacob could understand it now. They were forming a ladder. They were inviting him to climb on them. They were forming a kind of bridge for him between their world and his. He walked over to the pile of kings and the one on the bottom turned his knee out in Jacob's direction. Jacob took it to be the offer of a first step. The king lowered his head.

Slowly and carefully, Jacob began to climb. He tried not to think about the fact that this ladder he was ascending was made of the bodies of men who had been dead for centuries. *They don't feel very dead*, he marveled as he climbed. He struggled to keep ghastly images from overcoming him but it was difficult. Once a nasty picture creeps into one's head, it does not shake out easily. He slowly made his way to the top. At the top, the last king was waiting for him, seated on the back of the one immediately below. He reached out his hand and Jacob grabbed it. Exerting force in opposite directions, they pulled Jacob up until he stood on the king's thighs. At that moment, Jacob remembered his grandfather saying "we stand on the shoulders of giants, you know, we stand on the shoulders of giants." He wondered if he would tell his grandchildren someday, "we stand on the legs of great kings, you know, we stand on the legs of great kings."

Jacob reached for the ceiling and found two latches. He pulled each in turn and the floor gave way and swung down on its hinges. It was heavy stone. He reached up into Oran's chapel and found the edge of the stonework on the tomb recess. He pulled himself up and out of the hole. No one was in the small room and he gave thanks for that. He looked back into the hole in time to see the kings fade into the darkness and the stone slab slam back up and lock in place. Jacob sat back against the white wall of the chapel and took a deep breath as he looked around. It was light out, but Jacob had no idea if a moment had passed while he was in the chapel Perilous or if days had gone by. He tried to contact Nibblus Maximus but got nothing.

There was no way for the boy to know that the dragon pug had searched and searched the island for him and had gone back to Professor Niblick to seek his advice. He pulled his enchiridion notebook from his pocket and wrote a note to Jenny.

> Jenny,
>   I have more information, I think. Things are worse than we could have suspected there at Iona. I have seen things. I am in some danger here and have lost Nibbles. But when I get him, I will be off to help you there. Keep your head down until I arrive. And

Jacob replaced the enchiridion notebook and stood. He looked out the window and saw nothing but the graveyard and the sea with a few seabirds floating on the currents above. He walked to the door and peeked out. Seeing nothing, Jacob emerged from the chapel but hugged closely to the walls. He knew he was safe inside the chapel, but also knew he couldn't hide there forever. He moved leftward around the side of the small stone church, scanning the distance. He thought he would hug the perimeter of the building until he had scouted all the area and then, perhaps, well, he didn't quite know what he would do at that point, actually. He reached out to Nibblus Maximus with his mind again but heard nothing in return.

He moved further around. He was now at the back of the chapel and was looking out at the edge of the stone wall surrounding the graveyard and then the sea beyond. A voice, agitated and oily, broke in on the calm sounds of the breaking waves.

"So, you've decided to come out, have you?"

Jacob's head turned. Emerging from behind one of the grave markers was Mortimer. His black coat was flowing back in the breeze and exposing his silver broadsword.

"Predictable, you know, all so very predictable." The man said as he walked into a position straight in front of Jacob. "Children today have no patience. You could've stayed in there forever, you know. I could've done nothing to harm you. Now, you are out here among the dead and not the living. And, they will be company that you will enjoy for a long, *long* time!"

Jacob had frozen in place too long. The man was standing about twenty feet directly in front of him. Mortimer was in a perfect position to catch him whether Jacob went right or left. The boy called out to Nibblus Maximus but once again got no reply.

"Now, son," the man said, "why don't you just lay down that silly blade of yours and give me your sporran and that other old hunk of leather I suspect you are still carrying. Rubbish. It's all rubbish; just old myths and legends. Never true, really. Just rubbish. You don't want to die for rubbish, do you? You don't want to lose your life for old stories told by frightened old men, do you?"

To his own surprise, Jacob shot back, "Its not rubbish! I believe and so do you or you wouldn't care!" That was enough bravado for him, however.

Jacob decided to try a basketball head fake and run. He would start to the left, hoping to draw Mortimer that direction and then shoot back to the right. He hoped the extra step would get him to the entrance to the chapel ahead of Mortimer and his blade. Jacob met the man's eyes and then faked left. Unfortunately, the man didn't follow.

"Silly boy. Silly boy," he said. "Perhaps I will have to dispatch you after all. A shame. But, as you die, know that the cover of the book will be mine and because you did not give it to me freely, your precious sporran will emerge again in the world with some other undeserving punk. I will twist them until they give it freely to me. Unlike you, I am patient. Unlike you, I will live!"

Mortimer stepped forward and slashed with his sword. Starting low at his calf's height, the blade rose steadily upward as it approached ever closer to Jacob's open chest. The boy's eyes became fixed on the silver edge of the blade that was catching the blue of the sky and radiating it back up toward Jacob's eye. It all unfolded slow and steady in Jacob's mind, though it would take but a fraction of a second for the edge to reach his body. A black cloud came down over his face before the blade hit. Jacob heard the blade strike before he felt anything.

He fell back into the rock wall of the chapel and his eyes caught a black lump at his feet. Jacob instinctively reached for his chest and wondered when the pain would hit. He had heard of people being shot or otherwise injured but not knowing it at first. Here he was experiencing that strange open time, he thought. *Is that my heart, my lungs?* he wondered. Before he could puke, the lump moved and rolled off his feet. A face opened to the sky.

Fingus! Jacob recognized the little face instantly as one of the two small men who protected him a year before in the catacombs beneath the streets of Edinburgh. Before he could come to grips with what had now happened, he noticed blood running down his left leg and pooling at his feet. He saw the grimace of pain on the face of Fingus and came to understand the little remnant of the Weeling people of long ago had taken the blow from the evil blade. He had laid down his life for a friend. Jacob dropped to his knees in the bloody and spongy ground of Iona.

Mortimer took a step back in confusion and took up a defensive posture. He looked up on the wall and then to the roof.

"Fingus!" Jacob exclaimed as he reached his hands around the small man's head and lifted it slightly.

"Yes, Jacob," he struggled to answer, "but, forget me, get out of here while he is distracted ... go!"

Jacob stared, stunned as he watched drops of life drain from the little man's eyes which were changing in color, now slightly reflecting the blue and white sky above. Jacob looked up. Mortimer, assured that no other surprises were waiting on the roof, was now smiling down upon the scene from ten feet away.

The smile on the assassin's face worked in Jacob's imagination. It turned his grief and fear into a burning hatred. He slipped his hands from Fingus's head and stood defiant and full of anger. Mortimer's smile did not change as he pulled his sword back again into a position ready to strike. Jacob's rage boiled in his brain in a way he had never imagined possible before. He hated the man pure and hot. He stared at the man and his rage turned in on itself as molten lava rises and then falls again into its burning pool.

The sporran that hung about his waist burst open. A hot wind exploded into the damp atmosphere of Iona and furies rose from the pouch. Jacob didn't seem to notice the columns of flame hanging about the chapel behind him, but they would leave their marks forever in the surface they turned for a moment from cold rock to liquid ooze.

The man's smile disappeared as he breathed the warmed air. He took a step strongly toward Jacob. He was ready to bring his sword now finally crashing down into the victim intended for its earlier swing. Jacob yelled a shout of rage like never had exited his body before. He lifted his sword to engage the man. As his expression of anger lashed through the damp air, the furies that had been unleashed from the sporran descended. The flames cut through the air and met the man's blade on its track toward Jacob's vital organs. Drips of molten metal fell onto the cold grass and sizzled as the flame passed through. The man's arm kept moving but no blade was left to cut through Jacob's side. Mortimer turned around, confused, and looked into the flame as it disappeared into the air.

Jacob raged again and raised his own sword above his head. As it was raised, the sword spun in his hands. The dragons that comprised the handle and the crossbars were unfurling themselves rapidly. They broke Jacob's grip and the sword spun from his hands. The handleless blade stuck a few feet away in the soft ground of Iona. The long, thin, and wingless dragons rose in unison through the air, twisting like liberated snakes around one another as they ascended. They made a loop and twisted back down, flying toward Mortimer.

The murderer screamed. As he did, the dragons flew into his open mouth and gorged upon the blackened coal of the man's soul. He fell to his knees, his eyes showing the reflected agony of the conflagration within. He turned toward Jacob but before his body fell to the cold ground, Jacob could sense there was nothing left but a shell of human form.

Jacob would never forget the molten blackness and pain in those eyes and he would never quite forgive himself for allowing his anger to boil to the point it did that day. He felt like he had lost something in those moments; like the beasts he had unleashed had fed themselves on some of his innocence and he was left with a bit less goodness, too.

Long afterward, after much thought and study, he would come to realize there was a great storehouse of goodness in the universe that could replace any that had been lost if it was sought after freely and with faith. But at that moment he contented himself with the knowledge that this man named Mortimer had richly deserved his fate and his own anger that day had saved his life and the treasure he guarded, even if it could not save the life of poor Fingus.

Jacob dropped back to his knees and grasped the small man's head. "Fingus, Fingus?" Jacob called. "Please answer! Fingus!"

The Weeling's eyes slowly opened and the corners of his mouth turned up in a hint of a smile. "Is the danger passed, Master Boyd?"

"Yes, oh, yes, Fingus! We're alright now. Does it hurt much?"

Fingus did not reply but looked steadily into Jacob's eyes as if he were looking passed the boy that sat there and into the soul of the man who would come in time to replace him.

"Fingus? Do you have some of that healing water with you from the catacombs? You must! Don't you? We can take care of you!" Jacob spoke nervously and quickly. His mind had taken him back to the fountain he found a year ago beneath the streets of Edinburgh, Scotland.

"Master, don't ya worry yourself 'bout me. Old Fingus has seen what awaits him and is not afraid." He grimaced as a throb of pain expanded and then contracted within his belly.

"But, we can help you, I know we can. I'll get von Niblick, he will know what to do, or ..."

"Shh. . . the Master must not worry himself now about old Fingus. I have lived long and now get to see the Iona sky again and maybe, if I be lucky, will feel a cool drop of rain fall from the heavens again upon my head. It has been so long and I have missed the rain. My time in the catacombs is now over and I go on to where the evil ones have not been given the keys. It's a short walk from here, you know. Just a short walk."

"Fingus! We need you. *I* need you. Please don't go. I can get help," Jacob pleaded with the small man.

"Do not hold on to me, Master Boyd. My time is gone and is just beginning, too; my service has ended and is about to begin. It is just a wee walk from here ..." The man's face no longer looked in pain as his voice trailed off and his head turned from Jacob. The Weeling's eyes were now a perfect mirror of the heavens floating above.

Jacob pinched his eyes shut and a tear rolled off his nose and onto Fingus's forehead. As it did, Jacob thought he saw recognition on the small man's face. *Hopefully,* he thought, *Fingus felt that and thought it was an Iona rain drop just for him.* Jacob began to weep louder and harder, the tears beginning to run out of his eyes and down his face in streams as his chest rose and fell with release.

As he cried over the body of the Weeling who had so long served the Sporrai, he recognized his own head becoming wet. He opened his eyes and looked skyward. The Iona rain came down harder now and washed over his face. Jacob raised his hands and watched the blood wash off the edges of his palms and fingers then run down his arm and onto the ground at his knees. He sobbed louder as he bent near Fingus' lifeless body and mumbled, "There, friend. There's your rain!"

Jacob stayed for a long time on his knees by his friend. He watched the rain wash away the stains of blood on Fingus's cloak as it diluted the salt of his dwindling tears. Hearing something nearby, he looked up to see brown hands like roots rising up out of the ground and grabbing Mortimer's hollowed-out body. Slowly, the root-like arms twisted around the human's limbs and began pulling the man into the spongy soil of the island. Within a few minutes he was gone and the land began healing itself. Jacob looked over to see that the dragons had returned to form the handle of Isildane's sword. He would never look at it the same way again. He would never look at life quite the same way again.

When he had temporarily emptied his store of tears, Jacob stood and began to raise Fingus. As he did, Fingus's left hand fell out of the pocket of his cloak. In the palm of his hand lay a green emerald and a small cross of silver. *Two more parts of the cover?* Jacob wondered. He took the objects and put them into his own pocket. He would test his hunch later. With as much strength as he could muster, Jacob lifted Fingus's body and stepped away from the rocky wall.

"My friend, if you wanted to have the rain fall upon your face one last time, there is a better place than here among the dead," Jacob whispered as he turned to walk to the hill of Dun I.

Fingus' body was heavy for the boy. Jacob's arms ached from the elbows to his shoulders. His back bent in effort and strain. His legs got weaker with each step, but the rain kept falling upon his back as if it were urging him forward. Half way to the top, he had to stop and slip Fingus' body over his shoulder, for his biceps could take no more of carrying him across his arms without them ripping from his bone.

"Sorry, Fingus, I'm just a boy and it's the best I can do," he said.

The rain kept falling as he reached the top of Dun I. Jacob picked an area of soft green grass among the craggy rock outcroppings that seemed to protrude everywhere from the hill. He lay his friend softly upon the ground. He smoothed the small man's cloak, straightened his arms and legs, brushed the hair from his face, and then backed away so he would not block a single drop of rain from Fingus's face. As Jacob sat and looked over the Island and out at sea, he noticed the sun shining on the water and another island beyond. The rain seemed centered on the hilltop. He smiled. He lay down next to Fingus and let the rain wash over his own face until he opened his eyes to see that a slight rainbow had spread across the horizon and he knew it was time to get on.

"I wish you well on that short walk, my friend," Jacob said as he brushed his hand down across Fingus's face.

He marveled for a moment that he was touching a dead body and yet he wasn't concerned about that. It didn't bother him. He felt his confidence increase as if he could sense a man growing inside his own skin. He knew he was now different than he was earlier that day. He thought he was closer to being a man now. He knew he had to do more than be pulled along in this story.

He closed his eyes and over Fingus' body he said these words, "I am of the Sporrai. I am of the Remnant. I want to do good and serve what is right. I will play my part." It was a makeshift pledge that set his life on a new path. Years later he would look back and think that the truth was never more clear to him than it was on that day on Iona.

Where the blood of Fingus was spilled upon the land and where Jacob's tears had fallen like rain, a small tree would someday sprout. Born of the sacrifice of love and nurtured in the tears of sorrow, that tree would grow and bring forth fruit. One summer day a little girl named Sophia would come to visit Iona. She would play in the shade of the tree and put some seeds in the pockets of her dress to show her mother back home. Those seeds would eventually find a home in the fertile soil at the Iona Academy in America and they would help reclaim the scarred land produced by the withered and frost damaged fruit.

Homeward

igh above the north Atlantic, a dragon pug circled like a spy plane. It was using its eyes. But, more importantly, it was desperately searching with its mind, sending out signals and calling the name of "Jacob" down to every island he passed near. An old man sat upon his back, a pair of binoculars held to his eyes.

Nibs, is that you? Nibs? Jacob sat up and looked out at the sea. He spun around looking up at the sky. *Nibblus Maximus, where are you?*

Jacob! Jacob! Where are you?

On Iona, Jacob answered in his mind. *I am on the top of Dun I.*

The dragon dropped his head suddenly with excitement. The professor's stomach leapt into his throat as if he were on a fast and steep roller coaster. His hands came loose from his binoculars as he thrust them down to grab the horn of the dragon's makeshift saddle.

"Nibblus!" the professor yelled as he and the dragon continued their quick descent to the sea.

I have Master Boyd! The dragon messaged back. *He is on Iona. He sounds exhausted.*

Soon the dragon was drifting down to the highest ground on Iona. The professor hurried over to Jacob, who hadn't moved from Fingus' side. He scanned the area for threats and then he knelt silently beside Jacob and waited for the boy to open up and spill his story. When Jacob started, it was a non-stop string of action adventure that came from his mouth.

"Jacob, you speak of your story like it just happened. Do you know what day it is?"

"Well, no, I guess I don't, but I couldn't have been gone long."

"Master Boyd, you were gone for days!"

Jacob's head shot up as he looked into the professor's eyes. He wondered if the man was telling the truth. But, he wondered that only for a moment.

"Nibbles looked for you for the first day, and then he came to get me that night. I gave myself one more night's healing and then we went off again in search of you the next morning. We have been searching for you for two days, Jacob. You were gone down there in the chapel Perilous for three days."

Jacob looked at the ground in confusion and shook his head.

"But never mind that now, Jacob. You are out and have many stories to tell, so continue, won't you?"

Jacob did continue his story, though he kept wondering what had happened to him so long underground. Had he been unconscious for those days? Did his visions in the cup take up most of that time? The questions itched in the back of his mind. When he came to recounting the story of Fingus's heroic death and the end of Mortimer, Jacob became as solemn and serious as the professor had ever seen him. Mr. Nibbles, again the small dog, walked up to Jacob and snuggled next to his left leg.

"Jacob," the professor interjected when he could tell the boy was having a hard time finishing his thought, "you did nothing wrong. You acted courageously and correctly, lad. You did not cost Fingus his life. You must understand that. He *gave* his life in service of a good cause. He was strong and courageous until the end. That is what mattered to him, Jacob, and we should be happy for him."

"He said it would just be a short walk from here, Professor." Jacob choked on the words and knew he would have burst into tears if the professor hadn't been there. Like most boys his age, he didn't want to be seen crying.

The professor nodded his head and put his left arm around the boy's shoulders. Jacob leaned his head over to rest it gently on the professor's chest as he looked down at Fingus's lifeless body. But his quiet moment lasted no more than that.

"Professor!" he announced as he jerked up. "Professor, I saw things, more things than I told you. For a moment I had forgotten them somehow. I don't know how, but I did!" Jacob continued anxiously. "I saw all those things I told you of, but I saw more. I saw that Jenny and the rest of the kids at Iona were in danger. I saw fire and explosions. I saw strange animals and an awful evil force there, draped in red but with a soul dark and nasty. I saw Miss Witherspoon again calling out to me!"

"Alright, lad. Keep your calm about ya," the professor insisted with a firm hand on Jacob's shoulder.

"But I really have to get back there. I've gotta help. And, Professor— I think that Ian—" Jacob changed what he was going to say mid-sentence, "remember Ian? Ian Nelson?" Jacob asked. He didn't wait for a reaction, "I think he is wrapped up in this thing somehow, Professor. And it's not good, I know it."

Professor von Niblick's countenance turned even grimmer. "Jacob, you can't go back there. It's too dangerous for you now."

Jacob pushed back from the professor, "But I have to go back, I have to. I have to help them."

"Lad, I applaud your courage," the professor said, "but I am not well enough to make that flight with you now and I cannot send you back by yourself. I just couldn't put you in that kind of danger. It would be forbidden."

"I have to go back. I have to help. Why would I be given this image in the cup if I was not to help my friends?" Jacob had a point. He might not have known it at first, but he knew it now. He had a good case to make for going back. He expectantly watched the professor's grey eyes beneath the large furry white eyebrows that capped them like snow above two glacial lakes.

"Bearer, I cannot go with you now. I am not well enough yet and you are too valuable to be sent into harm's way unattended in days this dangerous."

"But, I won't be alone. I won't. I will have Nibblus Maximus with me, right little guy?" Jacob looked down at the small pug resting his head between his dark little paws. "He will protect me. Right boy? He

protected me before and got me out when it got dangerous. Right boy?
And, besides, I have been in more danger since I arrived here, it seems,
than I was in back there!"

"Oh, Jacob Boyd. I have to admire your courage, I do," the professor
was shaking his head. "Nibblus Maximus," he now spoke to the pug who
lifted his head from its resting place. "You take very good care of the
boy, is that clear? No chances; none. Do you understand your orders,
troublesome little dragon pug?"

Mr. Nibbles just turned away and looked out at sea. Professor von
Niblick, however, wasn't troubled. He knew his old friend very well and
knew he would not shirk his duty.

"Professor," Jacob said, "here is the cover of the *Book of Kells*. It was
right where *he* dropped it." He looked down at Mr. Nibbles who seemed
to be scanning the horizon. Jacob patted his head.

"Now, take a look at this, Professor." Jacob took the cover and
opened it flat on his lap. He then placed his right hand on the right side,
the side closest to the professor. He began slowly to drag it back toward
the left. Just like had happened before, Jacob's hand left a blue light trail
behind it as it moved across the page. In the blue light, both Jacob and the
professor could see the dark squiggles and words that instantly suggested
themselves as part of a map. The professor became visibly excited.

"Well I'll be!" he exclaimed. "I knew it must be something. I knew
it. Why else would the cover be lost from a book, I said! Why would a
book disappear and then eventually show up without its cover? I asked.
Why? Why? Oh, Jacob my boy, I knew it. I just knew it. The evidence
was clear, I thought. The evidence was clear."

Jacob felt pride in having made the discovery and being able to share
it with the man he admired so much. He remained silent to enjoy the
moment.

"It's the ring. It's the ring. The jewel in the ring, that must be what
is allowing your hand to show what is hidden in the leather, Jacob." The
professor was pointing to Isildane's ring and its red jewel that sat on
Jacob's right hand.

"Take it off and look through it," the professor gently ordered.

Jacob slipped the ring from his finger and pulled it to his right eye. He closed his left. Through the red jewel, everything took on a red glow. The ancient leather cover on his lap, however, waved and from it emerged the whole series of lines and words that Jacob could see only in parts when he moved his hand over it. Now it was clearly a map, though a very basic one. He handed the ring to the professor, who pressed it to his own eye and looked at the leather lying flat on Jacob's lap.

The professor smiled a slow and knowing smile behind his grey beard. "Yes, it is a map. It's a map of the British Isles. See, up here, Jacob, are the Hebrides where we are now. Over here is Edinburgh where we first met, up here is Inverness where old Nessie lurks, and down here, way down here is Dover." The man was pointing to the leather that to Jacob's unaided eye looked plain and unadorned.

"This is so basic … bare bones, lad, bear bones," von Niblick offered. "We have an outline, we have this line across the north here," the man traced his finger along the leather. "This must be Hadrian's Wall across the south end of Scotland, here. Yes, Jacob, this must be a map of the Roman occupation of the British Isles. When they couldn't defeat the ancient Picts who lived here in Scotland, they built a wall to keep us away, you know. It was named after Hadrian, their Emperor. They started it in the second century, about eighteen hundred years ago." He pulled the ring from his eye and handed it back to Jacob. "Very basic, lad, it hardly says anything. There must be more."

Hearing the word "more" reminded Jacob of the green stone and silver cross that Fingus had in his hand when he died. "Professor, would these have anything to do with it?" Jacob reached into his pocket and opened his hand near the professor. von Niblick reached over and flipped the leather cover closed, exposing the front with its empty spaces.

The man scratched under his grey beard and then reached over to Jacob's hand. He took the small silver cross and placed it in the cross shaped slot on the cover. It fit perfectly. He then took the green stone, rubbed it between his forefinger and thumb, and then tried to fit it into one of the circular holes surrounding the cross. It took several tries, but before soon it snapped into place above the cross. The man took a deep breath and lifted his head back and up, looking out at the sea.

"Astounding. This is astounding, lad," the man announced. "We now have three of the five treasures that belong on the cover. Each one of these is priceless, Jacob. Together they are of an importance that has not been known for five hundred years. Broken treasures from the past—meaning becoming clear again," the man mumbled these last words. He pulled on his beard and studied the cover.

"Sir," Jacob said, "if we could see things on the cover by looking through the red jewel, do you think we could see more things by looking through the green one, too?"

"That's my lad, that's my lad!" the professor exclaimed as he twisted the green jewel out of its socket. He took the cover and placed it open again on the ground in front of them. He pulled the green jewel up to his eye and looked through it. "By Jove!" he exclaimed. "Here is more," he repeated, "here is more!" He handed the jewel to Jacob who then pressed it to his eye. In the green haze he could see a different map with different markings. This one as mostly dots and squiggles and most of them were found toward the top of the leather.

"Looks to me," the professor instructed Jacob as the boy looked over the map, "like this green jewel is opening for us some knowledge of sites related to the ancient Picts or the Scotae. The red one must show some Roman sites in Scotland, you see. But, what do they mean?"

Jacob pulled the jewel from his eye, as what he saw meant nothing to him anyway. Then he offered, "what if we looked through both of them?"

"Combined?" The professor pulled on his long and bushy right eyebrow. "Yes, let's try it. You first, Lad."

Jacob took Isildane's ring from his finger and put the green jewel on top of the red stone of the ring. He then pulled them both up to his right eye. "I see them both, Professor. Both maps are there. The red one lays out the outlines of the map and then certain parts such as what you pointed out was that Roman wall. The green one then adds a bunch of dots and symbols and signs over top. They are all within the outlines that the red shows."

"Ingenius! You crafty Sporrai monks, you!" The professor stood and looked out at sea. "You crafty old monks!" Without turning toward Jacob he added, "Lad, put the green jewel back in the cover and be sure the silver cross is secure there, too."

"What about Isildane's red jewel in my ring, should I put it in the cover as well?"

The professor thought for a moment. "No, son. You need that jewel and Isildane's ring. It was given to you for a reason and you cannot be separated from it for now. I'll take the cover back with me to try to figure it out and keep it safe. We are all better off if we keep the treasures separated as much as possible. You being in America and the cover being in Scotland will protect us all from them falling into the same hands."

Jacob folded the leather cover back within the bigger and softer leather that had protected it. He stood and handed the cover to the *Book of Kells* to Professor von Niblick. The old man opened his coat and put the precious package in an inside pocket.

"Jacob, go back to America, then, and do what you have to do. I'll take this great treasure back with me and as I recover from my wounds, I'll study it. If all goes well, I'll come to America to lend a hand or at least help keep you out of trouble, when I'm well enough for the journey."

"What about dear Fingus?" Jacob interjected.

"Laddie, Fingus will have a funeral worthy of a king and fitting a servant in our Order. I will assure you of that. *Cuiridh mi clach air do chàrn*, is what he used to say to me when we parted. Now I say it to him, as a promise, not just a good wish."

"Professor, what does that mean?" Jacob couldn't even begin to pronounce back to him the phrase he just heard.

The man let a small laugh escape. "It means 'I'll put a stone on your cairn', lad. Cairn is a pile of stones that form a tomb. Now he will join his clansmen in a cairn in his ancient homeland and I will add a stone to those laid by his ancestors."

"Will you lay one for me?" Jacob asked.

The professor turned and looked into Jacob's moist eyes. "I think you will someday lay a stone of your own for our departed friend. I will leave that to you to do with your own hands."

Jacob looked down at Fingus's lifeless body and quietly said, "so long, friend. I hope you are enjoying that short walk."

"Now, off with you, lad. You forget that you have been under ground for three days. If your friends were in trouble several days ago, it might be much worse now."

Jacob had not thought of that. Was he too late? Had he delayed too long? The fear crept in upon his heart. "Nibs, let's go!" he ordered.

Mr. Nibbles jumped to his feet and moved over beside some of the craggy rocks atop Dun I. He moved his little body into the make-shift saddle he had crawled out of a short time before. He began to swell and his appearance began to change as the saddle lifted with him and grew tight around his mid-section.

Jacob mounted the dragon pug and von Niblick strapped him in tight, pulling the blankets up around his shoulders.

"Jacob, don't try to fly directly into the school. There might be trouble and you know they tried to do you in once. They will be looking for you. Go to where you left MacGregor and the rest. I will send word to them that you are on your way and they should watch out for you there. Do you understand?" The feebleness of the wounded man suddenly came over him again and he leaned on the dragon's right flank to steady himself. Jacob saw the sensation come over his face, but said nothing.

While he let von Niblick rest on the dragon, he took out his enchiridion notebook and scribbled, "Jenny, we are on our way. Stay strong."

Soon Jacob was high above the Atlantic working to steady his stomach. Professor von Niblick wrapped Fingus in his own coat and slowly carried him down the side of Dun I. He would carry him to the Island of Mull and then to the mainland of Scotland, where he would place the servant in the sidecar of his motorcycle to begin the long and lonely drive to the ancient Weeling homeland in the north.

RESCUE

"Friends, we have blinded the beast but that stick in the eye is bound to make it madder than ever, once it's discovered. We must move quickly now," Dr. Kirk spread out Bunting Boyle's map on the floor of the horse stall. "Bunting, give out the orders, if you would. I am going to try to get help. Godspeed."

"Good luck to you, Ramos," Boyle said as he patted Kirk on the back and knelt down in the older man's spot. Bunting Boyle was born with the look that demanded people listen to him. You could see he was in charge before he opened his mouth and in a darkened horse barn with a bit of warfare breaking out, there was not a soul that was going to question anything he said.

Boyle began by preparing the three newly arrived students, Landis, Emma, and Nolus. They were to gather all the students they knew with certainty they could trust. Boyle had already kicked in the door to the storeroom where the new administrators had locked up everything they wanted to remove from the campus. The room included paintings of old battles, statues of heroes long dead, various assorted forms of arms and armor, and the bagpipes that for more than fifty years had called clan Targe and clan Dirk to the gatherings. It was full of everything Finnius Creech decried as standing in the way of progress and proper educational attainments. Flat screen TV's, tofu bars and test tubes were in, old books and dead heroes were out.

Boyle handed the two boys each a set of bagpipes and said, "Boys, bagpipes were created as an instrument of war, you know. They were banned from Scotland by the English invaders, just like they have been banned from our Iona. But in Scotland they rose again and here they shall be heard again this night heralding the coming blow against these servants of this infernal 'Institute.' Get these to a boy in each of the clans who can be trusted to play and play loudly. Tell them to get to their gathering poles and begin to play at exactly midnight. Their sound will cause great fear in our enemy and should confuse them enough to get us the opening we need. As the students assemble, as God-willing they have remembered is their duty, they should be led down to the lions at the gate where we can hope they will be safe."

The boys nodded their heads and each in turn took Boyle's muscled hand. His hand was so large and strong that his mere grip gave the boys courage and confidence. Boyle then used the map to show them the darkest pathway on and off campus. Abigail Witherspoon hugged them tight and strong as she walked them out of the barn. Before she let them go, she pulled their heads close and said, *"Nemo Me Impune Lassicit."* They repeated the phrase and were off.

Abigail Witherspoon would prepare to lead a team of students into the administration building to try to uncover what they could from her old offices. She had worked and lived there for nearly twenty-five years and knew every inch of the administration building like an ant knows its hill. With luck, she would be able to navigate the place without the help of a flashlight, though she would take one in case Creech had moved things more than they hoped.

Jenny would help lead a small band of students up to the trailer where she would use her status as a student worker to pretend she was coming looking for her backpack. When she distracted the scientist in charge, the others would rush in to try to free Ian Nelson.

Copernicus Campbell was dispatched immediately into town where he would rendezvous with Dr. Kirk and help bring in supplies and the additional allies they could muster. Bunting Boyle would stay at the stables throughout this second phase and would get updates from Angus who was monitoring the battlefield from the watchtower of the Ashland mansion. They would communicate through the same walkie-talkies that he had given each of the team leaders.

This was all part of phase II of the battle plan. It was the part Bunting Boyle referred to as "clearing the field for battle." It was all only preliminary to the main action that would come after midnight, if all else happened successfully. Boyle called it "Operation Rescue and Reinforcements."

Nolus, Landis, and Emma returned from their mission with almost fifty others. They reported they could've gotten more, but these were the ones who they thought really hated the "progress" the school was making as it destroyed its traditions and curriculum. They were part of the band of rebels that had been forming within the student ranks recently and were attempting to keep some of the old ways alive. The three who were put on trial for keeping their old clan badges were also part of that group. Because Landis and Emma had kept a good list going of the kids that called themselves "The Old Ionans," they were efficient in their movements and got out, they believed, without being seen.

In the headquarters of Furangle's Guard, Jimmy Stalwart was working on the computers, trying to fix the software and get the cameras back up and running. Having started with the most complicated possible problem first, he had not yet come to the conclusion that maybe the problem was as simple as cut wires. Sabotage had not yet entered his feeble imagination.

Jenny was given the command of five students. Two girls and three boys were picked. All of them were strong athletes. The strongest were chosen in case Ian had to be carried. The old school nurse, Nurse Kelly, as they called her, was also going with them. She would be there in case a medical emergency came up and to evaluate Ian before he was moved.

Jenny got her orders. She did battle dragons with Will's fingers. Bunting Boyle led the group in a collective embrace and repeating the old school motto and motto of Scotland, "*Nemo me impune lacissit.*"

Then they were off. They worked their way up the north wood-line toward the trailers. Jenny was nervous, but the oldest girl kept putting a hand on her shoulder and giving a squeeze. The action gave Jenny some confidence. Nurse Kelly was slower than the kids and they waited on her every fifty yards or so.

Team Nelson, as Boyle had dubbed them, made it to just behind trailer #1 and waved to get the attention of Angus in the far watchtower.

It was too risky for them to talk into their walkie-talkies, so they were on radio silence unless an emergency arose. Angus was to watch them and report to Bunting Boyle.

Jenny leaned her head on a tire and looked up at the quarter moon. She smelled the cool night air and felt the dampness upon the back of her thighs. She worried about what would happen to her if she were caught. As they rested, though, she made her mind come back to focus on poor Ian instead of herself. She had to help rescue that poor kid, she knew. With a look only, her eyebrows rising and head nodding down, she communicated that it was time to move. They each leaned their right hand in and held the others. They closed their eyes for a moment and then broke. Jenny's heart raced. She took a deep breath and tensed her muscles in hopes of steeling her courage.

The team started along the back of the trailers, going slowly behind them and then rushing between the gaps. One of the girls took up her spot behind trailer # 4. She was to watch and if trouble occurred, bust down to the barns to get help. From his watchtower, Angus could not see the door side of the trailers where the action would unfold, so the girl's eyes were needed. The other two were to flank the doors of the trailers and rush inside after Jenny had distracted the occupant. Jenny was then to whip around back to trailer # 4 and wedge a pole Boyle had given her up against the door handle. This was just in case whoever was in that trailer might be able to see events in trailer # 5 through the monitor Jenny had seen. They didn't need to fight off another one.

Jenny approached the door. She knew if she paused she might never go through with it, so she pushed the button on the speaker without hesitation.

"Yes?" came a crackling male voice through the box. In the silence of the night, the sound that would be barely audible in daylight sounded to Jenny as if thunder were ripping the very air she breathed.

"Um. . . Its Jenny the student worker, sir."

"Student worker? At this hour? Go to bed, we don't need you at night."

"Well, sir, you see, I was in there earlier and think I left my backpack, can I come in and see, sir?"

"Oh, for the sake of ..." the box went dead. A deadbolt cracked open on the door. The handle turned and pulled back fast and strong. "There is no backpack here, girl." The man in the white lab coat was blocking the entrance with his body. He wore a surgical hair cap on his head and a mask pulled down around his throat.

"May I just check?" Jenny asked nervously.

"No, you may certainly not. And, you shouldn't have been in here today, either. Who would have let you in? How do they run things during the day around here, anyway?"

Out of the corner of her eyes, Jenny could see the shadows of the other kids moving along the silver siding of the trailer. They were readying themselves for the attack, the two biggest boys in the front of each side.

"Well, then, sir, can you please look over there under that desk?" Jenny was improvising now and hoping to get him to turn his back and bend down under the desk. The man huffed at her and rolled his eyes. He mumbled something about the hindrances to science that came from having children around. He turned. Jenny backed up and motioned the others to move in. They did just that as the man was bending over to look under the desk. The first of the two lead boys jumped on top of the bending man and threw his arms tight around his chest. The second dove at his knees, causing them to buckle. The man collapsed hard on the ground, sending the swivel chair flying into the back wall. The other girl rushed in next with the plastic cord handcuffs Bunting Boyle had given her. She slapped them around the man's ankles first and pulled tight. The oldest boy, who was nearly seventeen and had gone to Iona for five years, was whispering in the man's ear telling him to calm down and he would not be hurt. Not knowing who was on top of him and how many there were, the man went limp and let the girl slip cuffs on his hands. A gag was slipped over his mouth and tied before the kids got off his back.

Nurse Kelly had moved into the trailer and shut the door behind her. She was carefully studying the monitors and wires and tubes that connected to Ian. She looked him over. She filled her pockets with medicines that were on the shelf beside his bed. She grabbed the charts that hung near him and gave them a quick glance. The other kids looked around and wondered why they were rescuing a sick kid and what they were rescuing him from. But they believed the new crew on campus was up to no good and trusted Boyle, Kirk, Witherspoon and the rest enough to do what they said was right.

When the nurse had proclaimed the boy could be moved, she began unhooking the monitors and tubes.

"We have to take him with the bed. He is unconscious and certainly can't be carried around like a sack of potatoes. Help me put these monitors and fluid bags and such under the bed. See, they can hook here for moving the patient." She showed them the long metal railing under the bed that could hold the hooks on the equipment and fluid bags.

Jenny opened the door a crack and looked outside for any sign of movement. Seeing none, she opened the door wider and held it open. The nurse came next. Then the girl carrying extra blankets followed by the boys attempting to maneuver the hospital bed into a position to get out the door. It wasn't easy, trying to hurry the bed into place without jostling Ian more than was necessary. Bang, bang. Up and over the strip at the bottom of the entryway they roughly maneuvered the bed.

"Lift it up, lift it up higher," the nurse whispered aggressively.

Down the front edge went onto the steps. Then down again, this time into the grass. Snap. The front end buckled under the angle and pressure and collapsed into the ground. Ian started slipping forward in the bed. Jenny grabbed him and held. The nurse moved in and pulled him up. Then she reached under the bottom of the bed and lifted, snapping the front legs back into place.

"They weren't locked," she whispered. "Let's get him out of here!"

Jenny made one more look back into the trailer at the man tied and gagged in the corner. He looked angry and confused. She stuck her tongue out at him and locked the door behind her.

The ground was rough and uneven. The bed bounced wildly as the boys pushed it fast through the grass. Ian's body bounced more wildly still. He flopped and bounced. His head rose and fell. His arms flew wildly at his side.

"Boys," the nurse finally grabbed them and stopped. "You're gonna tear the young fella to pieces before we get him rescued! Come on, you're going to need to carry the bed. This is just too rough to wheel the boy over."

As they lifted, she snapped the legs up into place under the bottom shelf of the bed and they started off again. Ian bounced less, but still was bounced enough to dream he had fallen into a giant salad bowl and was being tossed into the air on blankets of lettuce. He would never really look as innocently upon salad tossing utensils again, though he never understood quite the reason.

The boys were tired and slowed by the weight of the bed and Ian. But, Jenny and the others hung back with them, searching always in every direction and stopping every fifty feet or so to listen for movement or activity. The doors to the barn opened as Jenny's team approached. When they saw the black chasm open against the dark red barn, Jenny and the other girl sprinted forward and into the dark protection of the stalls. The boys and the nurse quickened their pace as well and soon disappeared into the darkness. No light was lit until the doors were clamped shut. Though on almost any other occasion, Jenny would prefer the dim light of the outside to the pure darkness of a place like this, on this night she welcomed the darkness. She even welcomed the unmistakable pungent smell of the mix of damp hay and horse manure.

The nurse immediately started barking orders to prepare a suitable room for Ian until he could be assessed and then moved to a more secure place off campus. They each tried to follow her orders as well as they could make out.

Bunting Boyle was meeting with Ramos Kirk and Abigail Witherspoon in the stall where the map was spread out. Kirk had successfully returned with supplies and more than a dozen old friends and teachers from the school who had been thrown out with the coming of Furangle's and Creech's new regime. Abigail Witherspoon had not made it into the administration buildings because all the locks had been changed and the doors reinforced.

"No sense waiting any longer on Campbell, he must have gotten caught up somewhere on his way," Bunting said.

"I suppose you are right, Boyle, but it does trouble me that he is not back yet with those he was sent to retrieve," Witherspoon offered.

"Never saw hide nor hair of the chap on my rounds," Kirk added.

"Headmistress, my strong advice is to attack and attack, as we planned, upon the call of the pipes at midnight. We are near defenseless here, should they discover our activities and come after us. But, if we attack using the element of surprise, we will buy the time we need to get Ian out of here and, with luck and God's grace, we might even win." Boyle sat down on his haunches near the map.

"I wanted to get into my offices and gather more information, but, still, I guess the plan is now in motion and we need to follow-through. If we can't get Ian out of here now, we have to buy time. He cannot fall into their clutches again," Witherspoon said. She hiked up her dress slightly and knelt down next to Boyle to help refresh the plan with the new information they had.

Dr. Kirk muttered, "Down with the Neoterists!" and leaned over his walking stick to look at the map.

To Arms

Boyle gathered everyone into the show ring at the center of the great barn. There he rolled out a cart full of old weapons and supplies. Each participant was given two granola bars and urged to eat one of them immediately. They were also given two bottles of water and urged to drink half of one of them. Boyle then handed out weapons and other supplies to each of the participants depending upon their skills and strength. Having been the students' martial arts teacher for more than a decade, he knew the skills of all the students and most of the faculty and staff. To those who were good archers, he gave bows and a quiver of arrows. To those who were small and quick, he gave dark clothing and communications gear. To those good with the sling, he gave a sling and bag full of lead shot. Most everyone received a targe to protect him or her and a dirk, in case it came to hand-to-hand combat.

One of the older boys gave a quick lesson to the less experienced in the use of the targe and dirk. He demonstrated how each targe came equipped with a long spike stored on its back that screwed into the half ball on the front. It turned the defensive targe shield into a nasty and deadly offensive weapon as it's spike could be run through the ribs of an enemy who made the mistake of coming within range. He demonstrated how the targe was pulled up on the forearm so it could hang without taking away the use of one's hands. The dirk could then be held pointing down toward the ground in the hand that extended beyond the shield. The left side, then, held both a defensive shield as well as a spike for thrusting and a blade for slashing. The right hand was free to hold a flashlight or other weapon. Each newly commissioned warrior spread out in the ring and practiced jabbing and thrusting.

By the time everyone was ready, it was after 11:00 PM. Boyle called all team leaders together and dispatched them in the tinchel pattern he designed. They were grouped in teams of students and adults and given areas of responsibility. Together they would form a large circle around the school. The leaders called their teams together and delivered orders. Abigail Witherspoon led them all in quietly singing the alma mater of Iona. Then the small army moved off through the fields and the trees surrounding Iona Academy.

Everyone was in place and radioing in their position by 11:50. The next ten minutes seemed like an eternity to everyone in the field. Some prayed. Some gazed at the stars and wondered what would come next. Some kept a very careful eye on the school. All was quiet. All was still, until …

Bagpipes were originally created as instruments of war and if you have ever been close to them when played, you will know why. They stir the heart, but can also break the eardrums. In the stillness of a dark night, played by an unseen piper in the distance, they can seem to rip open the very atmosphere to allow a glimpse of some unknown country beyond. At exactly midnight, the Targe piper was first to blow a single note. The Dirk piper responded from over the rise. Then together as one they began to play "Scotland the Brave."

The courage of those in the field was strengthened and a tear or two was shed in the otherwise silent night. The story was different in the dorms. There, students were awakened from their sleep and were confused. They knew the pipes had now been banned, as had these nighttime gatherings. Still, they remembered the old ways and the old penalties for being late for such gatherings. They grouped in hallways where students who knew what was happening were waiting to usher them to their gathering poles.

The reaction in the homes around campus and in the scientific trailers was different still. Administrators and teachers, who had been asleep in their beds, ran out of their homes to see what was happening. A team of students had laid a trap for Lucy Furangle, knowing she would be one of their problems, but she did not emerge from her room. They waited in confusion. Finnius Creech did not emerge from his home. Those watching the Spur and Spoon from behind the stone wall noted that Dr. Frost did not emerge either. It was curious not to see the leadership of the new I.O.N.A. responding to the sounds in the night. But, they hoped they had gotten lucky and those adults were all very heavy sleepers or had left campus.

The leaders of the Targes and Dirks moved their students down toward the front gate and away from the action. They were all confused and some were a bit chilled in the night air. When they were gathered, they would be told some of what was unfolding on campus and would be instructed to keep their heads down.

The students and teachers and friends who were surrounding the school lay low and hidden and waited. Their job was to create the necessary diversions, once the security and administrators were up and counter-attacking. For now, there was no sign of a counter-offensive and so they stood still. Jimmy Johnston—a rather nervous boy from Connecticut—let an arrow fly prematurely from his string and it stuck fast and unseen in one of the poles of the empty gazebo. He was embarrassed and had lost one piece of ammunition, but otherwise there was no harm done.

Now that the need for silence was over, Abigail Witherspoon and a team of five students were up at the administration building again attempting to break the door down. She had to retrieve the paperwork from her files that would show she had never resigned and that the school was not operating according to its bylaws and charter. Bunting Boyle was getting reports via walkie-talkie from around the perimeter. He was also getting reports from Angus, who was watching from high in the Watchtower. Boyle was also monitoring the walkie-talkie Will had stolen from the New Guard Headquarters but he heard only static. All seemed to be progressing nicely.

Dr. Kirk had moved his way up toward the school with his team and they were watching for the opportunity to catch the scientists exiting the trailers to see what was going on. So far the scientists were not moving. Kirk radioed back in to Boyle and said, "We need more of a disturbance, Bunting, get a piper up here!"

Boyle called over one of the girls who was helping monitor the battlefield with him. "Can you play this thing?" he asked as he handed her a bagpipe.

She looked at it with an odd expression. "Well, I can make a noise of sorts, but I don't know if it would be called playing!"

"Good enough for what we need. Work your way up on the edge of the right woods," Boyle was running a long stick up the map showing her what direction she was supposed to go. "Then, when you get to this point, blow on that thing like you have never blown before. Do it for one minute and then bust your can back down here as fast as you are able. Understand?"

The plan had four basic components. Unaffiliated students would be gotten out of harm's way. Abigail Witherspoon's team would try again to enter the administration offices and get what documents and other information they could. They would then seek to hold that position through the battle, continually searching for evidence. Kirk's team would take over the science labs in the trailers and stop the experiments. Finally, the circle would be drawn tight onto the campus and the new administrators and security team would be rounded up and put into custody until Witherspoon had enough evidence from the files that the police could be called. Bunting Boyle was a military man and knew that no battle plan really works out exactly as designed. But, so far it was working as well as he could have hoped. Perhaps it was unfolding too well, he worried.

The sledgehammer came crashing down through the handle of the door, shattering the wood around it and bending the metal badly. The second blow separated it completely and Witherspoon pushed the door inward.

The pipe blew a horrendous sound near the trailers. It sent the animals inside into hysterics. The doors of the trailers popped open, one by one. Ramos Kirk and his team rushed in behind the startled scientists.

Students at the front gate looked on in wonder as the leaders tried to explain to them that the old leaders of the school were trying to take it back. All posts were reporting good news, as Bunting Boyle knelt over his map and listened to the walkie-talkies.

Suddenly, the stolen walkie-talkie cracked to life. "Mice are in the trap, spring it!" was all Boyle and the others in the barn heard. He looked up at the others surrounding him. "No!" he cried.

Floodlights suddenly snapped to life all over campus. They were on top of the buildings and on poles. They were in the tops of trees and on the sheds. Nearly the entire campus was lit-up like it was the middle of a June day. Everyone froze. A loud speaker suddenly cut through the still air. "Well, what do we have here?" It was the voice of Finnius Creech. From the shadows by the buildings, armed men in black stepped forward. Others were still hidden in the darkness behind the floodlights on the roofs, but the Old Iona teams that were close could hear the snap of their ammunition magazines into place in the bottom of their rifles.

"Getting a little uppity are we?" Finnius Creech's voice boomed throughout campus.

"What's going on, give me a report!" Boyle yelled into a walkie-talkie. The teams sat frozen like deer caught in headlights and bathed in light. None of them responded. Angus, however, the seasoned veteran of many Sporrai wars, broke the silence.

"Ambush. They have us, Bunting. Floodlights illuminate all our teams except Abigail's. I can see lights on in her old office now, though, too. She is almost surely caught. It's over." His voice was one of resignation and not panic or excitement.

Boyle dropped his head, but did so only for a moment. When his eyes rose again to meet those of his team he asserted, "I don't care what the nurse says, get the Nelson boy out of here and do it now! Angus will meet up with you at Ashland mansion. A truck is hidden in the carriage house. There are keys ready in the ignition. Get him out of here. Get him to a hospital if you have to. But, just get him away from here!"

The others stood stunned and silent. "Get moving, I said! They'll come soon to search here, too! We can't lose him to them again," he barked.

The team in the barn then heard a voice in the distance. "All of you," the voice came across the loudspeaker. "All of you, down on your faces. Toss your weapons in front of your heads. Come on, now, at least ten feet in front." As the teams slowly looked around at each other and did what the disembodied voice ordered, Creech continued. "I figured as much. Primitive old ideas being defended by primitive old weapons. Not efficient; not at all. But typical. Very typical." He was obviously watching, but no one could see him. The voice, being projected through more than a dozen loud speakers, must have sounded like what the tiny Lilliputians heard as Gulliver towered over them.

The black-clothed guards stepped forward into the light. They were frightening in their black jumpsuits, black berets and black automatic weapons. Lucy Furangle was with them. So was her father. Out of the administration building, Abigail Witherspoon and her team were marched in front of two men in black. They had also been caught. Behind them both were a couple of Lucy Furangle's New Guard.

When the lights came on to flood the campus with light, the leaders of the students down by the gate broke into the guardhouse. They were confused and concerned about what was happening. They hoped to be able to see what was going on from the video monitors. From the creative cutting Will had done to the wires in the guard headquarters up at the school, all the monitors and cameras were still out. Some of the more tech-savvy kids fiddled with the system in the guardhouse. But, the monitors would not come to life for another fifteen minutes, when Furangle's team discovered the problem and had it fixed.

Angus looked on from the watchtower in anger and confusion. Their teams of loyal students and teachers were all lying on the ground, disarmed and humiliated. The floodlights were so intense that Angus could see each and every one of them in their shame.

"Well, I see we have old lady Witherspoon here. Its not your school anymore Abigail, dear!" Creech was speaking through the loud speakers. "Oh, and there is dear Dr. Kirk, glad you are here for our moment of triumph, old friend." Creech's voice was dripping with sarcasm. "Oh, and I see so many old friends of Iona, the *old* friends of the *old* Iona. I am disappointed in so many of you kids out there, though. You are too young to care about dusty old men and dusty old ideas. A shame. But, you can all be replaced and you *will* be replaced. You are all replaceable, you know. Interchangeable, you are. Cogs in a wheel. Cogs to be conditioned to fit the wheel—or to be thrown away."

"Headmaster," Dr. Kirk yelled as loudly as he could muster from the ground. "Headmaster, I dare say, why do you treat your charges this way? If you truly do not care, let them go."

"What's that, Kirk? Sit up and talk like a dog, don't lie there like a worm. I am no longer to be called Headmaster. From now on, I am to be called The Director. I am no longer Finnius Creech, but The Director. "

A black truck was being backed out onto the grounds in front of the library. Finnius Creech stood in the bed of the truck with a half dozen students. He was wearing a black jacket with "The Director" embroidered on its left breast just above the initials I.O.N.A. He wore a wireless microphone coming off his ear and down to his mouth. "And, spare me your lectures, Kirk. From where I stand, my ethics seem to be bringing me victory. Yours seems to be bringing you a mouthful of dirt." Creech turned to one of the men in black standing near his truck. "Bring him to me, I have a little surprise for dear old Dr. Kirk."

The man walked over to Kirk and roughly pulled him up from the ground. He pushed Dr. Ramos Kirk up the gravel road toward Creech. When he got close, the new Director spoke again. "Speaking of old friends, Ramos. You might be interested to know how one of your old friends is doing. Let me introduce you to the *New* Dean of Faculty of the *new* I.O.N.A."

Abigail Witherspoon hung her head. In the watchtower Angus stuttered an unkind word into the walkie-talkie. Dr. Kirk stammered "No! Not you!"

"What is going on? Report," Bunting Boyle ordered into the walkie-talkie. Angus replied giving him the terrible news, "it was Campbell, sir. Copernicus Campbell sold us out. They were ready for us. The *rat* sold us out!"

Boyle slammed the radio he was holding down onto the ground where the battery door broke open sending AA's bouncing across the map. "They knew we were coming! They were ready for us! Blast the traitor!"

"Campbell, not you! Not with these … Gnostics!" Kirk spat in disgust as he looked dejectedly at his old friend.

"I'm tired, Ramos. I am tired of being on the losing side of history. For once I want to be with the winners."

Great Scot!, Abigail Witherspoon thought to herself as she watched the scene unfold. *What has Campbell told them about Jacob and Jenny and our plans to rescue Ian?*

The same fear-filled question was coursing through the minds of Boyle, Angus and Ramos Kirk as well. *How deep is the conspiracy?* Dr. Kirk wondered.

THE GORGON'S HEAD

"All of you get up on your knees. I want you all to bare witness to what is about to happen. The *New* I.O.N.A. will be concerned with two things. First, we are concerned to advance the human race beyond petty and old limitations. We will push the boundaries of science and will not be inhibited by silly artificial barriers put up by your churches and governments and weak teachers of ethics. Here, like the ancient dabblers in black magic, we seek power. The ancient world of magic will find its new expression in the cutting edge of advanced science. The whole human race will be our petri dish. To advance the species will be our goal."

"Second, we are also concerned with advancing our understanding of modern psychology so that we can cure our students of the old ways that would inhibit them from using the power we will have within our grasp to give." Creech was walking back and forth in the bed of the truck.

"Up. On your knees now to bear witness to our power!" Creech continued pacing nervously. He fingered the embroidery of his new title on his jacket as he spoke.

One young man over on the right stood up. He was afraid and was not thinking clearly. He didn't mean to make an example of courage and resistance, but he did. He stood on wobbly legs until one of the guards clothed in black marched over and slammed the butt of his rifle into the back of his knees. The boy collapsed.

"We now have the power to bring to life what was once just the imaginings of ancient fools. They stumbled upon the powers but without the tools to make them real. And so they made them evil and defeated them in their stories. Now, we have the power to make real the old ramblings of fools. We have the power to tame the ancient myths."

As he spoke, the front porch of the library slowly slid to the left. The grinding of brick upon cement was audible. Some of the kids who lived in rooms facing this side of campus recognized the sound. They had heard it occasionally in the night. As the lid moved away, a cage from within rose up through the ground.

"What? How?" Abigail Witherspoon muttered.

Though he could not hear her, Creech could see the confusion on her face. "Yes, Abigail, we have been here longer than you knew. We were here and you didn't suspect a thing. Under the ground, you see. Under your precious Iona, we were building, tunneling, undermining. Like an acid, we were eating away at your foundation until you got too weak to resist. Only then did we move above ground. The beasts are now hungry and ready to fly!"

The cage was slowly emerging from the ground. As it did, terrible shrieks and cries were heard coming from the pit. Those near the school buildings were the first to see their heads emerge—hideously swollen heads of eagles.

Some screamed. Dr. Kirk mumbled beneath his breath, "Neoterists! You know not how close to the root you hack!"

Creech laughed and, as the large bodies of lions emerged, he added, "Behold our gryphon!"

"No! They aren't *gryphon*," Dr. Kirk yelled over the cacophony of students screaming and the beasts shrieking. "Abominations of nature and ancient legend. Not gryphon! Mere abominations!"

"Oh, shut that bag of dust over there," Creech barked at a guard. The guard then roughly treated Dr. Kirk and gagged him with a black cloth.

A menagerie of emotions coursed through those watching the scene unfold. The sight of the hideous strength shaking the bars of the cage and fighting with one another sickened some. Some feared for their lives. Others contemplated running into the woods. Some cried. Others prayed. The sight of creatures they thought only existed in fairy tales awed them. A few, Will included, fantasized about how they might fight off the creatures when they were loosed. Jenny stood by Bunting Boyle in the barn and listened in disbelief as Angus told the story of what was happening.

"Watch out!" came the crackly shout through the walkie-talkie. Angus was watching the scene up at the library through a pair of binoculars and hadn't seen the team of guards sneaking down toward the door of the barn. By the time he pulled back his vision to search the rest of the battlefield again it was too late. Splinters flew as the door shattered open. Fifteen well-armed men in black rushed through the door in military formation. There was no use resisting. They had Boyle and his team by surprise.

"Down on your faces! Now!" one man shouted at them. "Jones, Masters, George, you three to the back room and retrieve the Nelson kid. The rest of you, cuff these ones and get them up to the Director," the lead commando barked. One of the men laughed and spit on Boyle's map as he cuffed the teacher.

Creech gave the order to release a gryphon. The eagle-headed lion leapt through the door in the top of the cage. It pumped its wings three times to achieve altitude and then swung down over the prostrate army of Bunting Boyle. Some screamed. Others dropped to the ground in silent fear. Creech pushed a button in his hand and the beast screamed in pain. It then turned back up to the library where it landed atop the cage.

"Just in case you get any ideas of running away, she will hunt you down and tear your flesh from its bone!" Creech announced.

"Now! Behold, the mistress of our new science. The most beautiful and most brilliant; the queen of our *new* I.O.N.A.; our Priestess of Progress; the mother of the new master race; Dr. Lilith Frost … ."

To the left of Creech and near one of the two dormitories, a square patch of sod began to rise. At first it appeared as if the grass and dirt were floating above the turf. In a moment most could see that it was a glass box emerging from the ground like an elevator. Its walls were milky, not clear. A form could be seen within, but it, too, was not very clearly defined. It rose to seven feet out of the ground and stopped. Slowly the door opened. On-lookers screamed. More than one fainted. Dr. Kirk attempted to yell through his gag but he could not be heard.

Some of the outer floodlights were redirected so that intense unnatural light focused on the box. Dr. Frost stepped forth and ran her hands down the side of her formal white dress. Her make-up was caked upon her face deeper than normal and from afar her face looked stunningly bright and clear. The screams and fainting were not the result of her fashion decisions, or her make-up, however.

Occasionally Jacob's mom would say that she was having a "bad hair day," but any such statement on this night would be the understatement of the millennium. The beautiful black locks of Dr. Frost had been shorn clean. Instead of hair, at least a dozen snakes writhed upon her head. She reached up and stroked them down as if she was doing nothing more than smoothing out some static hair from under a wool cap on a cold January day.

"You gorgon monster!" Abigail Witherspoon murmured under her breath. "Where is our Perseus? We have no Perseus! God forgive us!"

The crew from the barn were being ushered up into the field near the gazebo when Dr. Frost emerged completely from the box. Jenny's knees grew weak at the sight and Jenny dropped to the ground. She was caught by one of the other girls just as she hit. Boyle then came over and helped pick her up in order to help her obey the guard's orders to keep moving.

In the office once occupied by Abigail Witherspoon and now held by Finnius Creech, a man sat. He was alone. Only one candle provided light in the darkened room where the shades had been drawn to keep out the floodlights. He was looking up at the painting that hung behind the new Director's desk. He watched intently as the paint bubbled out from the flat surface, alternatively taking the form of a face and then disappearing. The man was reminded of more innocent times when he was a kid and played with pushing shapes through partly inflated balloons. "Come to us, Father. Come to us who beckon you," the man muttered.

Out on the grounds, Director Creech was barking orders. "Bring them all in toward the circle, guards. This is what you called a 'tinchel' or something isn't it, Boyle?" Creech was cocking his head slyly as he talked and mocking his opponents with how much he knew of their plan. Come, behold the crowning of the Priestess of our Progress!"

The armed men began pushing the captured enemy in toward the center of the school. The kids and old teachers had to leave their weapons lying on the ground as they were being herded toward a platform. The pyramidal platform had risen to two stories above the ground and it had two ornate and tall chairs at the center. Two women pulled a black rug up the stairs and two others smoothed it. Finnius Creech then led Dr. Frost up the stairs and to her seat on the left of the platform. Two gryphon flew over and sat on either side of the two thrones. Four more women carried great cauldrons of fire up the stairs and placed them on the very edge of the top of the platform. The gryphon on the left screamed at one of the women as she placed the cauldron. The woman was startled and fell back off the side of the platform. She lay there wounded but not a soul paid any additional attention to her.

Upon orders of Finnius Creech, armed men had taken Ramos Kirk, Bunting Boyle, Abigail Witherspoon, and Hammish MacGregor from the crowd. As MacGregor was led passed his old friend, Copernicus Campbell, he managed to dive at him, thrusting his head into the traitor's abdomen. Campbell flew back in pain. As the men grabbed MacGregor by the hair and arms and drug him back up, he said, "If they'd free my hands, I'd kill you, I would!"

The four members of the Remnant stood on a separate and much shorter platform next to the main one. "You conspirators will all die this night," Creech said into the microphone so all could hear. "To please our new queen and as a final sacrifice to the one who comes to sit and reign by her side, you shall die." None of the condemned flinched, but stood strong and looked out into the dark woods beyond the floodlights. "The spilling of your blood will be all that is necessary to bring our new king into his kingdom."

Truth Serum

The cameras and computers now repaired, the students down at the gate were watching events transpire up on campus. As many as possibly could fit were squashed into the guardhouse with the monitors. Others stood around in fear and curiosity waiting for reports from inside the small building. They mumbled among themselves about what they were learning. Some were agitating to head into the woods as a group and make for the protection of town.

Jacob had been sleeping most of the trip across the Atlantic. Near the approach of the North American coastline, he groggily came to life. He checked the straps that kept him tightly bound to the back of the dragon pug and then started a conversation with Nibblus Maximus about where they were and how the flight had been.

I need to stop for a wee rest when we come over the land, the Dragon informed him.

I could sure use a break myself, if you know what I mean, Jacob replied.

The pair had been flying most of the day and late into the evening. They came over New Jersey, Delaware, and the dragon brought them down in a field near an isolated lake in southeastern Pennsylvania. Before Jacob dismounted, the beast walked over to the water and took a large draught. Jacob got off with very wobbly legs and the dragon rolled over onto his side, extremely tired. *Just give me an hour or two, Bearer.*

Not a problem, big fella. I'm sure things can wait. Rest up for awhile and then we can take off again and make it back to the woods and get a good night's rest before meeting up again with Dr. Kirk and the rest. They are probably already asleep up at Ashland mansion, anyway. Let's take our time.

The dragon was already asleep when Jacob finished his short statement. The boy leaned up against the giant's belly and looked up at the stars. He pulled his sword from its scabbard and polished it with the tail of his shirt. He gripped and loosened the handle as he played out the battle with Mortimer over in his head. He tried to work out if he had made mistakes that cost Fingus his life. He wasn't sure, but he worried about it. He said good words to the small man's memory and shed a tear.

He thought about what he would do once he reached Iona. He knew something was wrong, but didn't know how bad things had gotten. *In the end, MacGregor or one of them will probably tell me what I have to do, anyway,* he figured. Though there was not much light, as his mind drifted there in the dark, he came to the thought that he should check the enchiridion pages.

He pulled the old notebook from his back pocket and flipped its pages back to the second half where the pages became blank. He turned the book over in his hands in several angles as he attempted to catch enough moonlight to see the page plainly. Something was there, but very faint. He remembered the matches in his pocket and pulled them out. He struck the match and watched it flame up, then settle down. He pulled it down next to the open book in his lap. The note had just seven letters, none very well formed. It was obviously written in haste and Jenny probably wasn't even looking at the page when she wrote, he guessed. His guess would be right. After being captured, Jenny had pulled the pages and a pencil from her back pocket, sat down in the grass with her hands tied behind her back, and scribbled as best she could. The letters were not exactly in the right order and were certainly not aligned. But Jacob made out the meaning loud and clear. "Bad Help"

THE BOOK OF KELLS

365

Nibbs! Wake up! Jenny's in trouble at Iona. Let's go!

What? The dragon was groggily trying to bring his tired mind and body back to consciousness.

Sorry, buddy, Jacob said, *but Jenny is in trouble and maybe the others are as well, I don't know.*

Within moments, the pair was airborne and heading southwest. Jacob tucked himself low and close to Nibblus Maximus to reduce wind resistance. He whispered encouragement to keep his friend pushing hard toward Iona Academy.

At Iona, all the "conspirators," as Creech referred to them, had been rounded up and were sitting in rows of a dozen about thirty feet away from the platforms where the bizarre rituals continued.

The woman who everyone had known as Dr. Lilith Frost sat upon her throne. She stroked her hair of snakes. Women all dressed in white attended her. The platform and the people on the platform seemed to be being prepared for something bigger to happen. The students and others mumbled to themselves, though when they talked too much, a black-booted guard would send his or her toe into their sides to shut them up.

Creech was now away from the microphone and stood on what was meant to be the execution block for the members of the Remnant. "So, Dr. Campbell tells us that Boyd kid is your charge and is one of these kids that carries whatever magic things you all believe in. I think it's all trash of course, but I take my orders in the name of science and psychology and cash and whatever I decide to believe in today. And today I believe in being the Director of I.O.N.A. and in following the orders of Mr. Furangle. He wants the kid. So, where is he?"

Witherspoon, Kirk, MacGregor, and Boyle all stood silently in their place.

"Well, let's see here. Gentlemen, please loose the cats' tongues a bit," the man was speaking to the guards standing behind the four captured members of the Sporrai. Creech's men jumped up on the stand and each simultaneously drove a hard fist into the right kidneys of the four members. The Remnant buckled and fell to their knees, grimacing in pain. None spoke a word. None raised their head.

"Stand them up!" Creech ordered. The men grabbed each of the four by the back of their shirts and forced them to their feet. "Now, shall we have another go at it? The Boyd kid; where is he?"

The four remained silent. Boyle looked over at Abigail Witherspoon and mouthed, "I am sorry." She winked back at him. Another punch landed in each of their backs and they all collapsed to their knees. They coughed and sputtered and grimaced in pain.

Ramos Kirk looked up and said, "It is not death that a man should fear, but he should fear never beginning to live."

"Spare me your outdated philosophies! You *will* find death this night and these children," he looked out at the assembled conspirators sitting in the dewy grass, "they will be forced to watch and will know that progress is at hand and your side is the losing side of history."

In Finnius Creech's office, Mr. Furangle sat in the darkened room, one candle bringing only a few rays of light into the darkness. The painting that had his full attention was now stretched out into the room. The red had mostly peeled back; the black filled the foreground and stretched the canvass into the room. "Father, come. Sporrai blood will soon run free upon this ground. Come."

"Let's try another way, shall we?" Mr. Creech said as he walked in front of the four condemned members of the Sporrai Remnant. "Dr. Wells, would you please bring the truth serum you've been working on?" Creech was talking to one of the scientists that had been doing experiments in the science trailers.

"Sir, its results are still highly irregular. It is still in the most experimental of stages and has not been tried on human beings," the doctor replied.

"Dr. Wells, I am offering you the perfect chance to continue the experiments. Are you too squeamish to continue working for the Institute?"

"No sir," the man said. He turned and hustled toward the trailers as visions of great scientific awards danced in his head. He grabbed one of his assistants who was standing quietly off to the side and ordered the man to follow him to the lab.

Fire from the Sky

Preoccupied by the developments on the ground, no one noticed the beast circling above the perimeter of Iona Academy. *Your eyes are better than mine, Nibbs, what's going on down there?* Jacob was straining to make sense of what he saw. Huge floodlights bathed the south end of the school in light. He could see the tall stage and a person sitting upon it. He could see people moving around and many more sitting in the grass watching what was happening. It almost looked like a concert.

It's bad, Master Boyd. Very bad. I can smell the evil drifting up like the nasty smoke of a tire fire: bitter and sharp.

Are they in trouble? Can we help?

I will help, if I can, but you will go hide in the woods, Bearer! The dragon said in the strong tone of an order.

I'm not gonna hide! I'm gonna help!

The dragon ignored the anxious boy for he now had turned north and could see more clearly what was happening on the ground. *Blasphemy and Dastardly Beasts!* The dragon's mind grew hot with anger.

What? Jacob called back. He could feel the rage growing in the dragon's mind as if it were in his own.

They have Kirk and MacGregor and the rest. They are preparing to kill them, I think. Get ready. I'm going to drop you off in the woods and come back to set their world ablaze!

Jacob raised his head and the two sides of his brow moved forcefully together. *No you're not! They are my friends, too. I can help. I have a blade and a fist.* Jacob punched solidly into the back of the dragon to show his power. *Don't leave me out. I had to lose Fingus and watch him die without being able to help. Don't make me lose more friends without at least trying!*

Nibblus Maximus did not respond. He continued scanning the situation and plotting his line of attack.

Why have I been given this sword and the sporran if I am not to fight for my friends? What good are they? I took a pledge over Fingus' body to do what I can to serve. You can't keep this from me!

The dragon was squinting trying to make out a new commotion on the stand where MacGregor, Witherspoon, Boyle, and Kirk stood uneasily.

"I bet this will make you talk," Creech whispered into Kirk's ear. The doctor with a large needle stood ready to inject his drugs into Kirk's left arm.

The students and staff who had been part of the failed rebellion sat frightened and mumbling and praying and looking intensely around for a sign of hope.

May the Power served by the Sporrai forgive me for this, but we have to go in, Jacob -- you, too. I think Kirk is in immediate danger and the rest will be soon. They are going to shoot him or inject him with something but I can't tell what from up here. I will distract them and then drop you off behind our friends. Take your blade and cut the ropes that bind them. Tell them to run as best they can. Then run as fast as you can north behind the buildings and into those shadows up there. I will rescue you and get you out of here. And don't be a fool! Just get out of there as soon as those ropes are cut, understand?

The dragon did not wait for an answer but immediately dropped his head and dove. Jacob's stomach bounced up into his throat like he was on the most intense roller coaster he ever imagined. The wind was blowing hard like sand into Jacob's eyes and causing them to burn. He found it hard to breathe as the air forced itself into his nose and mouth. Finally, he ducked his head to relieve his lungs and eyes.

Nibblus Maximus had his wings tucked back and was taking careful aim at the first silver trailer. He could feel a particular evil emanating from it, for it was Lilith Frost's own place and her heart had been twisted and turned in her many prideful hours spent within its walls. No one caught even a glimpse of him approaching in the darkened sky above and beyond the flood lights. Everyone, however, would immediately see the results of his work.

The belch of flame flew from the dragon's mouth and enveloped the silver trailer; then a small explosion; then a very big one. Nibblus Maximus banked back up. Jacob could feel the heat hottest on the bottom of his feet, but he could feel the hot air rising on his face as well. The students and staff sitting on the ground leaned back in a wave and then came slightly back up again. A smile slowly rose on MacGregor's face. A smile ripped across Abigail Witherspoon's face. Kirk drove his head angrily into the head of the man holding the needle next to his arm. That man dropped the instrument and collapsed on the stage. Kirk shook the cobwebs from his own skull.

Gasps went up all around. Lilith Frost rose with the snakes of her gorgon head waving in confused anger. She was shocked to silence for but a moment and then began barking angry orders. Jacob looked back at the flames and the secondary explosions that were now ripping through the series of kerosene tanks that sat behind the trailers.

Nibblus Maximus had risen above the buildings and banked left. He put his head down again. He was floating down, much more slowly and controlled than his last dive. *Ready yourself, Bearer. I will turn and drop you. Cut those ropes and get out of there, understood?* Jacob tightened and then relaxed the muscles in his legs, arms and stomach. It was a little trick he learned from baseball. Tensing his muscles and then letting them go helped his body relax. As the two descended into the lights, yells and gasps went up from the crowd. Jenny saw him and began to jump up in celebration. She wanted to not only stand, but to run to her friend. The fear of getting a rifle butt to the back of her head, however, made her settle back down onto the ground.

As the two floated down, they had to pass directly in front of Lilith Frost's throne atop the staircase pyramid. The beautifully hideous head of Frost turned as they passed and she looked Jacob directly in the eye. Jacob felt like the time was passing much more slowly now, as if the world had stopped spinning or that he was floating down through a thick and clear goo, rather than thin night air. He saw the snakes wriggling on Frost's head. He saw her mouth grow angry and her eyes squint ominously. Then, the world felt like it began to spin again and the dragon was banking to his left side. Jacob slipped off onto his hands and did a very poorly executed summersault, landing on all fours.

Jacob grimaced at his weak attempt at being a cool adventure hero. He jumped up onto the back of the platform where the Remnant stood tied and bound to a metal ring fastened to the floor. Jacob released his sword from its sheath and slammed it down through the ropes that tied their feet to the ring. He went to work on the ropes of Bunting Boyle. When Boyle was free, he stood in front of the others and sent a punch into the jaw of Finnius Creech. Creech fell off the platform. Jacob cut through Kirk's and then Witherspoon's and then MacGregor's ropes. He glanced up at Lilith Frost. She was looking down at him with her head cocked and the snakes moving about, each in its own direction and manner.

Nibblus Maximus had swung low over the crowd to divert attention from Jacob's rescue mission. If he had not, the black clothed guards would have descended on Jacob in seconds and the game would have been over. Students were screaming at the beast, not knowing if it was friend of foe. Only one guard was able to overcome his shock and fire at the dragon. The man was shaking and the brass jacketed bullets from his automatic weapon passed harmlessly above the dragon's head.

Down at the gate, the students who had not been involved in the uprising were watching the events unfold from the monitor in the guardhouse. They were confused and scared, but could see enough to know that the tide was turning, if only slightly, against those who held their friends hostage up on campus.

Jacob felt guilty about not knowing how to help next, but he stuck to the orders Nibbs had given him and ran back into the shadows behind the buildings. As he arrived on the other side of the dormitory, he looked up. He could see an inky shadow above the floodlights. It was coming in quickly down toward him.

Coming in, Master Boyd. Clear for landing. Jacob backed toward the wall to give the dragon plenty of room to land. He skidded to a landing and barked, *Get on!* Jacob ran toward him.

Wait! The dragon was looking curiously now up through the dark area between the buildings. He realized he was looking up the back end of the stepped pyramid upon which the new manufactured medusa stood. It was mere scaffolding, not solid and the dragon had a very devilish idea. *Jacob, go down with the kids at the gate. Rally them and get them into the woods down behind the sheds. We may need them.*

Jacob did as the dragon instructed. He started running as quickly as he could prudently do so across the roots that spread atop the ground from the great trees along the road. He turned once to see Nibblus Maximus begin to shrink toward his pug form. Jacob was confused. *Nibs, not now! We need a dragon, not a pug in a time like this!*

Just preparing a little surprise, Bearer, the shrinking dragon replied.

Mr. Nibbles jogged on his four little legs between the two dorms and looked up into the back of the pyramid stairs. He sat back and scratched his right ear with his back paw. He made some general calculations and then walked up under the scaffolding that supported the platform upon which Lilith Frost stood. He walked around smelling and looking in the dark.

Lilith Frost was standing above him barking orders to her men. "The gryphon! Release the gryphon!" she shouted. The one beast that had been standing beside her seemed agitated and was looking down at the floor of the platform. He could sense something was amiss. He could smell Nibbles but could not detect the dog's location. He cocked his feathered head left and then right as he looked at the platform beneath his feet. He walked on his four lion paws to the back of the platform and looked over the edge. Mr. Nibbles watched the shadows of its feet move above him. The pug knew he had no time to waste; that beast would eat him in one scoop from its unnaturally large beak, if he remained in the form of the small dog.

THE BOOK OF KELLS

373

Nibbles took a deep breath and blew his body up as fast as was physically possible. As he hit near maximum size, he launched himself up hard with his back legs and wings. His eyes changed to glow like liquid gold in the dark and he blew a great ball of fire up ahead of him. He lowered his head and burst through the wood. Splinters flew everywhere and caught fire. His right wing clipped the gorgon Frost and knocked her backward. The throne fell off the back of the stairs with the gryphon following it down. Everything began to catch on fire, including the bottom of Frost's dress. Students and staff in the crowd cheered loudly. Guns fired. The dragon dove and spun and turned in an attempt to avoid their shots. Frost screamed a hideous sound that was multiplied from the mouths of the snakes that were sunk deep in her skull.

In the headmaster's dark office, the paint that had been straining with life within the frame, started to shrink as the pain spread upon the countenance of the being within. Mr. Furangle stood and screamed, "Noooooo!"

A Battle Joined

The group of rebels pinned down on the lawn began to cheer. Jenny yelled, "Get 'em Nibbs!" at the top of her lungs, not caring anymore who heard or saw her. The black guards were too busy running for water, attending to Lilith Frost, firing at the flying beast, or just getting their bearings to worry about students making noise.

The dragon went down in the trees beyond the Spur and Spoon. No one was quite sure if he had been hit, if he had landed on his own, or if he was just turning in the dark to make another run.

Kirk, Witherspoon, MacGregor, and Boyle had jumped down from the platform the moment they were free. Because of the dragon's great diversion, they were able to duck into the shadows behind the buildings and were on their way running down toward the gate where they saw Jacob heading under the spotlights of the road. The gryphon that was on the platform with Lilith Frost was picking himself back up after his fall from the pyramid stairs. As he did, he saw the four running down behind the building. He blew out a loud screech.

MacGregor was the last of the line. He turned to see the gryphon flying just feet over the ground and closing fast toward them. MacGregor yelled for the others to run faster and then he paused. He would make himself a more enticing target so he could draw the beast away from the others. He switched directions and ran to the left toward the Great Hall. The gryphon followed. The diversion worked, but MacGregor's price would be high.

The beast descended on him. He glanced over his shoulder just as his pursuer screeched, its mouth remaining slightly open as it flew. MacGregor felt the wind from the wings only a split second before its front lion paws closed around his shoulders. The claws cut like razor blades through his clothes and one of every three punctured the flesh above his trapezes muscles. The beast lifted and MacGregor's feet left the ground.

Instinctively, the man reached up and grabbed the golden furry legs of the gryphon and held tight, fearing being dropped more than being held. "Beast of perversity and scientific Gnosticism you! Put me down! Monstrosity!" The animal was oblivious to his curses. It turned by the Great Hall and entered back into the light of the great floodlights. A shot rang out. One of the black guards had mistaken the gryphon for the dragon returning. The bullet flew at 1200 feet per second. MacGregor heard the bullet whistle in the air and then heard a thump above his head.

The bullet had ripped through the skin and some tendons on the back of the gryphon's left leg. The pain caused the animal to unclench its claws and collapse its wounded limb. It lost its grip on MacGregor's left shoulder. The man's weight was too much for his right claws alone and MacGregor swung over and then slipped from the grip of his abductor. He fell toward the building below. He had time to realize what was happening and yell out "Nibblus Maximus!" before he hit the roof of the Great Hall.

Immediately he began to slide down the roof. He was on his back and there was nothing to grip. He managed to turn just before he flew off the edge. He grabbed the gutter and slowed himself. The last second grab may have saved his life. He ended on the ground with a broken left ankle and a badly jarred back. He lay in great pain upon the grass, but he was alive.

The gryphon landed and nursed its left leg until the hideously headed Lilith Frost called him with a whistle. Some of the men in black were working to slide away the charred and twisted remains of trailer #1. Underneath was a large metal door like those used to go down into storm cellars or outside basements. Beneath the door was a storage area of strong cages. As the scientists created new beasts, they would remove them from the trailers down through these doors into their cages beneath the ground. Here they would study their creations and train them. Beyond the occasional cries in the night from some unknown place, none of the students ever had an idea of what foul deeds were going on beneath their feet.

Jacob reached the students gathered at the gates. They had watched him on the dragon and watched him rescue their old professors. They welcomed him with a great cheer. He motioned to them with his arms to be quieter. Boyle, Witherspoon, and Kirk had changed directions and rushed over to help when they saw MacGregor swept away and then dropped. Jacob began to take charge and rally the students. He was told of what the kids had seen on the monitors and he asked key students for advice.

"Ionans, for I guess that is what we are … fellows; brothers and sisters; old Targes and Dirks. Our friends are in danger up there. There is a terrible evil that has fallen on our school and may be spreading beyond. Who knows where it will stop and we all have loved ones beyond these gates. You will all have to choose your own course, but I ask you to consider joining the fight with me. Don't we owe it to our friends, our teachers, our school?"

Jacob was standing on a slight incline in the grass just off the road by the gate. The students, more than one hundred and fifty of them, crowded around and listened. After seeing him arrive on the dragon, there was no question that he deserved to be listened to. When he raised Isildane's blade above his head and asked for their pledge of support, they cheered and were completely with him. As he turned to lead them into the woods, only three girls and two boys remained behind. They locked themselves in the guard shack and ducked below the windows.

Jacob led his little defenseless army into the woods, not knowing what they would eventually do. The glow of the floodlights provided them some light to see as they moved through the trees. It was fortunate that the school was ringed with a well-worn path used by the cross-country team. The light brown dirt-clay path stood out against the dark ground around it that was covered with a mix of dead leaves, twigs, moss, nutshells, and assorted remnants of nature. They were making their way south along the western side of the school. Above them was the Great Hall, below them was the meandering creek and then the main road into town. Soon the maintenance sheds would be above them to their left and then they would arrive at the small observatory.

When they reached the field by the observatory, Jacob was approached by one of the older girls. She crawled up beside him and put her arm around his shoulder. Even in this terrible moment, Jacob felt a thrill from having an older and attractive girl whispering in his ear. She felt no such excitement. She was suggesting that if someone could get into the observatory, a telescope might be very useful to watch what was going on. Jacob agreed and pulled a couple of boys together and told them what was needed. He didn't order them to act and didn't even ask them, really. He wasn't sure how to ask, truth be told, but they took his words as a request and started crawling toward the observatory.

Jacob stood and pulled himself up on a low branch of a walnut tree. The school was up a rise from them and he could not see what was going on. He settled his feet onto the branch and pulled himself up on another. Up at the school he could see what looked like a bunch of moths floating around a porch light. They were gryphon flying around the floodlights, but Jacob could only guess at that from the distance. He got down just as the boys were returning with a telescope. Jacob looked into the faces of the kids. He saw mostly fear, but also some real strength deep beneath. He touched the shoulder of one boy who looked particularly troubled.

"Boyd, here is the telescope," Andrew announced. He was carrying the long object gingerly in his arms.

"Great," Jacob replied. "Good work." Now, he wondered what he was to do next. He reached out to Nibblus Maximus in his mind.

I am here, Bearer; just gathering a bit of an army of my own, the dragon answered.

Where are you? Jacob asked.

Where am I? Are you blind? the dragon replied.

Jacob looked down at his side. There was Mr. Nibbles, sitting back and looking up at him. Katie, a short, dark-haired girl from Cincinnati was sitting close to him and petting him sweetly behind his ears. The dog was clearly enjoying himself, but Jacob was not amused. *Nice!* He said with derision.

Jacob bent down to Katie. "He is such a cute little guy, isn't he?" Jacob was speaking in a baby voice that he meant to mock the pup for sitting there and getting a massage rather than being a dragon and kicking some gryphon butt. "I bet he wouldn't hurt a little flea, the little gutchy, gutchy, goo-goo, guy." Jacob reached under the dog's chin and tickled it. Mr. Nibbles had had enough and bit down on the boy's finger. "Ouch!"

Serves you right for not giving a hard-working warrior a break, the pug replied and then ran off back into the woods. Katie tried to grab him, but Jacob stopped her.

"He'll be safer away from us, he can hide well, the little guy. Don't worry about him."

Katie was even sadder when Mr. Nibbles left for she missed terribly her little miniature schnauzer that disappeared with the other dogs a few days before. She hoped he might be wherever Jacob's dog was heading and perhaps she would see him again in the morning.

The boys who retrieved the telescope were now perched in the tree above Jacob and the others. The one who climbed as high as he could go had the looking glass and was passing intelligence down through the other two, each perched a few branches below the next. The last whispered the information to those on the ground.

"In the name of the wee man!" the first exclaimed. (Dr. Kirk had taught the students that traditional Scottish phrase of frustration and anxiety.) "Gryphon, oh Lord, there are a dozen of them.

Jacob's heart sank.

"Looks like the people are cleaning up from that mess the dragon made," the boy reported. "All the kids and stuff that were captured are still there sitting. The guards in black are all around, pointing their guns into the air, probably waiting for that dragon to return. The field looks littered with something, but I can't tell what. They are all over the place, whatever they are."

"They are swords and shields and cool stuff like that," a small boy was at Jacob's side touching his sword belt cautiously and speaking.

"Puddles! What are you doing here?"

"I'm here to help and so are they," the small boy replied. He nodded his head back but without taking his eye off Jacob's sword belt and sporran.

"Who are *'they'*?" Jacob asked.

The boy did not reply but turned and jogged off into the woods, smiling as he went.

Jacob shrugged his shoulders and then sent a message back up the tree. "Can we make it up there to the weapons which Puddles says are in the field? And do it without being seen?"

"If we're careful, I think we can. The guards are all up by the school in the most intense light, so I think they would have trouble seeing out there in the darker field. If we had a distraction, I know we could."

A distraction! Jacob knew just who to call. *Nibblus Maximus, do you think you could create a little diversion for us?* he called out with his mind.

With enthusiasm, the dragon pug responded. *Diversion? Diversions are my specialty! Watch me pick off one of those man-made monstrosities! Nice and easy like; in and back out; a surgical strike with a big ending!*

Through the trees came the sound of cracking branches and rustled leaves as the dragon burst through the canopy fifty yards from where Jacob's little army of children crouched in the darkness. Jacob called everyone's attention back to him and gave the orders. In the need to move quickly, he found confidence to deliver the order.

"We think there are weapons laying scattered in the field out there. Probably they were abandoned when our friends were captured. We are going to go up to the edge of the woods and prepare. When I give the signal, we are going to rush out—as quietly as you can, keep in mind—and retrieve the weapons. Just drop and stay where you find a weapon and lie still. We'll move back into the woods after we know we've not been seen. Understand?" In the darkness Jacob saw or heard no reply. He appointed a dozen of them to be in the first line on the edge of the field. They would wait for his signal and then silently pass it down the line before leading those behind them onto the field.

Once they were all in place, Jacob gave a signal to Nibblus Maximus. *Ready, old fella!* Even as he said it, he could feel his stomach crunch with nervous energy. He wondered what the other kids were going through. He, at least, had some experiences, some terrible experiences, which helped give him some confidence in himself and the forces that seemed to look over him. *What must they be going through?*

The dragon circled in the darkness beyond. Upon Jacob's word, he turned and rushed in toward the light, his wings beating hard to pick up speed and power.

Tiny glowing eyes watched silently and waited in the darkness fifty yards or so from where the children lay in the grass.

The Howl of Battle

The dragon came in hard and fast toward the light. He picked his victim from among the gryphon circling the perimeter. He closed upon the beast. The bird-head turned and saw him coming, but it was too late. The dragon opened his mouth and slammed into the stapled throat of the half-lion-half-bird. He collapsed his jaws together, hoping to snap the spine of the beast before it could seriously fight back. The victim clawed wildly at the neck of the dragon but then went limp. Nibblus Maximus turned back out into the darkness. The people below were oblivious to what had just happened, but the children watching from the darkness silently celebrated. The gryphon looked like a large fish hanging from the dragon's mouth.

Jacob signaled his people to hold their positions. *Cool move, Nibbs, but that wasn't much of a distraction!* Jacob communicated.

When I mean to be a distraction, I am. When I mean not to be a distraction, I am not. Patience, little one. Patience. Now, behold the chaos loosed upon the land!

The dragon had turned and was now heading fast again toward the scene below. As he approached the floodlights, he bent his neck back to the right as far is it would go and thrust it forward hard. The dead gryphon flew from his mouth. Immediately behind it was a ball of fire. Flying faster than the dead beast, the flame caught up and engulfed the gryphon. Bunting Boyle looked up into the sky and swore he saw Greek fire being thrown from a medieval catapult.

The beast broke into pieces where the scientists had combined it unnaturally. The flaming head flew directly at Lilith Frost, standing now a few feet below where Nibbs had blown the hole in her stairs earlier.

She looked up just as it was about to hit. She dove. It hit and exploded. Her dress caught a flame and the heat melted several of her snakes. The gryphon body flew to the right, smashed into the platform that had been meant as the execution point for the rebels, and exploded. Parts of the flaming beast flew in various directions.

A flaming leg knocked over three of the guards. Lucy Furangle barely ducked out of the way of another leg, which went smashing through the window of the communications room of her guards. She turned and yelled as she watched her computers and equipment go up in flames. A flaming lion butt went crashing into the wall of Frazier House and exploded into a thousand small fireballs of meat and tissue.

After a moment of being mesmerized by the flame and explosions, Jacob heard Mr. Nibbles in his mind. *She's having a mighty bad hair day, Jacob. You better move while it lasts!* Jacob came back to the task at hand and gave the order to move out into the field. The leaders, all but one, signaled down the line to the next and their followers jumped and headed into the field to the weapons. Jacob grabbed a targe shield, already having a sword of his own, and slid to a stop. It was the kind of perfect slide every baseball player dreams of and he uttered "safe!" as he stopped.

A roar rang out through the air. Nibblus Maximus was claiming his credit for the chaos on the ground. The guards fired into the air. The sound of the shots caused all the kids in the field to drop tight to the ground and hug it as close as they had ever clung to a parent on a dark night after a bad dream. Katie felt a worm crawling near her nose, but with guns blazing, dragons bellowing, and gryphon catching fire, a little earth worm didn't seem all that bad.

Some of the gryphon turned and went after the dragon. Soon a half dozen were after him and he was dodging and weaving. The guards were shooting, some now in a panic. They took out two of their own beasts, thinking they were the dragon returning.

A howl went up from the woods. It sent shivers down the spines of the students. Jacob looked over at the trees just in time to see a pair of eyes emerge in the darkness. Then there was another. Then another. Then dozens. Another howl and then another.

In front of them was the gorgon-headed Lilith Frost and her army. To the left and behind them was a force heard and glimpsed but not yet seen. He looked over to the right and in those trees he also saw glowing eyes. *Trapped.*

Nibbs, we need help and we need it bad! Jacob cried out in his mind.

There was no reply for Nibblus Maximus was battling a half-dozen gryphon high above the school. They were diving at him and scratching at him. He was spinning and turning and lashing out. One crossed in front of him and gave the dragon the chance to make bar-b-que out of it. The charred and flaming beast dropped from the sky and landed not twenty feet from Joshua, a slight boy from Manhattan. On impact, sparks exploded into the air, but not as fast as Joshua exploded up off the ground. He didn't stop until he hit the woods and was knocked over by a force he could not see in the dark. He pulled himself up to a tree and sat begging for his life.

With no answer from the dragon, Jacob couldn't decide what to do. There was really nowhere to go. Finally, with nowhere to run, he decided it was time to fight. He passed the order to his inexperienced army to pull their weapons and ready themselves for battle. He turned half to watch the main force of the enemy on campus. The other half he positioned to watch the glowing eyes on the edge of the woods.

Another howl and then dozens of howls rose through the air from the trees. There was movement. The little boy nicknamed "Puddles" emerged from the woods. He stood silently. Then an army burst through the trees and charged hard toward Jacob and the others. Most of the children stood ready to fight. A few fell to the ground, but most put on as brave a face as they could muster atop shaking knees.

The army was large and small; long and short; lean and plump. They came from three sides toward the children. As they entered the light, their make-up could be seen. They were wild animals charging fast and

Puddles was with them. There were deer alongside badgers. There were beavers from the creek and hawks from the sky. Owls flew down over the scene and made a terribly frightful noise. There were foxes and even two wild boar with wiry hair and long, menacing tusks. Interspersed throughout the wild animals were the dogs that had been released from the kennels days before. As the students started to recognize the dogs, their fears began to drain away. Still, with everything that had happened, none of them thought they could be sure their dogs had not been turned against them.

The children stood ready, but as the animals approached, the creatures stopped their run a few feet before engagement and lowered their heads. The dogs slowly walked ahead of the other animals. Some of the kids saw visions of rabid dogs ripping at their flesh. But the dogs came in with their heads low then they lay down on their sides. The kids immediately recognized the sign and rushed over to greet their old friends. There were kisses and licks and hugs all around. Jacob looked to the sky and hoped Mr. Nibbles was winning his own battle. He did not call out to him again, fearing it might distract his friend from his fight.

A group of students surrounded Puddles and greeted him as a hero. They couldn't figure out what he was doing, but it was obviously special.

A large buck slowly walked into the circle of children, picking his way between them with his sharp hooves. He found Jacob in the group and approached him slowly. He had a mighty rack of twelve points and Jacob was sure he could fit his whole body between the tips of the animal's two front tines.

The great deer bent his head down exactly to eye level with Jacob. They could not communicate through speech or the way Jacob was able to with Nibblus Maximus, but they seemed to understand each other. Jacob looked deep into the animal's eyes and in those round brown marbles he saw an old world and a different time. In that older world he was able to see things a bit more clear than he could amidst the noise of his own time and amidst the pressures of his moment. His confidence grew solid and he was ready. The image lasted only a moment, though, and then he saw the floodlights reflecting again off the deer's left eye. He reached out and patted the animal on the forehead, not touching the antlers like he really wanted to. It was summer and the buck's rack was still covered in velvet. That velvet, however, would not last long as his tines would soon be sharpened in battle.

Jacob stood and took a deep breath. "Dirks and Targes, gather around. Pipers, prepare to play. It's nearly time ... ." He gathered the other student leaders and prepared them.

"These animals are here to help us, I am almost positive of that." He could read the confusion on the other kid's faces. "Don't ask me how I know that, because I don't have a good answer. But, I have seen stranger things in this world and just have a feeling about it."

"You have a *feeling* and we are supposed to just trust your *feeling* and risk our lives for your *feeling?*" one of the older boys huffed.

"Oh, shut up!" a girl interjected. "You saw him as well as I did. He rode that dragon and saved Professor Kirk and the rest. You saw that great deer over there approach him. I say if Boyd has a *feeling*, well, I'm willing to trust it. Unless any of you can also ride dragons, risk your lives like he did, and can talk to deer, I suggest you follow him."

Another boy interjected with, "Look, our school's in shambles, our friends are in danger, that hideous woman up there has already created some crazy new animals. Who knows what she's planning to do next. Experiment on us, maybe? Make us fauns or centaurs or something? Any of you want hooves?" The boy paused and looked at the animals. "Sorry, nothing wrong with hooves, if ya got'em, of course. I didn't mean anything. It's just that I figure we have what we are supposed to have and that's it." He put his head down wishing he had stopped talking much earlier.

"I'm going. Whoever is with me, our plan is to get up there quickly. We move when the pipers blow to distract the guards and that beast at the helm. Fight if you must, but if you can, just get as many of our friends out of there as possible. Any of you ever been to the other school up the creek?"

Two kids put up their hands. "OK. You two will be in charge of getting those we rescue up to the Ballard School," Jacob continued to take charge. "Ask them for protection. Tell them the leadership of Iona have gone crazy and are kidnapping the students. They won't believe the full truth, I'm sure. Where should we bring those we rescue to meet you?"

A boy named Treble from Montana said, "Down at the creek on the front of campus, under the great willow tree." The other student nodded.

"Then, you two make your way through the woods now and around the action so you don't get captured or injured. Position yourself and get them going in waves as soon as we are able to liberate them. The rest of you, upon the sound of the pipes, we start moving in. When we see the guards moving over toward the stables to find out who is playing, we move in fast. What the animals will do, I can't tell. Good luck!"

"Wait," a girl named Charlotte piped up, "Seems like a good time for Iona's motto, doesn't it?"

In unison the students recited, "*Nemo me Impune Lacissit.*" Then they all grew silent and bowed their heads or lifted them to the sky. No one said another word until the pipes cut through the air. They were playing "Scotland the Brave" and the affect was powerful. Many of the students, including Jacob, shed tears. They weren't tears of fear or sorrow, but the tears from experiencing something quite beautiful and very true.

Death to the Gorgon

The piper's music had a very different effect on Lilith Frost than it had on the student rebels. Her snakes squirmed and squealed in pain. She screamed into the night air. Her guards froze, some with a bit of fear creeping into their veins. They were experiencing what thousands of Scotland's enemies had experienced before—the fear of an unseen army bold enough to play music before they engaged in mortal combat.

"Don't stand there, you maggots! Shut that infernal screeching down. There is no room in *my I.O.N.A.* for such backward grunts of smelly air!" Lilith Frost clamped her hands over her ears.

"You heard her majesty! End that nasty sound, now!" Finnius Creech belched out. He was still dabbing blood from his broken nose.

Some guards were trying to put out the fires. Others broke down toward the stables to shut down the music and find out what was going on. A few were left aiming their rifles at the sky watching for the dragon's return.

The battle between the dragon and the group of gryphon was still going on and they were now miles away looping and diving and biting and scratching at one another.

Jacob's army of children began to run. Swords and shields clanged as they moved. Arrows were put to string. Fears were pushed down in their chests. Being faster than the children, most of the animals held back. As the kids got within fifty yards of the hostages, the fastest animals finally broke from their position. They rushed in following the children. Just as the kids were arriving, the animals burst between their ranks and rushed on the enemy. Their utter fearlessness spurred the children's own courage.

Dozens of deer, both buck and doe, rushed directly at the guards who were armed with small automatic weapons. They lowered their heads and crashed into the men's bodies. The doe were able to break ribs, when they hit just right. The bucks, with their antlers still tipped in summer velvet, were able to puncture soft bellies and limbs. They had them by surprise, but the guards had guns. Soon, a portion of the men were able to understand some of what was going on and began to fire. A deer fell by the pyramid steps; a fox by Frazier House. A badger was blown from the air as he leapt at Creech's face. Others would fall as the battle unfolded.

Until the sounds of gunshots shut their mouths tight in renewed fear, the children being rescued shouted and cheered at their rescuers. They were urged to rise and run. The army of children was doing a fine job of rounding them up and leading the others off the field of battle. They ran, hunched low to the ground, but as fast as they could move. Occasionally, a child would be attracted to a beaver or groundhog or fox rushing by them and reach out for a pet. Mostly, however, they ran for their lives.

Some of the kids let arrows fly, mostly wildly, at the gryphon that were now engaged in the battle with the animals. Except for the largest bucks when they got a lucky shot, the deer were no match for such a beast, but many of the smaller animals could dodge and hide and avoid them when they saw them coming. Others rushed upon the staff and guards who were serving Lilith Frost. The children wielded their swords and targes and dirks with skill and dispatched more than just a few of the enemy.

"Kill them!" Lilith Frost yelled. As her anger grew, Frost's beauty began to fade. When she had come out that night, only the snakes on her head were different. Otherwise she had most of the old beauty she always had. She was long and shapely with a face that attracted uncommon attention. Things had changed. Now, her face was swollen and round.

Her proud tan gave way to ashen skin. Her eyes were sunk with puffy patches like little pillows all around. Her eyes themselves had faded from a dark crystalline blue to soggy grey, as if a light was going out from within.

"Kill them!" she yelled again and again. The guards, however deeply they may have been sunk in her evil, were not in so deep that they could kill children. Some component of conscience, some spark of a moral imagination, kept them from firing. They shot and killed animals as they could, but none could bring themselves to fire directly on the kids. They fought back and punched and kicked, but did not shoot. The gorgon was furious. Her eyes grew greyer until the color had nearly disappeared completely.

Jacob had already found Will and they embraced and then quickly broke. He handed his friend the dirk he picked up and said, "Defend yourself if you have to, but get out of here. Follow the others up to the Ballard School. Where's Jenny?" Will pointed toward where he believed Jenny had been sitting. By now they were all on their feet and were running chaotically. There were screams and shrieks. Jacob watched between the running herds to try to find Jenny. Finally, as the crowd cleared, he noticed a girl lying on the ground and nursing her leg. The others had trampled her. Jacob ran to her and slid into place next to the girl.

"Jenny!" he exclaimed.

"Jake!" she threw her arms around him and pulled him tight in a way that would normally have been very embarrassing, but in a situation like this, it just seemed right. She hung onto him and her eyes became watery with emotional relief.

"OK, girl, OK!" Jacob tried to gently pull her back, but only gently. "We really have to get out of here. Can you walk?"

"I'm sure not staying here!" she answered, trying to pinch the tears from her eyes and get them to fall off her face before they were seen. If it was one thing she hated, it was appearing weak or showing more emotion than those near her.

Jacob helped her up and they started to hobble across the grass. Another boy grabbed Jenny's other arm and yelled, "Pick her up and let's carry her out of here!" Jacob did so and they started to move much faster. Jenny hated being carried like this as she hated appearing weak, but she didn't resist.

A man was picking his way quickly back through the rushing herd of humanity. Jacob saw it was Dr. Kirk, his thin black tie up over his shoulder, his hair disheveled, and his glasses twisted on his face. "Master Boyd, where is that beast of yours?" the man asked.

"I don't know, he was fighting some gryphon the last thing I knew. Let me try to reach him." Jacob gave Jenny's shoulder to Dr. Kirk to carry so he could clear his mind. He called out to Nibblus Maximus. Instead of a reply from the dragon, however, a terrible female voice slunk into his mind like a snake.

"Sssssooooo, it isssssss youuu," the words were drawn out and serpent-like. He turned his head. Lilith Frost was staring directly at him with white, empty eyes. Jacob could hardly recognize her. She was more a gorgon than a human now; she was more the medusa than woman. He felt a spike like a cold icicle drive down under his right shoulder blade and he bent forward in pain.

Jacob felt a tug in his back. He felt himself pulled backward. He stumbled back and turned. The great gorgon-headed Lilith Frost was staring powerfully at him. Her eyes were wide and light. Her right hand beckoned him to come to her. He felt it difficult to resist. He stumbled forward. Amidst the chaos, no one realized what was happening. Frost and Boyd were engaged in their own dance that the boy did not understand.

As Jacob reached the bottom of the stair pyramid, the gorgon spoke. "Gifted one, join me," she smiled. "This is the start of a new world order. This is the birthday of a new relationship of man and science. This is the birthing day of a new humanity with a new relationship to the heavens and the earth. Science, *my* science, is linking with the old hopes; purifying them and making their unrecognized dreams come true. Myth and science united. The dreams of profiteers, alchemists, magicians and scientists now linked. I am Medusa! I am the first of the gorgons to come! Join me." Her voice boomed through the night air as if she was speaking through a loud speakers and Jacob was not sure she wasn't.

"Who would you be? I can make you anything you want. What would you have me recreate you into? What do you want to be?" She asked, her voice now lowering and becoming gentler. "Come, tell me what you would be, Jacob Boyd."

Jacob's mind swam. "I would be," Jacob struggled to speak. "I would be, a boy!" He was defiant. "I would be a *good* boy!" Jacob was surprised at himself. He was being honest and strong in a way that felt good.

"Good?" she said incredulously. "Good? What is good is having power! What is good is purifying the race of vermin we must live among. Good is bringing science and magic into my service. Good would be bringing it all into *our* service. See the chaos unfolding? It was your power that brought it about. It is good because more of your friends will die tonight because of your power. Your power brought you here to cause this little rebellion. They were safe, all but a few, until you arrived. Feel the power, Jacob. Feel the power and know that it is good."

The woman's words dug deep into his soul. He looked around and wondered if he had caused more suffering than if he had never come to Iona and just let things unfold without him. He saw Jenny hobbling away; MacGregor over against the wall, badly wounded. He saw animals dead all around. He wondered about Mr. Nibbles and thought of Fingus, dead and on his way to his ancestral grave. It did not feel good at all. He felt sad, profoundly sad.

A moment more and his perspective changed. Looking over and seeing Jenny look back altered his view. She was not sad. She was not disappointed. She was happy to see him. She smiled. She supported him. It was not his fault, he realized. He became defiant again. "No! This is *your* fault, not mine. The blood is not on my hands, but yours!"

A half dozen deer, sensing what was happening, came and stood near Jacob in support.

The woman cocked her head and whispered at a gryphon standing near her on the pyramid. The gryphon launched itself. Jacob ducked and fear again crept in. The gryphon was not after him, however. The beast circled the escaping crowd. He picked out a young boy and swooped down, then rose. The boy squirmed in his paws. Jacob instantly recognized the victim. "Will!" Jacob called out. Medusa smiled, her new idea was working perfectly. If she could not reason with Jacob, she would threaten his friends with a horrible death right in front of him. Then he would give in, she was sure of that.

An eight-point buck stood twenty yards away. The animal burst into full speed and then jumped. The gryphon was on its second wing beat after picking up Will and the deer had to leap with everything his back legs could give. He launched himself high and ducked his head. He hit the back haunches of the lion-body and four of its tines punctured the unnatural beast's hide and stuck. The gryphon screeched. It dropped Will and the boy landed with a thump. Will stood and ran as fast as he could. The deer squirmed to get itself unstuck. His antlers held tight.

The gryphon rose, trying to shake the deer. Finally, the tines came loose, but the pair of adversaries were now high above the school and the deer had no wings. He plummeted to the ground, breaking his neck as he fell through the willow tree. His pain was gone before he hit the ground. The buck had given his life to save Will's and protect Jacob from blackmail.

Back in Creech's office, Mr. Furangle was willing the painting to life. "Nidalas! Come, Father! Come back from the place of eternal torture. Reign again with us in this silent world. The blood will soon be spilt. The young Bearer will soon be sacrificed for you. Come to the gate and ready yourself."

The black and red painting that had started to flatten and dry as the battle turned, was again growing wet and bulging. Furangle smiled. The black gathered itself again amidst the red and for the first time, Mr. Furangle heard a voice, hollow and pained.

"Take me to my daughter. Take me to where the blood shall fall. Take me to where the gate will open again." Furangle bowed solemnly then stood and removed the painting from the wall.

Lilith Frost grew angrier. She seemed to be tapped directly into the air around the school. Winds started to whip the flames of the fires. Trees began to bend. Students who were running away or fighting off the black guards turned and looked up at the sky to see the clouds circling slowly in the night. Something was very wrong in the world and everyone could feel it. Birds left their roosts and fled. The animals that were aiding in the fight howled in unison. Jacob's hair blew back and forth as he stood at the foot of the stairs. A spike of pain drove like a cold steel bar between his shoulders and his knees buckled. He went down.

In the corner by the girl's dormitory, Mr. Creech had pushed himself up tight against the wall. The self-described "Director" of the new I.O.N.A. had become the spineless kind of person he was trying to create with his reforms. He was sitting back and had pulled Lucy Furangle up tight against him, using the big girl as a shield. Lucy squirmed until the winds whipped and then she was afraid enough to be happy to sit back and hide in the shadows with him. A small spike buck and two badgers positioned themselves to make sure the two did not move. They were now prisoners of their own weaknesses and these three were their guards from the wilderness.

Having dispatched the gryphon, Nibblus Maximus was on the way back and was flying fast. He could feel Jacob was in trouble and called out to the Bearer. *Hang on Jacob. Stay strong. Keep true.*

"I can make the pain end. I can make all the pain go away," Lilith Frost was speaking to the boy who was on his knees at the foot of the stairs. "Come and sit upon the throne that I have prepared for you. Reign with me. Be my son. Join me in the new world we will bring about. We will reign over those who still live in the past. Our story is not yet written and we will do the writing!"

Jacob straightened his body slowly and stood straight on his weakened legs. He could hear the dragon again in his mind, *Bearer, you still with me? Get away from her, boy!*

There was no reply from Jacob. There was pain on his face. He began to move. He stepped slowly and deliberately closer to the stairs. He was not making eye contact with the gorgon, but was looking at the stairs below her feet. He got to the first rise and stepped up with one foot.

With his excellent long-distance vision, the dragon could see what Jacob was doing. A shiver of intense fear shot down his spine. *No! Jacob! I cannot let you join her! You must run! Do not go to her! You must not!* The dragon was shouting in Jacob's mind. *I won't let you. I can't let you. I love you, boy, but the force we serve is more important that either of us. I cannot let you give in to her temptations. You and I are less important than what we serve. I love you and will die with you, Boyd. We will both die if we have to in order to keep you and your gift from her evil ranks. Jacob, please! Turn back!* Nibblus Maximus was trying to find the strength to do what he feared he might have to do. He knew this day might come, but he dreaded it more than even he had known. He was sworn to keep Jacob's power and secrets out of the hands of evil at any cost. That terrible moment was at hand and he knew the boy might not survive.

A small voice, distant and sad, but steady like a strong little bird came back, *I love you, too.*

Then a picture came into Nibblus Maximus' imagination. It was the first time they had communicated from pictures in Jacob's mind. The picture was of Perseus, the hero who defeated the gorgon in Greek mythology. It was the kind of picture that Creech had banned from campus. It was the picture of a hero; it was a picture of victory. The dragon knew, now, that Jacob was not giving in, but he also now knew what the boy had planned. He was just as concerned.

The dragon called back. *No! Jacob, you cannot join her, but you cannot fight her, either. You are not strong enough. Jacob! Run!*

Another picture entered the dragon's imagination. He could see more of what Jacob was planning. The boy was not planning to try to take the gorgon on alone, but was asking for assistance in a developing plan. The dragon flew around the school in the darkness beyond the floodlights and then turned and dove down into the shadows behind the Frazier House dormitory. He shrunk like an untied balloon and then ran up under the pyramid stairs. He looked up at the hole that was the result of his earlier handiwork and waited.

Jacob undid the sword belt holding his sporran around his waist. He held it out in front of him and stepped up onto the next stair. Isildane's sword, hanging in its sheath upon the sword belt, brushed against Jacob's right forearm as it rose.

Hammish MacGregor was nursing his broken ankle when he saw what was happening. He stood and yelled, "Nooooo! Bearer! You must not!" He saw Jacob moving toward the woman with his sporran held out in front as if he was ready to present it as a gift to the snake-haired woman.

Jacob did not acknowledge his old mentor. The man hobbled as he could, yelling as he came. Jacob had never had a feeling like this before. The pictures had come to him in rapid succession. He saw the Remnant. He saw the pictures he was given in the cup in the chapel Perilous. He saw the scenes he was allowed to see in the eye of the great buck. He saw Fingus, both alive and dead. He was sunken deep into what great athletes call "The Zone." Nothing bothered him from outside. He was completely focused and unafraid. He was absorbed. He was ready. At that moment, with that feeling, he knew he could have hit the fastest fastball and the nastiest curve that ever was thrown. He was ready. He kept stepping slowly up toward Dr. Frost.

The gorgon's anger cooled. She was about to win. Her face was less bloated and grew more color. She became more beautiful again. Jacob looked up and was surprised that her returning beauty was more unnerving than her truer hideous face. Still, he was in the zone and remained unmoved.

Out from the shadows, Mr. Furangle emerged carrying the painting he worshiped like a god. The canvas was no longer flat. A face bulged in the center and looked up at the woman it considered to be its daughter.

She looked down and smiled. "Soon the long dream of the rebellion will be at hand! Come from your icy block of pain. Live again! Walk among us again. Be our sovereign and we will reign over the lands beneath you!" The canvass of the painting bulged further and stretched as a head pushed its way through the paint.

Jacob rose up another step. He was now standing just two steps below the woman who had been urging him to come to her. She turned her head back around toward him. She smiled and straightened her neck in pride. The wind was whipping stronger now. Fires grew with the new oxygen and blew sideways under the pressure of the wind. The woman's dress blew left and right in great ripples like a vertical white ocean. Trees waved like they were no stiffer than broom grass.

MacGregor was making his way toward the pyramid steps. He picked up a broken branch and used it as a crutch. He moved on slowly and in great pain. He yelled against the wind, "Bearer! You must not! Do not give in to the temptations of evil! Fight her! Resist! Flee!"

Jacob took another step to stand just a couple of feet from the great gorgon-headed woman. She smiled in pride. Jacob looked down at the white slippers that covered her feet. He had read the right books. At least sometimes he had read the right books and they taught him what the Medusa was and the importance of not looking her in the face. He wasn't sure this scientifically created one would have the power of the ancient beast slain by Perseus, but he was going to take no more chances this close. He focused on the curve of the front of her slipper.

"You are a good boy, Jacob. You are doing good things. Now, give me your sporran and be done with the pain. Share your power with me and I will share my great powers with you. Together, Jacob, we will make the rules. We will create the world anew. Just hand it to me and then come sit by my side. We will build a great throne for you."

Even as the woman spoke sweetly and gently, her imagination was full of darker images. She saw power; great power. She saw Jacob not sitting upon the throne in triumph, but being ritually cut by the terrible skien dhu that was once wielded by the evil one who now sought to emerge again into the world. She saw Jacob's blood being poured out onto the canvass and the portal opening to allow her master the chance to emerge again into our world. She saw Jacob serving to bring all the treasures together again to be used in her great plans of reformation for the human race.

Jacob looked at his sporran, hanging upon the sword belt in his hands. He lowered it back toward himself. The moment seemed to last forever. He looked over to the right. He searched the wall of Frazier House and found what he was looking for. There was one window on the third floor that caught the reflection of the gorgon perfectly in its glass. *Perseus' shield*, he thought, remembering how the Greek hero watched the gorgon in the reflection of his shield so he didn't have to look her in the face. He looked at her reflection in awe. He remained silent, as he had not spoken in many minutes, now.

The woman saw Jacob looking away and turned to see what had captured his attention. She saw herself and the boy in the reflection of the glass. Their eyes met. Without turning away, Jacob threw his arm into the air. The sporran, the sheath, and the belt they were attached to went high into the air. With his left hand, however, he had held fast to the handle of Isildane's sword. The blade slipped from the sheath as the treasures flew into the night air and over the great gorgon's head.

The winds seemed to stop and the world became still. The world itself seemed to be holding its breath in anticipation of the results that would determine the very fate of humanity. MacGregor saw the treasure leave Jacob's hand. He fell to his knees in shock and sorrow. Tears started to develop in his tear ducts. Abigail Witherspoon cried out, "Noooooo!" Dr. Kirk, though he was now out of sight, having delivered Jenny to safety, felt the change in the world and leaned against the wall of the Great Hall for support. Bunting Boyle had just driven a sword deep into one of the guards and turned. All seemed lost. A great doe, having watched the developments unfold from near the steps, bolted toward the scene.

The woman turned from the glass to see the sporrai treasure she coveted tumble through the air. Greed overcame her reason and she reached up awkwardly for it. She was dangerously near the front of the hole that had been created earlier by the dragon. Seeing his chance, Nibblus Maximus swelled and burst up through the stairs. The medusa was leaning back over the hole and the dragon smashed into her back, knocking her forward toward Jacob. He also bumped the sporran belt back up away from the woman's grasp as he passed and soared into the sky.

It took great discipline for Jacob not to turn and watch the event unfold directly, but he stayed steady watching it in the distorted reflection of the distant window. As the woman fell forward toward him, the boy shifted his weight to his right foot and lifted Isildane's sword. His feet steady, he twisted his hips and mid-section like he was at home plate. His arms came through with as much power as he could muster. His eyes closed so as not to be caught in the glare of the target's face. He hoped his blade would find its mark, but could not be sure. Jacob let out a scream. It was a yell heard on battlefields across the centuries. It was a soulful and manly sound that echoed off the buildings in the tones of a thousand fallen heroes.

The blade found its mark and began to tear. A sense of satisfaction surged through his hands and wrists with the feeling of a solid hit. His arms continued through the zone and the blade continued its work. The blade cut through the air in front of him and finished its path up by his left ear. He breathed for the first time since the final engagement started to unfold. Jacob opened his eyes and looked down. The body of the medusa had fallen back through the hole and was gone from his sight. The head lay at his feet, the last bit of life draining from its cold grey eyes.

Jacob rested his hands on his knees and took great gulps of breath. His insides were churning in a great jumble of emotions. His chest seemed full of twisting visions and feelings: a mix of anxiety, pride, fear, concern, sadness, sorrow, and lost innocence.

He had seen enough pictures of Perseus and his triumph and so instinctively reached down and picked up the head of the Medusa in triumph. He held it aloft, the dead snakes pressed between his fingers. It should have been gross, but he was lost in the moment.

Great cheers went up from those who had turned to watch the scene unfold and from those down at the guardhouse who were watching on the video monitors. Jacob smiled with pride. MacGregor stood, the tears that started in sorrow but flowed in pride watered his beard. In the triumph, Jacob let himself forget about the sporran, which had landed and lay upon the dewy grass. Furangle, momentarily stunned by the turn of events, had stumbled back. Now he saw the treasure lying unattended and started for it. He laid down the painting, whose bulge had stopped growing.

The female deer that had been rushing toward the stairs continued past Jacob and leapt off the pyramid. She tucked her front legs under her and turned her head to the left. She descended just as the man was about to reach the sporran. Furangle looked up to see the deer flying toward him. He started to reach up to defend himself, but it was too late. The right shoulder of the doe smashed into the chest of the man. The two flew to the ground, both suffering badly broken ribs. Jacob jumped to the ground and retrieved the sporran. He rushed to the deer's side. Furangle lay unconscious where the deer had crushed him.

A shriek was heard from the painting as it continued to dry and shrink back into its frame. Nibblus Maximus was descending fast and heard the horrible cry of suffering. His attention was called to the canvas and he flew down in its direction. Jacob felt the blast of heat from the ball of flame the dragon sent to consume the painting and destroy it forever. The fire struck the canvas and exploded out in all directions. The paint and canvas was utterly consumed, leaving the frame blackened and the grass scorched.

Jenny hobbled as quickly as she could back around the corner of the Great Hall. Will saw her going and rushed over. He swooped up under her arm and the two hopped like they were in a championship sack race toward their friend who had become a great hero. Jacob stood and watched them come the last few feet. Jenny launched herself at her old friend, her arms closing around his neck and her weight swinging to be supported by his. Jacob squeezed tight around her waist and then, amid the embarrassment of such a show of affection for a girl, his arms went limp. The boy had not yet left behind all childish things. Will watched the embrace and then moved behind Jacob and threw his own arm around his old friend. Jenny was unembarrassed and kissed him on the cheek before she pulled away.

The able-bodied children and staff went to help those that had been injured. The Great Hall was opened and the tables were used for giving medical care to the wounded. As they passed Jacob, the students patted him on the back or said a supportive word. Others worked to put out the small fires that burned around campus. As if the scene had released them from a spell or a duty they did not welcome, many of Lilith Frost's guards laid down their weapons and helped repair the damage they had caused. Others fled into the woods or sped off in black cars.

Having been left lying unconscious and then forgotten on the ground, Mr. Furangle was helped by Lucy to escape in the back of a car. Finnius Creech and those that worked with him were rounded up, tied together, and prepared for being arrested in the morning.

Jenny saw Jacob looking out into the distance as an orange sun started to arise in the east. She picked her way through the twigs and branches that were down all over the ground and hobbled to his side. Will approached next. Mr. Nibbles jogged up behind them and sat back, his corkscrew tail curling tight against his back. Jacob was thinking of Fingus and how the sun had already risen on his ancestral grave in the northeast. Without a word and without taking his eyes off the rising sun on the horizon, Jacob reached his right hand down and in front of him. The others recognized his move and put their own hands together with his. A round of "battle dragons" punctuated with *"nemo me impune lacissit"* welcomed the dawn of a new day.

Sleepless Night

Before they made their way back into the creeks, trees, and fields around the school, the animals dragged their dead up to the large wooden doors of the Great Hall. They respectfully laid them on the steps and backed away. As the sun started to warm the morning air, Miss Witherspoon saw Jacob, Will, and Jenny standing silently looking at the carcasses. She could see the confusion on their faces and approached.

"Don't let it bother you too much," she said as she put her arm around Will's shoulder. "They gave their lives willingly for a greater cause. They saw what was happening here. They probably could feel the evil seeping into nature, and they certainly knew of the beautiful trees felled and of the torture put to those poor animals in the trailers. They knew the stakes and risked their lives willingly."

Jenny bent down and raised the head of a small raccoon out of the dirt and laid it on the edge of the stair.

"This has been seen before, you know. These animals have now been given to us to remember their virtue and their sacrifice. If you would help me, let's take them to Mr. Dave's freezer in the cafeteria. Hopefully there is room in there. Jacob and Will, would you two drag the deer?" The children picked up the dead bodies of the foxes and dogs and badgers and the little raccoon and followed Miss Witherspoon.

A creepy kind of feeling came over Jenny as she hobbled on a makeshift wooden crutch. "Ah, Miss Witherspoon," she asked as she stepped quickly to catch up to the headmistress. The woman turned her head but kept walking. "We aren't going to *eat* them, are we?"

Witherspoon laughed out loud. "Heavens no, girl! Heavens no!" She laughed again. "They will live in our memories and they will be constant reminders of what happened here last night. We will have craftsmen make sporrans and other treasures out of their fur and hides. That is why their friends left them for us on the steps—in hopes that we will memorialize their sacrifice and would not forget. It all has happened before, you know, it has all happened before."

Later, Miss Witherspoon called everyone together for a headcount. Then she told them the cafeteria would be open all day and night for whenever they got hungry. An adult would be there around the clock, if they wanted to talk. She told them all not to work beyond 7:00 P.M. Then they were to call their parents and go to bed to get some much needed rest.

"Tell them you love them. Tell them you are okay. Don't try to explain to them what happened here over the phone. We don't want them to panic, and I'm sure they would panic if they learned of the little war we had and of the Medusa and all. Tell them that the school has had some problems and is shutting down."

At this, there was gasping and some booing around the Great Hall.

"Now, now!" Witherspoon offered, her hands stretched in front and her palms pushing down to try to quiet the students and alay their concerns. "Iona will not end this day. We will not shut our doors forever. Like the phoenix, we will rise from these ashes! But, for now I think it is best that you go to your families and be with them while we tend to the mending and the cleansing of this place. All will soon be made right, and you can return in the fall, if you wish and your parents allow." With this a cheer went up around the room.

"It's a time to celebrate, for we have reclaimed our school!" She turned her head toward Dr. Kirk and added, "We have reclaimed our home!" Turning back, she went on, "And, the night after tomorrow we feast! I declare tomorrow to be the eve of the Last Feast of Summer!"

Students stood and cheered and pounded on tables.

THE BOOK OF KELLS

403

Tears slowly grew in the woman's eyes and then overflowed down her cheeks. "Yes, the greatest feast ever!" she whispered as she stepped off the riser. Bunting Boyle was waiting with a strong and warm embrace.

Jacob got pats on the back all around, though a few of the kids seemed afraid of him and kept their distance. By 7:00 P.M. that evening, all were glad to be in their rooms, showered, and in bed. It had been the most stressful and confusing day of their lives and some had not slept in two days. They were all glad for sleep to come, though some slept with their lights on.

Jacob, however, lay staring at his ceiling and petting Mr. Nibbles long after Will's mouth went limp with drool. The images flashed in his mind like a constant slideshow. There was the gorgon's head; he couldn't believe he actually held it. There were the fires and the children running and the animals fighting; the hideous manufactured gryphon with their stapled necks; the visions seen in the deep pools of the deer's eyes; Fingus laying dying; the dragons of his sword handle being unleashed on Mortimer and the terrible things that happened to that man. Then there were the images of the cup, more important and deep and beautiful than the others. They all flashed in a confusing sequence.

Finally, Jacob sat up from his bed and carefully crawled out from under his light covers. Mr. Nibbles was so exhausted that he didn't even notice the boy move. He stopped his snoring but didn't stir. As Jacob looked down upon him, the dog with the flat nose started to snore again. Jacob smiled down at his friend. It took him awhile to get used to that pugly snoring, but at this moment, except for a hug from his mother, it was about the most wonderful thing he could imagine. "Sleep well, my friend. You've earned it."

The hallway was completely quiet and dark. The only light was from the nightlights at the ends of the hall. Jacob marveled that after all he had been through, the harmless shadows of night still caused his heart to flutter and his chest to tighten.

He paused outside Dr. Kirk's door and wondered if he should dare knock so late at night. He resolved to try only softly and then to return to his room if he was not answered. He rapped his knuckles on the door light enough, he hoped, to be heard if Dr. Kirk was awake, but not loud enough to disturb him if he happened to be asleep. He heard nothing and decided to rap once more before returning to his bed in hopes of sleep.

"Yes? Come in, come in," Dr. Kirk announced.

Jacob turned the handle and pushed the door open. The big lights in the room were all off, but there was a table lamp burning in the corner. Dr. Kirk sat at an old typewriter, peering over his black-framed glasses.

"Ah, my boy, come in, come in," the man announced as he removed his glasses and rubbed his eyes.

"Sorry to bother you, Dr. Kirk, but I've had trouble sleeping," Jacob said as his body fully crossed the threshold of the room. He closed the door quietly behind him.

"Jacob, you are not a bother, my boy, not a bother at all," Dr. Kirk said as he stood from his desk and stretched. "Just doing a report on tonight's rather unusual happenings. Sit down, son. I'll get us some hot cocoa."

While Dr. Kirk fiddled around with an electric kettle in the kitchen, Jacob sat in a brown leather chair and thumbed through a book of the fairy tales of George MacDonald. He remembered his father reading him *The Princess and the Goblin* a few years before and he had read and loved "The Golden Key." From the book's back cover he read of MacDonald being from Huntly, Scotland and his mind slipped over the idea that maybe his early reading had been preparatory for his own connection to Scotland and its ancient mysteries. He put the book down and looked up as Dr. Kirk entered the room again with two cups of piping hot chocolate.

"We will have to be a bit quiet, you will understand," Dr. Kirk said as he sat the tray of drinks on the coffee table in front of Jacob. He nodded his head toward the door to the spare bedroom. It was closed almost tight. "It is Angus. He is in there resting now after a difficult time coming to understand that his brother was killed without him being there."

A twisting hand of guilt slowly squeezed Jacob, though it shouldn't have. He knew it really wasn't his fault, but still Jacob couldn't shake the feeling that if he would have done something different, Fingus might still be alive. He stared down at the floor, lost in that thought.

"Jacob," the professor pushed a cup of hot chocolate under his nose. "Why don't you tell me about it?" the professor offered as he sat back, his cup and saucer balancing on his right knee.

Jacob found the telling of his story such a relief that he hardly paused as he went. The professor filled his cup twice before Jacob was finished. As he did, tears formed in the corners of Jacob's eyes. The boy was embarrassed and tried to blink them away.

"Jacob, you really can't blame yourself for what happened, you know. You can mourn for the loss of our friend, and it is a terrible loss, but you must not blame yourself. If you cannot understand that Fingus gave his life willingly for the cause he has dedicated his life to since he was a child, you are not honoring his life and his memory. Fingus understood that there are things worth dying for. You must understand that, too."

Jacob was exhausted from the battle, the cross-Atlantic flight, and the emotional pressures of all that had happened. He had had enough and the tears started to flow like the first slips over the top of a breached dam. Dr. Kirk reached over and took Jacob's cup and saucer. He filled it but left it sitting on the table, so as not to burden Jacob with the threat of spilling it as he sobbed. "Tears are a manly thing when shed in love or out of appreciation for true beauty and goodness, try to remember that as you grow to manhood."

Dr. Kirk handed him a monogrammed handkerchief and patted his knee. Jacob held his head in his hands silently as the well of tears began to dry up. "It is right to shed tears tonight," Dr. Kirk said, "but tomorrow we celebrate."

Jacob looked up. "Celebrate?" he asked, his left eye slightly closing and his mouth curling up on the same side.

"The night after tomorrow, Jacob, at the Last Feast of Summer, we will celebrate our, well, *your* great victory over the gorgon. Miss Witherspoon and I talked about it this evening. If you don't object, young man, we are going to have a very special ceremony. We are going to have a knighting!"

Jacob's heart fluttered. His mind crisscrossed between thinking that he himself might be knighted and reasoning that it must be someone else; or something else.

"You are young, I know," Dr. Kirk offered as he pulled a pipe from his coat pocket and fiddled with its bowl. "But, you have done an amazing thing. By taking on the Medusa, you saved who knows how many lives. Who knows what would have become of the school? Who can say what evil was growing back to life in that painting Furangle was clutching at the end? You didn't give up the Sporrai treasures. You kept the faith. You acted honorably and as a hero should. You proved yourself in combat. And according to the ancient rules of chivalry, even a boy like yourself can be knighted after proving himself in combat."

Jacob couldn't believe what he was hearing. Images of knights and medieval glory were passing through his imagination. Even with the excitement, the weight of exhaustion was descending heavy upon him. Dr. Kirk got up and walked silently to the kitchen. He paused at the threshold out of the room and watched. He knew if he just stopped talking, Jacob's eyes would be too heavy for the boy to keep open. Sure enough, Jacob's eyelids fluttered once and then shut tight. Dr. Kirk waited fifteen minutes and then struggled to pick Jacob up and slip him down onto the couch. He covered the boy with a blanket, brushed his hair from his forehead and then slipped off to his own room and to some much needed rest.

Preparation

Preparations began at first light. Not many students were out of bed at that point, but some were up and helping the early-rising teachers to clean up. Some were hauling up from the barn the old remnants of what the school was like before the coming of Finnius Creech while others were preparing the Great Hall. Mr. Dave, the cook, went out immediately after breakfast to buy special provisions for the feast.

Jacob didn't awake until nearly noon and was still groggy when he did. Ramos Kirk and Angus the Weeling were gone and the apartment was empty when he stood and stretched his aching limbs. Jacob awoke thinking about the knighting ceremony and wondering if it would actually take place as Dr. Kirk mentioned it. He wondered how he might find out without being inappropriate and asking. He shook the sleep from his legs as he walked to the door. Mr. Nibbles was lying in the hallway waiting for his friend to awaken.

"Hi, buddy!" Jacob bent down and rubbed the dog's head, finishing by scratching behind his left ear.

The two went up to Jacob's room where the boy changed. Everyone was at lunch and the hallways were completely quiet. Jacob got a treat out of his top drawer and tossed it to his pug dog before he walked to lunch.

For Jacob, the day was mostly spent in debriefing sessions with the Remnant. They made him tell his whole story and then tell it over again and again. After several times through, the recounting became a bit annoying. Kirk, MacGregor, Witherspoon, Angus, and Boyle were trying to get every scrap of information they could from him. For the rest of the staff and children, the day was spent continuing to clean up and replacing as many of the old images, sculptures, and books as they could find. The animals from the trailers that could be saved were; the others were gently put to sleep and buried in the pit that would become an animal graveyard for future pets of Iona. Just after dinner there was a bonfire of the busted wood, scraps, and downed limbs of campus. Jacob, Will and Jenny spent the evening catching up and flicking small twigs into the flames. Puddles sat near them saying little, but smiling much and giggling occasionally at Mr. Nibbles. The pug tried to ignore him.

At 9:00 PM, Ramos Kirk came and found Jacob. "Son, its time for you to prove worthy of the honor you are about to receive."

"Sir?" Jacob said. He acted like he was confused, but he was more hopeful than confused. He was hopeful that this meant the knighting ceremony was really going to happen.

"Excuse us, Jenny, Will, Nibbs, but your friend has a long night ahead of him."

Jacob bumped knuckles with Will and gave Jenny a gentle kick before he stood and followed after Dr. Kirk.

"Long night, Sir?" the boy asked as he caught up to his teacher.

"The longest of your life, the longest of your life."

Jacob's excitement started to slide away and apprehension set in.

Jacob was taken behind the dorms and across the small campus road to the headmistress's house where she was waiting. Jacob was given a hot bath and new white robes to put on. He felt very silly, but he was supposed to feel newly cleaned and ready, Miss Witherspoon explained. He was then escorted to the small chapel located behind the Great Hall.

"Here is where you will spend your night, Jacob." Jacob looked around for a place to sleep and Ramos Kirk saw it in his darting eyes.

"Oh, you will not be sleeping, no worries, there, son. You will be sitting and kneeling and pacing. You will be thinking and praying and learning. You will be readying yourself for the knighting."

Jacob said nothing.

"There is water on the table back there, Jacob," Miss Witherspoon pointed out. "You'll eat nothing, but can have as much water as you like. You are clean and must keep your innards clean as well as your body and soul. You will be visited, Jacob. Be not afraid. Be strong. Do not fall asleep. Think deeply. Pray hard. Hope and love. Know yourself and hope you are worthy."

Jacob listened, but was preoccupied by the "you will be visited," line. All kinds of possible visitations crawled through his mind from angels to ghosts to people trying to scare him.

"Are you ready?" MacGregor asked.

Jacob was not sure he was telling the truth, but he replied, "yes," in a low and barely audible voice. Each patted him on the back. Miss Witherspoon hugged him hard and strong and shed a tear. She pushed him to arms length and left her hands on the boy's shoulders. "Jacob, tonight you also must beg for forgiveness." Jacob's heart sank. He felt terrible. *What did I do?*

"Jacob, you did the right thing, but you still must beg forgiveness," she said as she looked strong into the boy's confused eyes. "Jacob, you took a human life on these grounds of the Academy. There was no other good choice for you. We all know that. You were courageous and true. You saved countless lives here on campus and elsewhere. You stopped the torture of the animals and of poor Ian. You were a hero. But, heroes, when they are called to take a life, must still pray for forgiveness. You must never learn to take such actions lightly and must understand the terrible price all such heroes must pay. Tonight, Jacob, think through your actions and beg forgiveness, even as you are thankful you had the courage to act."

Jacob shook his head and then remembered to ask about Ian, his old friend he had met the year before in Scotland.

"He is being taken care of in a hospital now, Jacob. He will be fine, we are pretty sure of that, and we will get him back to his parents just as soon as we can. Maybe you can visit with him before you head home." Miss Witherspoon pulled him closer again and hugged. Then she dropped her arms and backed away, another tear rolling down her cheek.

They all turned and left Jacob all alone in the old chapel. Jacob looked around, then sat and began his night of asking forgiveness for his actions. Soon, Jacob rose and played with the lights and messed with the piano a bit during the first hour. He wished he could actually play as practicing would have taken up some of the time. He found a small hammer in the back and did a little repair work where Creech had had a crew starting to remove the valuable parts of the furnishings before he was to have the building condemned and then bull dozed. Jacob was nervous, lonely, and scared, but he was awake, as he had been ordered. And, every few minutes his mind would wonder again to begging forgiveness and being thankful he was strong enough to act when he did.

At 11:00 PM his first visitor arrived. He jumped at the sound of the door handle turning. It was Bunting Boyle. He walked into the room and told Jacob to sit down where he was in the front pew. Boyle slipped in behind him and began to teach Jacob of the virtue of self-control. He handed him a string from an archery set and told Jacob of the importance of controlling himself like an archer controls the string. "Uncontrolled, it is a mere piece of string. Properly controlled by the archer, it is full of power and its movement can change history itself."

At each hour on the hour, a member of the Remnant arrived and taught Jacob about one of the other great virtues: chastity, perseverance, patience, kindness, humility, faith, charity, and hope. The last three were wrapped into one lesson during the hour between 6:00 AM and 7:00 AM and was taught by Abigail Witherspoon. Each also took the time to instruct Jacob on the need to avoid the great vices of lust, gluttony, greed, sloth, wrath, envy, and pride. Between lessons, Jacob was left to think and pray and work on the self-discipline of staying awake during the long night.

The Knighting

At 7:00 AM, Miss Witherspoon took Jacob to the cafeteria where his nighttime fast would be ended with juice and a cinnamon scone. As he entered the cafeteria, the few students who were already awake stood and cheered. They had been told what was going on with the coming knighting ceremony and were proud of Jacob and thankful for his victory over the gorgon and her allies.

Bunting Boyle, who was in charge of the festivities that would take place during this last day of the summer term, was waiting on Jacob's arrival. They greeted each other and the older man asked Jacob to sit with him and eat.

"I trust your night was one you will not soon forget," Boyle said. Jacob had a mouth full of cinnamon scone and so left a rise of his eyebrows and nod of his head suffice for his answer. Jacob knew that he would never forget that very special night and what he learned about himself and about life during the long hours in the chapel.

Boyle briefed Jacob on what would happen through the day and then set off to begin the festivities. Through the day there were a series of games that took place all over campus. Students could sign up for whatever they wanted to take part in. There were traditional Scottish games such as the caber toss in the morning. A picnic lunch was provided on the lawn in front of the library. After lunch there were softball games and sack races; fencing and fence jumping on horseback. It was a grand time, indeed.

As late afternoon drew to a close, all students were called together and then given orders to go to their dorms and clean up for the Final Feast of Summer. New robes had already been delivered to their rooms with fresh Dirk and Targe badges temporarily attached by pins as there had not been time for proper sewing. The student mood was joyous. Jacob, however, was a bit preoccupied by what yet might happen to him that night.

Not wanting to be caught bragging and therefore breaking his new dedication to humility so soon, he did not mention his feelings to Will. He showered and dressed in the best clothes he had. He pulled the robe over his clothes and attached the wire button and clasp together near his neck. Will was ready and waiting. They could hear other students already moving in the hallway and opened the door to follow them.

"Jake, old boy, its been a heck of a summer," Will said. He patted Jacob on the back and added, "even if I did seem to sleep through much of the good parts!"

Jacob laughed and slipped his own arm around Will to return the affection.

"Jake, I don't remember you visiting me while I was sick. Where were you?" Will asked as his memory crawled back through the events of the summer.

"Well, *old boy*, as you say, I was a bit preoccupied and ended up sleeping a bit more than I realized, too! But, that's all behind us now." Jacob turned back into the room and said, "Well, come on Nibbs, or you will be late for supper!" The pug dog jumped down off Jacob's bed and trotted out the door next to Jacob and Will.

Outside, the two boys split so that Jacob could gather with the Targes and Will could gather with the Dirks. Arriving at the Dirk gathering pole, Will could sense that something had changed in their attitudes. Lucy Furangle and some of her closest allies were not there. Those that were left were not nearly as arrogant as they were with Lucy in their company. They all had come to realize that the Targes had more to do with the survival of Iona than had their own members.

At the Targes' pole, Jacob quickly found Jenny. Beneath their long robes, their right hands extended from the shadows. Their two fists bumped and then retracted.

Jenny bent down and picked up Mr. Nibbles. "What a cute little boy he is," she said as she scratched him like a baby under the chin. The dog turned his face toward Jacob but communicated nothing to the boy.

Suddenly the Targe piper blew his instrument loud and strong. Those closest thought their ears would bleed from the shrill decibels. The Dirk piper responded from across campus and then both groups began a slow march.

They marched toward the front gate. Halfway there, the two groups merged into one. As they started down the hill, they saw the faculty waiting beneath the great willow tree that casts dark shadows on the stream and road. The teachers and administrators blended in among the students, creating one great community. At the gate, the leaders of the Dirks and Targes led the entire group in singing the alma mater of Iona, pledging their eternal fidelity and ending with *Nemo Me Impune Lacessit*.

The day was starting to grow into darker grays of dusk now as the sun was down behind the trees across the field. The pipers and two torchbearers led the group back up the hill and to the Great Hall. Before entering, the students greeted one another regardless of their rank or their status as Dirk or Targe. The faculty did the same. The two torches were placed in sconces on the wall flanking the door and the group marched in.

The Great Hall had been immaculately prepared for the Final Feast of Summer. Sporrans, targes, and dirks were hung from the walls. Candles were lit on the long wooden tables. Three white cheese balls about the size of softballs were on each table, a small dirk stabbed into the top of each. Next to each ball of cheese were two plates of uncut bread. Silver goblets sat at each plate and matching silver pitchers were on each table containing water with little ice cubes bobbing on the surface. The mood in the room was joyous and light.

Pipers announced the entrance of each course of salad and meat and vegetables. Mr. Dave's special red punch was served in great drinking horns that were passed around each table. Desert would come only after the meal and official festivities were over and would be served as a reception from a table in the back of the room. When they had entered, some of the students stood temporarily distracted by all the forms and manners of chocolate in every imaginable shade of brown and black that sat upon the table near the great door. Jenny was just such a self-proclaimed "chocoholic" who paused and fought the urge to sneak a little bite from the table.

After the meal was served and most of the students and teachers were done eating, Ramos Kirk stood to regain order among the revelry. It took him two shouts and banging his empty cup upon the table, for he did not possess a commanding voice, before he finally returned a quiet order to the room. He told the participants of the great traditions of these "Final Feasts of Summer" and the important place such meals have had to commemorate great moments in history. "We have survived a great trial. We have won a great battle. We have saved our beloved Academy!" he said as the room returned to jubilant shouting and the pounding of fists. Some of the faculty could be heard replying, "Here, here! Here, here!"

Abigail Witherspoon spoke next as Dr. Kirk and Bunting Boyle fiddled with items in a wooden box. "Ladies and Gentlemen, Dirks and Targes, Friends of Iona," she began. "Tonight we celebrate not only our victory as a community, but we also celebrate those individuals who demonstrated particularly outstanding service during our times of trouble." The room was filled with cheering. "Heroes must forever inhabit our imaginations and we have heroes among us this night."

Jenny was called up and given a medallion from the wooden box. Miss Witherspoon hugged her after Dr. Kirk placed it over her neck. Others were called up and similarly thanked for their service, including Will, Landis, Nolus, and Emma. Jacob was left sitting and wondering if he would get the same medallion. At last, he was called. Great cheers went up around the room. The kids all stood and clapped loudly as Jacob, his cheek's flushed red, made his way forward. Some of the kids who could reach him smacked him on the back as he passed. Though she wanted to hug him, Jenny knew Jacob would not appreciate that in front of everyone. She just brushed his shoulder as he passed. The little boy Puddles was sitting in the back of the room by himself petting Mr. Nibbles and wanting to feel like he fit in. He stood on his chair and hoisted the little pug above his head so the dog could see his master over the standing audience.

The medallion was placed upon his neck and he started back down off the platform. "Mr. Boyd," Dr. Kirk said, "we are not yet finished with you!"

Jacob turned, a mix of emotions running through his mind, and stepped back upon the platform.

"Members of the Iona community," Miss Witherspoon announced. "There is a long tradition that young men can earn a knighthood even before their time has properly come. When squires have proven themselves in terrible and glorious combat, they can be said to have earned their spurs. They can be considered to have earned a knighthood!" The students stood again and cheered. None of them had ever seen anything like it before, and they were caught up in the excitement.

"As headmistress of Iona Academy, I have witnessed the heroics of this young man. He did not lose faith. He did not cower and run. He risked his life for a higher cause. He won the field and saved the day!" Cheers and stomps broke out all over the room and Jacob's heart pounded in his chest.

"Jacob Robert Boyd, if you are ready to swear your oath of knighthood, we will proceed," Miss Witherspoon said as she looked Jacob straight in the eye and smiled.

Jacob nodded his head slightly.

"Dr. Kirk," Miss Witherspoon said, "if you would prepare the garments ..." Kirk nodded and the pipers blew a lonely and distant sound upon their instruments. Bunting Boyle walked across the front of the room cradling in his arms a new set of clothing. He stood next to Dr. Kirk.

Jacob become a little anxious at the new clothes and the fear of perhaps having to undress in front of everyone pierced his mind with embarrassment.

Miss Witherspoon moved to remove the medallion hung around Jacob's neck so that his dark grey robe could be taken off. As she did, Mr. Nibbles reached up and bit poor little Puddles on the little bit of his back end that the dog could reach through the back of the chair. The little boy shouted and jumped. Instantly every head in the room turned to look at him. Puddles was embarrassed as he rubbed his bottom and dropped back into his chair.

Jacob felt sorry for the little boy as the room echoed in light laughter. Then he remembered what the boy had done to help them all before the great battle with the gorgon. Jenny had also told him of the good he had done earlier. Jacob reached over and whispered in Miss Witherspoon's ear.

"Are you sure?" she asked.

"Yes, I'm sure," Jacob replied.

"Young man, you there in the back," Witherspoon was pointing to Puddles in the back of the room who just kept sinking lower in his seat. "Puddles, I think is your name, is that right?"

Puddles nodded his head slightly but wanted to run from the room and never come back to campus again.

"Come here, young man," she said. Jacob smiled at him and nodded in a way that was meant to convey confidence to the boy.

Puddles began to shuffle his feet slowly.

"Members of Iona; Master Boyd has just informed me that this young man has also performed heroic deeds and risked his well-being for the rest of us in this room and for the animals we liberated from the tortures of Lilith Frost."

Jenny started the clapping with loud applause. The others soon followed. Puddles, red-faced and slightly dirty, moved faster down the aisle between the tables. When he reached the front of the room, Jacob patted him on his shoulder. He then removed the medallion from his own neck and slipped it over Puddle's head. The little boy beamed with pride and the students cheered again.

"Master Puddles," Miss Witherspoon began but Jacob interrupted her.

"I think his name is Derek," Jacob said.

"Derek," Miss Witherspoon continued, "you are the boy that loves playing in the rocks and puddles, aren't you?" Derek nodded his head.

"Well, then I have a new role for you young man. And, it is a very important one, too! In many ancient cultures, including in Scotland, Wales, and Ireland, stones were piled up to form a small pyramid-shaped pile called a cairn. They were built to remind the people of great events. We are in need of a cairn so that we never forget what happened here this week. Will you search these woods and the stream for just the right stones and build us a cairn, young man?"

Derek smiled wider than he had ever smiled before. In fact, he could feel his cheek muscles grow tight like stretched rubber bands. The little boy jumped off the platform and ran down the aisle to shouts of "Derek! Derek! Derek!" He didn't stop or slow down until he burst out the door and into the night. The students giggled and wondered if he was out starting the cairn already. They never again called him anything but "Master Derek – The Cairn Builder."

When things calmed down again, the knighting ceremony began. It was a very solemn occasion and not a student or teacher made a sound until it was complete.

Dr. Withespoon removed Jacob's cloak. He was given a small bowl of water for washing his face and hands. He was given long brown socks to replace the blue ones that he wore beneath his brown loafers. The brown socks and shoes, Miss Witherspoon said, were to be a reminder of the dirt within which his body will eventually be laid to rest. They put a white robe over his shoulders to symbolize the importance of purity and goodness. Over the top of the robe, Miss Witherspoon placed a red cloak to remind him of the necessity and goodness of sacrifice. A golden rope tied the cloak at his waste and the tassels hung down between his legs. Golden spurs were strapped around his shoes.

Miss Witherspoon then asked everyone to stand, but Jacob to kneel. He did so as Bunting Boyle stepped forward. Boyle was carrying a sword in its sheath. He pulled it from its sheath and held it aloft.

"May the sharp edges of this sword remind you always of the necessity of justice in service of the oppressed. May its flat sides remind you of the virtue of forgiveness and magnanimity." He then stood silently holding the sword in front of him.

"Master Boyd, if you truly are worthy of this honor and wish to embrace its responsibilities, repeat after me," Miss Witherspoon said. As the headmistress began, Jacob chimed in immediately after her.

"I will always speak the truth. I will be loyal to my employers and my teachers. I will be devoted to my church. I will always be ready to serve my Iona. I will defend all women and never strike a lady. I will be charitable and defend the poor and helpless. I will always be brave. When I am on a great quest, I will remove my armor and my sporran only at sleep. I will never avoid dangerous paths out of fear. I will be on time for any engagement of arms and other important occasions. I will fight my opponents only in a fair fight, one-to-one. I will always be true and respect and defend the good and the beautiful."

Bunting Boyle stepped forward and handed the sword, hilt first, to Miss Witherspoon. She gently placed the broad side of the sword upon Jacob's left shoulder, then his right. She took a step back, turned the sword around, and extended its handle toward Jacob. Miss Witherspoon bid him to stand and handed him the sword. She then leaned in and kissed his cheeks. The room exploded in cheers. A tear slid down Jenny's cheek but she quickly wiped it away and fought against any more from escaping. Will pumped his fist in triumph. The applause and cheers were thunderous. There were a few tears amidst it all.

Hammish MacGregor, who had stood quietly watching it all happen then stepped up behind Jacob. He leaned down into Jacob's right ear and whispered, "Don't let it go to your head, lad. You haven't even begun to earn it all yet! And, don't expect me to call you 'Sir,' either!" Jacob's beaming smile closed only slightly as the applause continued to echo around the room.

❖   ❖   ❖

In the days ahead, most of the students went home to their parents, though a few stayed to help rebuild the damaged parts of the campus. They concentrated first on replacing the old artwork and books and landscaping the damaged grounds. Derek took weeks to pick out just the right stones and built a tremendous cairn that sits now at the very spot where the gorgon's lifeless body had fallen at the end of the great battle. Miss Witherspoon formed a committee to raise money to remodel the old Ashland mansion and make it part of the school again. Jacob, Will, and Jenny went home in the back of Mr. Boyd's car and now were getting a lot of rest. Two weeks after their return, Jacob walked down to the mailbox one morning and found a letter postmarked "333 Cowgate Street, Edinburgh, UK." A slight pain traveled up his right arm and then dug like a dull hook behind his shoulder. His eyes closed and he exhaled deeply. Mr. Nibbles barked from his yard across the road from the mailbox.

Jacob waited until he got back into his room before he opened the envelope that he knew was from Professor Chadwick von Niblick. Inside he found a folded and hand drawn map of Scotland that smelled of stale pipe smoke. There were only a few locations marked that he recognized the names of including Orkney, Iona, and St. Andrews. He didn't recognize others including "The Birnam Oak," "Sueno's Stone," or "Dalriada."

He blew open the envelope again and found a small note that had settled at the bottom.

That old cover is spilling her secrets, lad! Study this map. Don't lose it or let anyone else see it. Next I need that ring of yours so its stone can reveal more of the map. I'll be sending for you as I can. Remain ready. Stay strong. Be true. Until we meet again, I am,

Your friend,
Chadwick von Niblick

THE IONA CONSPIRACY

The hook dug again, but not unpleasantly behind Jacob's shoulder blade as he exhaled deeply before he leaned back.   "Well boy, it seems another adventure awaits ..." he said as he rubbed his dog's silky left ear. His eyes closed and his mind flashed through the recent events and then went blank. Mr. Nibbles lowered his face down between his own front legs and exhaled a pugly snort.

Discover the History behind The Remnant Chronicles

Many readers have asked if there is any real history behind *The Remnant Chronicles* and Jacob's trips through Scotland. The quick and true answer is that there is *a lot* of history behind the stories. Real people like William Wallace and Saint Columba were very important figures in Scotland's history. Nearly all the places Jacob visits are real and can be visited today—they all await exploration just a plane ticket away. Even Feddinch House is a real Bed and Breakfast overlooking St. Andrews and I have it on authority that Mrs. Woods continues to make her famous waffles to this very day. I hope you will take some time to pick up another book or two or go on the Internet to explore some of the real history and geography of Scotland. Who knows? You might even stumble upon a clue or two that Jacob will need as his adventures continue in *Remnant Rising*!

Here are some real-life places, people, and events related to *The Remnant Chronicles* that you can learn more about in books and on the Internet:

Columba	Feddinch House	Catacombs
Reilig Odhrain	Edinburgh castle	William Wallace
Fingal's Cave	The Highlands of Scotland	Robert the Bruce
Cairns	Lia Faile	King Arthur
Oran's Chapel	The Stone of Destiny	Scotland's Thistle
Dun I	Rob Roy MacGregor	Broadswords
Iona Abbey	The MacGregor clan	The Island of Iona
Sueno's Stone	The Boyd clan	The Book of Kells
The Birnam Oak	Niblick	Battle of
Dalriada	Pugs	Culloden
University of St. Andrews	Sir Walter Scott	Hadrian's Wall
(and Saint Andrew Himself)	Holyrood Palace	The Celts
Saltire Cross Flag	Kelpies	
(Saint Andrew's Flag)	The Royal Flag of Scotland	
Rule's Tower	The Royal Mile Edinburgh, Scotland	
Saint Rule (Saint Regulus)	Rampant Lions	

Other Titles of Interest

Repotting Harry Potter: A Professor's Guide for the Serious Re-Reader
Rowling Revisited: Return Trips to Harry, Fantastic Beasts, Quidditch, &
Beedle the Bard
Dr. James W. Thomas

In *Repotting Harry Potter* and his sequel book *Rowling Revisited*, Dr. James W. Thomas points out the humor, puns, foreshadowing and literary parallels in the Potter books. In *Rowling Revisted*, readers will especially find useful three extensive appendixes – "Fantastic Beasts and the Pages Where You'll Find Them," "Quidditch Through the Pages," and "The Books in the Potter Books." Dr. Thomas makes re-reading the Potter books even more rewarding and enjoyable.

The Hidden Story of Narnia:
A Book-By-Book Guide to Lewis' Spiritual Themes
Will Vaus

A book of insightful commentary equally suited for teens or adults – Will Vaus points out connections between the *Narnia* books and spiritual/biblical themes, as well as between ideas in the *Narnia* books and C. S. Lewis' other books. Learn what Lewis himself said about the overarching and unifying thematic structure of the Narnia books. That is what this book explores; what C. S. Lewis called "the hidden story" of Narnia. Each chapter includes questions for individual use or small group discussion.

Virtuous Worlds:
The Video Gamer's Guide to Spiritual Truth (pub 2011)
John Stanifer

According to a recent report, there were 34.2 million units sold of video game hardware or "consoles" in 2009. This does not include much larger sales numbers for the actual games. Popular titles like *Halo 3* and *The Legend of Zelda: Twilight Princess* fly off shelves at a mind-blowing rate. John Stanifer, an avid gamer, goes beyond a general overview and shows readers specific parallels between Christian faith and the content of their favorite games. Written with wry humor (including a heckler who frequently pokes fun at the author) this book will appeal to gamers and non-gamers alike. Those unfamiliar with video games may be pleasantly surprised to find that many elements in those "virtual worlds" also qualify them as "virtuous worlds."